SLEEP LIKE
THE DEAD

ALSO BY ALEX GRAY

Never Somewhere Else

A Small Weeping

Shadows of Sounds

The Riverman

Pitch Black

Glasgow Kiss

Five Ways to Kill a Man

SLEEP LIKE THE DEAD

Alex Gray

sphere

SPHERE

First published in Great Britain in 2011 by Sphere

A CIP catalogue record for this book
is available from the British Library.

HB ISBN 978-1-84744-391-5
C ISBN 978-1-84744-392-2

Typeset in Caslon by M Rules
Printed and bound in Great Britain by
Clays Ltd, St Ives plc

Papers used by Sphere are natural, renewable and
recyclable products sourced from well-managed forests and certified
in accordance with the rules of the Forest Stewardship Council.

Mixed Sources
Product group from well-managed
forests and other controlled sources
www.fsc.org   Cert no. SGS-COC-004081
© 1996 Forest Stewardship Council
FSC

Sphere
An imprint of
Little, Brown Book Group
100 Victoria Embankment
London EC4Y 0DY

An Hachette UK Company
www.hachette.co.uk

www.littlebrown.co.uk

This book is dedicated to Blake and Eloise with love.

We are such stuff as dreams are made on,
and our little life is rounded with a sleep.

William Shakespeare,
The Tempest

PROLOGUE 1

It always began in the dark. Not the crepuscular velvet blue of romantic nights but the sort of total blackness one would find deep underground – a coal-black cleft where one wrong move might mean stepping out into a bottomless void.

Darkness heightened every other sense, even the rank smell of fear prickling skin that was already damp and chill. And there was something else; something foul and rank as though some dead creature was buried underfoot.

The sound of a heartbeat hammering within a tightening chest was the only sign of life until . . . until that voice called out, soft and heavy within the thick blackness.

Then a sigh, relief that he had come again. That it would soon be over. Knowing he was here was better than the anticipation that had made this feverish sweat trickle down between thin shoulder blades.

Knowing he was here made what was to happen next inevitable.

The fingertips touched an unresisting throat, moving slowly in a mock caress. Then a pause, as though to consider the next move. But it was only the hesitation of a cat toying with its prey. That was understood.

With a suddenness that never failed to shock, the hands encircled the small white throat and squeezed hard. Then harder.

As ever, dark turned to red, raging behind each eyeball, protesting soundlessly as he pressed the carotid artery, cutting off breath and life.

Afterwards, blessed silence and a flicker of light from the street lamp outside as eyelids opened on the familiar room.

The bedside clock registered two a.m. Four long hours until daylight returned and life could resume its pattern; hours that would be witness to a creature fearful of sleep, desperate for rest.

It was always two a.m. when that nightmare act of murder was disturbed by wakefulness. And with it, the belief that one day it would finally happen.

PROLOGUE 2

The sound of the doorbell ringing was just part of an unremembered dream, wasn't it? Eyes still gritty with sleep, the man turned over but the noise continued to drill into his brain, commanding the wakefulness that he resisted.

Thrusting the covers from his body, he felt the cold floor on the bare soles of his feet. The red figures on the bedside clock told him it was still the middle of the night. Bad news. It was always bad news when someone came ringing your doorbell.

He thudded downstairs, one hand on the wall to steady himself, wondering what was wrong. Whoever stood there, one finger pressed on the doorbell, wanted his attention. Now.

Bad news. Wasn't that what his parents had always told him? The call in the night. The scream of an ambulance through the darkness.

He fumbled for the light switch but somehow his hand didn't find it and he opened the front door instead. Wanting to stop that incessant ringing. Curious to know what was wrong.

Out of the dark came a figure then a flash of white as his head exploded in a moment of agonising pain, kicking him through time and space.

Then darkness descended for ever.

The man with the gun shook his head at the body on the floor.

Bad news, indeed.

CHAPTER 1

Detective Chief Inspector William Lorimer felt the swish of the plastic tape behind him as he entered the crime scene. He glanced at the house, one eyebrow raised in slight surprise. It was such an ordinary two-up, two-down mid-terrace, a modest suburban home, like thousands of others in and around this city in a district not particularly known for a high rate of crime. And certainly not for ones like this. But impressions could be deceptive, that was something he'd learned long ago, and as the Chief Inspector took another look around him his mouth became a hard thin line: scratch the surface of any neighbourhood and the veneer of respectability could expose all manner of human depravity.

The entire garden was cordoned off and a uniformed officer stood guard at the front gate, his eyes shifting only momentarily to the DCI. Lorimer turned to look behind him. Across the street a huddle of people stood, clearly undeterred by the driving rain, their curiosity or compassion binding them in a pool of silent anticipation. Three police vehicles lined the pavement, a clear sign of the gravity of the situation.

The incident had occurred sometime during the night yet the bright glare from a sun struggling to emerge from layers of cloud made a mockery of the situation. This was an ordinary Monday morning where nothing like this should be happening. He could hear the hum of motorway traffic several streets away as people headed to work, oblivious to the little drama that was about to unfold. A bit in tomorrow's newspaper would command their attention for a few moments, perhaps, then they would dismiss it as someone else's tragedy and continue about their business, glad that it didn't impinge upon their own lives.

His business lay ahead, behind that white tent erected outside the doorway, keeping the scene free from prying eyes. Lorimer nodded, satisfied to see it in place. At least one journalist might be among that knot of watchers over the road, he thought wryly. Closing the gate behind him he ventured up the path then stopped. Someone had been violently sick out here, the traces of vomit splashed over a clump of foliage not yet washed away by earlier torrential rain. Whatever lay inside had been shocking enough to make one person's stomach heave.

With a word to the duty officer the DCI let himself into the house, his gloved hands closing the door carefully behind him.

The body lay spreadeagled on the hall carpet, the gunshot wound clearly visible in the artificial light. He was clad in thin summer pyjamas, the shirt open revealing his bare chest. Any traces in the immediate area would assist the scene of crime officers in learning a little more about the victim's end, as would the bullet lodged within his head. For Lorimer, the story was one that seemed sadly familiar; a gangland shooting, maybe drug related. The single shot to the temple indicated a professional hit man at any rate, he thought, hunkering down beside the body.

'What can you tell me?' he asked, looking up at Detective Sergeant Ramsay, the crime scene manager, who had arrived before him.

'Well, so far as we can make out there was no call from neighbours about hearing a weapon being discharged.' The officer shrugged as if to say that didn't mean much at this stage. To many people, having a quiet life was preferable to giving evidence in a criminal trial.

'The killer's weapon may have been fitted with a silencer, of course,' Ramsay continued, 'or the neighbours on either side could just be heavy sleepers. We haven't found a cartridge case, by the way,' he added.

'So who called it in?' Lorimer wanted to know.

'Colleague of the victim, sir. Was coming to give him a lift to work. Didn't get an answer to the doorbell so he looked through the letterbox, saw the body . . .'

'. . . And dialled 999,' Lorimer finished for him. 'Suppose that was the same person who was sick outside?'

Ramsay nodded. 'Poor guy's still shivering out there in the patrol car. Had to wrap a blanket around his shoulders. He's been trying to give us what information he can.'

'Okay. What do we know so far?' Lorimer asked, looking at the dead man, wondering what his story had been, how he had been brought to this untimely end. The victim was a man about his own age, perhaps younger, he thought, noting the mid-brown hair devoid of any flecks of grey. For a moment Lorimer wanted to place his fingers upon the man's head, stroke it gently as if to express the pity that he felt. No matter what his history, nobody deserved to die like this.

'Kenneth Scott,' the DS told him. 'Thirty-seven. Lived alone. Divorced. No children. Parents both dead. We haven't managed to get a lot else out of the colleague yet,' he added, jerking his head in the direction of the street. 'Too shocked to say much when we arrived. After he'd seen his pal.'

Lorimer continued to focus upon the dead man on the floor.

The victim's eyes were still wide with surprise, the mouth open as if to register a sudden protest, but it was not an expression of terror.

'It must have happened too quickly for him to have realised what was happening,' Lorimer murmured almost to himself. 'Or had he known his assailant?'

'There was no forced entry, sir, but that might not mean all that much.'

The DCI nodded a brief agreement. Men were less likely to worry about opening their doors to strangers, if indeed this had been a stranger. And a strong-armed assassin would have been in and out of there in seconds, one quick shot and away.

Lorimer sat back on his heels, thinking hard. They would have to find out about the man's background as a priority as well as notifying his next of kin. The pal outside had given some information. They'd be checking all that out, of course.

'What about his work background?' Lorimer asked.

'They were in IT, the guy out there told us, shared lifts to a call centre on a regular basis.'

Lorimer stood up as the door opened again to admit a small figure dressed, like himself, in the regulation white boiler suit. His face creased into a grin as he recognised the consultant forensic pathologist. Despite her advanced state of pregnancy, Doctor Rosie Fergusson was still attending crime scenes on a regular basis.

'Still managing not to throw up?' he asked mischievously.

'Give over, Lorimer,' the woman replied, elbowing her way past him, 'I'm way past that stage now, you know,' she protested, patting her burgeoning belly. 'Into my third trimester.'

'Right, what have we here?' she asked, bending down slowly

and opening her kitbag. Her tone, Lorimer noticed, was immediately softer as she regarded the victim. It was something they had in common, that unspoken compassion that made them accord a certain dignity towards a dead person. Lorimer heard Rosie sigh as her glance fell on the victim's bare feet; clad only in his nightwear that somehow made him seem all the more vulnerable.

'Name's Kenneth Scott. His mate came to collect him for work at seven this morning. Nobody heard anything last night as far as we know,' he offered, making eye contact with Ramsay to include him in the discussion. This was a team effort and though he was senior investigating officer Lorimer was well aware of the value everyone placed on the scene of crime manager who would coordinate everyone's part in the case.

'Hm,' Rosie murmured, her gloved hands already examining the body. 'He's been dead for several hours anyway,' she said, more to herself than for Lorimer's benefit.

'Rigor's just beginning to establish. May have died around two to four this morning.' Rosie glanced up at the radiator next to the body. 'I take it that's been off?'

'I suppose so,' Lorimer answered, feeling the cold metal under the layers of surgical gloves. He shrugged. 'It's still officially summertime, you know.'

'Could have fooled me,' Rosie replied darkly, listening to the rain battering down once again on the canvas roof of the tent outside. 'That's two whole weeks since July the fifteenth and it's never let up.'

Lorimer regarded her quizzically.

'St Swithin's day,' she told him. 'Tradition has it that whatever weather happens that particular day will last for forty days. Or else it's more of that global warming the doom merchants have been threatening us with,' she added under her breath.

'But this fellow's not been warmed up any, has he?' Lorimer said. 'Nothing to change the time of death?'

The pathologist shook her blonde curls under the white hood. 'No. Normal temperature in here. Wasn't cold last night either so we can probably assume it happened in the death hours.'

Lorimer nodded silently. Two until four a.m. were regarded as the optimum times for deaths to occur, not only those inflicted by other hands. He had read somewhere that the human spirit seemed to be at its most vulnerable then. And villains seeking to do away with another mortal tended to choose that time as well.

They'd find out more after Rosie and her team had performed the actual post-mortem and forensic toxicology tests had been carried out. Until then it was part of his own job to find out what he could about the late Kenneth Scott.

'It's okay, take your time,' he told the man sitting on the chair beside him. Paul Crichton was still shivering with shock, a mug of hot sweet tea clasped in his hands. The car had taken them back to police headquarters and Lorimer had insisted on using a family room, not one of the usual interview rooms. Here there were soft furnishings in unthreatening shades of beige and brown; Lorimer had chosen to seat them both in a couple of easy chairs, a low coffee table handy for the tea and biscuits he'd ordered up. Victims came in all sorts of guises; the dead man on the floor back there, his family and friends, this work colleague who'd had the misfortune to find him. He glanced at the young man again. What age was he? Late twenties, perhaps? His dark hair tumbled over his face as he drooped forwards, the call centre lanyard swinging into space.

Maybe he wouldn't find out much about Kenneth Scott at this interview, but it was always worth a try. Despite the horror of finding their mate lying dead, some people had a strange sort of fascination with the whole scene of crime process. He'd noticed the man's eyes following Rosie Fergusson as she'd left the house, bag in hand. But whatever questions were on his mind had remained unasked. Now it was the detective who sought information and Lorimer hoped that Crichton was in a fit state to give him the details he wanted to know.

'How well did you know Mr Scott?'

Crichton licked his lips. 'We'd been mates ever since he came to the call centre,' Crichton replied. 'Turned out he lived not all that far from me so we decided to car share. Cost of petrol,' he added, attempting a shrug and failing, his shoulders still raised like twin hillocks of tension.

'What can you tell me about him?'

'Oh, he was a decent sort of bloke. Lived on his own. No kids. Least not any that I know of,' Crichton gave a weak grin as though such a mild joke was permitted under the circumstances.

'Girlfriends?'

Crichton nodded. 'He had been seeing someone from work. A lassie name of Frances Donnelly. Don't think it was anything very serious, though. Just the odd drink and that.'

Lorimer made a note of the name. She'd be near the top of his interview list. Women were often better at giving personal details in between tears of grief.

'It's obviously a huge shock to you, Mr Crichton,' Lorimer continued, trying a different tack.

The man nodded his head. 'Can't believe it. Ken wasn't the sort of person you'd expect anyone to harm. I mean . . .' he tailed off, as though struggling to find the right words. 'Don't want to sound bad. But Ken was a really ordinary sort of bloke. Didn't do drugs, never really got plastered either. Nice fellow, but . . .'

'Not the type to keep dodgy company?' Lorimer suggested.

'Exactly,' Crichton nodded eagerly, 'Couldn't say he was a boring sort either, cos he was nice, you know? We talked about the footie on our way to work, mostly. And work itself, I suppose. There was nothing bad about him.'

'Did he ever talk about his previous marriage?'

'No,' Crichton shook his head. 'Subject never really came up. I only knew he'd been married when there was a whip-round for one of our young guys getting hitched. I remember Ken saying he'd tried that once himself.'

Paul Crichton leaned forward, cupping the mug of tea in both hands. 'It was as if he'd made a big mistake and didn't want to be involved like that ever again.' He looked sideways at Lorimer. 'Know what I mean?'

Lorimer merely smiled. Too many marriages ended unhappily nowadays and he was only grateful that his own had lasted the distance. But it would be worth finding out about the ex and asking questions.

'How long ago was it that he'd been divorced?'

'Sorry, haven't a clue. He was living on his own all the time I knew him. About eighteen months, I suppose since he joined the centre. So it must have been before that.'

'And you have no idea who might have wanted him dead?'

Paul Crichton shuddered visibly. 'Hell, no!' he muttered. 'It must have been a mistake. I mean, you hear of that don't you? Didn't the IRA shoot folk by mistake?'

Crichton had leaned back, relaxing a little, Lorimer noted, this new idea releasing him from the shock that had gripped him. The words would flow now, a reaction after the strain that had gripped him so tightly.

'That must be it, don't you think? A case of mistaken identity!' he finished, sitting up straighter as though he'd scored a point.

12

'That is always a possibility that the police must consider, Mr Crichton,' Lorimer told him blandly. Yet it wasn't something that happened often in this city. Still, if Crichton wanted a lifeline to rescue him from the awfulness of his experience, he could have it.

'I take it the car sharing scheme was pretty much a regular thing?'

Crichton nodded. 'Week about. This was my week, Ken's would have been next week. We always had the same shifts. We even had the same week off on holiday. This was our first day back.'

'Do you know if Mr Scott was away anywhere?' Lorimer tried to keep his tone as neutral as possible. This might be leading somewhere and he didn't want Paul Crichton becoming overexcited.

'I was in the Canary Islands with my girlfriend. Fuerteventura.' He shrugged. Ken said he might go up north to see some mates. No idea whereabouts, though.'

'But someone else from work might know?'

'Suppose so. Don't have a lot of time to chat at that place. Talk enough on the calls to IT support as it is,' he added. There was something rather defensive about Crichton's tone and Lorimer noticed he was digging his fingernails into the soft flesh of his palms. He was trying to hold it all together; not show any signs of the emotions churning his stomach. There was just one last detail Lorimer needed then he'd let the poor bloke go.

'Your workmates were aware that you travelled together week about?'

Crichton's eyebrows rose in surprise. 'I suppose so. It was no big deal. Loads of folk car share these days. Cost of petrol,' he repeated in case the police officer had missed it the first time. Lorimer ignored the slight. The man was still in the aftermath of shock.

13

'Okay, I think that's us done for now, sir. If you can leave us your contact details that would be appreciated. Anything else you might think of, give me a ring,' Lorimer drew a card out of the box on his desk and handed it over. 'Don't suppose you'll feel like going to work now?'

Crichton shook his head. 'Think I'll phone in sick,' he said. 'Pick up my car later on.'

'I'll find someone to drive you home, sir. But I'd be grateful if you don't mention the incident to anyone at the call centre until the police have had time to contact the management there first.'

Lorimer stood up and offered Crichton his hand. It was like shaking hands with a wet fish, the young man's hand was so sweaty and cold. A sudden vision of Ken Scott came to mind, his limbs dead and cold, rigid now with the onset of rigor.

A nice, ordinary bloke, his mate said. Perhaps. In Lorimer's line of work there were often hidden depths to the most ordinary appearances. Maybe there had been more to this victim than Paul Crichton could ever have imagined.

'No sign of the ex-wife, sir,' Detective Constable Annie Irvine shook her head, an expression of annoyance on her face. 'We have her last known address but there's no sign of any car ownership, so no joy there.'

'Employer?'

Irvine made another face. 'Hasn't signed on and there's no trace of tax being paid for the last few years.'

'What about full-time education?'

'Ah,' Annie's mouth took a little time to close as she pondered this option. 'She's well into her thirties, but I suppose . . .'

'New life after marriage? New directions?' Lorimer suggested. 'It happens, you know.'

'Oh, and talking of new things, there's that new detective constable in with His Nibs right now, sir. Omar something,' Annie risked a smile as she left Lorimer's room.

Lorimer nodded. His day was so full of distractions from the important matters like the sudden death of an ordinary man; he'd clean forgotten that this was the starting date for a new member of his department. Detective Constable Omar Adel Fathy had come with the highest recommendations from his previous division in Grampian Region. He'd passed out of Tulliallan with the best results of his initial training too, Lorimer remembered from reading the fellow's CV. *A fast tracker*, Detective Superintendent Mitchison had told him, pointedly. It was a matter of pride to the Superintendent that his CID team were mostly university graduates; and a matter for scorn that DCI Lorimer had chosen to drop out of his own university course to join the police force. He'd have to see Fathy sooner or later, he supposed, but he hoped Mitchison would keep him for now.

Lorimer's hopes were short-lived.

'Ah, Detective Chief Inspector Lorimer,' the nasal tones of the Detective Superintendent greeted him from the doorway and Lorimer gave an inward groan even as he stood up to receive his visitors.

Detective Superintendent Mark Mitchison strode into the room, ushering in the man by his side.

Lorimer's first impression of Fathy was how much of a contrast he presented to the super. DC Omar Adel Fathy was a slightly built young man, bright and quick in his movements as he came forward to shake the DCI's hand. Northern Egyptian, Lorimer guessed, from the darkness of the man's skin. Nubian blood somewhere judging by that gracefully sculpted head, he thought, recalling the statuary he had seen during his history of art years, though this particular man lacked the height he associated with those elegant people. Beside him Mark Mitchison looked washed out, his conventional handsomeness faded by contrast.

'It is a pleasure to meet you, sir,' Fathy told him, giving the merest hint of a bow as he spoke. But it was not an obsequious sort of gesture, more an innate courtesy. The direct way he looked Lorimer in the eye, a smile hovering around his mouth, was instantly appealing to the DCI. Here was someone he could work with, he thought. Someone who'd not suffer the sort of bullshit that Mitchison doled out on a daily basis.

'Detective Constable Fathy comes with a glowing report,' Mitchison drawled and Lorimer was heartened to see that this utterance had the effect of making the Egyptian frown slightly in embarrassment.

'Good,' Lorimer said. 'You'll be ready for anything then? Like a new murder case, hm?'

Fathy's grin was answer enough.

'I'll leave you gentlemen, then, must press on,' Mitchison nodded to them both. 'Door's always open if you need to talk, Fathy.' Then he was gone.

Lorimer exhaled in relief. His immediate boss was the only thorn in his flesh in a job that he loved. When his previous super had retired the word on the grapevine was that Lorimer himself would step into his shoes, but that hadn't happened, and, apart from a couple of secondments as acting superintendent, Lorimer still hadn't gained the expected promotion. It was only a matter of time, his wife Maggie had reassured him. But Lorimer wasn't so sure. The fast trackers with university degrees like the man before him were the ones destined for greater things, he believed.

'Sit down, Fathy. That's the correct pronunciation, is it? Fa-thy?'

'Yes, sir. The TH is hard, almost like a V sound. Of course many will call me fatty,' he grinned, showing perfect white teeth. Lorimer returned the smile. The officer's spare frame gave the lie to that.

'This murder inquiry, sir?' Fathy continued. 'May I be included in the investigation team?'

'Possibly,' Lorimer told him. 'The actions have already been given out but I think you might be able to accompany DC Irvine, at least for today. Hopefully we'll have it wrapped up soon,' he raised his eyebrows in a rueful gesture. It was every officer's hope that a murder case would be quickly solved. The longer it took, the harder it was to find the perpetrator.

Fathy's answering nod seemed to indicate that he understood exactly what the DCI meant and Lorimer wondered just what sort of cases this young man had tackled in his brief career.

Later, on his own, Lorimer had the opportunity to check on DC Fathy's past experience. It was just as Mitchison had said. A bright and able police officer who had taken part in some fairly high profile investigations. Yet he had asked especially for a transfer to Strathclyde Police. No particular reason had been given and Lorimer had a sudden uneasy feeling that it might not have been just to enhance the young man's promotion prospects. Had he been unhappy in Grampian? And if so, why? There were often jealousies within the police force, officers jockeying for the few senior positions available. Had someone resented Fathy's obvious potential? Or had he been too pushy? He was very keen to play a part in the new case. But perhaps as the new boy he should be trying to keep his head down for a bit and settle in. Lorimer stared out of the window, wondering. He'd taken an instant liking to the handsome Egyptian. It would be a pity if he failed to fit comfortably into his team.

CHAPTER 2

The man laid down the gun then fiddled with the straps on the worn leather bag. He had it down to a fine art, now, could strip down the weapon in seconds, transforming it into several parts easily stowed away in the holdall. The job had been simple enough. The guy had been sleepy, hardly registering his presence before the shot that had penetrated his skull. 'Didn't know what hit him,' he muttered under his breath. It was a mantra he often whispered to himself, partly to expunge the act he had committed. He'd forget the man, his address, anything he had known about him, as soon as the money was handed over. He was just another job, that was all. The hit man preferred not to know why he had been assigned to kill this man or why the target had deserved such an end. And there was certainly no room in a mind like his for false sentiment. Sitting along the edge of the unmade bed he stuffed some balled-up clothes into the bag, tucking the bundle closely around the pieces of hardware.

A quick look around the room sufficed to seek anything that might tell of his presence, but he saw nothing; the gunman was as meticulous in his habits as he was cautious, always choosing some bland, cut-price chain of hotel where there was a large client turnover. Soon a maid would come to clean this room, put on fresh linen and another traveller would lay their head on that pillow, oblivious to the identity of the room's previous occupant. He tightened the final notch, slung the bag over his shoulder and headed out of the hotel room, just another tourist checking out.

'There you are, sir. I hope you enjoyed your stay with us. Have a lovely day.' The girl with the sleek, dark ponytail barely gave the man a glance, though she did fasten a smile on her lips before turning her attention back to her paperwork. A pleasant faced, middle-aged man of medium build, wearing a khaki-coloured jacket and washed out blue jeans, he was out of her mind even before he had left the building.

Now he was ready to pick up his wages. His car's satellite navigation system would have to take him to the meeting place, across the city. He'd never been to that particular spot before. Then he'd be heading back down the motorway, safe in the knowledge that he had completed another satisfactory assignment. The wind whipped his jacket as he walked around the corner of the building to where he had parked his car, stinging his face with a hint of rain. Looking up at a sky full of grey clouds scudding across the heavens, he muttered a curse under his breath, hoping that he wouldn't have to wait too long for the handover.

Minutes later he was heading past Glasgow International Airport towards the city, one eye on the screen showing his route.

There were not many students about at this time of year. For most of them term did not begin for another two months though there were always those unfortunates with failed examinations to take again who pretended to themselves that physical proximity to the university buildings was going to make all the difference next time. So, as he lounged against a pillar in the draughty Gothic portico next to the quadrangle, the gunman had little to see of comings and goings. That suited him. The fewer nosey parkers who remarked upon his presence there the better.

A tall, grey-headed man strode out of a door and paused momentarily in his stride as he caught sight of the stranger. A sudden flare of nostrils at the wisp of cigarette smoke issuing from the stranger's lips expressed his disapproval. Then he was sweeping past on his way and into another massive doorway before the gunman could blink.

'Bang!' he said softly, making a pistol from his fingers and pointing it in the grey man's direction. Then he gave a low chuckle. Snooty academic! He could blow him away as soon as look at him. He'd had his fill of that type in the forces; the ones who enjoyed tormenting you because they could pull rank. He'd left a couple of them with souvenirs that they'd carry on their bodies for the rest of their lives.

A quick glance at his wristwatch made him frown. He was late. And he didn't want to hit the rush hour traffic further down the motorway. Flicking the stub of his cigarette towards the door where the donnish looking man had gone, he took a step forward, wondering if he could stretch his legs. It didn't do to look conspicuous. And if the tall guy reappeared and asked what he was doing, well, that wouldn't be good, would it? Maybe he could risk a stroll around that square of grass where he could keep one eye on this place?

Doctor Solomon Brightman emerged from the door opposite the quad clutching an overflowing briefcase tightly to his side. It was still a while until the new term began but for Solly and his colleagues the work was already well underway. Still, he'd done enough for today and now he wanted to drop this lot off before going into town to visit his favourite bookshop.

As the psychology lecturer stepped onto the grass he was aware of a figure strolling towards him. A stranger, dressed in casual clothes, a cigarette palmed in his right hand. A tourist, probably, visiting the University of Glasgow on the hop-on, hop-off bus that took visitors around the city. As they passed one another, Solly prepared to smile and nod, a common enough courtesy, but the man turned his head away, almost deliberately, as though avoiding Solly's glance.

It was enough to make the psychologist curious. He was perennially curious about human behaviour, of course, and looking at the departing figure of the man, he couldn't help but feel that here was a person who *wanted* to remain anonymous. And he began to wonder why.

An hour later the gunman realised that nobody was going to arrive. The wind that had threatened rain whipped through the cloisters with a ferocity that made the dried leaves scurry into the shelter of doorways. With one last look at the green square beyond the chilly pillars, he turned his heel, grinding the stub of a cigarette before moving into the warmth of a nearby corridor.

It had happened before and might well happen again. Sometimes it just took a little more time and not-so-gentle persuasion to get the money out of whoever had hired him. He clenched his teeth as he strode through the building, eyes alert for the nearest exit. Soon he was out and heading over the hill towards his car. He'd have to make a couple of phone calls then key in another address to the sat-nav. He swore as the blast of rain drove into his face. What he wanted was a few hours on the motorway then home, not hanging around this godforsaken city. The piece of plastic fluttering madly against the windscreen made him stop and swear again. Bloody parking ticket! With one swipe he tore it free from the wiper blades and stuffed it into his pocket. They could whistle for their fine. It was just one more aggravation added to the inconvenience of having to remain here a while. A grim smile hovered across his mouth.

Someone was going to pay dearly for this.

CHAPTER 3

'Once upon a time,' that was how stories ought to begin, Solly mused, walking slowly past the rows of books for the third time. Hadn't his own childhood reading been like that? Well, perhaps not, he smiled, recognising *The House at Pooh Corner* and a couple of familiar Roald Dahls. It was an interesting idea, though, that traditional phrases like 'Once upon a time' were somehow rooted in one's own consciousness. Perhaps he could use that in one of his seminar meetings for the second year students next term. The smile above the dark beard continued as Doctor Solomon Brightman, psychologist and expectant father, stopped beside a shelf of brightly coloured books for very small children.

Little blue men and flowers with grinning faces peered up at him. Shaking his head slightly, Solly picked out a cloth book that rustled as he touched its pages. Ah, this was more like it. He remembered a conference in Sweden where he had been in conversation with a fellow psychologist when the subject of tactile stimulation had been under discussion. Flipping the first page in his hands, Solly saw the black and white shapes, like petals, some large and some repeating a pattern. A young baby would receive visual information while being attracted by the sensual feel of its soft pages, crackling plastic portions cleverly concealed within.

Quite without warning he blinked away a sudden tear. A baby. *His* baby. His and Rosie's. Standing still in that bookshop, oblivious to other people moving past him, Solly experienced a moment of revelation. He was well aware that fatherhood could produce such feelings in an individual. Hadn't he been teaching that for some considerable time now? His rational self might well be able to identify each chemical and hormonal surge producing a physical sensation having no name other than the abstract: *joy*. But that he should have such feelings in his own breast was nothing short of a miracle. Wasn't that what he'd heard grandmothers call a newborn? A little miracle.

'Doctor Brightman!'

Solly spun around as his name was called out. A woman stood at the end of the aisle, a quizzical look on her face as though she wasn't absolutely certain that she had the correct person. Solly smiled tentatively, trying hard to recall the woman to mind. Too old to be one of his university students, and yet there was something familiar about that mane of red hair cascading down her shoulders, and those unwavering eyes.

'Fancy seeing you here,' she continued, sweeping her gaze along the row of children's books. Then she looked at him again, as though she were aware of his discomfiture and it amused her. Head held high, she regarded him boldly, a smile playing around her mouth.

'Yes, indeed,' Solly remarked, struggling to put a name to a face that he felt should be familiar. Was she one of his mature students? There were a few married women under his tutelage. Could he remember their names, though? His eyes fell on to her hands: no wedding ring, no help there, then.

'It's funny,' she said, staring at him, 'I've often imagined running into you, wondering what I would say if I did.' The woman regarded him steadily, her eyes dark with an unfathomable expression.

'I've got a lot to thank you for, you know,' she said, adding almost as an afterthought, 'See you next term.' Then, with a brittle smile and a wave of her hand she turned on her heel, disappeared around the row of books and was gone.

Solly stood for a moment, strangely disquieted at the enigmatic remark. She knew him. She expected to see him next term, so she must be one of his students, surely? And what had she to thank him for? Passing the exams? He frowned. Her words had been spoken in a tone of sudden gravity. So why couldn't he conjure up her name?

A frown creased his dark brow as the psychologist stared into space, struggling to remember. Mhairi. Was that her name? Or Marie something . . . Hadn't she been the one with the funny surname? Or maybe not. Names were not the psychologist's strong point but he did have a good recall for faces. But the woman he had just seen bore little resemblance to the student he remembered. This woman seemed altogether more confident, more . . . *alive* than the person he had taught all of last session.

Solly bit his lip thoughtfully. Alive. That was the correct word to use, right enough. For the Mari something or other who had sat through his seminars and scraped a bare pass in her first year exams was a mere shadow of the woman who had spoken to him moments ago. That stream of Titian hair had been screwed up into a messy bun at the back of her head, often as not, her pale face devoid of makeup, Solly remembered, casting his mind back to the seminars in his office at Glasgow University. There was a vibrancy about this creature that was at odds with his memory of her; Mari (was it Mhairi?) had dragged herself to his classes, a permanent air of grey exhaustion about her. At one point in the

27

session he remembered asking if she had been unwell. Her dull-eyed expression had given the lie to her assurance that she was fine.

The psychologist hadn't expected the woman to continue her course. But she'd gained the necessary grades and now she'd be back in his orbit once again. Whatever had happened to make her change so dramatically had to be good, Solly thought to himself. Love, perhaps? Or was it merely the escape from the drudgery of constant study? Shrugging his shoulders, the psychologist gazed at the spot where the woman had stood before resuming his inspection of the rows of little books.

In the weeks to come Doctor Solomon Brightman would have cause to consider this chance encounter and just what it had revealed. But for now his disquiet remained a temporary distraction, not the thing of darkness and despair that would come to haunt his dreams.

CHAPTER 4

He was really the only person in the world she could trust. Brother Billy. Wee toerag, his da had called him often enough before he'd been thrown out of the family home. No sweat, though. He knew his da had been right in his assessment of him. Billy Brogan, class A toerag, dealer in illegal substances, now doing a runner before all the shit caught up with him.

Billy chuckled to himself. She'd given him the 10K in used notes, dead careful not to have them traced to her bank account. Clever, she was clever all right, but not a match for her wee brother. No siree.

Billy swung the backpack onto his shoulders as he left the aircraft. The heat from the fuselage mixed with something else, a warmth that you didn't get even in the best of Glasgow summers. Man, this would be the life all right. A wee holiday in Spain first, since he had plenty of spending money, then off again to where the action was. Morocco, natch. Marrakesh. Where it all came from. He'd be the main man in no time at all, nae pushers coming in between him and the gear, giving him a hard time.

Billy strode up the corridor, glancing now and again out of the tinted windows. It was still daylight but the sky had a rosy pink hue where the light met the horizon. For a moment he slowed down, the bravado he'd been feeling lost in the realisation that he was in a different country now. Och, but it was Spain, Majorca, where Glesca folk came all the time on their holidays. They'd all speak English, eh? Billy tried to reassure himself. Then the corridor opened out into a large hall where loads of people were sitting waiting on rows of plastic seats. Waiting to go home again, he thought, seeing sun-reddened flesh and down-turned mouths. And ah'm jist arriving, he told them silently.

Joining a queue to show his passport, Billy kept staring straight ahead as though fearful that his expression might give the game away. But it was a quick in and out, a Spanish hand waving him along as the man in the booth barely glanced at his picture.

Further along past the luggage carousels he could see holiday reps with placards showing the names of their companies. But nobody was there to meet Billy Brogan. A shiver passed down the young man's spine. Whit the hell wis he doin' here onywey? The sudden panic made him want to turn straight around and get back on that plane bound for Glasgow. But that wasn't possible any more, was it?

A familiar sign just ahead of him quickened his step. An advertisement for Burger King was plastered across the wall. That was okay, then, he sighed, letting out his breath. It was just what he'd promised himself. A wee home frae home. Then on to pastures new.

Outside the airport building Billy glanced past the rows of palm trees till he saw what he wanted. Taxi. Another international word.

'Hey, pal. Any chance of takin' me intae Cala Millor?' Billy asked, pronouncing the Millor like Miller. He'd seen the place on the internet when he'd booked his ticket. Remembered a name he'd been given a long time ago.

The taxi driver seemed pleased as he slung Billy's pack into the back seat, the price of forty euros agreed as Billy shrugged his shoulders. Forty euros? An hour's journey. Sounded okay, he thought, settling back into the leather seats. Plenty time to chat the guy up, find a hotel he'd recommend. The driver looked the sort of person he could trust.

Billy smiled to himself, remembering what his big sister had told him.

'You're the only person I can trust, Billy,' she'd said. And it was true. At least for what she had in mind. He would find out the right person, he'd promised her. No contact made with her, personally; that was guaranteed. He'd be the go-between, the middle man; wee Billy Brogan, sure of himself, cocky as you liked, living somewhere in the shades where she dare not enter. It was just a question of how much. Ten thousand pounds didn't just drop off the trees. But luck had helped them with Amit's timely arrival into both their lives.

Handing it over to little brother Billy seemed to be as much a relief as knowing that it would all be over soon. And hadn't he promised her that it would be? He'd left her happy, assured that now she could sleep easy knowing that he was the only person in the world that she could trust.

31

CHAPTER 5

The flame burned low, melting the pale wood, then the wick spurted and she let the blackened matchstick fall, sizzling into the water, before it burned her fingers.

Lying back she slid down as far as she could, hair spread out like waterweed. Eyes closed, she could smell the fragrance from the scented candle: frangipani. Funny how evocative a scent could be. Memories flooded back now. Warm blue lagoons with sun umbrellas made from twists of thatch; sitting out on their own private deck at breakfast time, the mynah birds chattering; multi-coloured fish darting in the reef – electric blues and stripy yellows; flower petals strewn across their beds at night by some discreet, unseen hand.

In the beginning it had all been full of promise, full of hope. He'd lavished so much on that honeymoon, hadn't he? Seduced her into believing this would be paradise on earth, just the two of them.

She fingered the place on her neck where bruises had formed so often, so very often . . .

Despite the warmth of the bathwater, she shivered. Time to soap her arms, rub away the day's sweat and dirt. Sitting up, she displaced the volume of water, hearing it swoosh around her legs.

The spent match bobbed towards her, adrift on the scummy sur-face. She scooped it up on the third attempt and flicked it on to the floor. For a moment she let the water settle around her, trying not to imagine what it had been like at the end. Darkness. Gunfire. A sudden blast and then he was gone.

Like that spent match. All his fires out.

CHAPTER 6

'The wife's last address, sir,' DC Irvine laid the paper on Lorimer's desk. 'You were spot on about further education. She did a course at Anniesland College two years ago so she could apply for Glasgow University.'

Lorimer's raised eyebrows showed his unspoken question: *What then?*

Annie Irvine blushed. 'No trace of her after that so we don't even know if she's still in the country. But we're working on it. Sir,' she added earnestly.

Lorimer made a face. 'Tracing Mrs Kenneth Scott is becoming a nuisance. Maybe the current girlfriend, Frances Donnelly, can fill us in better anyway,' he raised a questioning eyebrow at his detective constable. 'Women like knowing things about their lovers, especially the other women in their lives,' he smiled wickedly.

Annie shook her head, giving Lorimer a mock smile. Did he think the divisional headquarters was a hotbed of sexual intrigue or something? If only.

'Take Fathy with you to the call centre, will you? We want to know all that the girlfriend can tell us about Scott, especially where he was the week before he was killed. Okay?'

'Sir,' Irvine backed out of the doorway and breathed a sigh of relief. The Scott woman had vanished into thin air, apparently. And that made it all the more suspicious, didn't it? Why would someone disappear like that, not want to be found, unless they had something to hide?

Annie Irvine gave a little skip as she crossed the corridor to the room inhabited by lesser mortals like detective constables. Out with Omar. That was a lucky chance. She ran fingers through her short dark hair then paused. A quick visit to the loo and a touch of lippy wouldn't go amiss before she called the handsome Egyptian to heel.

The call centre sat cheek by jowl beside a roundabout overlooking the M8 motorway on one side and a huddle of fifties terraced housing on the other. Its tinted glass windows caught the sunlight for a moment as Irvine parked the pool car, making her glance upwards.

'Looks an okay place to work,' she remarked to the man in the passenger seat.

'Better than your division?' Fathy asked, a crooked smile on his lips.

'Och, I'm happy where I am,' Irvine told him. 'It's not everyone who gets to stay put when you change from uniform to CID. And I've always liked working with Lorimer. He can be a moody beggar at times, right enough, but he's dead fair. What about yourself? Did Grampian not suit you or were you looking to see what this big, bad city had to offer?' She winked at him, then before he could reply, 'C'mon then, let's be having you. Or the boss'll have our guts for garters.'

Irvine watched as the young man slid out of his seat then brushed himself down. There was something both elegant and effete in the gesture, making her heart plummet. Was he gay? And if so, were the lascivious thoughts she'd been having about the new DC utterly pointless? She jerked her head towards the doorway. 'Right. You've been briefed about the girlfriend, but let me do the talking, okay?'

He was at the doorway of the call centre in two strides, holding it open for her with a twinkle in his eye as if her misgivings about his sexuality had been completely transparent.

Inside there was a curved reception desk made of blonde wood that took up a quarter of the floor space, its polished counter decorated with a stark display of white arum lilies. Irvine flinched. Was this a blatant show of sympathy for a deceased member of staff or did they just go for the minimalist effect? A glance around the hallway made her suspect the latter; the floor was a grey, polished stone and the walls were painted stark white between the huge glass windows.

'Yes, can I help you?' The ponytailed girl behind the desk looked up at them, her glance resting upon the Egyptian, her smile widening just for him. Irvine cursed inwardly, wishing she'd put on smarter stuff today instead of the jacket and trousers that were her staple work clothes. The collar of Miss Ponytail's white shirt was sharp enough to cut her, Irvine thought. And she would bet that sleek, black suit wasn't out of Top Shop.

'Detective Constables Irvine and Fathy,' she said sharply, commanding the girl's attention, her warrant card up close so the girl could read it if she wanted to. 'We're here to see Miss Donnelly in connection with the death of Mr Kenneth Scott.'

'Oh,' Ponytail gasped, one perfectly manicured hand covering her mouth for a moment. 'That was so awful, wasn't it?' she whispered, her eyes sliding back to Fathy, her voice so breathless and solemn that it made Irvine want to put a couple of fingers down her throat. The sympathy was so obviously fake. She probably didn't even remember what Ken Scott had looked like.

'Frances Donnelly?' Irvine reminded her.

'Oh, yes,' she gasped, wrenching her gaze away from DC Fathy as though it were something of an effort. 'I'll just call up and let them know you're here. Someone will be down in a minute. If you'd like to take a seat . . .?' Ponytail gestured to a row of seats upholstered in a bland grey fabric.

'Maybe you should do the talking after all,' Irvine whispered to her neighbour.

Omar Fathy laughed. 'Work some of my dusky charm, you mean?' he gave her a nudge with his elbow, dark eyes glinting with mirth. Irvine grinned back suddenly feeling loads better.

As the lift door sighed open both Irvine and Fathy stood up. Despite the fact that Frances Donnelly had obviously clocked them the moment she stepped into the reception area her eyes were everywhere but on the two police officers, betraying her nervousness. Irvine's first impression was of an attractive girl, taller than average, dark red hair (not out of a bottle, the detective constable surmised) but with the air of someone who didn't know how nice looking she really was.

'Frances Donnelly,' she said, extending her hand to Irvine with a smile hovering hesitantly around her wide-lipped mouth.

'DC Irvine. We spoke on the phone,' Irvine told her, 'My colleague, Detective Constable Fathy.'

'Hello,' Frances smiled shyly at Omar Fathy who gave her his customary little bow.

Irvine suppressed a grin. She was becoming used to the young man's courtesies now and it was amusing to see their effect on other women.

'Is there somewhere we can go and talk that's a little more

private than here?' Irvine asked, making an almost imperceptible nod towards the receptionist who was probably ear-wigging like mad.

'Not really, it's all open plan upstairs,' Frances began. 'Could we maybe just go out somewhere?'

'Got anywhere in mind?' Irvine asked.

'There's a wee coffee bar I know near Elderpark. It's just a few minutes' drive from here. It should be fairly quiet this time of day,' Frances told them, her eyes darting from one to the other as though she were being a little too bold in offering her advice.

'Okay. We can talk on the way as well. Just a chat,' Irvine gave the girl her best smile, willing her to drop the shoulders that were up around her ears with tension. It couldn't be very nice for this girl, though, could it? she reminded herself. Having to see two complete strangers and talk about your dead boyfriend.

Frances Donnelly glanced at DC Irvine, a flustered expression on her face, as Fathy opened the main door, stepping back with a flourish to allow the two women to leave before him.

'Egyptian manners,' Irvine whispered to the girl. 'We call him Omar Sharif back at the ranch.'

Frances Donnelly gave a silent giggle and Irvine was gratified to see her relax as they walked across to the pool car, Fathy quickening his pace to do his chauffeur impression.

'He's new to Glasgow,' Irvine confided. 'We've all got bets on that this sort of stuff won't last the month.'

She was glad to see her colleague opening the front passenger door for Frances, edging himself into the rear seat so that the women could talk more easily.

'Suppose you're all pretty shocked about Mr Scott,' Irvine began.

'Oh, yes. I mean, things like that just don't happen to ordinary people, do they? His friend, Paul, the one who . . .' Frances bit her lip, not able to complete the sentence; *the one who found him.*

'The guy who car shared with him?' Irvine offered helpfully.

'Aye, Paul. He reckons it was a case of mistaken identity. You know he might be right,' Frances continued in a rush of words. 'I knew this couple who were away on holiday and came back to find their cars had been covered with paint stripper. Police said it was the action of someone who held a grudge. But the couple thought it must be a mistake. There was this bent lawyer lived behind them; same sort of position in the next cul-de-sac. Probably meant for him. It cost them a fortune to get their cars fixed as well.'

Irvine let her rattle on. Get the nerves away with a load of blethering and she'd maybe be calm enough to answer the questions that were really important.

The Ritz Cafe was on Govan Road, just a stone's throw from Elder Park and diagonally across from the massive fortress-like buildings that comprised the old Fairfield's shipyard. The cafe had seen better days, like the yards that must have given it trade in the past, but it was clean enough and as Frances had said, it was quiet. The two women slipped into a booth, sliding along the red leatherette benches.

'What would you like, ladies?' Fathy asked.

'Large decaf latte for me,' Irvine replied cheerfully as though they were on a wee outing.

'Cappuccino, please,' Frances replied. 'I can pay . . .'

Fathy shook his head. 'No need, ma'am. Our treat.'

'Aye, we'll get it off expenses, Frances. Nae worries,' Irvine grinned.

The girl removed her grey linen jacket and pushed it aside wedging it into the angle of the booth.

'We need to ask you things about Ken,' Irvine told her quietly. 'Is that what you called him? Ken?'

Frances nodded.

'See, thing is, we don't have an awful lot of information about Ken's background and we would like to contact any family he might have. You know? Rotten for folk to find out stuff like this from the newspapers,' she added, appealing to the girl's sense of fair play.

'So, what can you tell us about him? Family, friends, his ex-wife, that sort of thing.'

Frances Donnelly opened her mouth for a moment as though to speak then closed it again, looking away.

So, something she didn't want to say? Irvine thought. Interesting.

'Did he talk much about his ex-wife?' she ventured again.

The woman opposite heaved a sigh. 'No,' she said at last. 'I got the impression he still had feelings for her, though. He was . . .' she bit her lip as though to prevent any adverse comment being aired. *It didn't do to speak ill of the dead*, so many Glasgow worthies were apt to say. And it was a habit that had stuck with the younger generation as well. So why did DC Irvine have the distinct impression that this was exactly what was bugging Ken Scott's girlfriend?

'I don't know how to put this,' Frances continued, 'but any time he mentioned her he was angry and sad at the same time. Like she'd hurt him but he still couldn't get her off his mind.'

'Who brought the subject up. You or him?'

'Funny you asking that,' Frances said, 'it was always Ken who began talking about her. He'd see a woman in the street, maybe, and say, *she's like Marianne.* Then he'd go dead quiet. I don't think he wanted to talk about her but somehow I felt that he couldn't stop thinking about her either.'

41

'A bit obsessed, was he?' Irvine laughed as though to make a light-hearted joke about it though the words were in fact completely serious.

The redhead nodded. 'I think so. In fact,' she frowned suddenly, 'I sometimes wondered if he was still seeing her.'

'Oh, what gave you that idea?'

'Things he said,' Frances shrugged. 'It wasn't anything you could put a finger on, know what I mean? It was just . . .'

'Your feelings?'

'Aye. I mean he was a dead nice guy and we got on well, but it wasn't a relationship that was going to go anywhere. I wasn't jealous of his ex.' She shrugged again. "Spose that shows I wasn't all that stuck on him, doesn't it?'

'Not a crime to have a casual boyfriend,' Irvine countered. 'Anyhow, here's coffee. Thanks, Omar. Ooh, biccies as well. My this is a treat!' she said, raising her eyebrows as Fathy handed out glasses of coffee and a handful of Amaretti biscuits individually wrapped in coloured tissue.

'Frances was just telling me that Mr Scott was maybe still seeing his ex. Funny how we don't seem to be able to trace her, isn't it?' Irvine told Fathy.

'But surely there's an address or a phone number? He was always saying things about her as if he'd been with her.' Frances frowned, puzzled.

'She went off to do a pre-uni course at Anniesland College. But there's no trace of her at Glasgow Uni or any other university for that matter,' Irvine said, blowing on her coffee to cool it down.

'Maybe she changed back to her maiden name?' Fathy offered.

'Brogan? Nah, we looked into that. No sign of a Brogan either.'

'But she might have given herself any name at all. You can do that,' Frances said slowly, looking at DC Fathy. 'I remember Ken told me. He said you could change your name legally under Scottish law without having to go through the registry office.'

'True,' Irvine nodded. 'And we have to look into that possibility. Police work involves loads of paperwork, you know,' she told the girl. 'Trawling through files and registry office databases. So long as we find her to let her know,' Irvine made a face as if to say this wasn't really such a big deal. But inwardly she was experiencing a frisson of excitement: Ken Scott's wife might have tried to do a disappearing act. Why? And did this tell them anything about her husband? Change the subject, she told herself. Keep cool. 'Any idea where he was on his week's leave?'

Frances shook her head slowly. 'Said he might go up north. That's all I know, I'm afraid. Sorry.'

Irvine wondered at that. Why keep his plans secret from the girlfriend? Had Scott been hiding something?

'Tell me what he was like, Frances. Nice guy? Well liked by his pals?'

'Ken was quite ordinary. Nothing special, but he was nice. He had good manners,' she blushed again, looking involuntarily at Omar Fathy. 'That's always a plus, isn't it?'

'What about other family?' the Egyptian detective asked.

Frances shook her head. 'Nobody. His parents were both dead and he was an only child. Never spoke about aunties or cousins or that.'

'What did he do at Christmas, then? That's a time for family gatherings.'

'I don't know. He was vague about that,' the girl said, her eyes narrowing as she tried to remember. 'Mind you, that was just after we got together. Too soon to ask him to join my family, you know?' she looked at the two officers guiltily then put her hand to her mouth as though to stifle a sob. 'I still can't believe . . .'

'Hey, it's okay,' Irvine put a comforting arm around the girl's shoulder. 'Isn't it better to remember good stuff about him? Eh?'

'I know,' Frances sniffed, pulling a hankie from her cardigan pocket. 'And it's not as if we were dead serious or anything. It's just such a terrible thing to have happened. First he loses his wife then . . .' she shook her head, not trusting herself to continue.

Annie Irvine's eyes narrowed. *Loses his wife.* An odd expression to use, surely. The ex-wife wasn't dead after all. But splitting up from her must have been a big deal. There was something more to all of this, she was sure. And if Frances Donnelly couldn't supply the missing pieces, then who could?

CHAPTER 7

Billy Brogan's flat was two floors up in an old Victorian tenement that had seen better days. As he dodged the crumpled chip papers and discarded beer cans that littered the entrance the man's trainers made no sound, stealth being a habit he practised nowadays without thinking. Getting in had been easier than he'd expected; the outer door had been left ajar for some reason and a young Asian boy had emerged just as he had been about to press the buzzer for Brogan's flat. The lad had scarcely looked at him. What would he see? A fellow in nondescript jeans and jacket, a baseball cap pulled down to hide his face, he resembled lots of other blokes in lots of other cities. Should anyone attempt to describe him, they would struggle to find any distinguishing features. Not that he had none, but so long as he was on a job his tattooed arms were kept out of sight.

Brogan's flat had a pair of old-fashioned storm doors that were pulled back, revealing a half glazed front door. A light was on in the hall but, as the gunman raised the flap of letterbox he could hear not a single sound coming from within. He stood, blinking for a moment, wondering what to do. The element of surprise was essential, after all.

He turned the ancient wooden doorknob and the door opened

with a sigh. Stepping inside, he closed it carefully, making certain there was no sound of a click to alert listening ears.

A few steps further into the flat showed him that his caution had been completely unnecessary.

The place was trashed.

In the main lounge tables were overturned, cupboards broken and lying on their backs, their contents strewn all over the floor. A damp patch of something sticky lay underneath a pile of papers. He took a step back then bent down to investigate a bit more. Eventually one gloved hand rolled over an empty bottle of Ribena that had been deliberately spilled on the dusty carpet.

Everywhere was the same; curtains slashed to ribbons in the back bedroom, dishes smashed on the kitchen floor, a jar of coffee emptied over the mess. His boots crunched the dark grains as he tried to step around the shambles.

The gunman's eyes narrowed; someone else with a grudge had got here before him. So where the hell was Brogan? And where the hell was his money?

Doctor Rosie Fergusson waddled around the stainless steel operating table, her eyes never leaving the naked cadaver. Apart from the obvious hole in the middle of his forehead, he looked perfectly fine. There had been no nasty toxins in his blood to suggest the victim might have been a dabbler in illegal substances, nor even a trace of alcohol.

In death, Kenneth Scott appeared to be a nice looking chap, the muscles in his limbs had been well toned, his fingernails and toenails were trimmed and not ragged like so many blokes' tended to be, and his white, even teeth showed evidence of regular dental checks. In life? Rosie tended not to think too much about what a victim had been like in life. Her task was to find out what had caused the cessation of that final heartbeat and to record it all as carefully as she possibly could. In this case it was fairly straightforward. The preliminary X-rays had shown the bullet lodged inside the brain after it had penetrated the skull, so this would be a delicate piece of surgery.

She glanced up at the viewing window where the ballistics officer stood, waiting for her to retrieve the bullet.

'Okay, Em, open him up,' she instructed her technician. Emma came forward, scalpel in her gloved hand, bent over the cadaver and opened his scalp from ear to ear, reflecting it back so that the interior was visible. She was good at this, Rosie thought, and she needed to be. One false slip with that metal instrument and the rifling on the bullet might become damaged if it were close to the surface.

Rosie lifted up a pair of plastic forceps, ready to delve into the mass of tissues whenever the technician had finished her part of the job. The sound of the saw filled the room with its metallic buzz as the skull was opened for surgery. The pathologist stepped forward and paused. Forceps or fingers? It was a tricky bit of the procedure now to remove the object. Rosie decided on forceps. Carefully, carefully she reached into the wound, dipping her instrument into the exposed tissues. Then her steady hand drew out the bit of metal that had killed the man on her operating table.

Rosie let the bullet fall into the kidney-shaped dish, hearing it clatter. The man at the viewing window above would take possession of it, Rosie signing the production bag before he took it away. Every step of this long process of determining the man's death and finding his killer needed to be executed following all the rules of bagging and recording evidence. One slip and a later court case could come tumbling down with serious repercussions for the professional involved.

'Need to keep the brain and fix it for neuropathology so we can determine the precise track of it with regard to its direction,' Rosie said aloud. It was important that the ballistics officer could not only see what was going on but could hear everything the pathologist said through the sound system in the post-mortem room. 'We also need to determine what structures are damaged,' she added.

Rosie kept some thoughts to herself, though. It was a professional job, all right. She'd seen enough of them to say that with a high degree of certainty should she be asked in her capacity as an expert witness. He'd probably used a silencer. They all did, the pros. Her glance fell on the waxen body. He probably hadn't even seen it coming.

There was no mystery being found out in this post-mortem. It was a routine job, like so many others. The only mystery was who had killed him and why. And that was something for Lorimer and his team to discover.

'Couldn't it be a case of mistaken identity?'

Lorimer looked up sharply. 'What makes you say that?'

Detective Sergeant Niall Cameron drew in his breath before replying. 'He seems to have been such an innocuous sort of person, sir. No previous. No toxins in his bloodstream. Place of employment giving him a glowing character.' Cameron shrugged a narrow shoulder as if to reinforce his argument.

'A man opens his door in the middle of the night. He's shot at point-blank range, killed instantly. Nobody can make sense of that at the best of times, can they?' Lorimer replied. 'But I see your point, Niall. Scott had no known association with the criminal world. As far as we know he hadn't hacked anyone off enough to deserve this.'

'Not a football referee, then?' DS Alistair Wilson joked. A ripple of laughter ran through the officers assembled in the muster room. Wilson's remark harked back to a case they'd had involving a Glasgow football club, where a referee had been shot dead on his own doorstep.

'That's actually not a bad point to make,' Lorimer told them. 'We had no idea at the time about the referee's entire background. He looked as squeaky clean as this victim,' he turned to tap the photograph behind him. All eyes followed his glance. Kenneth Scott's blown-up photograph stared back at them, the black circle in his forehead looking for all the world as if some wag had drawn it there with marker pen.

'We need an awful lot more on this man's background before we can put it down to a case of mistaken identity. No matter what his chum thinks,' he added.

'Sir,' DC Irvine spoke up. 'There's something worrying me about the wife. I mean, the ex-wife. His girlfriend gave me the impression that he might still have been seeing her. And,' she paused for a beat, 'if he was, why haven't we found any address or phone number for her at his house?'

There was a murmur amongst the other officers at this.

Lorimer raised his hand to quieten them. 'Okay. This is just what I mean. You need to look for anything that's unusual or unexpected in this man's life. Sometimes it's the things that are missing that we need to consider,' he nodded at Irvine who reddened with pleasure at her boss's approval, 'And right now it's an ex-wife. What do we know about her so far, Annie?'

'Marianne Brogan, born 28th May 1977. Married Kenneth Scott on January 1st 2000.' She looked up, making a face, 'Like thousands of other couples all over the world. Anyway, they were divorced more than two years ago. No children. She worked as an admin assistant in local government out at Cowglen before she was married but according to the Department for Work and Pensions she didn't appear to have had a job at all after the marriage.' Irvine looked around her to see how her colleagues would react to this snippet of information. DI Jo Grant met her glance and raised her eyebrows.

'How many women nowadays just give up working once they're married?' Irvine persisted. 'And with no kids to look after? Makes you wonder, doesn't it? Anyway after the divorce she registered for a course at Anniesland College.'

'In her own name?' DI Grant wanted to know.

'That's the funny thing,' Irvine replied. 'She registered as Mrs Marianne Scott. But there was never an application made to the university in that name.'

'Most divorced women would surely revert to their maiden name,' Cameron remarked.

'You'd think so,' countered Irvine. 'But somehow we've lost her in the paperwork.'

She looked up at Lorimer. 'It's almost as if she wanted to become someone else, isn't it?'

'How about DWP? Was she ever a claimant before or after her marriage broke up?' Grant asked.

Irvine shook her head. 'Not a Scooby there either. And her last bank details were just after her admission to Anniesland College when she withdrew all of her funds and closed the account.'

'So she could be anywhere? Abroad, even?' Jo Grant persisted.

'Well, we've no reason to think of her as a murder suspect, have we?' DS Wilson broke in. 'And if she's started a new life for herself we can hardly ask Interpol to trace her just so's we can let her know her ex-hubby's dead, can we?'

'Okay. We keep looking for her, but not as a top priority. Maybe the girlfriend's intuition is wrong,' Lorimer said. 'Maybe Scott hadn't seen his ex-wife for a long time. It would certainly explain why a house he's been living in for the last eighteen months shows no sign of her.'

'Wanted to give himself a fresh start, probably,' Cameron chipped in.

'We still have several of Scott's associates at work to interview. See if any information about Mrs Scott emerges, okay? And find out what he was doing on his week off. Ask the neighbours if he was about. Talk to the postman. You know the score, Annie.'

DC Irvine tried not to grimace as she nodded. It would be a case of grinding through family members (of whom there appeared to be none) and his workmates.

'And you'll continue having DC Fathy to help you,' Lorimer added.

Annie Irvine's mouth twisted into the semblance of a smile as if she were keeping her pleasure to herself.

Lorimer glanced at her, eyes twinkling for just a second, but it was enough to let her know he could see right through her.

'Now, soldier, you're going to have to make something of this,' the hit man whispered to himself. He was sitting on an armchair that he had turned right way up, gazing at the debris littered around the room. If there was anything of value, then he was going to have it, but better than that, he might be able to find some address book or other that would give him a clue to Brogan's whereabouts.

Outside the bay window he could hear the noise of traffic mingling with the thud of some heavy machinery from a nearby building site. It had been a while since he'd visited this godforsaken city full of mad Jocks and the hit man realised that it had changed a lot. He'd noticed new blocks of flats that had sprung up around the riverside and more bridges spanning the Clyde's oily waters. Across on the south bank he had glimpsed the BBC and STV buildings, their roofs sporting a mass of satellite dishes. The whole area seemed to be on the up, he thought. Maybe Brogan's place was worth a bit of money these days.

'Right,' he sighed, easing himself out of the chair. 'Let's see what you've got hidden away, Billy boy.'

The bedroom was the obvious place to begin. But whoever had been here before him had well and truly gone through every drawer and cabinet, emptying the contents onto the manky carpet. The hit man wrinkled his nose. The whole place reeked of cannabis. He stopped for a minute, considering. There was no finesse in the search that had happened before his arrival. Just an angry rampage through the place, as though whoever had been here had scattered the stuff around in a furious temper. A drug fuelled temper, perhaps? Brogan was now a weaselly little Glasgow dealer, that much he knew from his enquiries about the man he remembered from the old days. And he'd obviously made himself some enemies. 'There's someone here who'll do more than throw your stuff, around, Billy Boy,' he promised the silent room.

Wearing these thick leather gloves to rake through all of this mess was a nuisance, but he did not dare leave his prints anywhere. The hit man hunkered down and patiently sifted through every piece of discarded paper, turning each bit over and reading it as he made a neat pile on the space beside the overturned bedside cabinet.

There was a reporter's notebook, some pages ripped out and the rest blank, a plastic wallet full of old bank statements that made the man's eyebrows rise in surprise at the last paltry amount in credit. Still, the bloke was a dealer and dealers invariably used cash in their business transactions. Somewhere, Brogan was out there with ten grand of his, he reminded himself.

He'd given up finding anything of value when his hand slipped on the last few papers, making him lose his balance and fall sideways against the bed. It was then that he saw it: a small, black bound book lying amongst filthy clumps of dust under the top end of the bed.

Flattening his hand, the hit man reached for it, but the space was too narrow. Swearing softly to himself, he drew off the left hand glove and tried again. This time his fingertips reached the edge of the notebook and he felt its grainy surface under his fingernails. Slowly and carefully he drew it out then sat up, resting his back on the side of Brogan's bed.

It was an old diary from a year back. The hit man flicked through it from front to back until he came to the section for addresses. None of the names meant a thing to him, but there were a few with telephone numbers against them so at least that would be a start.

What to do now? If he were to check into another hotel and Brogan came back, he might miss his chance of nailing the little bastard. On the other hand, if the dealer had had to scarper in a hurry, perhaps he had simply been unable to keep to the agreed rendezvous?

The man closed his eyes as he considered his options. He'd been in worse places. A flash of white hot desert came to mind, the heat beating down, sweat gluing his hair to his helmet. He opened his eyes again, seeing the dust motes thick in the air as a shaft of sunlight crept into the room, smelling the rank odour of spent joints. Aye, he'd been in hellholes worse than this crummy little pad that Brogan called home.

CHAPTER 8

The short, dark-skinned man in the ill-fitting leather jacket whistled a tune between his teeth. It was a sunny day here in the city and the long shadows reminded him of home. Just for a moment, though. Home was so very different from this place where total strangers might try to engage him in conversation, just to be friendly. It had taken Amit a long, long time to become accustomed to the '*y'all right, pal?*' a passing workman might toss over his shoulder as Amit hesitated at the margin of some busy road. But now he was safe. His papers were in order, he had a legitimate reason to be here. The dark threat of deportation had gone and in its place was the prospect of a sunny future.

Amit rounded a corner and shrank back against the wall as two uniformed police officers strode towards him. It took all of his courage to continue walking, eyes cast downwards, praying that they would pass him.

Sudden memories came back as the pair drew nearer: the blows from the baton raining down upon his head; yells that were accompanied by kicks in the tender parts of his body until he held himself tightly, foetus-like on the ground.

When the police officers had passed him by and crossed at the traffic lights, Amit let out his breath and wiped the sweat from his palms onto his trouser legs, trembling uncontrollably. If they should find out . . .

So far Amit had been lucky. The Scottish *polis*, as his friend Dhesi in the restaurant called them, were no' sae bad. But they *were* policemen and where Amit came from that meant fear and suffering, sudden visits in the night and brothers taken away, never to be seen again. He dragged his feet along the street that led to Glasgow Central station, the shadows from the railway bridge a comfort after the brightness of this summer sunlight. '*The Hielandman's Umbrella*,' his friend had called it the first time they had walked together along this darkened stretch of road. '*Where all the Teuchters came to meet their pals when they'd come down from the Hielands.*' It seemed a strange sort of meeting place, this gloomy space below the massive railway overhead, but Amit supposed it had at least served to keep these Northerners dry. Hence its nickname.

Amit recalled days of monsoon rains when everybody laughed and danced to feel the warm drops cascading down, the welcoming waters breaking the thunderclouds that had built up such terrible tension for weeks on end.

Then the rivers of his homeland had run red with the blood of family and friends.

It was better to forget such a past if he could. Scotland was his home now. Some days Amit found himself welcoming the strange, fine mist that enveloped the city; and he had been here long enough now to find that the sunshine could break through at any time.

'*Wait five minutes an' the weather'll change*,' an old lady had cackled in his ear one day. This city was full of them, little old ladies who bustled about, crossing the busy roads fearlessly, too impatient to wait at the designated traffic lights. Amit always waited for the green figure before moving off the pavement, more afraid of drawing attention to himself than of the traffic that criss-crossed the city.

The station suddenly loomed ahead and Amit turned into its noisy, echoing entrance, eyes searching for the escalator that would take him up to the higher level above the street. Their agreed rendezvous was a better meeting place than that dingy street, a bustling coffee shop whose very anonymity Amit found reassuring. Strangers came for a time, drank coffee, their lives suspended between where they had been and where they were heading, coffee filling the gap. Was that what he had with Marianne? A gap between his past and his future? The sudden longing that came to him was tinged with a sense of hopelessness.

As he entered the coffee bar he could hear music being played in the background, the tune and lyrics masked by the barista banging coffee grounds into a bin and the hissing of steam as milk was frothed up for the waiting customers. In one corner a bald, bespectacled man carried on a one-way conversation with his mobile phone. Nobody cared any more about discretion, Amit thought, overhearing snatches of the man's words; business was regularly conducted in such public places.

She had arrived before him and was sitting with her back to the window. There was no mistaking that cascade of red hair tumbling down her back. Marianne looked up sharply as Amit approached her table. Her large black handbag had been placed on the seat next to her as if reserving a place for him and, as she removed it, he bent over to kiss her cheek.

'Hello, Marianne,' he murmured.

'Okay, that'll do. No need for any of that stuff, Amit,' she said. But there was a smile upon her lips as she looked up at him. 'How're you doin' anyway?'

The small dark man shrugged his bony shoulders, making the leather jacket seem even more shapeless than usual. 'I have a day off today,' he replied, carefully. His English was perfect, that of an educated man and better than most of the people who lived in this city, but sometimes even that made him feel set apart. 'Sunday the restaurant is closed.' He shrugged again. 'So I can buy you lunch, perhaps?'

Marianne smiled again. 'That would be lovely, thanks. D'you want to go out of town since it's a nice day? We could get a train to Ayr, if you liked. See the seaside. Eh? How about it?'

Amit looked thoughtful for a moment then shook his head. 'I am sorry,' he said. 'I need to see somebody later today.' He gave a stiff little nod that might have been a gesture of apology or even a little bow.

Marianne raked her fingers through her hair then let it fall over her cheeks. 'Och, well, never mind. It's good to keep in touch, though. See you're doing all right.'

She looked around, noticing a group of travellers with pull-along luggage trolleys enter the coffee shop. 'Come on, it's getting too busy here. Let's go and get some sandwiches and sit in George Square.'

As they came back into the main concourse of the station, the woman sensed her companion slow down and move closer to her side. Marianne looked up to see two British Transport Police officers standing talking together outside the entrance to the disabled toilet. She took Amit's hand and pulled him towards the middle of the station where streams of people were walking to and from the platforms. The intimate gesture reminded her suddenly of another man whose hand she had once held. But that hand was cold now, cold and gone. The woman squeezed Amit's hand, suppressing her shiver.

58

'It's okay,' she urged him. 'You're just part of Glasgow's rich and varied landscape now. There's no need to worry any more. I promise. Nobody's going to send you back.'

Yet, as they headed for the Gordon Street exit, something made the woman turn her head, just to see if the policemen were watching them.

CHAPTER 9

Detective Chief Inspector Lorimer frowned at the papers on his desk. The ballistics report was complete and Rosie's pathology results were all there, including the toxicology report. Some background information about Kenneth Scott had been written up by his officers and so far it made pretty boring reading. There was nothing there. Not a thing to show why a supposedly upright member of the community had been gunned down in the hallway of his own home. And it had all the hallmarks of a professional hit, the gunman even taking time to remove the cartridge case from the scene of crime.

Perhaps Cameron and Scott's mate, Paul, were right. Perhaps this had been a case of mistaken identity. If so, he reasoned, would there be another killing soon? Finding the correct target this time? His mouth hardened. Trust something like this to come up just when he had planned his summer leave. Usually Lorimer and his wife, Maggie, took a break at the beginning of July but this year it hadn't happened. Instead he had allowed the roster to be filled up by fellow officers who had young families and needed to fit their plans in with the Scottish school terms. Having no kids of their own, the Lorimers had decided to let the holidays drift, even though Maggie was similarly constrained in her teaching profession. Next week was the final week of her summer vacation, then it would be back for a couple of in-service days at Muirpark Secondary School before the kids came streaming into the playground once again.

This last week had been earmarked by the DCI, however. One of the officers in the division had cancelled his leave and Lorimer had jumped at the chance to take Maggie away to their favourite hideout, a cottage miles from anywhere on the isle of Mull. Now, he reflected gloomily, even that small respite might be denied them.

The telephone rang out twice before he yanked it off its cradle.

'Lorimer,' he said. There was a pause before the voice on the line identified itself as Doctor Solomon Brightman.

'Um,' Solly said, then paused again. 'I have a problem. Not quite sure what to do about it.'

Lorimer leaned back in his chair, letting it swivel around from side to side as he smiled at the sound of his friend's voice. Despite his years in Glasgow, Solly's accent was still one hundred per cent that of a Londoner. A well-educated, Jewish Londoner who had the annoying habit of filling a conversation with lengthy blanks.

'Okay. Shoot,' Lorimer told him.

'I have had a letter from the Assistant Chief Constable,' Solly began. There was another pause and this time Lorimer stopped swinging in his chair and sat up, listening.

'It seems that there has been a change in policy and that my services may no longer be required by Strathclyde Police,' Solly said quietly.

'Good Lord! What else did it say? Does she give any reasons for that?'

'Only that there has been a change in policy regarding the use of criminal profiling,' Solly said.

Lorimer could hear the hurt and disappointment in the man's

voice. Doctor Solomon Brightman had been instrumental in helping to solve various murder cases in which Lorimer had been the Senior Investigating Officer and the policeman had learned to value his insights.

'Did she hint at budgetary constraints?' Lorimer asked, wondering if the credit crunch had been to blame.

'No,' Solly said. There was a silence then the psychologist blurted out, 'Is it me? Are they not happy with something I've done?'

'Hey, don't even consider that for a minute,' Lorimer told him. 'You're well thought of around here, surely you know that!'

'Then why . . .?' Solly left his question unfinished.

'I really don't know, Solly. But leave it with me and I'll see what I can find out. Anyway, you've got enough to do right now, haven't you? A book almost ready for publication and a new baby on its way. Got that spare room made into a nursery yet?'

The psychologist's voice brightened up as he took Lorimer's lead and chatted about the changes he had made to the spacious top floor flat that overlooked Kelvingrove Park.

Lorimer put down the phone and looked at it, thoughtfully. Why had Solly been so summarily dismissed from the police service? Was it money? Or was it something to do with that case south of the border where an eminent criminal profiler had got things spectacularly wrong? Lorimer thought about the case for a few minutes.

Doctor Richard Thackeray (*Doctor Dick*, the less salubrious newspapers had taken to calling him) had profiled a young man with some pretty serious mental health issues as being the perpetrator of six prostitute murders. The man had been taken into custody, the southern police force thoroughly relieved to have found their killer. Or so they had thought. After being brutalised by his cellmate, the young man had committed suicide. The press had been less than charitable, hinting at justice being snatched out of the hands of the courts.

Then the whole shebang had collapsed with the killing of a seventh victim and the apprehension of another man, one who appeared to be, ironically, completely sane. The man's DNA was all over the other victims and so a confession of sorts had been obtained.

Yet again a furore had broken out, the redtops changing their stance once more, this time baying for the blood of Doctor Richard Thackeray. This had all taken place last year but now the killer was due for sentencing. Alongside the media fuss, the future career of Thackeray was being mooted. Several of the better papers had run features on criminal profiling, not always portraying it in a positive light. Was that it, then? Had police forces around the country decided that profiling had had its day? As a mere DCI, Lorimer was not party to the sort of policing politics that determined things like that.

Perhaps he might have a word with Her Nibs, as they all called Joyce Rogers, the Assistant Chief Constable. She was a fair-minded individual and would at least give Lorimer a chance to put forward Solly's case.

Omar was staring at the open door of his locker. Instead of the clean grey metal interior there was a piece of A4 paper fixed with Blu-Tack. The scrawl of words jumped out at him.

GET THE FUCK OUT OF HERE BLACK BASTARD

The officer felt the sweat prickle under his collar. Giving a quick glance to see if anyone was watching, he tore the page off the door and crumpled it into a ball then thrust it right at the back of the locker, behind his gym kit and the rest of his stuff. His fingers felt stiff and clumsy as he tried to shut the locker and, as he turned the key, Omar noticed that the doorframe now sat at a slight angle. Someone had clearly broken into his locker. You didn't need to be a CID officer to work that one out. But that wasn't why the young Egyptian was having difficulty in controlling his trembling hands.

It wasn't the first time.

Racist slurs like this had been the officer's main reason for quitting Grampian region's police force. He'd thought to have put it all behind him now. But, unless this was some sort of fiendish coincidence, it seemed as if his unknown tormentor had followed him all the way down from Aberdeen.

'Okay?' Annie Irvine smiled at the young man who approached her, his eyes looking everywhere except in her direction. DC Irvine groaned inwardly. Had she come on to him too strongly? Embarrassed the poor guy? She sighed. Och well, better get on with the job in hand, pretend it never happened. *Like it was ever going to*, a small voice whispered into her ear. *Why imagine that he'd fancy you?*

'Hello,' Fathy's smile was strained but he was still being the polite foreigner, Irvine thought, waiting for her so he could open the car door.

'Right,' Irvine said brusquely. 'Boss's orders. Let's get gitting, partner,' she attempted a smile to lighten the atmosphere but the man beside her seemed occupied in thoughts of his own, turning away and looking out of the window as she drove away from headquarters.

By the time they had reached the motorway Irvine had reconciled herself to a merely platonic friendship with this particularly attractive male specimen of the human race.

'Been to Glasgow before?' she asked brightly.

Fathy turned as if he had forgotten there was another person in the car beside him. 'What? Oh. Glasgow. Yes, loads of times. We came here for quite a few cultural visits when I was at school.'

'You went to school in Scotland?' Annie's eyebrows shot up, her notions of the man as an exotic stranger suddenly disappearing. 'Sorry, it's just that you don't sound all that Scottish.'

'Oh, yes,' Fathy replied, his mouth twisted into a strange little grimace of a smile. 'Both my parents are Egyptian but I was born here. Went to boarding school in Perthshire. Father was insistent that his sons all had the best education possible,' he continued. 'And St Andrews University was the natural choice after that,' he shrugged.

'What did you study?' Irvine glanced away from the road ahead for a split second, curious to see his expression.

'Philosophy and maths,' Fathy told her. 'Perfect degree for anyone wanting to be a copper.'

His tone held just a trace of irony and Irvine wanted to push a wee bit harder, to nosy in to the Egyptian's past to find out more, but something stopped her. Be cool, she told herself. Keep to neutral ground. It was something she'd learned from watching Lorimer with people in interview situations.

'Did you not go on to do honours, then?'

'Yes, actually. Got a first as it happens.' He shrugged again as if it was no great shakes or else he was shy of being seen as a brainy type.

Irvine kept her eyes on the road as she digested this snippet of information. 'Och, I just did an ordinary at Strathclyde,' she told him. 'Never could do maths.' She gave him a wicked grin. 'I'll get you to do my time sheets if I ever get stuck, eh?' She moved her elbow as if to dig him in the ribs, a gesture that said at once that she was only being a pal, a mate, nothing more.

66

Irvine drove on, her thoughts taking a different turn. Fathy's well-educated voice had made her think he'd received his education abroad, at an international school perhaps. Or maybe that he'd been sent to the UK by his family. It had never once dawned on her that he might actually consider himself Scottish. Don't be so small-minded, woman, she scolded herself.

What made you join the polis? she wanted to ask. But again, something prevented the words from being uttered. He might well ask her the same question. And Annie Irvine knew that her standard answer to such a question, *to help the community*, might not fool this man as it had fooled so many. No, better to keep these things to herself. She was doing okay now, wasn't she? CID might be a sideways move but it felt like progress. Annie Irvine could be proud of her career path so far. Joining up, for her, had been purely cathartic; a move to signal that she could face her fears head on, maybe even be rid of them for good, one day.

'Right, let's see what this lot have to say for themselves,' she muttered, turning into the car park of the call centre. 'See if anyone can throw a bit of light on Mr Scott.' Thoughts about Omar Fathy had to be shelved for now.

And any thoughts about her own past would be easily forgotten in the process of this investigation.

CHAPTER 10

Amit drained the last of his coffee. It was the quiet part of the day when the staff had an hour to go about their own business. Some, like Paramsit Dhesi, drove over to the south side of the city to spend a little time with families. Others drifted away from the restaurant in twos or threes, chattering in a Punjabi dialect that reminded him all too clearly of the streets of Lahore.

Visions of the city came to him like snapshots: the still lakes of water reflecting sun-drenched skies at noon; the market with people constantly coming and going, its smells of ripe fruit, cattle and dust wafting in the stifling air; the train cutting through the city, its open windows full of travellers staring out at the wonders of Lahore. He remembered the family house in Gulberg, its pink washed walls and curving windows: each sill and lattice detail decorated in the style of a Mughal's palace. Then there were the clubs, his father's meetings at the Moslem League, the polo matches. But these pictures in his mind were like something he had seen in a film or a dream, not part of his own history.

The images of bloody bodies, his mother's scream as the Inter-Services Intelligence dragged his father away, these were the stuff of nightmares, locked away in some deep, dark part of his brain, never brought out willingly for examination.

The sound of crates being delivered to the back door made Amit stir from his reverie. He was in Glasgow now, safe in the place that he was beginning to call his own.

His mouth turned up at the corners as he recalled the first time he had sat at this very table. A coffee, that was all he had asked for, but that one request had brought him so much more.

Dhesi had sat down beside him, his hand extended, the light of recognition in his eyes as Amit had spoken.

'You are an *Aitchisonian*!' Dhesi had exclaimed, his hand ready to shake Amit's own.

'Yes, but . . .'

'I could tell, my brother, I could tell!' Dhesi had clasped his hand with such warmth that Amit had suddenly heard the familiar inflection in his voice. Only a person who had attended Aitchison College, Lahore's premier educational establishment, would speak in such dignified tones. But here? In this Scottish city? It was nothing short of a miracle.

'This is nothing short of a miracle,' he remembered Dhesi's words and how he had grinned as if he had been able to read the stranger's thoughts.

And, for each of them it was just that. Dhesi had sat for the best part of that quiet hour, lamenting the problem he faced with his establishment. A partner who was not to be trusted any longer. Dhesi's desire to buy the man out. 'But what can I do?' he had shrugged, his upturned hands expressing his helplessness. 'I don't have the sum of money needed to send the rascal packing and the banks are simply unwilling to lend at this time of recession.'

By the end of that hour, Amit and Dhesi had not just clasped their hands together in recognition of their joint past, but had shaken on a deal that would mean much to them both. Amit would buy out the other partner and invest in this business (once

70

he had examined the books. *Of course*, Dhesi had said hurriedly, *that was understood*.)

And for Amit it had signalled a new beginning. He had a place of business now, a partnership in a thriving restaurant and a friend upon whom he could rely.

Money had not been a problem. The *Hundi*, the fixer, had arranged everything just as he had promised. Trust of a different sort had been all important, of course, but Amit had been in a situation where even had he been robbed blind by the go-between, he would have given the man his hefty commission. Nonetheless his funds had been transferred to an account in a Glasgow bank and to his surprise they had not been reduced by more than the agreed fee. Honour was still intact, even in this cold, Western land.

His rental flat was comfortable but it was time now to make another sort of investment. A place of his own, here in Glasgow's West End.

Amit thought of the woman with the long red hair. Marianne. If he could run his fingers through those silken tresses . . . touch her in a way that brought a smile to her lips . . .

He dismissed the sudden fantasy. She had been useful to him, wasn't that all? And Amit knew the time was approaching when his friends would expect him to be rid of her for good.

CHAPTER 11

'Dinner'll be ready in a minute,' Maggie called out, hearing her husband closing the front door behind him. 'Salad again.' She turned and made a face. 'I've tried to go easy on the avocados but there's plenty of chicken and bacon. Okay?'

Lorimer sidestepped the ginger cat that was attempting to wind itself around his trouser leg and walked across the room to where his wife was putting the finishing touches to a dressing. The scent of oranges wafted from the breakfast bar where she was standing and he sniffed the air appreciatively.

'Smells good. New recipe?'

Maggie smiled and shook her dark curls. 'No. Just made it up as I went along. Inspired by what was in the fridge.' She looked up at the tall man who was leaning against the counter. He was, Maggie Lorimer thought, the sort of person who filled a room just by being there.

She was suddenly reminded of the first time she had seen him. A crowd of her pals had been gossiping in the students' union, a few weeks into the beginning of term, when this tall young man had wandered in, his eyes fixed on somebody at the far end of the room. He had walked past Maggie and her girlfriends, and as he passed she had turned to follow him with her gaze. His loping walk, the intent expression in his face, something . . . what had it been? A quality of stillness within, perhaps? So different from the clowning, posturing of so many of the lads trying to impress. Maggie had gone out of her way after that to look for this one.

He told the story his own way, of course: she had been sitting alone in the crowded cafeteria and he'd given her that crooked smile of his. 'Is it all right . . .?' he'd asked and she'd gestured for him to sit down beside her. He'd been watching her for weeks, he said, waiting for a chance to say hello.

That same crooked smile made Maggie's heart turn over now as he put out his hand and touched her hair.

'Good to be home,' was all he said but those few words and that blue gaze spoke far more to Maggie than any earnest proclamations of love. Scotsmen didn't go in for flowery speeches and this one was no exception.

'Just as well it's salad,' was all she said, opening the refrigerator door and sliding the bowl back in.

Later, as she watched him pull on his jeans, Maggie wondered at the chemistry that had brought them together and the bond that held them now. Okay they'd had their ups and downs but each storm had been weathered: the nights of sobbing into her pillow after each miscarriage, the bereavements as sharp as if these poor half-formed babies had been family members already; the endless weeks when she hardly saw him during a difficult murder case; the months of separation when she had left him to work in America. Somehow each of these things had made their marriage more secure. Or was it that their need for one another was deeper than mere desire?

A lift of his eyebrows as he turned to look at her made Maggie's cheeks glow.

'How about some food now? Dragging a poor man off to bed before he has a chance to eat his dinner!' He gave a little laugh then, fastening his jeans, came over and bent to kiss her gently. 'Thanks for starters,' he murmured in a tone that had Maggie wanting to pull him back into bed again.

'Ow!' she exclaimed, sitting up abruptly. 'Cramp in my toes!' she added.

'Come on, stand up and it'll be better.'

He lifted her out of bed, his hands warm against her naked flesh, holding her against him for a long moment.

'Right,' he slapped her bottom gently. 'Now I really need some food. See you downstairs.' Then, releasing her, he picked up a discarded T-shirt from the floor and was gone.

Maggie flexed her foot, willing her toes to uncurl again. She hobbled across the room, pulled her cotton dressing gown from the back of the door and slipped into the shower room, glad of the cool shower tray beneath her feet.

Minutes later she was dressed and heading back down to the kitchen, her hair wrapped in a towel. There was no sign of Bill but the open door suggested that they were eating out of doors this evening. She yanked off the towel, draping it on the back of a chair to dry then pulled her fingers through her long, dark curls. It would dry in minutes out in the garden.

'How was your day?' she asked. Her husband made a face, his mouth still full of food.

'Hm, good as that, eh? Or was it murder?' she joked.

'Had a call from Solly,' Lorimer began, then, as Maggie shot him a look, he began to relate what the psychologist had told him.

'That's peculiar, surely,' Maggie said at last. 'With Solly's track record the force should be letting him know he's a part of any investigation into multiple murders. Come on,' she reasoned, 'he's been feted by the media up here, so why should another man's mistake affect our Solly?'

Lorimer shrugged and made a face. 'Not fair, is it? But I can't see what I can do about it other than have a wee word with Joyce Rogers. It'll have been decided at a policy meeting. Still,' he went on, 'it would have been nice to have had some prior warning. A memo from on high, at least. Solly seemed really hurt.'

'Is it true what the papers are saying, then?' Maggie wondered aloud. 'Do they really think that psychological profiling has had its day?'

'I hope not,' Lorimer replied. He ran his fingers through his dark hair. 'Och, I can remember when I was completely against it myself. Thought it was interference from outside.'

'But that was before you saw the great Doctor Brightman in action,' Maggie laughed.

'Aye, so it was. Though I wouldn't really say Solly had been guilty of a lot of running around. It's more the way he sits back and views a case from different sorts of angles. Working with statistics and maps and things. Almost scientific,' he added in a mumble.

Maggie gave a hoot of laughter. 'Now that is an admission, Detective Chief Inspector. *Almost* scientific.'

'Anyway, he's not likely to be involved in the murder case we're investigating just now. Unless there's a mad gunman about to hit the Glasgow streets.'

The hit man tried again to turn the key in the lock but it was no use. Whoever had been responsible for breaking into Brogan's pad had done a damned good job of wasting the front door. Chucking the key behind him into the mess of stuff lying on the floor, he pushed the door back and forwards, testing it. He considered the

76

security of the place. A pair of bolts had been nailed to the inside, top and bottom, but neither was flush with its original hasp any more and a thorough search of the flat had failed to turn up any decent tools to fix them. It was typical of Brogan. Always had been a lazy, careless sod. He cursed him as he stepped onto the landing.

The man's boots made hollow echoing sounds as he headed down the stone steps. Okay. He'd have to risk leaving this place for a while. His own toolkit was locked inside the boot of his car. He paused at the entrance to the close before setting foot on the Glasgow streets. There were calls to make this evening, but he could do that from the car. It was parked not too far away and it would be sensible to move it to another place before it was remarked upon by any nosey neighbours. Care and attention to detail had always been his watchwords and he wasn't going to neglect either now.

'Hello?' Marianne lifted the telephone from its hook after two rings. *Never give your name*, Billy had always dinned into her. After the last couple of years that advice had become second nature to the red-haired woman. And not just because her wee brother was a drug dealer, mixing with a strange assortment of folk.

The voice on the other end of the line was unfamiliar, an English accent that Marianne couldn't place.

'Hallo. Is Billy there?' the voice asked, in a tone that was friendly enough to make Marianne relax a little.

'Sorry, no, he's not,' she answered. 'May I ask who's calling?' she added politely.

'Oh, I'm a pal of Billy's from the old days. In Glasgow for a bit. Thought I'd look him up,' the man added.

Marianne frowned suddenly. 'How did you get this number?'

'Billy gave me it. Said to ring if he wasn't at the flat.'

'Oh,' Marianne stood for a moment, wondering. That was okay, then, wasn't it? Billy never gave out any details of her number or whatever address she was using. So this old friend must be from his army days, someone who had no earthly idea of the Brogan family or their affairs.

'Haven't seen him since we came home together on leave that last time. Man, that was some night!' the man on the other end of the line chuckled.

It was a warm, friendly sort of laugh and Marianne found herself smiling. Its very normality made her feel good.

'Well, I'm sorry I can't help you . . . what did you say your name was?'

There was a long pause and no reply then an unintelligible voice that faded until she could make out the words *line breaking up* and the connection was dead.

For a moment Marianne looked at the receiver then replaced it on its stand. Pity, she thought. He sounded nice. But not nice enough to break her promise not to give out her brother's mobile number. Then she frowned. Why wasn't Billy at home?

Curious, she lifted the telephone again and dialled. As she listened to the unfamiliar ringtone, the woman sat down suddenly. Now she knew why that man hadn't found Billy Brogan in his flat.

And if her suspicions were correct he would not find him anywhere in Scotland, never mind Glasgow.

He put the folded handkerchief back into his pocket, thinking hard. Either this woman really didn't know where he'd gone or she was lying to protect him. She hadn't sounded too put out. A pleasant, educated voice, someone he'd enjoy talking to in another time and another place. And who was she anyway, this

Marianne whose name had been written in red ink and under-lined? A girlfriend? He didn't think so. There had been an absence of any sort of proprietorial tone to her voice. Maybe she was an ex? Hadn't seen Billy boy for a while. One way or another he had to find her, make her tell him what he wanted to know – the whereabouts of Billy Brogan. And his ten thousand pounds.

CHAPTER 12

The slate blue sky was streaked with salmon pink clouds when Annie Irvine stood looking out from the balcony of her top-storey flat, a glass of wine in her hand. The Glasgow cityscape twinkled before her, though how long she might enjoy gazing at it was anybody's guess. Planning consent had been given for a multi-storey building that would be constructed right in front of her block of flats but so far there was no sign of any start to the project. So Annie was determined to enjoy the view while she could. Far ahead was the dark spire of the university, just visible on the edge of the skyline. The roads between were a blur of dark shapes punctuated by lozenges of lit windows, reminders of other lives out there, other people with hopes, dreams and fears like her own.

Once Annie's fears had included the monthly mortgage payment. She'd bought her flat when property had been at a premium, worried sick by how far she had extended herself. But the credit crunch had taken the sting out of that, with interest rates tumbling down so that now the policewoman could enjoy a reasonable standard of living. She swirled the red wine round and round, though she doubted whether it made any difference to aerate a bottle of stuff this price. Probably not, she told herself, taking another mouthful. Ach, it tasted fine to her, anyway.

For a moment she wondered what sort of fine wines Omar Fathy was used to drinking. With his expensive schooling and posh accent (*not fair, Irvine, he's just a nicely spoken man!* she scolded herself) he was probably accustomed to the sort of bottles that came all cobwebby from a real vintner's, not cheap supermarket plonk like this. The woman gave a sigh then leaned forward, resting one arm on the railing. She'd never fancied a fellow officer like this before. Maybe it was because Omar was a bit different. Well, a *lot* different, she admitted, giggling a little at her thoughts. Certainly he was drop-dead gorgeous and she was sure she wasn't the only female officer who couldn't take her eyes off him. But it was more than that. Annie had felt at ease with him, as if they could be good friends. *Or more*, a little voice whispered in her ear.

So far DC Annie Irvine had managed to work happily with her colleagues without being asked out on dates. Maybe her manner had been a trifle wary, giving out the signal that she wasn't up for that sort of stuff? Annie grinned. Doctor Brightman would no doubt be able to suss out that one, wouldn't he?

But would the good doctor be able to plumb the depths of her heart? A heart that had been sorely tried and that even now fluttered uncertainly as she contemplated a situation where she might be able to trust a man in her life again. Annie tipped her head back, letting the last of the wine slide down her throat, determined to blot out any glimpse of threatening memories.

Omar Adel Fathy flicked the remote until the programme reached his chosen channel. He had eaten a chicken ready meal out of the hoard that he kept in his tall fridge freezer, a stack of meals supplied by M&S. Fridge to oven, to plate to stomach. He sighed, watching the football teams run all over the green space on his plasma screen. It wasn't like the old days when he had been at home, cosseted by loving parents, given choice dishes by their resident cook. But then rebellion on his part had put an end to that sort of lifestyle, hadn't it? Joining the police force and making his own way in life had been his way of escape.

'Ah!' he cried aloud as someone missed a sitter, the ball ricocheting off the crossbar and back into the defence. His eyes were glued to the game but Omar's mind was half on his past and the ties he had chosen to cut. Nepotism had not been a dirty word in his family. On the contrary, it was expected that the children would follow their father's steps in his multi-million business. He could have been ensconced in a nice office job with a fantastic salary if he had toed the family line. Instead here he was in a bog-standard flat eating the same dinner as hundreds of other single men as they watched television. And it felt great!

'Come on!!' he urged the striker who had gathered up the ball at his feet and was now running towards an open goal.

'Yes!!' Omar stood up, still clutching his dinner plate, then sat down again, grinning. Here he was, free to pursue his own life, doing a job he loved. What happened tomorrow was unpredictable and that was one of the things he enjoyed about being a police officer. Would there be a development in the case he was on, perhaps? There was something strange about this murder, he mused. Why would an innocent man be gunned down on his doorstep in the middle of the night?

His partner had given a cynical reply to that question, hadn't she?

Irvine had smiled at him in that funny way she had and tapped a finger against the side of her nose, 'More to this than meets the eye. Wait and see what we dig up, pal,' she had told him. And Omar had felt something stirring in him, an excitement about being part of this Glasgow team, a thrill at having DCI Lorimer as his boss.

Omar put down the half-eaten chicken and sat back, arms folded as the teams regrouped on the pitch. Superintendent Mitchison had said to come to him for anything he wanted. And so he could. But if he was going to share the knowledge of that note inside his locker it would have to be with someone he could really trust. DC Irvine? he wondered. Or would she think him a wimp for having left Grampian? Her opinion mattered, somehow. Did she fancy him? If so, she hadn't been pushy with it and he found himself admitting that he liked this policewoman with her quirky smile and sense of humour.

Who, then? The image of a tall man with dark hair flopping over his forehead came clearly back to Omar. His was a face that had seen too much suffering and pain, too many dead bodies and grieving relations. But there was an inner strength about this man, a core of toughness that was tempered, Omar felt sure, with a genuine kindness. He'd be able to talk to Lorimer. But not yet, not till he was ready.

'Och, Fraz, he'll no be back therr again, he'll have gone tae crash at anither pad. Know whit ah mean?' whined Andy Galbraith. The taller of the two men outside Brogan's flat did not deign to reply, simply shouldering his way into the close mouth with a swagger that betokened his superiority.

'Ah mean, Brogan widnae came back efter we turned his pad ower, ah mean, wid he?' Galbraith danced at the other man's side, an anxious hand raised as if to ward off any blows.

Fraser Sandiman took the stairs two at a time. The shotgun held neatly against his body was a mere shadow in the dim light.

'C'mon, Fraz, wait fur me!' Galbraith panted up the stairs.

'Shut it, Gubby,' Fraz replied in a quiet but menacing tone, his face turned towards the man several steps below. 'D'ye want the entire neighbourhood tae hear ye?'

Galbraith waited till the other man had recommenced his ascent then stuck out a childish tongue at his back. He was Gubby to his mates, not just in token of his surname but because ever since primary school he had been unable to keep his gub shut.

'Cannae even say a wurd but yerr on tae me,' he grumbled, clenching his fists, hard man style.

The door was easy enough to open, but Fraz pushed it gently, just in case someone was inside.

'Made a richt job o' that, eh? Eh?' Gubby laughed gleefully as he brushed a manky hand across the splintered wooden frame.

'Aye,' said his mate, moving cautiously into the flat.

'He's no in,' Gubby rattled on. 'Ah telt ye, he's no comin' back here. Let's jist get onything we can and split.' He followed the other man into the wreck of the lounge.

'Shut it,' Fraz snarled, raising a hand in warning. 'Someone's been in here. See this? He lifted a khaki-coloured kitbag that rested behind an overturned chair.

'That no Brogan's?' Gubby asked doubtfully. 'Cannae mind him havin' wan like that,' he scratched his already tousled hair then scratched a bit harder as if to stimulate his thoughts.

'C'mon, let's see whit's in the kitchen. See if onybody's bin doin' the business,' Fraz commanded.

Gubby followed him out of the lounge. If there had been any drug taking going on, surely they'd find traces? Crumpled tinfoil, maybe? A few roaches chucked into the dustbin? Gubby wrinkled his nose in disgust. He'd never touch the stuff, nor would Fraz. They'd both seen too many dealers go the way of addicts, money slithering through shaking fingers as they dipped into their precious goods. Fraz and he made their money out of men and women desperate for what they could sell them, and so did Billy Brogan.

Was Billy on the stuff? He'd seen him smoke a few joints at parties, but had he gone onto the hard stuff? Whatever the story was, Billy Brogan had skived off somewhere, owing them a whack.

Outside the Glasgow streets were slick with a damp rain that had begun to fall as the clouds gathered steadily, drifting from the west. The hit man locked his car and strolled across the street, not looking back. The kitbag was back at the flat and he had some spare clothes heaped inside the boot. He hoped he wouldn't need them, though this thin rain was already soaking his jacket. Maybe Brogan would come back tonight? Then he would conclude his business with the dealer and head on home.

The man bent his head against the wind that was gusting scraps of paper and old leaves along the pavement. He rounded a corner. Two more doorways then he was back to Brogan's pad. Looking up, he hesitated. A red car that had not been there earlier was parked outside the close. A smile crossed his mouth.

'Welcome home, Billy boy,' he chuckled softly.

The worn stone steps made no sound under his soles as he stepped swiftly up the two flights of stairs.

Then he stopped. Voices from Brogan's flat made him shrink against the wall, one hand curled around the gun hidden under his jacket. He grinned, anticipating the look on Billy boy's face when he made his entry.

The front door was open just a fraction and he could hear the voices coming from a room along the far end of the flat. The kitchen, he thought.

'Yerawanker!' one of them shouted out and then there was a thump.

'Gerrofff Fraz! Leausalane!' another voice whined, obviously hurt in some way.

The hit man stopped halfway along the hall. Glasgow accents, both of them, but neither reminded him of Private William Brogan. So where was the little sod?

Before he could think of his next move, two figures rushed out of the kitchen, one of them brandishing a shotgun.

'Whit the . . .?' Fraz's question was cut off even as he began to aim his weapon.

The sound of gunfire resonated off the walls of the flat, booming and echoing, masking any cry from the men. The impact of the shots lifted each of them off their feet, one after the other, backs curved, arms flung heavenwards before they hit the ground in two dull thumps.

The hit man listened to the silence, the sense of stillness that followed every death: the scent of gunfire drifting above those crumpled heaps on the floor a malevolent incense.

The man took a step back, regarding the dead men. If he turned them over he would see patches of crimson staining their chests, dark bullet holes piercing their pale, northern brows.

Heart, head. That was how he had been trained to kill in the service of Her Majesty. It was second nature to him now, that sudden reflex action. Not like the deliberate hit of a commission where he simply fired into the middle of a man's (or, occasionally, a woman's) skull.

Taking a piece of worn cloth from his pocket, he wrapped the gun carefully before replacing it in his jacket. Had he been a wild west cowboy he'd have blown into the barrel, he thought. The image made him smile.

'Right, Billy boy, what have we here?' he murmured, hunkering down to have a closer look at the men on the ground. But his examination was to be short-lived.

He stood up almost immediately, tensing as he heard noises coming from the stone staircase outside. Time to get out of here, he told himself, thinking rapidly as he grabbed his backpack; no wasting precious seconds scrabbling around on hands and knees trying to retrieve four cartridge cases.

Mary Murphy turned up the television a fraction more. Maybe it had been a car backfiring. Did a car backfire in a series of bangs like that? But even as she listened to the canned laughter from the comedy show, she shivered, knowing instinctively what it was that she had heard downstairs.

A bad lot, that Brogan. People always coming and going, pushing past her on the stairs as if she was so much rubbish, some of them queer-looking folk with eyes rolling in their heads from all the stuff they took. The old woman shuddered again. If Alec had been here . . . But Mary knew that Alec would have told her the same thing: *keep out of it, hen, ye cannae change that sort.*

So, even as she sat shivering in her chair, Mary Murphy decided that she had heard nothing at all.

The hit man pulled the baseball cap lower as he left the shadow of the close mouth and walked out into the damp Glasgow night. Keeping his eyes fixed to the ground, he knew that nobody could see his features, nobody would be able to identify him as the man who had emerged shortly after eleven-thirty that particular evening. The wet pavements muffled his footsteps as one stride after another took him to the street where he had parked the car less than an hour before. Gloved fingers reached down for the key in his trouser pocket and, as his hand slid down, he was aware of the hard shape nestling in his jacket.

A small smile of satisfaction spread across the man's face. That would show anyone who knew Brogan that he meant business. Then the smile faded into a frown. He had to find somewhere else in this city to hide out now. This whole business was becoming more and more complicated. But until he had that money in his hand, Billy Brogan could consider himself a marked man.

Mario stopped by the open door, pursing his lips thoughtfully. The man who lived across the landing hadn't been around for a little while now. So why was his door lying open like that? He sniffed the air, smelling an unfamiliar, acrid sort of scent. Was something burning? A human instinct to help overcame Mario's reluctance to intrude on another man's privacy.

Pushing the door a little wider, he began to step forward then stopped at the sight before him.

'Holy Mother of God,' he whispered, crossing himself before backing out of the hallway once more. Trembling fingers reached for his mobile phone. Three buttons were pressed then there was a pause before a female voice asked him a question.

'Police,' Mario said, swallowing as the words stuck in his throat. 'There's these two men . . . I think they're dead . . .'

CHAPTER 13

Long before a squad car arrived to investigate Mario Bernardini's call, the hit man had driven for several miles, seeking somewhere safe on the margins of the city. The bright lights of the cinema made him glance up briefly, letting him catch a glimpse of a neon Marilyn, her white skirts fluttering in a permanent arc above the parking bays. Maybe a nosey around there would help to establish an alibi, should he require one? A discarded ticket was easy enough to find. It was no more than a passing thought. Nobody was going to associate him with the carnage he'd left behind in Brogan's flat. The Travel Inn loomed closer and he turned the car into its dimly lit forecourt. It was one more anonymous place to rest his head. A place where nobody would see anything other than one more stranger passing through.

Detective Chief Inspector Lorimer stood by the bay window, looking down into the busy Glasgow street. Normality reigned here with cars, taxis and trucks moving slowly between sets of traffic lights, their collective aim to arrive at a destination before the nine a.m. cut off. However, the vehicles parked below and the lines of blue and white tape were making things more difficult for the steady stream and the policeman could imagine the swearing and dirty looks that were being directed towards this particular tenement.

The entire flat was being picked over by scene of crime officers, a horrible task given the state of the place. Had the killer ransacked Brogan's home before shooting these two men? Flashes of light behind him made him turn away from the view. The photographers were taking pictures of the scene of crime, particularly the two corpses lying in the middle of the hall, before the on duty pathologist arrived. A shotgun lying near the bodies had also attracted their attention; it was not the murder weapon, though, Lorimer knew. Those neat holes through the heads of each man had been made by something like an automatic pistol. Sadly such types of gun were all too easily available nowadays, the market from eastern Europe having flooded the country with a variety of ex-military hardware. Once ballistics had identified the bullet they could begin to build up a picture of the assailant, but meanwhile the policeman had to content himself with finding out what he could from the drug dealer's flat. At least this time they had found the cartridge cases, something that would help to pinpoint what kind of weapon had been used.

For the moment Lorimer was keeping out of the way, not just to avoid any contamination of the scene but also to have a closer look at Brogan's home. A man could disguise himself, wear clothes to try and hide his real personality, but one of the things that gave him away was his own personal space. So often Lorimer drew knowledge about a person from the way that he lived.

It was a big flat for one person. Three bedrooms lay off the long narrow hallway, two with single beds that were now turned on their sides. There had been no bedclothes in either of the smaller rooms and one of them was full of empty cardboard cartons, their lids turned neatly in as if someone had stacked them like nesting boxes before the rampage had begun and they had been tossed around. But it was such small details that Lorimer had learned to see; did it indicate that Brogan was a methodical sort of fellow?

It was going to be a tough job to read these surroundings, given the mess in most of the rooms. Only the bathroom seemed to have avoided the onslaught of an enraged punter. Was that it? Had Brogan's flat been targeted by one of his customers? The man was a known drug dealer, one that had slipped and slithered out of the reach of Strathclyde CID for far too long. But his name and those of his associates was certainly on their files.

Lorimer's eyes roamed over the bright room that overlooked the west end of Argyle Street. Narrow twin shelves above the massive plasma television looked as though they had been built to hold compact discs; the charcoal-coloured carpet beneath them was now littered with dozens of broken plastic boxes. In his mind's eye Lorimer saw angry feet stamping on them, destroying things that might have given Brogan some pleasure. With one gloved hand, he picked up the cases. Brogan's taste was mainly for hard rock music but Lorimer did raise an approving eyebrow at a boxed set of Rolling Stones Greatest Hits and a David Bowie re-issue. The films were a mixture of horror and soft porn but there was one copy of *Lost in Austen*, still in its original wrapping. A gift for a girlfriend, maybe? If so, its choice showed a more thoughtful side to the owner of this flat. And who was the intended recipient? Lorimer wondered.

As he looked around he saw a bronze-coloured sculpture that was supposed to represent grasses blowing in the wind. It had been partly wrenched off the cream painted wall and was swinging loose, a pathetic piece of junk now rather than an attempt at modern art. Had Brogan fancied himself as a Mr Big? His taste in decor was reasonably muted; a dark carpet with matching grey tweed curtains (that had been professionally lined) against clean cream walls. The red leather settee was the only brash colour in the room. It looked as if it had been expensive, Lorimer thought, eyeing the slashes made by someone's spiteful knife, and for a moment he wondered if drug dealers bothered to insure their possessions.

Voices outside indicated the arrival of a newcomer, but before he left the room, Lorimer walked carefully around the debris, seeking something more personal. So far he had little clue as to how Brogan had lived, other than his penchant for rock music and tacky films. And a woman somewhere, he thought, remembering that brand new DVD.

He found it in one corner under a pile of scattered magazines, shards of glass sticking out from the splayed pages of *FHM* and *GQ*. A framed picture of a woman, smiling back at the camera. She was in her late twenties, perhaps, with a distinctive sort of pallor, her alabaster skin tone reminding him of some of the Pre-Raphaelite paintings. That long red hair cascading down upon one bare shoulder might have come from any era. But the background to the picture was entirely modern and Lorimer recognised the building at once: it was the library of Glasgow University, a place he had frequented during his time as a student. Dusting away the remaining fragments of glass, he let his finger linger on the glossy photograph. 'Who are you?' he whispered softly.

'Probably between nine and midnight,' a familiar voice intoned, making Lorimer straighten up, pocket the photograph and step into the hallway once more. The white-suited figure crouching beside the bodies paid him no attention, looking instead at her colleague who was busily taking notes.

'Never one to give us an exact time of death,' he said, shaking his head in mock despair as he noticed DC Fathy who was evidently absorbed in the pathologist's examination.

'Sir,' Fathy said, straightening up and looking guiltily at his senior investigating officer.

'It's all right, Fathy. Watching this one will teach you plenty,' he chuckled.

'That you, Lorimer?' Rosie turned her head a fraction, trying not to overbalance.

'Aye, and shouldn't you be the note taker these days?' he answered, smiling at the woman below him whose figure was now quite altered by her pregnancy.

'Och, just this last one . . . well two . . . then I'll leave the nasty stuff to the rest of them,' Rosie replied.

'Dedication to duty,' Lorimer explained to Fathy in a loud whisper behind his hand that Doctor Rosie Fergusson was meant to hear.

'Any idea when the PMs will be done?'

'Well, seeing this is the first murder since your pal Kenneth Scott, we might just be able to fit them in today. That all right for you?' Rosie asked waspishly.

DC Fathy looked from one to the other, mystified by the bantering between his SIO and the consultant pathologist.

'No worries, son, Rosie and me, we're old pals,' Lorimer explained. 'She just likes to give me a hard time of it.'

'Aye, and that's because you want everything done yesterday,' Rosie shot back. 'Right, give me a hand up, that's us all done for now.'

Lorimer reached down and helped the pathologist to her feet, allowing the detective constable to see a fresh faced woman with curly blonde hair escaping from her white hood. Despite the voluminous overalls, Rosie's pregnancy was evident for all to see and Fathy noticed her eyes crinkle in a friendly smile as she regarded his boss. For a petite and pretty young woman like this to be involved in something as harsh as the examination and dissection of dead bodies was a novelty to the detective constable, whose experience of such folk had so far been limited to much older and much less attractive practitioners.

It was well after noon when the team reassembled at divisional headquarters. The rain that had earlier washed the streets had eventually disappeared in a haze of rainbow colours and now a glaring sun was shining through the dusty windows.

'The car's registered in the name of Fraser Sandiman,' Irvine told the officers assembled in the muster room.

'Ah, dear old Fraz, wondered what kind of a sticky end he'd come to,' murmured DS Wilson. 'Known drug dealer,' he added for DC Fathy's benefit, giving the young man a wink.

There was a murmur amongst the other officers, some of whom were only now being brought up to speed on the latest murder case. Stuff like this happened not infrequently within the Strathclyde area. Drug dealers falling out, men gunned down for reasons that only became partly known, if ever, in a court of law.

'Galbraith was identified from his credit cards and Brogan's not been seen in his flat for a wee while, according to the neighbour who called us,' Irvine continued, her voice rising above the noise.

'His place was really trashed when we saw it this morning,' DC Fathy put in. 'Someone doesn't like Mr Brogan very much.'

'Naw, son, he's no very well liked by a lot of folk,' Wilson explained as a ripple of laughter rang out, leaving the young officer red faced.

'Okay,' Lorimer raised a hand and immediately all talk ceased as they turned to look at the senior investigating officer. 'The post-mortems have still to take place but our initial impression is of a professional who knew what he was doing all right. There was a shotgun inside the flat, registered to Sandiman, and I believe we will find that victim's prints on it.'

The word victim served to remind the officers that, yes, these were Glasgow dealers who may have made hundreds of lives miserable through the supply of drugs, but they were still citizens whose murders deserved to be investigated. *Some mother's son*, DS Wilson was fond of saying, whenever a fellow officer became cynical about such deaths.

'The injuries to their chests and heads suggest a marksman, maybe a trained sniper. So one immediate line of investigation has to be into any known associates of the deceased who are or were regular army. Alistair, you knew Sandiman from the past, can you take on this action?' Lorimer nodded to DS Wilson. 'We've still to get the ballistics report as well as other forensics from the scene of crime, but until then it's a case of asking questions of neighbours like Bernardini, local shopkeepers and,' he fixed Irvine and Fathy with a stern eye, 'relatives of the deceased.'

Annie Irvine swallowed. This was becoming a habit. She was accustomed to being picked for this sort of action: dealing with the victims' families fell to a female officer all too often. *You've got that sympathetic touch*, she'd been told. But this was a little different from giving bad news to the relatives of an accident victim. Sandiman and Galbraith's families might well be a tough lot, not easy to handle.

'What about Brogan?' someone asked.

Lorimer's face creased in a grim smile. 'Finding Billy Brogan is our top priority. It's looking likely that he's the man who can answer all of our questions. Billy's ex-army remember,' he added, raising one eyebrow suggestively. 'There's plenty of reasons for thinking he could have been the one behind these deaths.

Something tells me he's in for more trouble than a fight with his insurance company.'

Marianne spread out the books on her bed. She had enough to keep her busy until the beginning of the new term. One by one she lifted the volumes, reading the back covers where the various psychologists had been given their accreditations by the marketing departments of different publishers. Some were written in a more academic style than others. The last book she looked at was the one she wanted to read most. A slim black volume with the author's name picked out in silver: Doctor Solomon Brightman.

The woman smiled. The psychologist would never know just how much he had turned her life around, would he?

When the phone rang she paused before rising to answer it, almost as if she had an instinct of bad news. Marianne's stomach lurched. Something had happened to Billy!

But when she lifted the handset and said *hello*, the voice on the other end was not that of her brother at all.

'Yes?' she asked, leaning back on the bed.

'Still no sign of my pal Billy,' the voice said ruefully. 'And here I am all on my lonesome, no one to hang out with. Thought we could at least have a pint in that place he likes so much, what's it called? The Scotia?'

Marianne suppressed a laugh. If that wasn't an invitation to meet up, then she didn't know what was. 'Well . . .' she began, then paused, listening. The woman frowned, sitting up suddenly. He was waiting for her to make a mistake, she thought, her intuition sharpened by the intensity of the silence between them.

'I don't know where he is,' she said at last then added, 'sorry,' before ringing off.

She stared at the telephone in her hand. What was wrong with her? The guy seemed okay. Knew Billy's regular bar, as well. Was every approach from a stranger going to make her turn and run like a frightened rabbit?

Amit had been a stranger once, she thought. But then Billy had arranged that for her too and now she felt perfectly safe with the man from Lahore.

Billy. Where was he? And why was this innocent call from one of his old army mates making her so nervous?

Marianne looked at the telephone thoughtfully, deciding to store that number so she could call him back whenever she wanted. *If* she wanted, the voice of caution reminded her. She gave a sigh and rolled onto her back. She was tired of this constant running, moving from place to place. Surely now she could find somewhere to settle down for good?

Her dreams were changing after all and there was no longer any darkness taking her down into the place from which she could never escape.

CHAPTER 14

'Ye wantae score?'

Billy Brogan whirled around at the familiar Glasgow accent. A pair of dark eyes twinkled at him from behind a counter full of flimsy women's garments. Had he passed him by, Billy Brogan would have taken the lad for a genuine Spaniard, but now that he looked closer, that skin was too dark for even southern Spain. Asian, then, he guessed. And maybe even second or third generation Glaswegian. So what was he doing on the other side of this Mallorcan market stall? Clearly it was more than ladies' panties he was selling.

Brogan's curiosity made him hesitate. The evening market in Cala Millor was pretty crowded but he managed to squeeze his way closer to the edge of the wooden trestle table.

'You talkin tae me, pal?' Billy asked, chin up in a show of defiance.

'Aye. You're Brogan, aren't you?' The boy was probably no more than seventeen, his thin arms protruding from the sleeves of a black shirt, its cuffs unbuttoned.

Covering himself up in this heat? thought Billy, wondering what sort of marks these loose sleeves might be concealing. Or was he just dodging the mosquitoes? 'What's it tae you, son?' he replied.

The toothy grin faded for a moment. 'Ye know ma faither,' he said at last. 'Mr Jaffrey.'

'You're Sahid's boy? Whit're ye doin' out here?'

The boy's grin grew wider once more. 'Could ask you the same thing,' he replied cheekily.

'Holiday,' Brogan shrugged.

'Gap year,' the other replied. 'Dad says I have tae make myself useful.'

Brogan gave a derisive laugh. 'An ye're supplementing yer wages wi sellin' ither stuff. Eh?'

'Aye, why no? Anyroad, are ye wantin' some?'

Brogan laughed out loud this time. 'Me? Buy stuff affa wee Jaffrey's laddie? Naw, son, whoever telt ye aboot me's given ye the wrang story. See, I buy tae sell. In bulk. Know whit ah mean? Nice try, though, pal.' He paused for a moment then turned back again, bending closer so only the boy could hear him. 'An' how did ye know who ah wis? Eh?'

That smile again, winsome and full of the desire for approval. 'Ach, Mr Brogan, everybody roon ma bit knows who *you* are. I mean tae say, ye're *famous*!'

Dropping his gaze, the boy managed a convincing blush.

'Aye, well,' Brogan shook his head and gave a desultory wave of his hand. 'Keep yer nose clean, awright?'

As the older man made his way through the narrow street he was quite unaware of the pair of dark eyes following his progress.

When he was quite sure that Brogan was out of sight young Jaffrey reached into the pocket of his tracksuit trousers and pulled out his mobile phone. Stepping back from the fray, he slipped into the shadows behind a rail of hanging garments and tapped out a number.

'Hi, it's me,' he said after a few moments. 'Guess who ah've jist seen.'

Amit wandered into the back of the restaurant, mobile phone to his ear. He nodded his dark head, eyes fixed to a spot on the carefully swept floor. That morning's news on the radio had given him a real jolt.

Police are looking for the owner of a flat where two men were found shot dead. Mr William Brogan has not been seen for several days and police are keen to make contact with him.

Now Amit was being presented with a real dilemma. Alerting the authorities was totally out of the question. Not only did he owe a measure of loyalty to this man, but he had other worries. Gnawing his lip, Amit listened to the Hundi's words. If he were to be associated with Brogan, they might come after him again. But could he bring himself to sever the ties that held him to the drug dealer?

'Okay, I hear what you are saying,' he told the man. 'Of course I'll be careful. And, no, I won't leave any traces.'

The man from Lahore clicked the mobile shut and stared out of the window. The morning was one of these bright days that presaged rain to come, but while it lasted there was a radiance to the streets outside, making this part of Glasgow almost continental. Across Great Western Road a cafe had set out silver-topped tables, the blue and white striped awning above shading them from the glare. Already several women were sitting drinking their morning lattes, chattering together. They had probably dropped off their sons at Glasgow Academy and were now indulging in a post-school-run half an hour before heading back to the suburbs. But, no, the Glasgow schools were still on holiday, weren't they? Dhesi's kids had been around the restaurant with their mother, prior to being kitted out for the new term.

Amit remembered his own mother, kissing him before school each day. Their farewells had been in the garden, Father had been the one to take them to Aitchison's on his way to work.

Suddenly he was back in Lahore again, in one of the public parks beside a rectangle of silken grey water; his father talking to other gentlemen, their freshly laundered white linen garments lending them a certain gravitas. As a boy, Amit and his brothers had always been dressed in proper shirts and long trousers, not the baggy shapeless T-shirts and tracksuit trousers favoured by the young around here. If he could go back . . . but returning there was impossible now and he had to make the best of the life he had here. As so many others had done.

Amit sighed. He would have to make contact with Marianne again. Had she heard from her brother? he wondered. And if she had, was Brogan now aware of what had taken place in his Argyle Street flat?

Marianne smiled as she waited on the bridge. The sun was out, the day was hers for the taking and soon Amit would be here. *Lunch somewhere nice*, he'd told her. *How about The City Inn, you could meet me on Bell's Bridge*, she'd answered, giving him the details of how to get there, where best to park his recently acquired Mercedes.

Marianne had arrived early, not because she was over anxious but because she wished to savour the freedom of standing out in the fresh air a while. She lifted her face to the sun, eyes closed, letting the breeze from the river wrap her cotton skirt around her bare legs.

'Hello,' he said and she started, surprised to find him standing there when there had been no sound of a footfall.

'How have you been?' she smiled, casting her eyes over the

man's face. The smile faded as she saw the frown lines between his eyes, the agitated manner he had as they turned to walk side by side along the footpath.

'What's the matter?'

Amit stopped and looked at her gravely. 'You haven't heard, then? I wondered if you knew.'

'Knew what? Amit, what's happened?' Marianne took a step back, clutching at the painted railing that separated the path from the waters churning below them.

'It was on the news,' Amit told her, then he stopped, his eyes looking beyond her. Marianne turned to see two joggers bearing down on them. They moved a little to one side, allowing the pair to pass, then Amit took her arm and led her around a corner of some thick shrubbery to a bench.

'Sit down,' he told her. 'I have something to tell you.'

Omar scrolled down until he came to the page he wanted. He read the information then sat back, frowning. Had he read that correctly? Leaning closer to the computer screen once more, he read the lines that told him of certain familial relationships. A few minutes passed while he typed in other names and dates, then his mouth fell open as he realised just what he had uncovered.

He wanted to call her, say 'Hey, Irvine, see what I've just found' but something stopped him. It was vital that this went straight to Lorimer and to no other officer first. Omar Adel Fathy was not going to be upstaged if he could help it. He recalled several times in his last post when other officers had claimed the glory for work that he had done. Well it wasn't going to happen here.

He printed off the necessary sheets and slipped out of his seat, heading along the corridor to the DCI's room.

*

'Come in,' Lorimer called out, his eyes not on the door but on the document in his hands. This ballistics report was making interesting reading.

'Sir.'

Lorimer looked up. It was the handsome Egyptian who was making such a stir in the department. The DCI had eventually started to notice that all the single women (and several of the married ones) were paying the young man a lot of attention.

'Jist like thae Arabian nights,' wee Sadie from the canteen had snorted, her gravelly voice testament to a lifelong nicotine habit. 'This place is becoming a right *har-eem*,' she had added for Lorimer's benefit. 'Nivver seen sae mony o' your plain clothes lot in skirts! Mind you he's a nice looking laddie and his manners wid pit maist o' this lot tae shame,' she'd growled, head nodding towards a group of male officers gathered at a nearby table. Lorimer had chuckled at Sadie's words. The canteen lady could always be depended upon to tell things just as they were, neither glossing over nor embellishing the facts.

He gave the young officer a curious look. There was something he recognised in the man's expression; an eagerness that reminded him of his younger self.

'Okay, what have you found?' he asked, swinging his chair back, one hand indicating the chair at the other side of his desk.

'It's about William Brogan, sir,' Fathy told him. 'I think you ought to see this,' he continued, handing the sheets of printed paper across to the SIO.

They were all assembled once more in the incident room but this time there was a definite sense of anticipation.

Irvine looked across quizzically at Fathy. He was deliberately avoiding her eye and there was an air of suppressed excitement about him. Oho, what have you been up to, pal, she thought.

'Right,' Lorimer began. 'We've had a bit of a breakthrough, thanks to Detective Constable Fathy,' he nodded in the young man's direction, causing a stir of murmuring from the others.

Omar felt prickles of sweat on his forehead from the warmth of the room. He was the new boy being singled out for praise; whoever had put that notice in his locker wouldn't like that one little bit. Was someone watching him at this very moment, hostile eyes boring into the back of his head? Omar itched to turn around but forced himself to concentrate on the SIO at the front of the room.

'Is this about Brogan?' DS Wilson wanted to know.

'Funny you should ask that. I was just going to tell you all a little story about Mr William Brogan,' Lorimer smiled. 'DC Fathy has discovered that our Billy's sister is a lady we already want to question in connection with an ongoing case.' He paused to make the moment a little more dramatic, sweeping his gaze over the assembled officers.

'Marianne Brogan was Kenneth Scott's ex-wife,' he told them, nodding at the exclamations from all corners of the room. 'And I now have some rather interesting stuff here from forensics,' he said, waving a sheaf of papers in the air.

'Ballistics reports confirm that the weapon used to kill Kenneth Scott was the same one that shot Galbraith and Sandiman.' He let both pieces of news sink in, then raised a hand to quieten everyone down.

'The bullet that Doctor Fergusson retrieved from Scott's head showed a wipe mark at its nose cone, so we can be pretty sure that means a silencer was used. Same bullet type but no wipe marks on the ones that killed Sandiman and Galbraith.' Lorimer watched their faces. 'I'll distribute copies of the ballistics report

107

for you all,' he continued. 'Just want to draw your attention to the part that refers to marks caused by the extractor claw and ejector post. Seems to indicate a good match.' He nodded at the papers. 'I want each officer to spend what time they can afford catching up with the finer details. But not right now.' He fixed his blue gaze on the men and women assembled around him.

'Now more than ever it is imperative that we locate Brogan and his sister,' he said. 'I want every one of Brogan's known haunts investigated.'

Omar opened the locker carefully, feeling the hinges grind against the metal hasps. But when he looked inside there was nothing to see, just his kit and a plastic lunch box. No racist notes, no reminders of his ethnic origin or anything that might make him reconsider his decision to become a police officer.

'Okay, Fathy?' The tall, lanky figure of DS Cameron loomed behind him and Omar felt a friendly touch on his shoulder.

'Good work that, finding out the sister was Scott's ex. We could've been running round in circles for ages without that particular snippet of information,' he smiled.

Omar Fathy ducked his head as if in embarrassment. The detective sergeant's lilting voice sounded so genuine, so why was every sinew in his body stiffening in suspicion? The man from Lewis was a nice guy. They had Asians up there who spoke the Gaelic like natives. So why would Cameron target the young Egyptian?

'You all right?'

Omar looked round to see an expression of real concern in the man's eyes.

'Yes, thanks. Just worried someone might think I'm overstepping the mark, you know?'

Cameron gave him another tap on his shoulder. 'Nobody will. Lorimer takes notice of everyone's contribution. There's no pecking order with him,' he grinned. 'He might be a DCI but he's not forgotten what it's like for the foot soldiers. Besides,' his grin widened, 'he's not averse to getting his hands dirty, if you know what I mean.'

Omar frowned.

'Och, I often think he'd rather be out and about with us than stuck in his office with all that admin,' he continued, shrugging. 'But sometimes he just does that anyway. Drives the Super nuts of course.' Cameron laughed. 'You should see Lorimer questioning a suspect. There's no one can hold a candle to him in the interview room, I promise you.' And, winking at the detective constable, Cameron moved on towards the door.

Omar stood perfectly still. If what Cameron said was true, then more than ever he believed that Lorimer was the man who would listen to his story and take it seriously.

CHAPTER 15

Lorimer listened to the liquid notes of the thrush. How any bird could sing its heart out like that in the middle of this city, was something akin to a miracle. It was a sound he associated with the countryside, reminding him of deep, green swards of grass under shady stands of trees. But why this fellow had chosen to compete with the constant din of Glasgow's traffic was anyone's guess. He had heard the bird several times now, from its perch on top of a lamp post just outside his window. For a moment the detective forgot all about the bodies lying in Glasgow City mortuary and the ever-growing files upon his desk. It was the thrush's total innocence that moved him, its unconcern for anything except filling the whole of its small body with that song.

The shrill, peremptory ring of the telephone broke the spell and Lorimer turned back to the world of crime and criminals.

'Lorimer,' he said, a slight frown upon his brow. But as he heard the woman's voice at the other end of the line, he straightened up as though she were with him in this very room.

'Ma'am,' Lorimer said, listening as the deputy chief constable, Joyce Rogers, took time to explain the meetings and discussions that had preceded the letter that had gone out to Doctor Solomon Brightman. Lorimer's email to her might well have been a little on the terse side, but now she was being fulsome in her praise of the psychologist, assuring Lorimer that it was nothing personal, simply a slight shift in policy.

'A temporary shift, perhaps, ma'am?' he enquired.

'We'll see about that, Lorimer,' Rogers replied. 'And, talking about shifts, have you had any thought about my proposal?'

'Not yet, ma'am. Still thinking it over,' Lorimer replied. He bit his lip. Being asked to head up the Serious Crimes Squad with promotion to detective superintendent ought to be a no-brainer, but he had put it to the back of his mind, not even mentioning the matter to Maggie.

'Hm, well, don't take too long about it, will you? There are always plenty of other officers hungry for a chance like that. Meantime,' she continued briskly, 'any joy with those two men who were shot?'

Lorimer spent the next five minutes filling the deputy chief constable in on the recent progress, even going so far as to mention DC Fathy's part in the investigation.

'Good man, that. Lots of potential. See that we keep him in Strathclyde, won't you, Lorimer. Don't want his feet to become itchy again. Besides,' she continued in a tone that made Lorimer imagine her eyes twinkling, 'We need all the diversity we can muster within the force in these modern times.'

Lorimer put down the phone, grinning. For two pins he would bet that even Joyce Rogers would apply her lipstick if she anticipated a visit from DC Fathy. He had them all around his little finger, he chuckled, storing up this little nugget to share with Maggie when he got home.

But it did not alter the situation with Solly. Not that this case required the psychologist's input. There was nothing remotely resembling a serial killer on the loose. No, it was a case of drug dealers falling out, if he was not mistaken. Yet there was something odd about it, too. Scott had seemed a decent citizen to all intents and purposes. Yet he had been married to the sister of a known dealer. *Had* been, a voice reminded Lorimer. Perhaps Scott had wanted to sever links with the Brogans. But the man's divorce had been effective for over two years now. So why had he been targeted by that marksman? Had there been bad blood between Billy Brogan and Kenneth Scott?

Lorimer chewed his lower lip thoughtfully. Scott had no family to talk to and they had already spoken to his workmates. But surely there were others in his life who had known the man more intimately? If only he could speak to Marianne Brogan, or whatever she was calling herself these days. But the woman seemed to have vanished off the face of the earth, suggesting that she had in fact relocated to somewhere overseas. They would have to continue their inquiries to see if that was indeed the case. Or did her disappearance give a hint that she had something to hide? Lorimer asked himself, his suspicions shifting his thoughts down a different route entirely. One way or the other he was going to be working flat out, he realised with a grimace.

The prospect of a holiday during Maggie's summer break was becoming more and more unlikely as the days went by. It wouldn't be the first time they had had to cancel something due to the pressure of his work, Lorimer thought. Perhaps they could have a last-minute break during the school October week, he told himself, ruefully.

The detective leaned back in his chair, his eyes on the Van Gogh print that he had placed across on the far wall. There was something alive about the painting: the art dealer seated on that rush-covered chair, bright splashes of colour behind him, depicting some of the paintings in his shop. And that timeless quality in the man's wizened face appealed to him too; he could have been a Tibetan monk about to deliver some piece of ancient wisdom. It was as if the subject might turn his head and speak from the frame at any moment.

He could do with some words of wisdom right now, that was for sure, he thought, standing up suddenly and pacing the room.

It was something he simply could not help; an anxiety to be up and about, searching for the next clue in a puzzle about human life. A restless spirit, Maggie had called him once, a tinge of regret in her voice. But it was how he was made, he reflected now, his mind roaming into dark avenues where other people might fear to venture. Being a policeman was not just a job, it was a way of life. And hadn't he just recently told that to some new recruits in his lecture at the police training college in Tulliallan? And Maggie knew that. Had he opted for a life of academia, like Solly, would life be very different now? Would he be traipsing across the globe lecturing on fine art, as he had once imagined?

The telephone ringing once again took Lorimer's thoughts back to the present and the portrait of Père Tanguy seemed to diminish as he let his eyes slide away, focussing on the papers on his desk instead.

Several minutes later, Lorimer was tapping words into his BlackBerry, fixing a date to speak at a course in the University of Glasgow. Rosie had wheedled in such a convincing way that he had found himself agreeing almost immediately to her request. It might take a bit of time to prepare, though, he frowned, wondering if he could wing it in front of an audience of medics, legal folk and fellow police officers. No, he thought, glancing up at the painting once again and noting Père Tanguy's calm gaze. This was something that would demand a proper amount of thought and effort.

He stood up once more and strode to the open window but the thrush had flown away and all that he could hear was the noise of traffic rumbling around this great city's beating heart.

'We've already tried Martha Street and The Department for Work and Pensions,' DC Irvine moaned. 'What more can we do?'

'She went to Anniesland College to take the necessary qualifications for entrance to university. What name did she use when she registered there?' Fathy asked.

'Scott. But that doesn't get us anywhere. We've eliminated all the Scotts as well. The registry office at the uni confirmed there are no Marianne Scotts or Marianne Brogans currently attending any courses.'

'And she would have needed to register under the name that was on her SCE certificates, wouldn't she?'

'Of course.' Irvine narrowed her eyes. 'What are you getting at? You've got that look again,' she said.

'What look?'

'Hm, the sort of look that means your exotic brain's about to churn up something interesting that the rest of us mere mortals have missed,' she replied, smiling in spite of herself.

'Well,' Fathy began, 'what if she didn't register for her exams in her married name. Or her maiden name, come to that.'

'You mean she used an alias? How would that work?'

'You know as well as I do that under Scottish law you can call yourself anything you like. See,' he swung round in his chair to face her, 'I had this pal at school, foreign bloke like myself, his surname was Lo. L-O,' he added with a wave of his hand. 'Sort of gave away his different ethnic origin – except his mum was Scottish. Never got on very well with his father. So when he went up to university he decided to change his name to Lowe. L-O-W-E, see?'

'But didn't everyone think it was the first spelling, I mean when they looked at him?'

'That was just it,' Fathy explained eagerly. 'James didn't look all that Chinese, really. Dark haired and all, but much more like his mother,' he mused, gazing beyond Irvine as if to conjure up the woman.

'Okay, so what's your point?'

'James could have changed his name by deed poll but he didn't. He simply began using the other spelling for all his legal documents: driving licence, bank details, you name it . . .'

'So you think Marianne Scott, née Brogan, might have done the same sort of thing?'

'Well, we could check with the SCE exam board to see what names come up for the year before she was meant to begin university.'

'If she ever did,' Irvine replied gloomily. 'I'm beginning to think she's not in Scotland at all.'

'Worth a try, though, isn't it?' he persisted.

'Aye, suppose so. Lorimer'll want no stone unturned.' She looked thoughtful for a moment. 'There is another possibility, though. D'you remember that case of the medical student who faked his school exam results?'

Fathy shook his head.

'Och, it was ages ago. The bloke had been knocked back to study at Glasgow Uni so he forged a load of stuff and began attending lectures, doing exams, the lot. Pretended he was just a young guy when he was . . . oh I can't remember, thirty-something I think. Nearly got away with it an' all.'

'Would have to have been a good forgery,' Fathy pointed out.

'Aye, so it would,' Irvine answered. 'And I wonder just who would be doing stuff like that in Glasgow nowadays.'

*

Marianne lay with her eyes closed, willing sleep to come. The nights were beginning to darken earlier now so there was no reason why she should find it difficult to rest and relax. Everything had been so carefully worked out, hadn't it? But now all of her plans seemed to be unravelling at the seams.

Where was Billy? And who was the man with the seductive voice who wanted to see him? An old army pal? Or was he something else? These thoughts chased themselves around her brain like hamsters on a wheel.

And now there was so much more to worry about. Two men had been found dead in Billy's flat, Amit had said. Known drug dealers. The newspaper item hadn't even made the front page of the redtop she'd bought. Just a couple of column inches tucked away at the foot of a page dominated by the shenanigans of a blonde celebrity. *Fraser Sandiman and Andrew Galbraith*, the paper had written. The names didn't mean anything to Marianne, but then she had deliberately steered clear of her brother Billy's mates. Only saw *him* when she needed to. And then, only on her own terms. In fact, she thought, she had never once set foot in that particular flat over in Argyle Street. He had always come to her.

'Where the hell are you, Billy?' she whispered into the gathering darkness.

Dreams came at last, not the old nightmares of suffocating pain, but of Amit waving to her, laughing as he ran across the bridge over the Clyde. He's going to catch hold of my hand then pull me into a hug, she thought, panicking . . . choking me like Ken used to do . . .

Then everything changed. And he was falling, falling in slow motion before disappearing below the oily waters. Marianne heard a voice screaming aloud as she knelt on the bridge, desperate to see the man who had been about to embrace her.

The sound of her own voice emitting a hoarse croak made her sit up suddenly, awake and sweating.

It was only a dream, wasn't it? But then she frowned. Was it something that Doctor Brightman had said? Or something she had read? Symbolism, she thought, savouring the word as much as the concept. Was she afraid of losing Amit? Or was this a dream signifying something much more sinister?

CHAPTER 16

Omar waved his hand as the policewoman said goodnight. She might raise her eyebrows at his staying on late, but he didn't care. This was something that he had to do. The university registry officer had given him a list of all last year's new students as well as those who were just waiting for freshers' week. The woman for whom they were searching might have gained enough points for entry but delayed enrolling for a year, he had told the registry officer. Even so, the list of every girl and woman in those categories whose first name was Marianne was surprisingly long. If Lorimer okayed it, he and Irvine might be in a position to visit and interview every one of the forty-seven Mariannes on record.

He thought about James Lo. He had kept his first name all through the changes, hadn't he? But what if this woman had completely changed her name? Biting his lip in a moment of self-doubt, Omar wondered at the zeal that had kept him at this task all afternoon. What was he trying to prove? That he was a better officer than all of the rest of the team? Or that it was his endeavours, not the colour of his skin, that was of any significance?

Lorimer had taken away the photo of that red-haired woman he'd found in Brogan's flat. Could this be the sister? He'd let all of the members of the investigation team have a good look at it and then they had compared it with recent images of Brogan. There was not a shred of familial likeness and most of them had gone along with DS Wilson's suggestion: *probably Brogan's bird*.

Now he looked at the photograph on his desk. It wasn't evidence as such, so there had been no requirement to send it down as a production. The woman gazed out of the picture, that smile on her lips directed towards whoever had been behind the camera. *Say cheese*, his dad had always told him as a little lad whenever he had wanted another snap for the family album. And women liked nice photos of themselves so invariably they put on their prettiest smiles for the camera. There was nothing provocative about her, he thought. That bare shoulder was probably on show simply because it was a sunny day. No smouldering looks for a lover. And just because the picture had been in his flat did not mean that Brogan had taken it himself. So was this lady Brogan's girlfriend or not? Maybe he had a better snap of her secreted in his wallet, Lorimer thought, absently touching the pocket where he kept his own photograph of Maggie. Perhaps the drug dealer was at this very moment with this woman somewhere.

It's what's not there as much as what is, that we have to focus upon, Lorimer had insisted earlier that day. And apart from Brogan himself, there was a fair amount missing: passport, bank details, address books, all sorts of personal stuff. *And Kenneth Scott's home lacked some of these things too,* the DCI had reminded them.

Now, sitting at his desk, he wondered. Each of these killings had the same signature about them as far as the ballistics were concerned and had probably been undertaken by a trained marksman. But now there were more links between the two cases. He closed his left fist and stuck his thumb upwards, counting.

Marianne Scott was Brogan's sister; paperwork that one might expect to find in a home being used by its occupant was missing. He raised his index finger then paused. Was that all?

His hand relaxed on to the desk as he thought hard about each of the killings. Maybe they ought to look at the differences too. Scott's home hadn't been ransacked; he wasn't a known drug dealer (or user come to that); nobody in Scott's neighbourhood had heard or seen a thing. And one of the two men had been carrying a shotgun. Was that significant? Had the more recent killings happened in a chaotic situation? Where Scott's death bore the hallmarks of a planned attack, Galbraith and Sandiman's killer seemed to have stumbled upon them. Or was it the other way around? Had they come across the killer after they'd entered the flat? Traces of DNA in other rooms would help to establish an answer to that particular question.

Lorimer sighed. He'd asked for Marianne Brogan to be found as a matter of priority but was that really such a good idea? The woman had no police record of any sort and the very little he did know about her seemed to indicate that she had been an ordinary housewife before her marriage had broken up. DC Irvine had been adamant that it was weird for a woman to stop work like that after a wedding and most of the officers had agreed. Nowadays it usually took the combined salaries of a husband and wife to pay for the mortgage. And Scott hadn't exactly been rolling in money. See what you can find out from the GP she was registered with, he had suggested. She may not have been fit to work for health reasons. If so, then there might be a trail of benefits paid in her name that they could source. And that would be another bit of the jigsaw that took time to find. He sighed again. Try as they might to make progress in a case as quickly as they could, there were always elements that demanded patience; lab reports, ballistics,

121

pathology results ... things that had to wait for their slot in another professional person's busy schedule.

The DCI stood up and stretched. It was time to go home. Maggie had so few days of her holidays left and he suspected she had begun to do some work for school, having given up on the thought of them both enjoying a break away. At least their evenings could be spent together.

'Sir?' DC Fathy whirled round as the DCI entered the room.

'Working a bit of overtime, Fathy?'

'It's the sister, sir,' Fathy shrugged as he glanced back at his computer screen. 'Just can't stop thinking about where she might be, so ...'

'So?' Lorimer cocked his head to one side, interested suddenly.

'Well, I thought if we looked at all the students from last year's intake and next year's new ones to come whose forenames were Marianne, we might find something.'

'And have you?'

Fathy shook his head. 'No, sir, but I did wonder ...'

'Yes?'

'Well, what if we called on these women and asked about their backgrounds? Asked to see ID like birth and marriage certificates?'

Lorimer took a step backwards and laughed. 'Any idea how many man hours that might take? And can you see Superintendent Mitchison agreeing to extra bodies for an action like that?' The DCI frowned suddenly as he uttered Mitchison's name. There was no love lost between the two senior officers but that wasn't something that young Fathy needed to know.

'No, sir,' Fathy hung his head for a moment and looked so disappointed that Lorimer gave in to his natural impulse, reached out and patted the young man on the shoulder.

'Look, it's not a bad idea and in ideal circumstances we might even go that far. But until we have evidence that Marianne Scott is still in the country we'd be in danger of wasting taxpayers' money.'

'So that's still to be determined, sir?'

Lorimer nodded. 'Aye. There's no trace of the woman having worked, paid stamps or anything in the last year so chances are she's somewhere overseas.' His mouth pursed in a sudden thought. 'Or working at some occupation that doesn't require official papers,' he said with a sigh.

Fathy nodded. He knew what the DCI meant. 'You think the woman might have slipped off our radar because she was involved in criminal activity or maybe was on the game?'

'She has to have supported herself somehow since her marriage broke up,' Lorimer reasoned. 'And it might even give us a clue as to why that happened.'

'You mean she could be an addict?' Fathy asked.

'Who knows?' Lorimer replied tiredly. 'Brother Billy mixed with plenty of them. Wouldn't be the first time a lassie got hooked then had to resort to selling herself to fund her habit.'

'Do we have anyone looking in that direction, sir? Maybe checking the usual drop-in centres used by local prostitutes?'

'Not as yet,' Lorimer continued, mentally adding that to his tally, wondering if Fathy was about to offer to take on that task.

'Why not pack up for the night and come back tomorrow with a fresh mind, eh? It's still a lovely evening out there,' Lorimer added, nodding at the pale blue space above the city skyline.

'Right, sir. And thanks,' Fathy smiled a little uncertainly. There was a momentary pause and Lorimer stopped, waiting for the DC to continue.

'Good night, then,' the young man said at last. 'See you tomorrow, sir.'

Lorimer was still frowning as he reached the foot of the stairs. Had Fathy something else on his mind?

But as he reached the car park his thoughts were already heading homewards, all notions of what the newest member of his team had or had not been about to share already forgotten.

As he turned the car into the driveway, Lorimer slowed down. Maggie was on her hands and knees, weeding the flowerbed under the dining room window. She looked up at the sound of the car and the way her face lit up as she caught sight of him made his heart turn over.

'Hiya, you,' she said, straightening up and rubbing the small of her back as he stepped out of the car.

'Mm, hiya yourself. You smell lovely,' he added, sinking his face into her hair as he bent to kiss her cheek.

'Already showered twice today. This heat! Weather forecast says we're in for thunder before the night's out.' Maggie broke away from him, shading her eyes with her hand as she looked up at a pale sky already flecked with pinkish clouds.

'Red sky at night . . .' Lorimer began.

'Is a load of . . .'

'Mrs Lorimer!' He gasped in mock horror.

'Sorry,' she grinned. 'It's what the kids at school say. Think we can't hear them half the time and the other half they know fine well we can.'

'Itching to get back are you?'

Maggie made a face as they entered the house together. 'Not yet. Wish we could have had a bit of a holiday first,' she mumbled.

'Sorry about that.' Lorimer sighed. 'Maybe we could take off to Mull for the September weekend, though.'

The bright smile his wife gave in response was pasted on to

cover up her discontent, Lorimer knew. But she wouldn't complain. Maggie Lorimer knew that crime didn't take a holiday nor did criminals plan their misdeeds just to thwart her own spells of vacation.

'Good idea,' she replied. 'Now come through and fire up that barbecue. I'm starving.'

'One, two, one, two, up, down . . . you must be joking!' Rosie muttered, darting a black look at the TV screen where an enthusiastic young lovely in a pink leotard was encouraging viewers of her DVD to bend all the way down to the floor.

She picked up the remote control and froze the screen, leaving the instructress with her mouth open mid-command.

'Ooh,' she puffed, her steps becoming faster as she approached the loo. This pregnancy thing. You heard all the other women's moans and didn't believe them really, till it happened to you. Like needing to go all the time.

'Ah,' Rosie exhaled a sigh of relief as she sat on the toilet. It was the baby's pressure on her bladder, of course. Any doctor could tell you that. But it had been happening ever since this wee one in here had been no significant size at all.

As she washed her hands, Rosie thought about her impending leave and what she might do in the days running up to the birth of their child. Solly was not back officially until the end of September when his students began their first term. He was already preparing stuff, of course. In some ways he never stopped, she thought, pulling the light cord and waddling back into the large airy lounge that overlooked Kelvingrove Park. Take this evening, for example. Instead of coming home, he was lecturing on a course for young offenders.

Rosie shrugged as she sauntered across to the window. Would it do them any good? It depended on their level of willingness to respond, Solly had told her. The pathologist sat on the rocking chair placed at an angle in the bay window so that she looked out on the park and over the Glasgow rooftops towards the west. They were so lucky, she reminded herself. Their baby would be brought up by educated parents who were loving and caring. Too many of the inmates of these young offenders institutions came from dire backgrounds of deprivation and crime.

As she gazed at the sky, Rosie let her mind wander. The colours of the setting sun seemed more vibrant than usual, reds tinged with streaks of purple like bruised flesh; the horizon's pale lemon reminding her of the waxy pallor of a bloodless corpse. She shivered, suddenly wishing it was dark and she could be rid of the images scudding violently across the heavens.

That was another thing about this state of pregnancy. Her imagination seemed to be working overtime. Hormonal activity making you ultra sensitive, she told herself wryly. Wait till the baby's born, a colleague had warned her; your mind becomes like a vegetable. Rosie smiled. Well, she'd be off on maternity leave for a good enough spell to let her brain recover from the shock of the birth.

The telephone ringing made her turn around. Clutching both arms of the rocking chair and heaving herself up, Rosie wondered who on earth wanted to call on a week night. She was no longer on call at nights, but had somebody forgotten that?

'Maggie!' The pathologist's expression changed from apprehension to delight as she heard her friend's voice on the other end of the line.

'We're having a barbecue out in the garden. D'you fancy coming over?' Maggie asked.

Rosie made a face, glad that the policeman's wife couldn't see her. 'Sorry, His Nibs is out and I feel too fat and squashy to be bothered driving over on my own tonight. Do you mind?' She felt a sudden pang of guilt. Maggie had never managed to carry a baby to term, had never known what it felt like to have a burgeoning bump cavorting inside her.

'Och, that's okay. Maybe you can make it over at the weekend. If you feel okay?'

'Yes, I'm sure we can do something. Just a bit hot and bothered tonight. They said on the evening news that it was to be thunderstorms later on.'

'Right, well we better get on with it before we're rained off,' she heard Maggie reply.

Rosie put down the telephone then looked back out towards the west. The streaks of cloud were moving a bit faster now, driven by an unseen wind. Lorimer was home with his wife, then. No late nights chasing after murderous gunmen. Gun*man*, a little voice corrected her. It looked all the more likely from the ballistics report that the three men had been shot by the same weapon. Some kind of automatic pistol. Brogan, the man in whose flat the two drug dealers had been found, was ex-army. Had he killed them? And his former brother-in-law? Rosie sighed. Such matters were not really her business, but it was something that all her colleagues did regularly: speculate on the types of persons responsible for the damage that they saw down in the city mortuary.

The pathologist rolled her shoulders, feeling a sense of restlessness that made her get up and walk about the room. As she paced back and forwards, past the open door of her husband's study, Rosie noticed a mess of papers strewn upon the floor. Rosie glanced at the curtain blowing inwards. She had opened that window earlier to let in a draught of cool air. 'Hm,' she sighed, 'better clear that lot up, hadn't I?' Crouching down, she gathered up the loose sheets, not really paying much attention to what they were – lists of students' names, she thought – more intent on collecting them neatly together and placing them back on his desk. She gave a quick glance around, searching for the large Caithness glass paperweight that they had been given as a wedding gift. There it was, just beside a basket full of journals. Rosie placed it on top then smiled. He'd never know they'd been scattered around now, would he?

As she wandered back into the lounge Rosie forgot all about the papers. Behind her, the topmost sheet was rippled by the breeze as if it sought a means of escape from the weight of the pale purple glass, the name *Marianne* flickering back and forth, tossed in the power of the gathering storm.

When the first drops began, the woman turned towards the window, suddenly awake. Her heart was hammering in her chest, but there was no dream lingering in her thoughts, nothing to make her sweat in such fear. The noise had been enough; a drumming on the window pane like a scattering of pebbles flung by some unseen hand. Marianne shivered, remembering. He had done that often enough, hadn't he? Woken her up to let her know he had found her again.

But that could not happen any more and this was simply a storm beginning. Marianne turned on her side, tucked the sheet close about her chin and closed her eyes, willing sleep to return.

Across the city lightning cracked the sky, illuminating the streets below in sudden flashes as if daylight were breaking through the inky darkness. The hit man rolled over in his narrow bed, listening as the rains coursed down the gutters outside his rented room. A sudden flash made him open his eyes, the unfamiliar shapes of the furniture giving him a sense of where he was and why he had not yet returned to the place he called home. For a moment he lay still, wondering. The shooting of those two men had complicated things. Why not simply get into the car tomorrow and leave? On a night like this it was a tempting prospect to simply cut his losses for once. He rubbed his eyes as if rubbing the idea away. Ten thousand pounds was too much money to forfeit. Besides, he had his reputation to consider and nobody was going to pull a fast one on him, least of all scum like Brogan.

CHAPTER 17

Cala Millor was bathed in its usual sunshine, pooling the room with yellow light when William Brogan awoke. He had left the curtains of his hotel room open the previous evening to watch the streaks of lightning fork downwards into the seas. He sat up, screwing his eyes against the dazzle, stretched out his arms then sank back onto the pile of snowy pillows behind his head.

'Ah,' he sighed, breathing out as his lips widened in a smile of utter contentment, 'this is the life!'

He glanced down at his arms, noting with satisfaction the tinge of bronze that had appeared over the past few days. Another week of this and he'd be ready to move on. Marrakesh, first, then maybe further east. See what pickings there were, he thought to himself. He had booked this hotel for an entire fortnight, though he had no intention of paying for it when push came to shove. Dear me, no. Waste of good money, Billy grinned to himself. He'd just push off one fine day as though he were going to the beach, then catch a plane out of here and the hotel would be none the wiser. Wasn't as if they'd kept his passport or anything, was it? He'd given it over for them to check but now it was secreted in that safe inside the massive wardrobe, just waiting for him to decide on his next move.

A noise outside the room made him look towards the door. Throwing back the covers, he stepped on to the tiled floor, glad of the cool beneath his bare feet. He padded across the room, unlocked the heavy door and peeped out from behind it, careful to hide his naked body from the gaze of any passing chambermaid.

There, on the floor, was a British newspaper. Giving a quick glance to left and right, Brogan scooped it up and let the door swing shut.

'Tough luck, pal,' he said, grinning at whoever had been unlucky enough to have had his morning paper delivered to the wrong room. 'Okay, let's see how you're all getting along back home without me,' he chuckled, turning the newspaper over to see what the sports headlines might be. The footie season had begun after a summer of British clubs wrangling for the best players at a price that would keep them on the right side of solvency. Brogan skimmed the pages, turning until he came to the one that gave the latest Scottish Premier League results.

'Och, no' again!' he moaned, tossing the paper onto the bed as he read the report on his favourite Glasgow team. 'Anither year chasin' yer tail at the foot of the table,' he told the newspaper in disgust. Then he looked up at the glass doors that separated his room from an extensive balcony: sunshine was flooding the entire area with a brazen light. Suddenly the air-conditioned room felt too close and cramped and Brogan decided it was time to breathe some fresh air. He picked up the white bathrobe that he'd discarded the night before and shoved his arms into it, luxuriating in its soft fluffiness as he tied the belt around his waist. As he caught sight of himself in the bedroom mirror, his mouth turned up at one corner. A tanned face with several days' stubble looked back at him, the eyes narrowing speculatively. 'Aye, no sae bad, son, no sae bad,' he muttered to himself then, grabbing the newspaper, he headed towards the balcony and the beckoning sunlight.

This time Brogan began reading the newspaper from the front page, glancing briefly at the main news items before turning to other snippets inside.

It was written in a small column on the left hand side of the fifth page. Later, Brogan wondered how he'd even managed to notice it, the news item was so small. But at that moment it seemed to loom large on the page as if some magic were magnifying the words as he read them.

Men found dead in Glasgow flat, he read, not even remotely surprised by the headline.

Perhaps it was that inner parochialism that dogs so many Glasgow folk, especially those away from home, for, instead of flicking to find some more interesting stories, Brogan read on. It was *his* city, he told himself. And he'd see what was going on there.

But, as his eyes scanned the few lines of print, Billy Brogan realised that it wasn't just his city that was at the heart of the story but *his* flat. He licked his lips nervously as the final sentence glared at him.

Police would like to speak to the flat's owner, Mr William Brogan, the writer of the article informed him.

Billy dropped the paper on to the metal table. Now the sunshine seemed too bright, a menacing thing that might trap him in its beams. He picked up the paper again almost against his will to read the article once more.

'Gubby and Fraz,' he whispered to himself. '*Gubby and Fraz!*' Then he read the article for the third time, still unable to believe what it was telling him. Had it been him at home, and not these two dealers he'd been trying to avoid for weeks, then one of these shots might have found its mark in Billy Brogan's skull. He'd got away just in time, it seemed.

'Fraz and Gubby,' he murmured once again. 'Well, youse two willnae be botherin' Billy boy ony mair, will yese?'

His lower lip jutted out, the mark of a petulant child, giving him an expression that his sister, Marianne, would easily have recognised as a prelude to a strop. If he were to go back . . . he could show them he'd been here all this time, prove it by the hotel register . . . they couldn't pin anything on him for Fraz and Gubby, surely?

Brogan turned away from the balcony to step inside the cool of the room once more. He had a good idea who'd fired that gun. More than a good idea. And going back to Glasgow would be too much of a risk right now. He glanced at the newspaper folded in his hand. Lucky he'd seen that. Now he knew the police would be after him, he had to make a move. Checking out of here was definitely the wrong thing to do. They'd only be able to trace his movements. Check flight lists . . . Brogan paced back and forward, his feet making damp imprints on the tiled floor. Flying out of Palma might not be such a great idea either. Would they have alerted the Spanish police to watch all airports? Brogan felt the sweat trickle down his neck. Could they trace him from that incoming flight roster? Suddenly this island with its swathes of bougainvillea tumbling over stonewashed walls and green crested waves licking the miles of sandy shores was not the safe haven he had imagined.

But it was an island. And islands attracted thousands of yachts to their marinas. And there were loads of fishing boats as well. He scratched his head, wishing he'd not dogged off school so much. He tried to remember the map of Europe and where he was in relation to Marrakesh. Palma was just across from that coastline, wasn't it? He remembered Fraz talking about a holiday there and nipping over to Morocco. Brogan sat down on the edge of the bed, twisting the sheet in his fingers as a plan began to form in his mind. He still had plenty of money. All he needed to do was find some willing sailor to let him buy his passage out of here.

'Love you,' Lorimer whispered, turning his head to look at Maggie. Her naked body lay close to his, her limbs languid now and her hair tumbled out upon the crumpled pillow, a disarray that made his heart swell with renewed longing. He put out his hand and touched her cheek, feeling its warmth. He'd need to be up and about, should have been up and ready for work before now, but he had lingered, sensing an unspoken need to reach out to his wife.

'Sorry to leave you, love. Must get up now,' he murmured, sighing.

'Mm,' Maggie replied, her eyes still closed, a small cat-like smile hovering on her lips.

'You stay in bed. May as well make the most of your last day of freedom,' he told her.

Maggie put her hand on his arm and patted it gently. 'Go,' she said. 'I'll be fine.'

As the water cascaded down from the large shower head, Lorimer found his thoughts clearing and, as he washed Maggie's scent from his body, he was already thinking ahead. Today they should have more reports to help them push the case forward.

Brogan hadn't been seen anywhere near his flat either that day or for several days before the shootings. And none of his known associates admitted to having seen him around lately. So where the devil was he? As he raised his head to let the hot water flow over his face, Lorimer closed his eyes. Had they sufficient manpower on this one? Should he ask the super to put out for extra help? Fathy's suggestion about tracing the ex-wife might not be such a bad idea, he mused, reaching out blindly and fumbling to turn off the shower.

He towelled his dark hair vigorously then glanced at the bathroom mirror, but it was quite steamed up and all he could see was a hazy reflection.

'Want to try to catch up with Solly and Rosie later on?' he heard Maggie's voice drift through from the bedroom next door.

'If we can,' he answered shortly. 'See how today goes. Okay?'

There was no response. Maggie knew how these things panned out, she was well used to making arrangements that had to be subsequently cancelled. It went with the territory of being a policeman's wife. So the silence from the bedroom was most likely an acknowledgement of that fact. If he could be home in time to socialise with their friends then he would. She knew that.

Flinging the towel down on the top of the linen basket, Lorimer strode into the bedroom, expecting to see his wife still curled under the duvet. But she was gone and he could make out the familiar morning sounds from the kitchen downstairs; the dishwasher being emptied, Chancer, the cat, yammering for his breakfast, a kettle being filled. Lorimer frowned, the earlier joy of their coupling vanishing as he considered why Maggie had decided not to lie in on her last morning off. Were these pots and pans being banged into the cupboard with unnecessary force? He listened, wondering. What had made his wife suddenly so annoyed? Maybe the thought of going back to school without the two of them having had a break together, he decided gloomily. He'd make an excuse to leave right away, avoid any confrontation.

Lorimer gave his tie a final tug against his collar and headed on downstairs.

'Right, I'm off. Love you,' he said, planting a kiss on Maggie's mouth before she could speak. 'See you later.'

'But you've not had any breakfast,' he heard her protest as he made for the front door.

'You spoiled my appetite for food, wicked woman that you are!' he grinned over his shoulder, gratified to see a smile appear reluctantly on her face.

Maggie listened as the door slammed behind him. Heaving a huge sigh, she stood, clutching the back of a chair as though for support. Another day gone and still she hadn't told him. Why? What was it that was so difficult about this?

Wearily she pulled the chair to one side and sat down, burying her head in her hands. The doctor had said it was for the best, hadn't she? And she had mentioned the consolation of being off school for several weeks. Though for Maggie it wasn't really a consolation at all. She had smiled and put on a brave face but inwardly she had been in turmoil. After all these years of failed pregnancies she was not to be allowed one more chance. The scans had shown both ovaries full of tiny cysts. Nothing cancerous, but the perpetual bleeding twice monthly had been dragging down her general health and now Doctor Reynolds was advising a hysterectomy. They'd save her ovaries if they could, she had been told. Just so she wouldn't begin an early menopause. Thirty-nine years old, Maggie told herself. Not that much older than Rosie who was to have her baby in a few weeks' time.

Was that why she hadn't mentioned a thing to her husband? Was it the sense that she was doomed for ever to be a barren wife? So many of her colleagues at school had wee ones to go home to. Her best friend, Sandy, had a teenager at home. *More trouble than*

137

they're worth, Sandy often grumbled. But Maggie knew that was an exaggeration put on for her own benefit.

Maybe that was the problem. There hadn't been anyone to talk to over the last few weeks. And somehow she'd been unable to confide in Bill. If only Mum . . . Maggie bit back the tears that threatened.

'Stop it, woman!' she said out loud. 'Feeling sorry for yourself won't solve a thing.'

He hadn't said much about these shooting incidents and Maggie was experienced enough not to ask questions, but now her thoughts turned to those who might be left behind; parents, brothers and sisters, close friends . . . It was like seeing ripples emanate from a pool when a stone is suddenly cast into the water, Lorimer had once explained to her: a criminal act like murder created wave upon wave of victims.

Maggie Lorimer gave herself a mental shake. What was she worried about, after all? It was only an operation. There were far worse things going on in other people's lives.

The young woman in Glasgow University's registry office sat crouched over her computer screen, one hand upon her aching belly. If only she hadn't had so much to drink last night . . . Joan screwed her face up at the pain. A couple of joints would have been so much nicer, but her friend, Billy, was nowhere to be found for that particular requirement. Joan bit her lip. Billy Brogan was a wanted man. Once that would have made her smile, the thought of him being one of the big men around town. But this was different. A couple of men had been found dead in Billy's flat. She'd been there plenty of times, sleeping over after parties, sometimes sharing Billy's bed.

A sudden thought came to the woman: would the police find

traces of her DNA? Her stomach turned over in a moment of panic. But there wasn't anything they could do, was there? After all, Joan Frondigoun didn't have a police record, did she? Her eyes fell on to the list that she was typing out. Billy had given her loads of gear as well as nice presents to do him that favour, hadn't he? All she'd had to do was make a few changes here and there, delete one particular name from the university records whenever it was necessary. But now it might be a little more difficult to keep up this pretence. Okay so Billy's sister had changed her surname again, but that police officer had been asking about *any* students from a two year period whose forenames were Marianne. Had Billy's sister done anything criminal? Was *that* why she'd been trying to cover her tracks?

Joan Frondigoun sat still and thought carefully. If she were to reveal the extent of her cover up then she would not only lose her job, she might lose Billy as well. But what if Billy really had shot those men? Her lip began to tremble. He'd taken off somewhere, not told her anything about his plans. So perhaps he hadn't intended to include her in his future after all?

'You all right, Joan?' her line manager looked up from an adjoining desk, a frown on her face.

'Aye, a bit of stomach cramp. Need to go to the loo,' she said and scurried out of the office, down a short corridor and into the relative cool of the ladies' toilets.

Once inside the cubicle, Joan Frondigoun sat down and stifled a sob. It was no use kidding herself any longer. Billy Brogan had made promises that he would never keep and wasn't it just like her to have believed them?

She blew her nose loudly before flushing the toilet. Stupid cow. Stupid, stupid cow, she told herself angrily.

Then she gave herself a mental shake. Maybe it wasn't too late to get out of all this mess. Perhaps the best thing she could do now was to look for another job, leave the registry behind. She'd managed to hide Marianne Brogan from prying eyes. Now it was time she looked after herself.

CHAPTER 18

Doctor Solomon Brightman lifted the pile of papers from his desk and shuffled them into a new card folder. This year's student intake was still to be sent out to him once registry had satisfied itself that all the new applicants were processed and their classes finalised. The basic class in behavioural psychology had been oversubscribed last year and there were still some students entering their second year who wanted to add this to their timetables. Solly's mouth turned up in a small smile of pleasure. His was a popular subject all right, and those students who passed through his department would benefit from the teaching in all sorts of ways, not just those who wanted to enter the profession. Being aware of certain things about human nature was always going to be an asset in life, he'd often told them.

Opening the top drawer of his filing cabinet, Solly pushed the folder into the relevant section then flicked across until he came to the subject he wanted.

'Ah, here we are,' he murmured to himself, drawing out a green folder. 'Dreams,' he added, sitting down at his desk and opening the file. All of the psychologist's notes were saved on his hard drive but he always kept a hard copy with a duplicate for the department's files. It meant that any lecture could be given at a moment's notice, even if the member of the department who had written it was absent. He grinned. It was just as well. He'd be taking off the statutory two weeks' paternity leave once the baby arrived and that was scheduled to be a few weeks after the start of term. Still, he enjoyed giving this particular lecture and he wanted to amend some of the contents before the new session began.

As he riffled through the documents he noticed that one page at the back had come adrift from its paperclip. Solly pulled it out and glanced at the list of names that had comprised one of his tutorial groups. Eight names conjured up only a few faces. He shook his head, berating himself for having such a terrible memory. But then he stopped as he read the last but one name on the list. Scott. That was her name, the red-haired woman who had spoken to him in the bookshop. Marianne Scott. Now he remembered her. An older student, pale faced, with an air of defeat about her, he recalled. Hadn't she always sat in a corner away from the others, as though she had wanted to fade into the woodwork? That alone had made her an interesting subject. It hadn't just been the fact that she had been the only mature student in that particular group that had made him think about her. The aura of unhappiness around her had been almost palpable, if one believed in such things as auras, he chided himself. Whatever had been wrong must have sorted itself out, though, as she had seemed a different person that day in the children's department of the bookstore.

Tucking the list more firmly in its place, Solly began to read his lecture notes on dreams and the preamble that always included the great twentieth century figures of Freud and Jung.

Sitting back, the psychologist relaxed as he read his notes.

Dreams are what pass through the human mind as we sleep. While they appear to us as pictures and may include other sensory input like sounds they are usually associated with strong emotions and thoughts. Although there is no definitive reason for why we dream this is a topic that has fascinated mankind since the beginning of time. Solly read on, skimming the references to Biblical characters and those in various mythologies. He had included Joseph, of course, and had gone on to relate his own knowledge of the Judaic ceremony *hatavat halom*. This was a ceremony where through ritual a rabbi could transform bad dreams, making them good. Not a bad ceremony to have, Solly thought to himself. If he had long since given up being a practising Jew, he still retained a strong respect for the traditions and felt it was important to include this snippet in his lecture.

He skipped the pages referring to REM sleep. Students new to the neurology of sleep and dreams loved this bit, especially those who craved empirical evidence. Solly chuckled, turning the pages until he came to the section on the psychology of dreams. So much of it was theory, of course, and students had to balance what many psychologists had said upon the subject, some of it quite contradictory. Were dreams an emotional preparation for solving problems? Did they create new ideas? Did they function as a mental dustbin for all the sensory input that had taken place before sleep? Solly read on, once again acknowledging his own fascination with the subject.

Rosie had told him of the vivid dream she had experienced when she had been in hospital. She had felt as though she were leaving her own body. The memory of that time still had the power to disturb him. That she had hung between life and death following her terrible accident was never in doubt. But had she been given some sort of premonition of the afterlife in a dream? Or had the massive amounts of drugs been responsible for such pictures in her brain? It was interesting, he always told his students, that more women than men recalled their dreams. And also that those remembered dreams were more often than not associated with anxiety rather than with a feeling of well being.

Solly laid down the folder full of papers and gazed into space. *To sleep, perchance to dream*, Shakespeare had written. Distracted for a moment, he wondered if he ought to write a paragraph or two about characters from the plays. Undergraduates often combined the study of psychology with that of English literature. Hamlet was an obvious choice, of course. And Lady Macbeth, though she, poor woman, was often wrongly attacked as being a psychopath. Such persons did not experience her level of guilt, he would have to remind his students. And did psychopaths have the necessary mental equipment to be dreamers themselves? That was another interesting question that might be worth including. The better students would enjoy following up that one.

A door closing shook Solly out of his reverie and he turned around to listen to the familiar sounds he held so dear; Rosie letting her keys fall into the porcelain dish on the hall table, then her voice calling him as she entered the lounge.

'Hiya. I'm home.'

Solly rose from his chair, all thoughts of dreams and dreamers banished in that moment as he caught sight of his pregnant wife. There was something that caught at his heart as he came forward to fold her in his embrace: a new vulnerability that made her seem fragile despite her robust shape. She was sheltering their child, keeping it snug and warm, protected by her body. *Flesh of my flesh*, Solly thought, the phrase coming to him suddenly.

'Here, sit down. I'll make you something nice. Lemon and ginger tea?'

Rosie slumped down in her favourite rocking chair, settling a couple of cushions at her back. 'Ah, that's better. Yes, some of that nice tea would be wonderful. And maybe a wee ginger biscuit as well. I've been having horrible heartburn again. Wee rascal's probably lying up against my tummy. Oh,' she added in a sigh. 'All those poor bits of me squashed up. Can't think what a relief it'll be to be back to normal again.'

The pathologist closed her eyes, feeling the warmth from the early evening sunshine through the glass. Their bay windows faced west and it was a treat to bask in the last rays of the setting sun. Theirs would be an autumn baby, due to be born on the twentieth of October, Rosie mused. A Libran, Emma in the mortuary had informed her. They had chosen not to know whether it would be a boy or a girl. *So long as it's like the world*, her old aunty had said. And she was right, of course; a normal, healthy baby was what mattered. Solly's mum and dad didn't seem to care either way, or so they had said. Rosie sighed. It was such a shame her own folks were no longer here to see the next generation of wee Fergussons.

'Here you are,' Solly handed his wife a mug of tea and hunkered down beside her. 'Good day? Or shouldn't I want to know?'

'Thanks, love, not bad,' she replied, taking a sip from the china mug. 'I'll spare you the details,' she grinned.

Solly smiled back. Theirs was a strange union in many ways; a man who was squeamish about all things to do with blood and gore and a woman whose profession it was to delve into the innards of a human cadaver. Early on in their relationship Rosie had learned to be sensitive to the psychologist's weakness and was always careful not to dwell on too many particulars of her day to day work.

'Interesting case this one that Lorimer's got on just now. Probably some gangland falling out, if you ask me, but ballistics are having some fun with it.' She turned away from the sunlight to look at her husband, sitting by her side. 'Two men gunned down in the flat of a known drug dealer. The flat belongs to the man whose former brother-in-law was killed by the same weapon. Or so they believe.'

'Not very mysterious, then,' Solly shrugged.

'Shouldn't think so. The dealer is ex-army so as it stands things seem to point at him. Lorimer's team will likely turn him up then that'll be another case for the records.'

'Will you be required to give evidence in court?'

Rosie bent her head from side to side trying to ease the neck muscles that had stiffened up. ''Spect so. But they have to catch him first and it'll only come to trial if he pleads not guilty.'

'Is that likely?'

Rosie snorted. 'Och, they all seem to plead not guilty these days. Hope that they'll have one of our famous celebrity defence lawyers who'll get them off.'

'Well, at least you won't be performing any more post-mortems now,' Solly said, a hint of warning in his voice.

'No, 'spect not,' she replied casually. But as she drained the mug of tea, Rosie wondered if the recent post-mortems she had performed on the two drug dealers would be her last before going on maternity leave. It was becoming more and more difficult to lean over the operating table and sometimes she had experienced tingles in her fingers, not the best thing when wielding a scalpel. Solly was probably quite right, even though it felt as if he were being a tad over-protective. Somehow this case had intrigued her. The memory of that nice looking chap with a single hole to his forehead had lingered with her. Especially when Lorimer had expressed his surprise that Kenneth Scott had been targeted by a hit man.

Ah, well, it wasn't her business.

'Look!' Solly laid a gentle hand across her belly as a ripple appeared, moving from one side to the other. And as both of them gazed at the tiny miracle that was their unborn child, all thoughts of dead bodies and gunmen were forgotten.

'Lorimer always tells us to look at the victim's home,' DS Cameron said, as he strolled down the corridor with Detective Constable Fathy. 'We didn't have too much chance of doing that with Scott so he wants me to take you back there today to have a look around.'

'To see what isn't there,' murmured Fathy.

'Right,' Cameron replied. 'We seem to have reached a bit of an impasse with Mr Scott. Far too little known about him. Lorimer reckons we might turn up something back at his house.'

Fathy nodded, increasing his speed to match the other man's stride. 'And he's happy for me to tag along?'

'Of course,' Cameron said. 'Especially as your pal, DC Irvine, is off with DS Wilson to see Sandiman and Galbraith's families,' he added. 'Think we've got the better of the actions today, don't you?' he grinned.

Omar Fathy gave a smile in return. It would be good to have an opportunity to see the detective sergeant in action this morning. He had warmed to the tall Lewisman who had gone out of his way to make him feel welcome. They had spent time playing pool one evening and he'd noticed that the other man had kept to soft drinks, never making a big issue about it. 'Don't drink,' Cameron had shrugged when offered something alcoholic, as if it was no big deal. Fathy had been impressed. Up in Grampian that might have been remarked upon and he knew some officers there who would have taken the mickey out of Cameron. But the detective sergeant seemed wholly unfazed about being a teetotaller.

147

It was a short ride across town to Scott's house, a small terraced property in the suburbs that was remarkable only because of the manner in which its owner had died.

The crime scene tape was still tied across the pathway, supposedly keeping anybody from nosing around. It hadn't, of course. Images of the house had been circulated around all the tabloids, though now it was old news and there was no sign of any reporters hovering in the vicinity.

'Okay, here we are. Gloves on. Keys at the ready,' Cameron grinned. It was important not to contaminate the scene in case further forensics were required so both men put on a pair of latex gloves before leaving the pool car.

As it was a week day the neighbourhood was virtually deserted, a British Telecom van being the only other vehicle parked in the street. Omar Fathy looked around him as Cameron fiddled with the keys to the front door. It was such an ordinary looking place, every garden neat with well-trimmed hedges or low stone walls. The hanging baskets at the neighbouring doorway were full now, their colours a blaze of crimson geraniums and bright blue lobelia in contrast to the victim's home. There was a patch of lawn, fairly recently mown, but no baskets or tubs full of flowers and only a few shrubs placed next to the garden path. Filling a garden with annual plants was often a woman's pleasure, Fathy thought. It had certainly fallen to his mother to choose what flowers their gardener was to plant each year in their extensive grounds. Something missing, Lorimer had said. Well, a woman's touch out here was missing at any rate, but they already knew that, didn't they? he thought as he followed DS Cameron into the darkened hallway.

Cameron stopped suddenly then flicked on the light switch. 'That's where he was killed,' he said, pointing to a patch on the carpet just feet from the front door.

'He opened the door and was shot right away?' Fathy asked.

Cameron frowned. 'From where the body was it looks as though he had taken a couple of steps backwards before the gunman shot him. That's what ballistics have told us, anyway.'

'Right,' Fathy nodded, then stepped gingerly to one side as the other officer sidled past the spot where the man had died. He shuddered despite the warmth in the house. A man had died just there; one moment he'd been a living breathing person and the next all that remained was a piece of dead meat for the pathologists to pick over.

Fathy exhaled, his eyes fastened on that spot on the carpet, unaware that he had been holding his breath.

'The main room is through here and the kitchen off to the back of the house. Two bedrooms and a bathroom upstairs,' Cameron said, waving a hand as he entered the living room.

'You'd make a great estate agent, Sergeant,' Fathy chuckled and was gratified to see the senior officer smile in reply.

'Well, maybe we should look at the house with different eyes. As if it's a place we would want to buy. What d'you think?'

Fathy shrugged. Whatever the DS wanted was fine with him.

The main living room had been split into two distinct areas, one with a two-seater settee and a matching easy chair facing a large screen television and the other housing a small square dining table with four chairs. The furnishings were fairly bland, to Fathy's eye; mid-brown laminate flooring and a marled beige throw over the darker brown sofa. Everywhere he looked it was the same; plain tones of beige or brown except for the black television screen dominating one corner of the room.

'And no plants. Nothing living here at all,' Fathy remarked as he moved from the main room into a kitchen that was almost clinical, the cupboards a stark white against dark grey granite worktops.

149

'Kept the place really tidy, so maybe he didn't have much time for plants and stuff cluttering it up,' he murmured to himself. 'What's in the cupboards?' he asked himself, opening one after the other. The detective constable raised his eyebrows as he caught sight of the contents; rows of jars neatly labelled, tins of food stacked in perfect symmetry. He wiped a latex-covered finger across the floor of one cupboard and was unsurprised to see it come away with not a trace of dirt or dust.

Kenneth Scott had been a fairly young man, he reminded himself. Most of the young men Fathy knew were too busy enjoying themselves to become obsessed with having a perfectly neat and tidy home. The young officer felt a sudden sadness for the victim: what sort of life had he had? Too much time on his hands by the looks of it, if he'd always kept things in such meticulous order. He hadn't had much of a life at all, it seemed. No wife to clutter the place up with knick-knacks, no sign of any bottle racks full of booze to entertain pals of a Friday night.

'Come on upstairs,' he heard Cameron calling. 'See if you can make head or tail of this.'

Fathy left the kitchen and took the few steps through the living room back into the hall then climbed the steep staircase to the upper level. A single window at the top should have let the light in but the blind had been kept closed for some reason. Fathy stretched out one hand and pulled on the blind cord, letting in a stream of sunshine. Dust motes hovered in the air as though suddenly released and the young detective stopped for a moment, considering the man who had been killed. He'd been in his pyjamas, hadn't he? He would have stood on the very step Fathy was standing on now, making his way downstairs to answer the front door. Was that how it had happened? Fathy gave himself a shake as he entered the victim's bedroom.

'Look at this,' Cameron declared, standing beside a neatly made bed.

Fathy stared at his DS then looked around the room. What was it he was supposed to be looking at? The place was as tidy as the rooms downstairs. No clothes were lying on the back of the chair by the window, not even a dressing gown. That was hanging on a hook behind the door, he saw as he continued to turn around, examining the room. 'Tidy beggar, wasn't he?' he offered.

'You don't see it, do you?' Cameron said at last. 'Think back to all the scene of crime photographs you've seen so far.'

The young detective constable frowned in concentration then shook his head.

'The bed,' Cameron said at last, an eager light in his eyes. 'Look at it.'

Fathy looked, thinking about the night Scott had been killed. Then it dawned on him.

'It's made.' He looked up, bewildered. 'Someone's made the bed!' he exclaimed.

'Aye, took your time to see it, though, didn't you?' Cameron smiled ruefully. 'Entire crime scene's supposed to be left exactly as it was found. Any copper knows that. So, who's been in to do a wee bit of housekeeping?'

Fathy stared at the bed. Not only was the coverlet smooth, but there was a crease folded under the bump where the pillow lay.

'You think someone has been in?'

'Certain of it. We're going to have to get the fingerprint lads back here pronto. And see if we can find out from the neighbours who else had a key to this house.'

'Maybe he's got a cleaner who comes in,' Fathy suggested.

'Could be. I'm reasonably tidy but I can't say it's anything like my own place,' Cameron said ruefully. 'Never seem to have the time to keep it as orderly as this. Maybe you're right. Maybe someone does come in. But why wouldn't any of the neighbours have told us?'

'And if he didn't have a cleaner, if he kept the place as spick and span as this, maybe it tells us something about him.'

'Aye,' Cameron agreed. 'If he was ex-navy or something you might understand it. Someone who was used to keeping things in a really meticulous fashion. But maybe it says something about his personality. I don't know . . .' he tailed off thoughtfully. 'Point is, someone's been in here without our authority and we'll need to find out who that was.'

'True, but let's not abandon this till we've seen the rest of upstairs,' Fathy answered, moving towards the doorway. 'I'm willing to bet that the bathroom and the spare bedroom are equally shipshape, but maybe we should take a minute to see if there's anything else unusual. Like Lorimer said, look for what should be there but isn't.'

'Already looked in the bathroom and guess what I didn't find?'
Fathy looked blank.

'No condoms. No spare toothbrush. Nothing. It's as if the bloke had been a hermit.'

'But he had a relationship with that woman, Frances Donnelly,' Fathy said.

'Aye, but it doesn't look as if he ever brought her back home, does it?'

'Weird,' Fathy said at last. 'Unless she only came round to do a bit of housework?' he added.

'You think the girlfriend would come round and make up his bed after he'd been killed here?' Cameron's tone was sceptical.

'No, suppose not. But it seems odd that *anyone* would do a

152

thing like that, doesn't it? I mean, it doesn't fit with what we know about him.'

'And what's that?' Cameron asked, folding his arms and looking at the younger man with interest. 'What sort of a person do you think he was?'

'Frighteningly tidy, and I'm willing to bet he suffered from obsessive compulsive disorder. *And* he was a very private person,' Fathy decided. 'Doesn't that make you wonder if there was something he wanted to hide from the outside world?'

Annie Irvine stood outside the high-rise flat, wondering how often she had been in this situation before. *Send Irvine,* she could hear the voice clearly. Any voice. It didn't really matter who was in authority, they seemed to recognise that here was a woman who would be useful in keeping a veneer of calm whilst distraught relatives gave vent to their emotion. The front door that had once been some shade of red was scuffed from repeated kicks and knocks and there was a faint smell in the corridor that might have been cat pee. The whole place was redolent of despair and neglect, she thought. Lorimer had often ranted about the iniquity of the skyscraper flats, wondering why on earth these planners from the sixties had thought it a good idea to upend streets and leave them hanging in the air like this.

She looked up at DS Alistair Wilson, seeing more than the thinning dark hair and the worn leather jacket. He was a middle-aged cop, a family man whose years in the force had given him a hard-bitten edge. But Annie had always known Wilson as a policeman whose humanity lay just under the surface of that outward gruffness. Too many cops became inured to the suffering of others, but, like Lorimer, Wilson wasn't one of them.

'Whityewantin'?' A large woman had suddenly appeared in the doorway, eyeing them suspiciously. Her wild shock of grey hair looked as though several birds might have roosted in it overnight and her pink T-shirt hung loosely over a pair of unsupported breasts. Annie stared for a moment then realised that the woman had probably just got out of bed even though it was early in the afternoon.

'Mrs Galbraith?' Wilson was proffering his warrant card for her to examine and, as the woman peered at it short-sightedly, he took a step towards her. 'Detective Sergeant Wilson, Detective Constable Irvine. We're here to see you about your son.'

Three quarters of an hour and two pots of tea later Annie found herself out in the fresh air once more.

'Christ!' Wilson swore as they walked across to the car park. 'How does she do it? One fag after another!' he exclaimed. 'Betty'll create tonight when I walk in smelling like this,' he added.

'Never mind how she does it, how can she afford to smoke like that?' Irvine retorted. 'No husband around and existing on benefits,' she exclaimed. 'Still, maybe it's what's keeping her going. That and tannin.' She grimaced. 'How many teabags d'you reckon were in each pot?'

Wilson took a deep breath, face towards the sky. 'Whew, that's better. My poor lungs were fit to burst in there. Anyway, young lady, what do you think? Reckon we're any further forward after speaking to Gubby's old mum?'

Irvine shook her head as they approached the car. 'No. She obviously didn't see him much. Still hell of a shock to find your boy's been blown away by some mad gunman, isn't it?'

'Aye,' Wilson replied. 'I know some who would say: *she'll get over it, her type always do*, but here's a thing. She's a mother and mothers never get over losing their kids, no matter how estranged they might have been.'

The Detective Sergeant's words stayed with Annie on the journey to Langside where Fraser Sandiman's father lived. In contrast to the Galbraith home, his was positively middle class. The short terrace of town houses ended in a narrow cul-de-sac, forcing Wilson to manoeuvre the car with some difficulty so that it was facing back out towards Langside Avenue.

The appearance of the houses was deceptive, however, and as they drew closer to the Sandiman house, they could see that many of the properties had been split into flats. Some had annual plants brightening up the patches on either side of the steep front steps but at number eleven it looked as though its residents had lost heart long ago. Here the tiny front gardens were choked with long grass and summer weeds, rose bay willow herb blowing its feathery seeds skywards.

'Wonder what else they're growing down there,' Wilson joked, motioning towards the overgrown plots.

'If it was cannabis they'd be taking a lot more care of it,' Irvine muttered.

There were five names on a list by the security buzzers, Sandiman being the only one properly typed and slotted into its metal plate. The rest were scribbled but legible, possibly evidence that the residents were mostly students who would have shorter tenancies.

In answer to Wilson pressing the buzzer Irvine heard a crackle then a man's voice asking, 'Who is it now?'

There was no mistaking the irritation in that tone and the two officers exchanged a glance before Wilson answered, 'Strathclyde Police.'

'Top floor,' the voice said and they stepped into a darkened hallway as the door clicked open.

Charles Sandiman was waiting for them at his door. Irvine saw a tall man with a military bearing and a small, grizzled moustache. He looked at them fiercely, eyeing them as though they were officers on parade to be inspected, then stood aside. 'You'd better come in,' he said.

'It's about Fraser,' Irvine told him as they entered a large lounge that overlooked the street. She resisted the impulse to touch the man's arm. Talking about the death of his son was surely going to be as painful for this man as it was for any mother?

It was Annie who made the tea in this home, allowing DS Wilson to fill the father in on how his son had been killed. She left the two of them sitting side by side, the father gazing unseeing out of the window as Wilson tried to engage him in some form of conversation. From the adjacent kitchen she could then hear the detective sergeant's voice explaining why they had to come, why questions about Fraser's background had to be asked. But until she re-entered the room, bringing a tray with mugs and a plate of digestive biscuits, the man did not say a word.

As she approached, Sandiman stood up, a mark of courtesy that she recognised as belonging to gentlemen of a different generation. Or class, Annie reminded herself, thinking of Omar. But his stiff-backed stance was probably from years of that military background.

'We're looking for William Brogan, sir,' Wilson said. 'To help us with our enquiries,' he added.

'Never met the man. Knew he was one of ours, though,' Sandiman said gruffly.

'You were an army officer, sir?' Irvine asked.

'Black Watch,' Sandiman replied, adding, 'before they re-arranged us into a *battalion*!' He spat the word out as though it had a bad taste. 'Best regiment there was. Top Brass never get it right, though,' he added bitterly. 'Didn't then and aren't doing so now,' he shook his head angrily.

'Brogan was a Black Watch officer?' Irvine asked in surprise.

'Not an officer. Private,' Sandiman corrected her.

'Did Fraser ever speak of Brogan to you, sir?' Wilson wanted to know.

The man turned to face the two police officers and Irvine could detect a trace of tears in his eyes. His mouth trembled and she felt a sudden sympathy but as he began to speak she realised that he was shaking with suppressed fury.

'My *son*! *My* son!' His voice cracked as emotion swamped his self-control. 'To consort with low-life like Galbraith and Brogan! What was he thinking about?'

Irvine watched, fascinated, as he clutched the mug of hot tea, his fists gripping it with such intensity that she feared he would break off the handle.

'Fraser was educated, Sergeant,' he said, gritting his teeth. 'Brought up to respect people. To respect his country. Not to make his living from other men's misery!'

As he bowed his head Irvine stepped forwards and took the mug from his grasp, letting her fellow officer be the one to console the man in the torrent of grief that followed.

Annie stood behind them, wondering. It was bad enough to have a son who was found dead, but the shame of being found in the home of a known drug dealer was something this proud man would find hard to forgive. Fraser Sandiman had been given a decent upbringing, by all accounts; Galbraith's background on the other hand was rooted in poverty and deprivation. But from her limited experience Irvine knew that it was wrong to make a judgement about people based on that. She thought about the blowsy woman they had left over in Glasgow's East End and then looked at the man weeping into his hands, Wilson's arm around his shoulders. They were also victims of whoever had pulled that trigger. And their suffering would likely follow each of them to their graves.

DCI Lorimer looked at the report from Irvine and Fathy. He'd read it and reread it but there was still something that didn't add up. Marianne Scott seemed to have vanished. There was no trace of her after her course at Anniesland College though they now had her list of SCE Higher passes. She had certainly gained enough for entry to the University of Glasgow. But had she gone elsewhere? Abroad, perhaps?

Frances Donnelly's statement contained the idea that Scott had still been seeing his ex-wife, though there was no concrete evidence for this. It was only the girlfriend's impression. But what if the Donnelly woman had been wrong? What if Scott hadn't seen his ex-wife for one very good reason?

And for the first time the DCI had the chilling thought that perhaps there was another body still to be found.

CHAPTER 19

The August sun beat down on his back as Billy Brogan strode along the path towards Cala Bona. The Catalan name meant *the good bay*, one of the hotel waiters had told him. And Cala Millor meant *the better bay*, the man had added, smirking as well he might. The hotel was possibly the most expensive in the area and its guests would be pleased to know how well they had chosen their holiday destination, his expression had seemed to suggest.

That wasn't an issue with Brogan right now as he headed towards the small fishing port that lay a few miles along the curving coastline. The morning was already stifling hot and he had nearly finished the bottle of mineral water that he'd taken from the refrigerator in his room. Brogan winced as he walked along, feeling a blister begin where his toes were being rubbed by these cheap flip-flops he'd bought at the market. He glanced at a couple of older men who passed him by, bare chests showing enviable suntans; both sported sensible panama hats and each carried a large bottle of chilled water as they headed towards the miles of silver sand. His T-shirt was probably showing large patches of sweat, he thought, wiping his brow for the hundredth time as the perspiration trickled into his eyes. Not a pretty sight for any of the yachties he was hoping to cajole into giving him passage.

Brogan paused for a moment under the shade of an awning that jutted out from one of the many restaurants. Maybe he should nick around to the shopping area in the street that ran parallel to this one? Buy a clean shirt, freshen up a bit?

The thought seemed to lead his weary feet back into a shaded side street and past the blocks of apartments where women hung out of their windows talking loudly to neighbours in the street below. Brogan watched them, not understanding a single word as they called to one another, waving their hands in the air as though to emphasise whatever it was that they were discussing. The sunlight cut across the openings between the buildings, making him blink even behind the shade of his sunglasses, then a noise just behind him made Brogan turn and he stepped quickly to one side as a motorbike roared past, a pair of Spanish men on board. Neither of them were youngsters, Brogan noticed; both of them were dressed extravagantly in cowboy gear, even sporting colourful boots with fancy patterns cut into the leather.

He looked down at his own clothes, a grey sweat-stained cotton shirt and a pair of shabby cut-off jeans. No, he thought, this wouldn't do at all. Lengthening his stride, Brogan emerged into the main shopping thoroughfare and began searching for a half-decent men's outfitters amongst all the outlets laden with tourist tat.

Twenty minutes later he was back on the esplanade and heading on to Cala Bona looking for a waste bin to ditch his old clothes. Catching sight of his reflection in a window he saw a man wearing a fine linen shirt hanging loose over cream-coloured chinos, his bare feet thrust into a pair of comfortable tan leather sandals. He ran a hand through his hair, making it stick up in spikes, a fashion look that made him grin in appreciation.

It was better up here, he thought, as the path twisted through high sided buildings that created some shade from the late morning sun. The two towns simply ran into one another and only a large notice proclaiming that this was now the town of Cala Bona allowed a stranger to know where one stopped and the other began. Then suddenly he was out in the sunlight once again, the path taking him straight to a picture postcard harbour where several large boats were moored.

Brogan strolled around the harbour side, glancing at the fishing boats and yachts as any tourist might, all the while taking note of the names on the hulls and the various countries of origin. Among the craft were a couple of glass-bottomed boats, their crew nowhere to be seen. But from the placards fluttering from the booms, Brogan could see that they were pleasure craft for taking tourists on trips around the area.

Retracing his steps back around the harbour, he took a path back up to the edge of the esplanade and found himself looking out at the water. It was choppy today, the waves rolling in more fiercely after the thunderstorms of previous nights. Would these pleasure boats put out to sea in conditions like this? He glanced behind him and saw a small booth set against a wall, the names of the boats displayed brightly against the desk. A bored looking lad of about eighteen lounged in the shade of the booth, gazing at the folk who constantly passed him by.

Then, as another man approached him, Brogan smiled. The furtive exchange between the two Spaniards was something Brogan had seen a thousand times on the street corners back in Glasgow. This was a wee glimpse into his own world, he told himself, moving towards the lad with increasing confidence.

'Doin' the business, pal?' Brogan grinned, giving the Spanish boy a slap on his shoulder.

The way the lad gave a quick look to his left then his right told Brogan all he needed to know.

'You lookin' to score, señor?' he asked Brogan nervously.

'Well, now I'm lookin' for something, that's true, but you can keep your weed, son. What I'm after is a bit bigger.'

Shifting from one foot to the other, the boy eyed him suspiciously.

'That your boat out there?' Brogan pointed to a large craft bobbing at anchor.

'*Sí*,' the boy answered sullenly.

'No custom today?'

The boy shook his head and nodded towards the sea. 'Too much waves. No go out today.'

'How about tomorrow?' Brogan persisted.

'No tomorrow. Maybe day after,' the boy shrugged. 'You wanna book a ticket?'

Brogan grinned and sidled up to the boy. 'Maybe I want to take a private trip,' he said, slipping one hand into his pocket. 'Just me and the captain,' he continued, watching as the boy's eyes fell greedily on the bundle of folded notes he had produced. 'How about it? Where can I speak to your boss?' he whispered, lowering his sunglasses in a way that made the boy look at him more closely.

Marianne handed over the application form to the librarian, watching to see her reaction when she read the name on the piece of paper. It came, just as she had thought it would, a surprised lift of the eyebrows and a swift once-over of the red-haired woman standing on the other side of the desk. Marianne waited, unsmiling, for the card to be printed out and re-issued. If anyone were to question her . . .? But it was only minutes before the girl returned and handed back her renewed library card, staring at Marianne with blatant curiosity. Dropping her gaze, Marianne saw that the librarian's hands were carefully manicured, pale pink shiny polish

162

on perfect ovals, all the better to display the two rings, one gold, the other a single diamond that sparkled under the artificial light.

'Thanks,' Marianne mumbled, then, deliberately avoiding the girl's curious stare and pushing the card into the depths of her shoulder bag, she turned on her heel to head for the barrier that would take her into the heart of Glasgow University's library.

Well, she thought, letting out a sigh of relief, that was that, then. A new name and a new term ahead. Between Billy's young friend in registry and this latest twist to her life, Marianne could breathe more easily knowing that the secrets of her identity were safe.

There were more than five weeks now until the start of the session but this time she was determined to be ahead of the game. Plenty of time for all the required texts on this year's reading list. A little smile played about her mouth. She was one of the fortunate students who did not need to work at part-time bar jobs in order to fund their courses. Marianne sighed. Another couple of years, or more if she were lucky enough to make honours, then the world of work could beckon once more. A new beginning somewhere else, the States, perhaps, where a degree in psychology might be the necessary passport to a job of some kind. Glancing behind her at the librarian who was now busy with another student, Marianne's face took on a wistful expression. She hadn't appreciated how much fun she'd had all those years ago having colleagues to gossip with, girls' nights out. The girl back there at the desk looked as though she had it all: a steady job, decent salary, nice place to work, a husband and maybe even kids . . . Well, times had changed and she had changed with them.

Be careful what you wish for, she told herself. It might just come true.

CHAPTER 20

'Brogan. B-R-O-G-A-N. That's it. Billy Brogan. How did I get your number? Well that's for me to know and you to find out, pal.' He looked back at the notebook in his hand with its list of names and telephone numbers. 'Right now I want to find our friend, okay?'

The hit man waited, listening to a rumble of voices in the background, straining to make out what language was being spoken. It was more than a minute before the man he had called made any reply. Then it was to apologise. *He was busy, had a business to run. Not convenient to talk right now.*

'So when would it be convenient, mate? I think we might have something to discuss about Billy Boy,' the hit man said slowly, his voice full of steel.

'I'll call you back,' the man replied.

'No,' he said. 'That's not possible. Arrange to meet up now. Give me a time and a place and I'll be there.'

There was more hesitation and a spluttering of excuses but eventually a rendezvous was suggested.

'Okay by me. Today suit you?'

Again there was some humming and hawing, until a time was fixed for the following day. 'I have meetings, many meetings. I am a very busy man, you know,' the voice on the line insisted. 'I will send someone to meet you.'

The hit man listened, hearing just a hint of anxiety, understanding that the very mention of Brogan's name held a lot of significance for the man who was listed in Brogan's notebook simply as Dhesi.

Glasgow in late August was better than he had expected. The weather was clear and sunny, the summer heat intensifying just as the school term had ushered the population of Scottish schoolchildren back indoors for a new session. The hit man grinned as he sat on a bench in the middle of the city watching the lanes of traffic circulate around George Square. It was not unpleasant sitting here watching the world go by but he did not expect to be in Glasgow for much longer. He glanced at his wristwatch. Soon he would be joined by another man, someone who could help him to recover the money he was owed; someone who had an interest, like himself, in finding Billy Brogan.

The chosen rendezvous had been easy to find and he had arrived early, wandering around the square for a while, admiring the City Chambers, a pale grey building that dominated one entire side of the square. It was impressive by anyone's standards, even someone like himself who knew nothing about architecture, its towers leading the eye upward. A pair of stone carved lions flanked the white cenotaph, a few yards from the building, reminding him of lives lost in a duty to Queen and country that he himself had once followed.

The hit man watched as a large black Daimler glided to a halt right outside the entrance to the City Chambers. From a professional point of view the security was spot on. Darkened windows hid the passenger from view and he caught only a brief glimpse of

166

a woman's figure as she alighted from the big car and entered the main door with some lackeys in tow. He cocked his head to one side. Now, if he had been positioned up on that rooftop, belly down, rifle in his grasp, that would have been an entirely different matter.

'Mr Smith?' A voice behind him broke the reverie, making the hit man stand up immediately.

'Aye, maybe,' he replied evasively. 'Who wants to know?'

A dark-skinned man who may have been Indian or Pakistani stood smiling at him then gave a small bow, one hand across his corpulent stomach. 'I come to you as an intermediary, Mr Smith. I believe that was understood by our mutual friend?'

The hit man sniffed and threw the man a sideways glance. 'So what are we waiting for?' he asked. 'I take it he's ready to begin discussions?'

'Oh, yes, sir. If you'd like to follow me, we have a car parked just along the road,' the Asian motioned with one hand, willing the other man to accompany him.

'I suppose you've got a name, pal?'

In reply his companion tapped one side of his nose, an age-old gesture that signified that it was not wise to ask too many questions.

The hit man frowned suddenly. This man's voice sounded so like the one he had spoken to on the telephone yesterday. Was *he* actually Dhesi? And had it all been a bit of nonsense about sending someone else?

The hit man walked just a little behind the stranger, cautious in case he had to make a sudden run for it. He touched his pocket, feeling the gun's reassuring hardness. But it wasn't something he could make use of here, in the city centre, if things suddenly went wrong.

167

The Mercedes was parked outside a large pub just past the square. As he was ushered into the back seat, the hit man glanced at the driver, a middle-aged white man with rolls of fat coming over his collar, clearly sweating under his smart black uniform. Not in good shape, he told himself, dismissing the driver as posing no potential threat, then turned to face the Asian who had climbed into the back to join him.

'Brogan,' he began. 'He's known to you?'

The Asian inclined his head a little. 'He is known to my client,' he said.

'Client? What are you? Some sort of lawyer?'

The man beside him chuckled. 'Not at all, my friend. I am what you might call a fixer. A middleman. Those from my home-land know me better as *The Hundi*.'

'So you're not the man I spoke to on the phone?'

'No, Mr Smith. That was my client. Someone, it appears, who has a mutual interest in Mr Brogan. Now, while we drive to our meeting place, let me tell you something about this lovely city of ours,' he said. Turning towards the window he pointed up at the buildings that swooped up on either side, their windows glittering in the sunshine. Then, as though the hit man was simply a tourist visiting Glasgow for pleasure, the Hundi began to enthuse about some of the city's architectural gems.

Dhesi stood, hands behind his back, looking out of the window. This was his home now, this city whose fine buildings were a con-stant reminder of past glories, Glasgow's tobacco lords and ship owners gaining their immense wealth from their trade. It was a city that suited him, Dhesi thought. He, too, traded in things, though those commodities were less welcomed by the city fathers than the bales of Virginia tobacco that had been shipped to the docks in times past. The restaurant was his legitimate enterprise, of course, and he was proud of it. Things had become so easy in the months following Amit's arrival, that it would be a pity if they were to be upset by these latest incidents. But his partner's complete integration into their world here in Glasgow was of the utmost importance and it might even be to their advantage that Brogan had disappeared, leaving his sister unprotected.

The Pakistani had deliberately chosen this suite of rooms in a West End hotel in which to meet Brogan's contact. Someone calling himself Mr Smith (he'd laughed derisively at that) had insisted that he wanted to find Brogan. A mate, he'd said, from the old days. Knowing Brogan's past as well as he did, Dhesi guessed that this was another ex-soldier. And from what he had read in the newspapers, he wondered if the man might be useful to them right now. If he turned out to be just another druggie, they'd get shot of him faster than he could say chapatti. But that voice on the line had sounded intelligent and, besides, he could only have found out his number from Brogan himself. Was this a set up, perhaps? Was Brogan using this old chum for purposes of his own? Nobody in Glasgow had any idea why the dealer had disappeared, though two dead bodies in his flat might give even the least cynical person some sort of clue.

The sound of a door opening behind him made him turn away from the window. His friend, the Hundi, was ushering in a man whom he judged to be about forty-five, short mid-brown hair, thinning on top and of medium height and build. Dhesi took all this in as he strode towards him. An ordinary looking man, he thought to himself, except for the face and its pale grey eyes. These were eyes that had seen terrible things, Dhesi told himself; and that face, with its sharp cheekbones and firm jaw, might have been carved out of granite. Glasgow folk had a name for someone

169

like this: *a wee hard man*. His visitor stood ramrod straight, gaze unwavering as he looked Dhesi in the eye.

This is someone you don't want to mess with, he suddenly thought, hearing Brogan's voice in his mind.

'Mr Smith,' Dhesi smiled, stepping forward and extending his hand in welcome, 'So good of you to come.'

'Dead? What makes you think that?' Joyce Rogers leaned forward in her chair, one hand clasping her chin as she considered the DCI's idea.

Lorimer made a restless movement before he answered, immediately revealing to the deputy chief constable that he was less than comfortable with this suggestion himself.

'She's nowhere to be found, ma'am. No trace of her leaving the country, no records of employment, nothing in the university registry or in any other UK registry that we can find.'

'I see,' Rogers nodded briefly. 'And you think we might want to investigate her as a missing person?'

Lorimer sighed. Thousands of people went missing each year, many of them at their own behest. But there would always be some who had been killed by a person or persons unknown and whose bodies would rot in their unmarked graves for generations. The police knew that from experience. And from the results of their cold case units around the country.

'We have no idea when she was last seen, nor do we have a recent photograph of her. No marriage photographs at Scott's house, nothing for matriculation at the college . . .'

'Oh? And why is that? Isn't it mandatory for all the students to have photo ID?'

'Yes, ma'am, but the college doesn't keep them for more than a year after the student leaves.'

'She could be shacking up with someone, of course,' Rogers mused. 'Another drug dealer like brother Billy.'

'That's true,' Lorimer conceded. 'And if she is alive we might try to ask her to come forward, to speak to us in confidence.'

'Why do I have the feeling that you're about to suggest putting out a televised appeal on *Crimewatch*, Lorimer?'

Lorimer spread his hands open and smiled, 'Because you know me so well, ma'am?'

'And you haven't been able to ask Superintendent Mitchison, I take it?'

The DCI's smile slipped a little. 'Not available at divisional HQ at present, ma'am,' he replied stiffly.

It was common knowledge that the superintendent and DCI Lorimer did not rub along easily together, Rogers reminded herself. If she had had her way, it would have been Lorimer running his division, not Mark Mitchison, but her vote at the time had been only one of many, something that grated to this day. Promotion for this man was long overdue, Joyce Rogers thought, watching Lorimer as he tried not to fidget, hands clasped but fingers rubbing each other as though unable to settle quietly. There was an opening in the Serious Crime Squad and she had thrown this man's hat into the ring, pleased to see that her other senior colleagues approved of the idea.

'I'm happy to authorise an appeal so long as a photograph of the woman can be found,' Rogers said at last. 'You will have been sent the last passport photograph from the passport record office, I take it?'

'Yes, ma'am. It was taken over nine years ago so she may well have changed in that time.' Lorimer bit his lip, considering his next request. 'Perhaps we might consider local radio stations first?'

'Ah, you're thinking of Radio City? They put out regular calls for missing persons, don't they?'

'Yes, ma'am, they do,' Lorimer replied. It had been DS Cameron who had suggested this at their last meeting. The Lewisman was involved in church work in the city and knew the presenter of one of City's evening programmes. The sound of a telephone ringing on the deputy chief constable's desk was the cue for Lorimer to take his leave.

'Keep in touch,' she told him as he stood up.

The DCI had just emerged into the daylight outside Pitt Street when his own mobile rang.

'Lorimer,' he said.

'Sir, it's DS Cameron. There's something we think you should see. Are you coming back right now?'

Fathy and Cameron were waiting for Lorimer in the incident room, an expression of excitement on both of their faces.

'Sir, it's the scene of crime file from Kenneth Scott's house. They've sent over prints of photographs that were taken from a camera that was logged at the scene.'

Lorimer nodded, taking the large A4 manila envelope from his detective sergeant. It was usual for items like cameras and computers to be taken from a crime scene for forensic examination.

'Anything interesting?'

'Oh, yes, sir,' Cameron replied, sharing a quick glance with Fathy. 'Wait till you see . . .' he tailed off as Lorimer strode towards the window and sat beside a low table.

Opening the envelope the DCI saw that there were four packets of prints within clear plastic packets, labels denoting the dates on which the various photographs had been taken.

He looked up at the two officers. 'There must be over one

hundred pictures here,' he said then looked back at the dates on the labels. 'Taken from more than six months previously to the week before Scott was killed,' he murmured.

'Right, let's begin with you lot,' Lorimer said, lifting the pack of photos that had been taken most recently and laying the others on a low table. 'Maybe we'll find out where Scott went for his holiday.'

The DCI's eyebrows rose in astonishment as he drew out the first photograph. It was of a Glasgow street with a young woman walking along, her red hair blowing in the wind.

'Good Lord, it's her,' he whispered, recognising the same woman whose framed photograph he had found in Brogan's flat. 'Did you realise?' he asked, looking up at Fathy and Cameron.

The two men shook their heads, coming around to have another look at the pictures for themselves.

'This is the woman whose photograph was found in Billy Brogan's place.' He looked back, studying the picture for confirmation. 'Thought it might be one of Brogan's fancy women,' he muttered.

Then, as he picked up the next photo and the next, he saw that the subject was the same. 'It's her,' he said again, flicking through the entire pack. 'You've seen what's been happening, eh?' he said, looking at his two officers. 'Whoever the photographer was he's shot the same woman from different angles and in various locations around the city.'

'We assumed it must be Kenneth Scott who took them, sir,' Cameron said.

'Mm,' Lorimer's reply was non-committal as he turned his attention back to the remaining photographs. The other three packs showed an identical subject – the red-haired woman.

'Look,' Lorimer pointed at the array of photographs laid out

173

upon the table. 'She's not looking up at the camera, or even smiling towards the lens for the benefit of the photographer, is she?'

Suddenly Lorimer rose from his place by the window and motioned for his officers to follow him back across the corridor to his office.

Cameron and Fathy watched as Lorimer stepped towards his desk and lifted the file on top of a mass of other papers. In seconds he had found the passport image of Marianne Scott née Brogan. Nodding to himself, Lorimer gave a sigh. 'It *is* her,' he said, glancing across at the bundle of photographs.

'Who do you think it is, sir?' Cameron asked.

'It's Marianne Brogan. Marianne *Scott*,' he corrected himself. 'Look at this,' Lorimer handed over the small square of passport photograph. 'Same face, same hair colour. A lot younger but it's her all right.'

'It's weird that he took all these photos of his ex-wife,' Fathy began, indicating the pile strewn across the table beside the window. 'Well, more sinister than weird really, isn't it, sir?' he said, as they looked at the images of the woman.

'Very strange, Fathy,' Lorimer agreed. 'It would be interesting to know just why this man took so many pictures of her. Suggests an unhealthy obsession, doesn't it? And we have to see if this has any relevance to his death.'

Before the day was out Lorimer had obtained the necessary authorisation to have Marianne Scott's image spread across the media. The press office had agreed to release her picture to the press as soon as the *Crimewatch* programme went out.

This was not the first time that Lorimer had appeared on national television. One of his earlier cases had included an appeal for information and the results had been crucial in following up their initial leads.

And it had been down to Doctor Solomon Brightman that good use had been made of that programme, hadn't it? Lorimer thought to himself, remembering. A flicker of irritation crossed his mouth. Solly's expertise was something he had come to appreciate, admire even at times, and now it was to be consigned to oblivion because another psychologist had got things spectacularly wrong. Still, he reminded himself, this was a pretty straightforward case. Everything now pointed to Brogan being the killer, didn't it? He'd done a runner, leaving three men dead behind him, men who had been well known to the drug dealer. And he'd been ex-army, had handled firearms.

Lorimer nodded. Solly's skills in profiling a potential serial killer simply wouldn't be needed in this case.

CHAPTER 21

The hit man drained the last of the whisky, putting down the glass with a thoughtful look in his eyes. The name *Brogan* had opened a particularly interesting door for him. He had not mentioned anything about his reason for being in Glasgow, preferring instead to continue the fabrication about being an old army mate. Had that washed with the man calling himself Dhesi? He doubted it. There had been something in the man's expression as they had discussed their *mutual friend*, as the Pakistani had insisted on calling Brogan, that implied friendship was in fact the last thing involved. And how could he forget the man's words, directed at him in that soft, suggestive tone of voice?

A lot of money might be made for anyone who was willing to assist in disposing of troublesome elements from their part of the city.

A steely glint had entered these dark eyes as he'd dropped that bombshell into the conversation. Did he know? Or was he simply guessing that he'd blown these three men away?

The pub was busy at this time of the evening, a crowd of customers around the bar, calling to one another in loud voices that competed with the football match being shown on the television, a Manchester derby. He'd thought it safe enough to mingle with the populace here, knowing so many would be crammed into the place to see the widescreen TV. And so it had transpired. Nobody gave him a second glance as most eyes were fixed on the players. It was, he had to admit, a cracking match: there were players of international standing whose skill commanded that sort of attention. The hit man could not give it his full concentration, having an habitual tendency to glance around him, his gaze often straying towards the door, just in case.

Part of him wanted to get out of Glasgow and head back south but a sense of caution stopped him. He hadn't committed himself to anything more than an agreement to meet up again with the Pakistani. He'd been treated with respect, he thought, remembering the tray of coffee and cakes ordered in that upper room, the dignified way in which Dhesi had handed him his cup and saucer. And that other chap, who called himself the Hundi, he'd been graciousness itself. They needed something from him and he had guessed what that might be. Also, he wanted to know what it was he was being offered. Money, certainly, but perhaps the security of a bigger organisation within this city that might provide him with a better way out.

They wanted Brogan, that was clear. But there was more to it than this. A subtle hint that another job might be in the offing. *Elements*, Dhesi had said. The man sitting in a corner of the pub, nursing his glass, was oblivious to the sudden roar from the punters around him as Manchester City scored a goal. His grey eyes narrowed in thought.

Licking his lips, he savoured the taste of whisky in his mouth. There was money to be made, a lot of money. Well, perhaps he'd hang about and see what was on offer.

CHAPTER 22

Marianne imagined that she could feel his breath on the back of her neck, hot and moist as she ran. The street was in total darkness, the slippery cobbles under her feet threatening to trip her up. If she could just make it to the corner where the amber light from a street lamp spilled onto the pavement, then she'd be safe.

Her chest hurt and she could hear the footsteps behind her, pounding along in a purposeful rhythm.

She could tell without looking around that her pursuer meant her harm. If she didn't escape, she knew she would be killed.

With one almighty effort, Marianne lunged forward towards the light then felt herself falling, falling, falling through space.

'No!' She sat up, heart thumping.

It had been a dream, only a dream.

Turning, she looked at the illuminated digits on the clock by her bedside. Almost three, the dead hour.

Marianne forced herself to take a few deep breaths. The chill night air crept across her skin making her shiver. With one movement she stripped off her nightdress, rolling the sweat-sodden garment into a ball and hurling it away from her.

What did it mean? Her dreams had always been imbued with some meaning before, hadn't they? Some people were visionaries, their dreams prophetic of things to come. Doctor Brightman had told her as much in his lectures, hadn't he? She frowned, unable to recall everything that the psychologist had said. Maybe she had read that somewhere instead? That other dream was past now, the terror gone for good. But this? What was *this* dream trying to tell her?

Marianne threw back the damp covers and scrabbled in the darkness for her clothes. She had to get out of here, she thought, the rising panic making her breathless.

That figure in the street last night, had he been following her? Just like Ken used to. She shivered suddenly, the memory of his shadowy footsteps, his obscene whispers as he walked behind her vivid in her mind.

And these wrong numbers on the telephone. Wasn't that proof that something bad was happening? They were coming for her, that was the significance of this latest dream, surely?

It was not until she had drawn the bedroom curtains against the night that she dared switch on the lamp beside her bed. No one must know that she had gone until she was well away. Nor must anyone know where she was going. She gave a rueful smile. Even *she* didn't know where that would be, yet. Silently the woman dressed, aware of every creak as her feet hit the wooden floor. Everything seemed unnaturally loud at this early hour, as if the room was holding its breath, listening.

She reached under the bed and drew out a well-worn suitcase then stood up to open the single wardrobe that contained most of her clothes.

The first coathanger clanged against the metal rail, making her jump. It was imperative that she made as little noise as possible.

The other tenants in this service flat might be light sleepers. She didn't know if that was the case but every nerve in her body cautioned her to take the utmost care. Slowly she drew her clothes off the hangers, folding them into the case with an expertise born of much practice. Soon the wardrobe was empty and she turned her attention to the chest of drawers. Ken had trained her well, demanding that she be fastidious in her habits so all of her other garments were already folded neatly and it was a matter of seconds to place them in the suitcase.

Marianne looked frantically around the room. What else must she take? Books, of course, and her laptop. And toilet stuff. She tiptoed into the adjacent bathroom, picking items off shelves and cramming them into a plastic carrier bag. They would go into the rucksack along with the books.

In less than an hour she was ready. Her hand was still trembling as she tapped out a number on her mobile phone.

'Taxi, please,' she said, her mind already focussing on her destination.

She gave the driver the name of a hotel. It was in a busy part of the city, close to a railway station with an ever present line of taxis, convenient for the next step in her escape. It would do for a few nights until she could find another place to stay, somewhere near the university, she hoped, though by this time in the summer lots of student accommodation would already be taken.

Once or twice the driver tried to engage her in conversation but she remained silent, head turned towards the window, watching as the city drew closer. Blue lights in the trees shimmered, caught like stars in a web of foliage as they drove through the night. Her head turned from one side to the other as they entered an underpass, its shape outlined in dazzling purple. Glasgow at night was a myriad of colours, the city fathers having brought brightness into the inky dark. Marianne smiled, thinking of the different bridges that spanned the river. At this time of night a traveller might see lines of red, blue and violet reflected across the water's surface.

The journey from the West End into the heart of the city took only minutes. But in that short time Marianne had regained some of the calm that had deserted her. The woman who alighted from the cab straightened her back, head held high as she took a deep breath of night air.

'Okay, miss?' the driver asked and she turned, seeing him take her bags and lead the way into the foyer of the hotel. She gave him a handful of silver, noticing the gap toothed grin as he made a mental count of her generous tip.

'Have a good night, miss,' he said, nodding at her. Marianne pretended not to see the expression of curiosity that flicked across the taxi driver's face. *What was a woman doing out at this time of night and checking into a hotel?* Instead, she walked towards the reception desk to another man whose eyes were already full of questions.

Amit drummed his fingers on the steering wheel, his eyes fixed on a point ahead, wondering if he could be bothered to find another parking space. By the time he returned his own space might well be taken, legally or otherwise. It was a fairly short walk from his own place to the curving terrace that bordered the river Kelvin. As he considered his options, the sun emerged from behind a cloud into a stretch of blue. He unbuckled the seat belt, letting it fall back against the leather seat. He would walk there, he decided, getting out of the Mercedes and pointing the key towards it. The big car gave a blink and a click as though in acknowledgement as Amit strode along the pavement in the direction of Byres Road.

This was the very heartland of student life: streets full of

Victorian flats that criss-crossed all the way from Great Western Road, sweeping past many of the university buildings then bisecting Byres Road until they marched in an upward curve to meet Great Western Road once again. Amit's present home was two floors up in a tenement flat above a delicatessen. The Mercedes he kept parked around the corner in a space designated for residents only.

Despite the fact that the new term was still a month away, the place was teeming with young people. Amit watched them as he walked along; girls with long hair in earnest conversation with a group of young men or giggling in a huddle with their pals. With a pang Amit realised that he had never known such careless freedom. His own youth had been hedged about with rules, both from his family and also by the state, university life a matter of serious studying and only the occasional social engagement.

He left a group of youngsters laughing in his wake, wondering if they realised just how privileged they were. Probably not, he told himself. But there was no bitterness in the thought, it was merely one of the many observations Amit allowed himself as he continued along the road.

Marianne would be expecting to resume her studies soon, he told himself. A frown crossed his dark brow. Was there really any way he could make that happen? Or was her time at university coming to an abrupt end? Biting his lip, Amit walked more hurriedly until he reached the end of the road. A large church building dominated the corner, sprawling between the junction of the two main roads. Amit looked up as he waited to cross towards the botanic gardens. It was no longer a place of worship and was now known as Oran Mor. He had been inside once, climbing the staircase that was decorated in colourful murals that had somehow reminded him of many of the places in Lahore. A restaurant and a pub took up some of the building but it was possibly best known for its basement theatre. A group of young men and women lounged outside on the steps clutching bottles of beer. Amit glanced at them. Seeing the confidence on their faces reminded him of what he was about to take away from Marianne and he experienced a moment of sadness that it had to end like this.

The lights changed and he crossed to the curving railings surrounding the park. It was not far now. Once across the bridge he turned left and followed the graceful line of terraced houses until he stood outside her house, looking up at the curtained window.

She was at home, then. He breathed a sigh of relief then walked up the five steps that led to the main entrance, pressing the bell next to the name that she used, a name that made him smile.

The smile changed to a puzzled frown when no answer came. After repeated attempts Amit decided to wait. Perhaps she was in the bathroom and could not immediately come to let him in. Five minutes passed before he tried again, then ten.

Amit paced back and forth on the top step, looking around to see if anyone was watching a dark-skinned man hovering on the threshold of this house. Only a young man walking his dog passed him by but he did not give Amit a second glance, absorbed in the music coming from his iPod.

Biting his lip, the man looked up again at the curtained window. His brow creased in worry. What if something was wrong? They had always agreed that he would not have a key to her flat. She required privacy and that was something that Amit understood. But now he wished that he had pressed Marianne on this point.

Taking a deep breath Amit pushed the first buzzer in the row, knowing that this ground floor flat was the home of Marianne's landlord, the man who owned the entire building. He waited then glanced to his left as a curtain was twitched to one side and a familiar face looked out at him.

'Mr Shafiq, my friend, come in, come in,' the Asian ushered Amit into a square, tiled hallway that had a case of wooden letterboxes set on to one wall.

'Marianne,' Amit began. 'She is not responding to the bell.' He shrugged his shoulders in a casual gesture but, seeing the worried look reflected on the landlord's face, he knew his attempt at nonchalance had failed.

'I have a spare key, my friend,' the landlord waddled off to his own apartments, his cotton slippers flip-flopping across the stone flags. Amit waited politely in the inner vestibule, regarding the stairs to one side as if Marianne might descend at any moment, making a fool of him and quietening his anxious heart.

'Aha!' The landlord beamed and brandished a set of master keys in his chubby fist. 'Now we'll see,' he said, stepping up the stairs with a nimbleness that was surprising for a man of his girth.

Amit followed, cursing Marianne for leaving these curtains drawn in the middle of the afternoon. But what if she were ill? He swallowed, forcing down worse images as he clattered up behind the landlord.

As the key rattled in the lock Amit could feel the sweat on the palms of his hands. Hastily he rubbed them against the sides of his trousers. What was wrong with him? Why such anxiety for this woman?

When the door was flung open, both men stood for a long moment saying nothing.

Then the landlord strode to the window and drew back the curtains. As light flooded into the room they could see why nobody had responded to these repeated rings of the bell. The bedclothes

185

had been left in an untidy heap and the wardrobe doors hung open, showing empty rails.

The landlord screwed up his eyes and Amit knew he was looking at him to see how he was reacting.

'So,' Amit cleared his throat, amazed by the emotion that made speech so difficult.

'So, she's gone,' the landlord said, throwing his hands up in a gesture of dismissal. 'Pity she hadn't washed the bed linen,' he grumbled, pulling the sheets off the bed and rolling them into a large ball. 'But at least the rent was paid up,' he added, giving Amit a sly tap on his arm. Then, cocking his head to one side, he seemed to see the sorrow on Amit's face.

'Don't worry, my friend,' he said, putting down the bundle and grasping Amit's arms in his hands. 'Better off without her. Plenty more fish in the sea for a handsome young fellow like Mr Shafiq.'

CHAPTER 23

'I know where Brogan is,' Jaffrey told the man sitting a little apart from him on the park bench. He waited, a small smile hovering on his lips as he anticipated the next move in this game. Information like this had its value and he would not be short-changed by this person, no matter what importance the Hundi felt that he had.

As the other man suggested a suitable figure Jaffrey's smile changed to a frown.

'You insult me,' he said, then waited once more as the Hundi remonstrated with him.

'Things are not so easy, Mr Jaffrey,' the Hundi pouted. 'We are in a recession still. Money is always hard to come by,' he lied.

Jaffrey knew that this would take time. Such matters always did. It was all part of the procedure; he would be given a figure, knock it back, suggest an impossibly inflated price himself until a bargain was agreed upon. There was no take-it-or-leave-it about their methods. He had something to sell and he knew the Hundi would be buying.

'The police might want to know this,' Jaffrey said slyly, looking to see what effect his words might have. But there was not a flicker of change in his companion's expression.

At last an acceptable sum was offered and he could tell the man what he wanted to know.

'Brogan was seen by my son,' he said proudly, nodding as he eyed the Hundi's bulky black jacket. The man had arrived not too long after Jaffrey had called him but he knew that a thick wad of notes would already be secreted about his person, ready to hand over once the information was given.

Jaffrey edged a little closer along the bench. 'He's in Mallorca. A town called Cala Millor,' he said, raising his hand to his mouth as though to prevent the words being overheard. He slipped his hand into his pocket and pulled out a piece of folded paper. 'My boy is a smart one,' he grinned. 'Followed Brogan back to his hotel. Even found which room he was in,' Jaffrey held the paper in the air triumphantly.

In one quick movement the Hundi stood up, snatched the paper and dropped an envelope onto the bench. Then, hardly pausing to read its contents, he stuffed the paper into his wallet, slid it into the inside pocket of his jacket and walked away from the other man without a word.

Jaffrey watched him go, making a rude gesture at his unseeing back. The Hundi commanded a lot of respect in the community and it would not do to openly cross this man. Still, he had what he wanted, he thought, opening the envelope and counting its contents greedily, giving absolutely no thought to what consequences this encounter might have for Billy Brogan.

'*How* long?' Brogan's mouth was an O of astonishment at the Spaniard sitting next to him on the jetty. He'd never been on a boat longer than the half hour that it took to travel from Wemyss bay to Rothesay.

'The wind may alter that,' the man shrugged, looking up at the skies as though to see what the weather might tell him, 'but, yes, I think it will take at least fifteen hours.'

Brogan followed the man's gaze. The skies had little whippets of cloud scudding across an expanse of searing blue. Sailors knew all about such things, he supposed. This man had the expertise he needed – he could set off from Mallorca at dusk and be on the African mainland by noon tomorrow. Marrakesh! The very name conjured up mountains of hashish, just waiting for someone like him to come and buy.

Brogan licked his lips, tasting a saltiness borne on the incoming breeze. They had discussed a price and he'd agreed to it, mentally calculating how much money he would have left.

'You come tonight?' the Spanish captain asked, his small dark eyes never wavering as he looked at the Scottish man beside him.

Brogan had spun him a tale about needing to leave Mallorca in a hurry, not being able to buy a plane ticket in time for an important meeting in Marrakesh, but he knew fine the Spaniard had seen through his lies. That nut-brown face criss-crossed with wrinkles had seen enough of life to know what was going on. The price he'd asked reflected that, too, Brogan guessed.

'I will take you to a village. Near to where you wish to go,' the Spaniard told him. 'I know a harbour,' he nodded and turned away, looking out to sea as if their destination was clearly imagined in his mind's eye. 'The harbour master is a friend. He will not ask questions.' The Spaniard turned back to look at Brogan, smiling a knowing smile. 'Or ask to see passports,' he added.

Brogan nodded, trying not to seem too relieved by this. He'd keep up the pretence as long as he was with this man, but he was acutely aware that the Spaniard had a good idea of his fugitive status.

'Okay. I'm cool with that,' he said, nodding his head. 'But how do I get to Marrakesh after that?'

The man shrugged. 'Plenty of buses. Not difficult. You'll see.'

'Right, I'll be here at seven o'clock, then,' Brogan said, proffering his hand for the man to shake.

'If I am not here, remember to ask for Carlos,' he told Brogan. 'One of my sons will be preparing the boat for departure. Adios,' he nodded.

As the drug dealer walked back along the esplanade he failed to see the expression on the Spaniard's face or see him chuckling to himself.

Carlos smiled as he shook his grizzled head, watching the Scotsman head back to his hotel. Such fools as this could make him a wealthy man, he thought. Marrakesh!

He laughed silently imagining Brogan's face when he found out his true destination.

CHAPTER 24

Annie Irvine sat perched on the edge of a desk, listening as Lorimer updated them all on the case.

'You've all had a chance to see the images and as you can see from those I have selected,' the DCI turned to indicate the blown-up photographs on the board behind him, 'there was definitely something going on between Scott and his ex-wife.'

Annie took a deep breath. The pictures spoke for themselves: it was a clear case of stalking as far as she was concerned.

'Why would he stalk his ex-wife?' someone asked, putting Annie's thoughts into words.

'What motivates any stalker?' Lorimer returned. 'The profile we're building up of Scott is of someone who led a very private sort of existence. According to the girlfriend she says she had never been to his house.'

'Someone had,' Cameron interjected. 'What about that bed?'

'We'll come to that in a bit,' Lorimer said, acknowledging the detective sergeant's point. 'But I think it may be very pertinent to our case to see what sort of man Scott really was. He had a casual relationship with Frances Donnelly, was friends with his work colleagues but he doesn't seem to have given anything away to any of them about himself, does he? And stalkers are notoriously private people.'

Annie shuddered, remembering the disgusting letters, the used condoms and filthy underpants deposited in her parents' garden and the shadow that had seemed to follow her every day on her way to university. Derek had been too clever for them to pin him down, to find enough evidence to link him to the stalking campaign that had lasted for more than three years. But it had given Annie one thing: her resolution to join the police force had sprung from a determination to see that other women were given more protection by the law.

'Did she know she was being stalked?' DC Fathy asked.

'Now,' replied Lorimer, 'that's a good question. None of the photographs indicate that she was aware of him. But the dates on the photographs show that he was following her on a regular basis, so, perhaps she knew what was going on.'

Too bloody right she did, thought Annie bitterly, edging herself off the desk and leaning against it, arms folded. But she kept her thoughts to herself, waiting for another officer to suggest as much.

'If she did know, why not contact the police?' Fathy asked.

'It's not an offence yet,' Annie couldn't stop herself blurting out. 'The proposed amendment to the Criminal Justice and Licensing Bill hasn't been put through our Scottish parliament. So the laws around stalking on this side of the border are still the same. Stalkers can only be charged with a breach of the peace. *If* you can make it stick!' she added passionately.

There was a sudden silence in the incident room and Annie listened, hearing her own breathing come thick and fast. It was the nearest she had ever come to admitting these horrible things from her own past and she reddened as she imagined what her colleagues might be thinking.

'Thank you for that DC Irvine,' she heard Lorimer say at last. 'And it is good to be reminded of the way such matters are currently dealt with. If stalking does become a statutory offence we might alleviate quite a lot of the suffering that women – and some men – currently endure.'

As Lorimer's blue gaze fell on her, Annie felt that he was looking right inside her. Could he guess at the years of persecution she had been subjected to? Or was that penetrating look simply a mark of respect for an officer who had done her homework?

'These photographs are only suggestive, not proof, of the fact that Scott may have been stalking his ex-wife,' Lorimer continued, addressing the room. 'But if Marianne Scott was indeed the target of a stalking campaign, then perhaps we have found a possible motive for Scott's murder.'

He looked around at them all in turn, his gaze coming to rest on Annie.

'One way or another, it is more important than ever to locate Marianne Scott. And her brother.'

There was a murmur of agreement and Lorimer nodded at the policewoman briefly before addressing the team once more.

'We're still waiting for fingerprint results from the SCRO to establish the identity of whoever came back to Scott's house.' He paused. 'Someone made up that bed. Was it the ex-wife? A neighbour who did it out of a sense of compassion? We need to find out who had a spare key to the house and I'm afraid that means going back over old ground; asking the neighbours, talking to Frances Donnelly and the human resources people at the call centre. Maybe even Paul Crichton,' he added as an afterthought. 'This could be nothing or it could give us more of a clue to Scott's background and why anyone might want to have him killed.'

'It's still being regarded as a hit, then?' DS Wilson asked.

'It looks that way,' Lorimer replied. 'It has all the hallmarks of a professional killing.'

He turned to where Omar Fathy was sitting. 'DC Fathy suggested a trawl of the students at Glasgow University,' he began. 'Any student in the first or second year whose Christian name is Marianne. Registry found nothing, but I suggest that for a time we bypass the red tape and begin to ask questions elsewhere and show people this photo of Marianne Scott.'

'Most of the students are still on holiday, sir,' Cameron pointed out.

'That's true, but the admin staff don't take long summer breaks, do they?' Lorimer asked. 'What I'm proposing is for a search to be made at departmental level. And while you're at it, ask around at the students' union, the clubs and societies, the list of accredited landlords who let out rooms during term time.'

The DCI's face hardened. 'Somehow this woman has managed to slip through our net. What should have been a relatively simple task to find her has become hugely complex.'

Annie listened as her boss handed out new actions to members of the team.

She wanted to shout above his voice, make herself heard, but was too afraid that everyone would see this thing that she had succeeded in hiding from them all.

Detective Constable Annie Irvine had been a stalker's victim.

And she knew fine why it was proving so difficult to locate Scott's ex-wife.

The policewoman turned her gaze to the photographs of the red-haired woman striding along various city streets.

You don't want anyone to find you, Annie whispered to herself. *But I understand. I promise you, I understand.*

'You okay?' Fathy asked as they trooped out of the incident room.

'Aye, fine,' Annie replied.

'Well you don't look fine,' Fathy persisted. 'How about a coffee before we tackle Frances Donnelly again?'

'No, you're okay. C'mon. Sooner we get this over with sooner we can give the boss something to go on, eh?'

'You think she had a key to his house?' Fathy asked as they descended the stairs to the back door.

Annie shrugged. 'Doubt if she'll let on until we can tell her that fingerprints have been found.'

'Well, maybe it *was* her,' Fathy went on. 'And another thing. We don't know for sure that it was Scott behind that camera. Maybe it was his girlfriend?'

Annie looked at him in disbelief then shook her head. 'No chance,' she said at last. 'That was Scott all right. Anyhow, why d'you want to make it more complicated than it already is?'

Fathy opened the door and stepped aside, saying nothing.

'Right, Sir Galahad,' Annie grinned suddenly, her good mood restored. 'Let's get going.'

Lorimer put down the phone. It was all set, then. By the end of this week he would be appearing on national television, appealing for information on the case, asking for Marianne Scott to come forward. If they hadn't found her by then, he reminded himself.

He heaved a sigh. Was she a frightened woman? And if so, who did she fear? Not her husband: he was dead. Her brother, then? But the photograph in Brogan's flat scotched that idea. The two of them had been close. Well, was she avoiding detection because of something else? Her whereabouts had been unknown for much longer than the short time since her ex-husband's death, he reasoned. Had she only gone into hiding since that event, then the finger of suspicion might well have fallen on her.

Had she been stalked by her ex-husband? Almost certainly.

195

Lorimer frowned as he remembered DC Irvine's impassioned little speech. She was well up on the law concerning stalkers. A coincidence? Or had she been involved in something personal? Lorimer tried to recall a case that might have sparked off such outrage in the time that Irvine had been in the force – and under his command – but nothing came to him. Well, if she had a friend who had been stalked, she might tell them about it. It was her business, he reminded himself.

The telephone ringing cut off his thoughts, as it so often did, and he picked it up, giving his head a shake as though to clear his mind.

'Lorimer.'

'Call for you, sir. From a call box. Putting you through, now,' the operator said.

'Detective Chief Inspector Lorimer? I have some lovely news for you, sir.' The voice on the line was definitely that of an Asian, Lorimer realised. Second generation, perhaps, but still with echoes of another tongue. Hindi? Urdu?

'To whom am I speaking?' he asked, but the voice on the other end simply chuckled.

'*You* know who this is. Just listen, Chief Inspector. You want to find Billy Brogan?'

Lorimer picked up a pencil ready to jot down the information as the man continued.

'Here is where he has been seen,' the Asian said. 'Someone from Glasgow spotted him.'

Lorimer listened carefully, his eyebrows rising in surprise as the details were given.

Lovely news, his informant had said. Well, maybe it would be if he could verify that it was true, his more cautious self reminded him.

'Jaffrey? Is that you? How did you get this information?'

Lorimer asked. But the click at the other end told him the question was destined to go unanswered.

'Hello?' he said. 'Hello . . .?' but even as he spoke, Lorimer knew that the call had been terminated and he was left with a feeling of frustration that whoever had been in touch knew an awful lot more than he was letting on.

'Call box from the south side of the city, sir. Pollokshields. We're pinpointing the location as I speak,' the operator informed him.

'Okay. And we'll need to run a check to see if there are any CCTV cameras nearby. But I have a feeling this chap's been taking no chances,' Lorimer sighed. What was Jaffrey hiding? And how on earth did he know about Brogan?

They might well find out which particular call box had been used. But by the time they did their caller would have slipped away into the area that had been largely taken over by the Asian community, mingling with his own folk. Glasgow had become home to many different races, some fleeing oppression in their homelands, many integrating well alongside the Glasgow people. And certain areas had become enclaves for them. But this man might well be on the shady side of society, Lorimer told himself. How would he have been able to supply this kind of information? Why else would he have failed to give his name? Surely that had been Sahid Jaffrey, one of his occasional informants? Who else could it be?

He studied his computer screen; in a couple of minutes he would have the number of the hotel he had just been given, then he could verify this information. And if it was correct, his next call could be to the Spanish police.

'Billy Brogan's been seen in Spain,' Lorimer was standing opposite Superintendent Mitchison who was leaning back in his chair, regarding the DCI with only a faint interest.

'We have his hotel room number and an officer from the local police who is going to see if they can apprehend him on our behalf.'

'And the caller was anonymous,' Mitchison drawled.

'Yes, sir, Asian. Educated voice. Spoke clearly. Asked to be put through to me so he obviously knew who was in charge of the case.' Lorimer crossed his fingers behind his back. There was no way he was going to reveal his sources to Mitchison.

'Reads *the Gazette*, then. Or watches the evening news on television,' Mitchison said in a dismissive tone that set Lorimer's teeth on edge.

'Well, Brogan can't get very far on an island, I suppose,' the superintendent continued. 'And if he's your prime suspect, then perhaps you'll have this case wrapped up before the week's out.' He smiled, baring a set of perfectly capped teeth. 'Once Brogan is extradited from Spain there will be no need for your little performance on *Crimewatch*, will there?'

Lorimer refrained from answering. The man's dislike of him was palpable and the less fuel he gave him for stoking the flames of his enmity, the better.

As he left the superintendent's room, Lorimer managed to smile. Brogan was almost in their clutches! Perhaps by this time tomorrow he would be facing the drug dealer in one of the interview rooms, asking questions about the deaths of three men.

His eyes narrowed as he recalled that Asian voice. Someone in the city knew all about Brogan and was grassing him up. And if it was Jaffrey, why was he doing this? Somehow that question took the edge off his present excitement. There was more to this than he could read right now. But would Brogan be able to supply the full story?

CHAPTER 25

The thin linen shirt was sticking to his skin as Brogan made his way back along the esplanade towards Cala Bona. He'd left some of his stuff back in the hotel room; dirty clothes and a few toiletries, just so it looked as if he was going to return. He shouldered the new backpack that contained his possessions. All he needed was in here. He gave a grin remembering the mantra that his pals recited before they left for holiday: *money, tickets, passport.* Well he still had enough money to keep him going, some of it already changed into American dollars, the favoured currency in North Africa, he'd been told. His passport was tucked inside his trouser pocket and as for his ticket? Well he'd paid his new mate, Carlos, for that trip, hadn't he?

The sun was a red ball in the sky, sinking towards the edge of the sea when the receptionist looked up to see two officers from the local police.

'Can I help you?' the girl smiled at them. But as they motioned her to a back room out of the hearing of several guests who were gazing at them with unashamed curiosity, the receptionist's face became grave.

'A Señor Brogan. Englishman,' one of the officers began.

'He is *un Escocés*,' the girl corrected him primly. 'Not *Inglés*.'

'Where is he?' the other officer demanded, clearly quite uninterested in the distinction.

'He left his key in reception,' the girl nodded to the desk. 'Went out hours ago. Probably gone for dinner by this time.' She glanced at the clock. 'Almost nine. He'll likely be in one of the tavernas, I would say. What d'you want with him, anyway?'

'Where's his room?' the first policeman asked. 'We need to look at it.'

'Has he done something wrong?' the girl's hand rose to her mouth in alarm.

'Key to his room, please, *señorita*,' the other officer said, holding out his hand in a manner that brooked no argument.

The glass doors to the balcony were open, thin muslin curtains blowing upwards, letting in a draught of the night air when the two Spanish officers entered Brogan's room.

'Doesn't look as if he's gone for good,' one of them remarked.

'No,' the other agreed. 'And see here,' he opened the wardrobe to show the clothes still hanging upon their rails. 'Look in the bathroom. See if he's taken his razor and stuff.'

Moments later the other man returned. 'All there. He's not done a runner by the looks of things.'

'So he doesn't know anyone is looking for him,' the first officer said, nodding. 'And he will not be expecting us to visit him when he returns.'

'What are you suggesting?'

'Park the car round the back. We don't want to warn him off. Remember what our instructions were.'

'To keep a low profile,' the other officer said as though he were repeating someone else's words. 'But what are we actually supposed to do?'

'We'll wait here for him to come back, won't we? I could do with a couple of San Miguels,' he grinned at his companion. 'How about phoning down for a little room service while we cool our heels up here?'

The boat had slipped quietly out of the harbour, unnoticed by the mass of tourists seeking their evening's pleasure onshore. It was a good time to leave the island, thought Brogan, as he watched the twinkling lights recede. Taking a deep breath full of salty air, he stood on deck, watching as the old sailor guided his boat out into the choppy waters. This was it, then. A new adventure! Billy Brogan laughed softly to himself: he'd done it! They could look high and low for him all over the damned island but they'd be chasing shadows. He was off and running with this tide, evading anyone who might try to takes him back to Scotland to face a mess that was not of his own making.

Brogan frowned. Was he in any way responsible for what had happened to Fraz and Gubby? He sniffed. Och, they'd run close to the edge, that pair. Not his fault if they'd come to a bad end. And Marianne? Och, she'd be fine. Amit would be looking out for her, he reasoned. But the creases on his brow persisted and he chewed a guilty lip, wondering just what was going on back in the place he had once called home.

A full moon made a track across the waves as though leading them onwards into the dark seas. Brogan shivered, rubbing his arms. Carlos had advised him to wear something warm but he had ignored the man, choosing instead to wear this thin linen shirt that now flapped in the gathering wind.

As the lights from the shore grew smaller and smaller, the island appeared as a large brooding mass, frowning across at the boat bobbing uncertainly on the rising waves. Brogan staggered from the deck to the safety of the large inside cabin, sliding open the door, feeling unbalanced in the heaving swell that made the timbers beneath his feet rise and fall.

His stomach gave a queasy flip and he caught hold of a wooden rail to steady himself. Fifteen hours, the Spaniard had told him.

He let out a yelp as the boat rose and fell over a particularly high wave. Oh. That wasn't funny. A feeling of nausea came over the man as he clutched the rail harder then shuffled to the nearest seat. Fifteen hours of this? Brogan groaned aloud. Just what had he let himself in for?

CHAPTER 26

'It's entirely your decision,' the man told her, sitting back in his swivel chair, watching her face.

Maggie Lorimer nodded, too unhappy to give a verbal reply. It was her body, her cramps brought on by the endometriosis that was filling her womb with knots of fibrous tissue. And that persistent pain, she reminded herself. Yesterday she had been quite certain of the way forward. Abandoning a classroom full of kids halfway through a lesson to stumble along to the ladies' toilet was just not on. She'd have the damned operation, she'd told herself then, splashing water on her face, cursing the weakness that was dragging her down.

But now, in the cold light of day, faced with the surgeon who would open her up and remove that poor part of her, Maggie was not so sure.

Babies had been started there, nascent little creatures whose forms never developed to term. Such hopes each of them had brought! And such grief when they had aborted from her unwilling body. There was no hope left, one gynaecologist had insisted. Better to face up to the facts. But Maggie Lorimer had clung to shreds of longing, waiting for a time that might come. Now that time seemed to have run out and she was making herself ill by delaying what was surely inevitable.

Mr Austen's voice had sounded quite calm but a small frown furrowing the consultant's brow showed Maggie that he was genuinely concerned.

'If it was your wife . . .?' she asked, hearing the breathy catch in her words.

He smiled then, a sympathetic smile. 'I'd tell her to go ahead and have the surgery,' he said, his eyes full of pity for her dilemma. 'But then, we already have two boys,' he shrugged.

Maggie nodded again, glad of the man's honesty. He hadn't just told her what to do: he had understood the turmoil in her heart and mind. Probably used to women like me, she reminded herself.

'Okay,' she sighed. 'When can you do it?'

Omar lifted the bundle of mail from the dark space by the door. Most of it consisted of flyers – for a local grocery store, someone offering car insurance and a tree surgeon. He smiled at that last one. There were no trees in this block of flats: he supposed that the sorting office was given loads of that sort of stuff to thrust through letterboxes in a wide area, irrespective of how appropriate it was to the householder. The rest of the mail consisted of a bill from his electricity provider and one handwritten envelope that looked as if it might be an invitation to someone's birthday party.

Omar opened this one first, hopeful of adding a date to his somewhat empty calendar.

He drew out a plain piece of card, neatly folded down the middle, then turned it over, expecting some sort of picture on the front. There was nothing and its stark whiteness made him grit his teeth, anticipating the contents.

GET OUT BLACK BASTARD

The words, scrawled in dark felt pen, jumped at him, making Omar flinch. So. They had found his address already. That was bad.

Heaving a sigh, Omar Fathy nodded to himself as though he had come to a decision. He had endured so much up in Grampian and had thought that this move would mean a fresh start. But someone must have followed him here. Picking up the envelope, Omar examined the stamp to see if the franking mark might give him any information: it did. The card had been posted locally, here in Glasgow.

It was time to do something about this. His dark face hardened as he dropped the junk mail into a recycling box. Taking the card carefully between his fingers, he walked through to his kitchen, looking for a clean plastic bag.

DCI Lorimer turned slowly into his street, willing the old car to roll into the driveway. He came to a stop and turned off the engine, sensing the sigh of relief from the Lexus as it began to cool down. Pressing a button, Lorimer saw that he'd clocked up the best part of two hundred thousand miles now, surely more than could be expected from even the trustiest workhorse. The old girl was losing oil at an astonishing rate these days and he knew in his heart that it was time for a change of car. The detective was surprised at his attachment to what was, after all, a heap of metal. A fondness for this machine that had carried him to so many destinations was surely bordering on a sentimentality that was unworthy of his calling? But he sat still, fingering the worn leather on the driver's seat, feeling as much at home here as he did in his own front room. He'd miss driving this car but there was no denying it was time to trade it in for something newer. His fortieth birthday was a few months away now, Lorimer reminded himself. Perhaps he could justify the purchase of another Lexus?

'Hi,' he called, closing the front door behind him.

As soon as he saw her tense white face Lorimer knew something was wrong.

'Hey. What's happened?' He was at her side in two long strides, arms around her shoulders as Maggie began to weep silently.

A pot of tea and several man-sized Kleenex tissues were required before Maggie could explain her health problem.

'You have to do what you think is right for *you*, love,' Lorimer told her gently, stroking her hair back from the tear-stained cheeks. 'You know we'd given up any notion of a family,' he added quietly.

Maggie nodded and blew her nose again. 'Uh-huh,' she gulped. 'I know. It's just . . .' Her voice disappeared in another swell of emotion and Lorimer held his wife close to his chest, patting her back, noting the irony as he did: it was a gesture a father might make to comfort a child.

'With Rosie . . . and everything . . . it's hard,' she sniffled.

'It'll always be hard, love. Other people's bairns will be like the gifts we've been denied. But we've got a lot to be thankful for, haven't we?' Lorimer turned her face to his, searching her eyes for answer.

A tremulous smile and a nod gave him what he'd wanted. They had one another. Okay, there had been periods of difficulty caused mainly by his work, but they'd weathered such storms and were still together, stronger for those times, Lorimer believed.

'What did the consultant say?' he asked eventually and Maggie told him, haltingly at first then with growing confidence as she began to see that her decision was the right one.

'No date yet, then?'

'Possibly just before the October break,' Maggie said. 'Mr Austen goes on holiday then and wants me done before that.' She giggled a little at her choice of words. 'Says I'll be off school for about three months, depending on what he finds inside.'

'So, a break till the end of the year? Manson won't like losing his favourite member of staff, will he?' Lorimer replied, referring to Maggie's head teacher.

'Plenty of teachers on the supply list,' she told him. 'He'll have no bother replacing me for a while. And I can visit Rosie and her new baby when it arrives,' she said, looking past her husband at a point in the distance.

Lorimer followed her glance but there was no indication what, if anything, his wife was seeing.

The wee small hours of the morning found Lorimer awake, his arm around a sleeping Maggie, her drowsy body curled into his side. Thoughts of her impending surgery had been supplanted by other notions. Sometimes in the cold hours before dawn his mind was suddenly alert, full of ideas. What had happened in the days before Ken Scott had been gunned down? That he had been stalking his ex-wife seemed almost definite, Lorimer reasoned, given the host of photos taken in the streets of Glasgow. A chilling thought had taken hold of the detective and he drew back slightly from his sleeping wife as though the very idea might contaminate her.

Stalkers had been known to become so obsessed by their victims that they eventually killed them. Nobody but the crazed killer knew just what took place on such occasions but psychologists and police officers had attempted to piece together the likely steps that had led to the stalker finally descending into that ultimate violence. Memories of high profile cases flooded back to him now; women who had been the object of someone's fantasy and desire and whose rebuffs had led to their slaughter.

Is that what had happened to Marianne Scott? Had she been killed by her ex-husband, a seemingly mild-mannered man who had given little indication of his obsession to those who claimed to know him best?

Marianne Scott was certainly missing and in Lorimer's experience that could mean one of two things. Either she was playing a very clever game at deliberately disappearing or she was dead, her body concealed somewhere. Now, as the grey light crept into his bedroom, Lorimer felt certain that the woman had been murdered. It made sense of Scott's killing: could it have been an act of revenge for taking his ex-wife's life? Brogan might well have undertaken a hit against his former brother-in-law if he had any reason to believe the man had killed his sister. He'd had her picture in his flat, a sign of his fondness for her, surely? The man wasn't just a known drug dealer. He was ex-army, undoubtedly with contacts in the underworld where guns were readily available for the right money.

As he rolled onto his other side, Lorimer became more and more convinced that his theory would stand up in the light of day. Why had Brogan done a runner? He grinned to himself. Maybe they'd find out today. The Spanish police might even have the man in their custody by now, he thought. And once they had Brogan extradited back home he might supply answers to all of these questions.

As the night clouds rolled away and a thin line of scarlet bled onto the horizon, Billy Brogan groaned with relief. Only half a day more and they would be free of this tumbling sea and the endless heave and swell that had turned his stomach inside out. He shivered, rubbing his arms in a vain attempt at making them warm again. He'd been awake most of the night, only dozing fitfully on the bench by the window. Carlos had thrown a blanket over him some time during the night and he had heard voices, speaking in Spanish, as he'd drifted in and out of sleep. Now, fully awake, Brogan knew that there were two men on board, not just the old man. It made sense, he supposed. Carlos had to rest some time during this voyage and he'd taken one of his crew with him. The Spaniard had never said they were sailing alone, had he? The other guy must have been down below when Billy had set foot on board the boat, doing whatever sailors did. But it had been done in a furtive sort of way that made Brogan uneasy. Why had Carlos not simply introduced the other man when he'd stepped down the gangway? Brogan tried not to let his ideas go any further. He was at the mercy of these Spanish seamen and sitting tight and not asking any questions until they had completed the journey was probably for the best.

Another massive wave made the boat rise high in the air and descend with a crash, sea spray flying past the window where Brogan was clutching the edge of his seat. All he could think about was his present condition; the bucket on the floor beside him skittering away from his hand as he reached out to grab it. Whatever was going on up on deck or in the wheelhouse wasn't his affair. So long as the sun continued to rise and the boat was heading for land, that was all he cared about right now.

CHAPTER 27

'Fax from the Spanish police, sir,' the duty officer handed a sheet of paper to Lorimer as he walked along the corridor to his office. 'No sign of Brogan. He didn't return to his hotel room last night. And he wasn't on any of the flights leaving Palma yesterday.'

Lorimer nodded and took the fax into his room. Brogan would still be somewhere in Mallorca, then. And shouldn't be too hard to locate. The fax added that no hire car had been taken out in his name. And he'd have needed a valid driving licence for that, wouldn't he? Lorimer wasn't too worried. The local police would pick him up pretty soon, he reckoned. It was an island, after all, with few places for a Glasgow drug dealer to hide. Then a frown crossed Lorimer's face. They'd had that tip-off from this end. Did that mean Brogan had friends in Mallorca? But why check into a hotel if that were the case? No. The caller had mentioned that Brogan had been spotted by someone from back home. That had been unlucky for the drug dealer. And Lorimer hoped that was a sign that Brogan's luck was rapidly running out.

Meantime he had a pile of paperwork that would take most of the morning to sift through. He was quietly confident that by midday they'd have had news of Brogan's arrest.

But there was something else he wanted to do first. Opening up his laptop, he composed the message in his head. It wasn't anything official, nor something that could be seen as contravening the present command about using the services of a psychological profiler. It was just a friendly enquiry from his personal address, Lorimer reasoned, as he typed in the email for Doctor Solomon Brightman.

'Stalking,' Solly said the word aloud as he read the heading on Lorimer's email message. A slight frown creased the man's brow. He'd been hurt by the police decision to withdraw from his services and now here was Lorimer asking him questions that would take up some of his time. In one way it was gratifying that his friend continued to have faith in him but in another way it was just plain annoying. Had he let any pettiness creep into his soul, Solly Brightman might have told himself that if his services were not required by Strathclyde Police then he'd simply ignore the email. But such ignoble thoughts were not part of the psychologist's make-up and, as he rose from his desk, he was already thinking of well known cases like that of TV presenter, Jill Dando. There had been good evidence at the start of that investigation for supposing that Dando had been gunned down by a stalker, though what had actually taken place might always remain a mystery.

'Stalking,' he said again, this time standing by his filing cabinet and leafing through his notes.

Ken Scott would be an interesting subject if he were proved to have been a stalker. Not only was he an ex-husband whose wife had rejected him publicly by the divorce but he must have harboured the delusion that she was still in love with him. For, Solly knew, that was the hallmark of a stalker. The person stalking was

212

convinced that his or her target was capable of returning the devotion that they felt. And with patience and perseverance the notion was that their victim would eventually fall into their arms, capitulating to their desires. For it was not about love, Solly reminded himself. It was all about power and powerlessness. The stalker, once a rejected lover (whether in reality or in his or her mind), regarded themselves as in a position of power while they followed their prey. Overpowering their victim became a necessary part of the game. They might tell themselves that they only wanted their loved one to return some affection, to give a smile or a kiss. But what they craved was their victim's ultimate submission. And when it became clear that wasn't going to happen willingly, they sometimes resorted to violence.

Frustration breeds violence was a phrase Solly remembered from his early days as a student of behavioural psychology. And he could cite many instances in the world of stalkers where that held true. Filthy messages sent through the post or by email, unwanted gifts (some of them with sinister overtones) and plain harassment were the outpourings of a rejected and frustrated stalker. Had there been any evidence of such things in Scott's case? The photographs were all that the police had to go on so far. It was a pity that Lorimer had drawn a blank in locating any of the ex-wife's friends or family. If he had a fuller picture of the couple's relationship then perhaps he might be able to make some useful contribution. But, failing that, he could give his friend some general pointers about the sorts of violent stalkers whose deeds had been recorded.

Annie Irvine watched her colleague as he lifted his lunch tray off the table and headed towards the canteen door. Omar had deliberately chosen to sit by himself for the last few days, she'd noticed, facing the window that looked out on to the street, avoiding eye contact with any of his fellow officers. There was something about that figure hunched over his sandwiches that troubled Annie. Something was wrong and it wasn't to do with the ongoing murder case, she was certain of that. Omar had been full of enthusiasm not that long ago, hadn't he? So why this sudden change in his manner? The policewoman had been sensitive enough to know when to leave the handsome young Egyptian alone. Besides, what chance would she have of furthering their friendship if she barged in on him when it was obvious that he wanted nobody's company?

A tall dark-haired woman planked herself down next to Annie. It was Maureen, the civilian officer who was in charge of processing and recording all the productions from scenes of crime. Annie would have moved away but her lunch was barely started and she was incapable of being rude even to Maureen, whose loud-mouthed comments were known to make others cringe.

'What's up with Omar Sharif?' she asked, nudging Annie's arm. The woman's shrewd glance showed that she had been following Annie's gaze as Omar walked out of the canteen.

Annie didn't reply, trying to focus on the salad and ham baguette that had suddenly become quite unappetising.

'Had a tiff, then?' Maureen gave a short laugh that sounded like a dog's bark.

Annie coloured up, watching as several heads turned their way, Maureen's strident tones carrying right across the canteen.

'Don't know what you mean,' Annie mumbled, stuffing the baguette into a napkin. She opened her handbag and drew out her mobile phone. There was no message on the screen but Maureen wasn't to know that, was she? Sometimes a wee deception had to be played out and this was one of those times. 'Have to go. See you,' she said, then rose from the table as fast as she could.

'Ach, he's no worth the heartache, Annie,' Maureen persisted. Then, catching hold of the policewoman's arm she dropped her voice to a whisper. 'An' I reckon he's the wrong colour for a nice girl like you, eh?'

Annie stood stock still for a moment, shocked at the woman's blatant racism. Had she been overheard, Maureen might well have been given notice to quit her job. She blinked then shook her head, showing the other woman that such a remark was not to be condoned.

As she turned to go, Annie kept hearing the words in her mind like a hiss of malevolence. Really she should report the woman, but there was something nasty about Maureen Kendall that gave her pause for thought. Somehow, Annie felt, there would be repercussions if she tried to put that little incident into a formal complaint. And right now she could do without the bother.

Omar was walking down the CID corridor when Annie finally caught up with him.

'Hey, what time do we have to be at the university?' she asked, still slightly breathless from her encounter in the canteen.

Omar turned round and when he saw Annie he stopped and gave her a smile. Was there really nothing worrying him behind that nice polite face? she wondered. Was she seeing things that weren't there? None of her business, anyway, Annie reminded herself.

'Remember we've to get our tails up to Gilmorehill and start quizzing the departmental secretaries,' she reminded him.

'Yes, of course,' Omar replied, the faintest of frowns producing a crease between his dark eyebrows. 'Would you like me to drive?'

The spire of the University of Glasgow could be seen for miles around, dominating the skyline as it stood proudly on the heights of Gilmore Hill. It was a strange piece of architecture, harsh spikes emanating from that narrow spire, reminiscent of a knight's mace. What the story was behind that particular feature, Annie didn't know. But it always held a sense of foreboding when she looked up from University Avenue at the dark points outlined against the sky.

'No problem getting parked today,' she remarked as Omar slipped the pool car into a space not far from the main gate. In term time it would be a different story, parking spaces close to the university buildings becoming as rare as hens' teeth.

'Wonder if she ever did apply for a course here,' Annie mused as they walked over the hill towards University Gardens.

'Lorimer thinks she's dead,' Omar replied shortly.

Annie stopped and looked at him. 'Well what on earth are we doing here? It's just a waste of our time, surely?'

Omar gave a faint grin. 'Your DCI isn't right all the time, is he? Besides, he has to cover all the possibilities.'

Annie kicked a stone that appeared on the pavement. It skittered onto the railings with a metallic ping. 'In my experience Lorimer's hunches usually turn out to be spot on,' she said gloomily.

'That's funny,' Omar said. 'I feel certain that she's alive.' He turned to face Annie. 'Don't ask me why. It's just this gut feeling I have. Maybe I'm totally wrong. But then again,' he grinned wickedly, 'maybe it's Lorimer who's got it wrong.'

'Well, let's see if anyone can remember Marianne Scott or Brogan or whatever damned name she was using, shall we?' Annie raised her eyebrows as they continued down towards the rows of departmental offices that were tucked away from the main road. She glanced at Omar's profile. He was smiling still, happier than she had seen him in days. Was that all that had been bothering him: worried that his own ideas about Marianne Scott were clashing with Lorimer's? He'd certainly spent loads of time trying to trace the missing woman. Maybe that had made her all the more real to him. And if it transpired that Marianne was actually found dead how would this young policeman react? Annie wanted to reach out and touch Omar's hand, warn him not to become too involved.

But then she thought of the tall brooding figure of their DCI. Lorimer felt things deeply, too. Didn't say much, but you always knew that he cared for the victims of crime. Would Omar Fathy become like that? She stole another glance at the Egyptian and nodded silently to herself. He'd go far, she realised. Not because he was ambitious but because he shared the same qualities as their boss.

Marianne was not dead but sometimes she felt as though her life was ebbing away from her. The nights she had spent in this hotel had not been free from the recurrent dreams she had so longed to escape. Certainly the constant noise of traffic had kept her awake for long spells until exhaustion had forced her into a troubled sleep. Waking to a morning that was bright behind the heavy hotel curtains made her realise that another day must be faced and decisions made.

The truth was that Marianne had no real idea what to do. The telephone calls she had tried to make to Billy were left unanswered, the first foreign ringtone telling her that his mobile, at any rate, was somewhere across the Channel. Why hadn't he called her? Was he somehow involved in these deaths? Marianne shook her head slowly as she sat on the edge of the great white bed. That ringtone had preceded the events in his flat. Billy had left Glasgow before all these things had happened, hadn't he? But why? They trusted one another, didn't they? Surely Billy would have let her know if something was wrong. Amit had broken the news of the two dead men to her solemnly, as though she was one of their family, one of the bereaved. Remembering his grave tones, Marianne realised what the Pakistani had been thinking: Billy Brogan, her brother, had killed two known drug dealers and had fled the scene.

Marianne knew better, but it galled her to realise how Billy would be being perceived by Amit, a man who had been helped by her brother in the not-so-distant past. Besides, she knew Billy Brogan better than anybody. Including Joan, that daft wee girl in the registry who fancied him so much. Marianne gave a sigh. Billy Brogan simply didn't have it in him to kill another human being in cold blood. Wasn't that why he'd quit the army, after all?

Lifting her mobile phone from the bedside cabinet, Marianne scrolled down until she came to one particular number. Should she try to see if Billy's army pal was still in town? Maybe they could meet up for a bite to eat? He'd sounded nice and uncomplicated. He was a friend of Billy's from the old days, she told herself. And if there was anything she needed right now it was the company of someone outside all of the tangled web that was threatening to close in on her.

The hit man smiled as he put down the phone. Sometimes luck simply came your way. He had suggested meeting the woman in the entrance of the NCP car park in Cambridge Street, the idea being that they take a trip out of town. She'd sounded keen. His smile widened into a grin. And no wonder. With both the police and the Asians looking for her, Marianne Brogan would do well to keep out of the city as much as possible. He whistled as he opened the wardrobe door, wondering what to wear for his next performance.

CHAPTER 28

September wasn't Rosie's favourite month of the year and she was glad her baby would be born later, once the nights had really drawn in and the darkness settled. Now she fretted as the summer drew to a close, the warmth making a mockery of the shorter days and fading leaves. Down in the park the dust was blowing in swirling clouds as though some unseen force was changing everything. Girls and boys still strolled slowly along the paths, their sleeveless T-shirts paying homage to the fact that it was still officially vacation time and the good spell of weather had lasted.

The bird man was there again, she noticed, standing stock still beside a line of bushes, outstretched hand resting on the railing. She had seen him often over the last few months, his little packet of seeds scattered onto his palm. Sometimes, if he stood quietly, a blue tit would come down from branch to branch, peck at the offering then fly off. From this upper window Rosie couldn't see if he had a bird on his hand or not, but she recognised him all the same: his shock of dark hair falling over a pale face, the same khaki jacket that he always wore, camouflage for the purpose of feeding the wee birds, she supposed. One day, she mused, she would push her pram along the path and stand to watch the bird man, his quiet patience usually rewarded by a tiny visitor to his hand.

Rosie was not aware that she had begun to smile. The expression on her face was one of calm serenity, all the lines that so furrowed her pale brow when she was bent over a cadaver in the mortuary had disappeared with this pregnancy. Instead of being in pain or discomfort, the pathologist was at that enviable stage in her third trimester when all seemed well with the world and she could revel in her swelling body. A first baby could arrive early or late, Em had warned her. Two weeks either way, her technician had said, wagging a finger at Rosie.

'If you do come early it'll be nice to get to know you,' Rosie whispered, circling the bump gently with her fingers. 'See who you look like,' she added fondly. If it were a boy, she would love him to have Solly's dark looks, but she'd prefer a wee girl to have her own fair hair. 'Maybe one of each,' she said dreamily. 'In time.'

Solly's mum fretted whenever she called from London, asking if Rosie was all right, reminding her to eat properly; she was eating for two, remember. The pathologist hadn't the heart to remind Ma Brightman that she was a qualified doctor and knew exactly what was going on inside her own body. Let her mother-in-law have her say. After all, Ma Brightman had given birth to her beloved Solly, hadn't she? And she couldn't fault the job she'd done in bringing him up.

The street buzzer sounded in the hallway, cutting short Rosie's thoughts. Waddling through to the hall, she picked up the handset and listened.

'It's me, Lorimer. Can I come up and see you?'

'Sure, come on up,' Rosie said, pressing the entry button. She was surprised to hear the policeman's voice. What was he doing over in this neck of the woods in the middle of the afternoon? Well, that was something she was about to find out, wasn't she?

Lorimer climbed the winding staircase, admiring the banister's graceful sweep and the delicate plasterwork coving picked out in creamy white against the russet walls. This had once been a gentleman's town house but was now divided into high-ceilinged flats. The builder had made a fine job of it, whoever he was, thought Lorimer as he reached the top floor. He'd kept all the original features within the hallway and landings including one Art Nouveau stained glass window that reflected lozenges of blue and green light onto the carpeted stairs. Solly had bought his top floor flat at just the right time, he mused; before house prices had rocketed in this part of the city. But would they stay here once a baby arrived?

The door swung open as he rang the bell as if Rosie had been waiting for him.

'How are you?' Lorimer stepped forward, kissing her on the cheek.

'Great,' she smiled. 'Never better. In fact if it goes on like this I might just decide to be the Old Woman who lived in a shoe.' She chuckled as they moved into the spacious lounge, a room that Lorimer loved with its huge bay windows overlooking Kelvingrove Park and the swirling abstract paintings that Solly had acquired from a local gallery.

'Thought you might be contemplating a move to suburbia,' Lorimer said.

'No, I don't think so,' Rosie said, settling herself on a couch with the help of a couple of squashy cushions at her back. 'We can leave the pram in the downstairs hall. Besides, I'm really looking forward to walks in the park.' She gave another smile that softened her features, gazing out towards the window where the afternoon sunlight was streaming in.

There was a new vulnerability to the pathologist that Lorimer had never seen before, a fragility that surprised him. With her halo of blonde hair shining in the light, she looked much younger than her thirty-five years. No one seeing her right now would imagine her in scrubs, scalpel in hand, exploring the mysteries of a corpse on her clinical metal table back in the mortuary. The tough, resilient woman he had come to visit dissolved in an instant and Lorimer knew at that moment he could not bring himself to discuss Maggie's predicament. It had been selfish of him to think that Rosie might give his wife some friendly medical advice, reassuring her that all would be well. How could he talk about a matter like Maggie's hysterectomy when Rosie's baby was filling its mother's womb?

'Nice to see you,' Rosie began and Lorimer found that she was looking at him quizzically.

'I was just passing. Had a meeting nearby. Thought I'd come and see how my favourite pathologist was faring,' he lied, smiling his most charming smile and fixing her with his blue eyes.

'Fancy a cuppa?'

'No, you're fine, thanks. Just wanted to have a blether, see what you're up to. Missing the day job yet?' he grinned.

'As if,' Rosie laughed. 'Can't perform any surgery now but I do have plenty of paperwork to keep me going before I hand the university work over to my locum. Things to do before term starts,' she added.

'So you're not wanting to hear what we've found in the Kenneth Scott case?'

Rosie shook her head but she was smiling. 'Suppose you're going to tell me anyway,' she said giving a theatrically exaggerated sigh.

'Well, the answer is, not a lot, I'm afraid,' Lorimer replied, suddenly serious. 'We can't locate either Brogan or his sister, though word has it that Billy boy was in Spain recently. As for the woman, well,' he shrugged and turned away from Rosie's gaze. Suddenly he was reluctant to talk about the case. How could he begin to relate his thoughts that Marianne Scott was dead when his friend was sitting there, blossoming with that new life inside her?

'We're still working on that,' he said instead. 'Doesn't look as though we're getting anywhere fast, though.'

'Can't win them all,' Rosie replied in an indifferent tone that Lorimer read as distancing herself from his world.

'So, what else have you been up to?'

'Watching the bird man. Do you know him?' Rosie asked.

Lorimer got up and moved to the window. 'Ah, that man,' he nodded. 'Aye, he's one of the RSPB volunteers from Kelvingrove Art Gallery and Museum. Sometimes takes visitors around the park to tell them about the local wildlife. Can't remember his name offhand. But we've spoken a few times.'

'And not about low-life hidden in the undergrowth,' Rosie commented dryly.

Lorimer chuckled. 'No. More about the goosanders and whether a kingfisher has been sighted.'

'I like to watch him,' Rosie said dreamily. He stands so still, so patiently, waiting for the little birds to come.'

Lorimer recognised the note of longing in her voice. Hadn't he heard that over and over whenever his own wife had raised her hopes for the child she had been carrying.

'Maggie sends her love,' he said, turning to leave. 'I'm sure she'll be in touch but she's pretty busy with school stuff right now. Curriculum for something or other,' he added vaguely.

'Sure,' Rosie said, heaving herself out of the sofa and standing beside the tall policeman. In her flat shoes she barely came up to Lorimer's chest and had to stand on tiptoes as he put his arms round her for a farewell hug.

What had that all been about? Rosie wondered as she closed the door. With her swirling hormones heightening her perception of everything around her Rosie could see that something was troubling the DCI. And it wasn't anything to do with the murder case they'd both been involved in.

'Someone told the police,' the Hundi said, watching for Dhesi's reaction. 'They know Brogan's in Mallorca.'

'Not our friend? Not Amit?'

The Hundi shook his head. 'I don't think so. We've been keeping a close eye on that one. I think,' he said slowly, 'that Jaffrey has been a greedy man. Not content with just giving his information to us.' He raised one shoulder in a shrug of resignation. 'Not much we can do about it now. Though we may be able to put feelers out to his boy. See just what he knows about Brogan.'

'If the police do find Brogan, if he tells them about us . . .' Dhesi's voice rose in alarm.

'We'll find him first, don't worry,' the Hundi reassured him. 'Remember we've got Mr Smith now,' he added with a crocodile smile that made his lips curve but failed to reach his narrowing eyes.

Mr Smith had decided to be Max Whittaker today. Of the several names by which he was known it was the one he liked best. Besides, it was the name on his driving licence and on one of his collection of passports. Marianne would be expecting an ex-army chum so he kept to his faded denim jacket and combat trousers with a clean white T-shirt making the outfit both respectable and authentic. He slicked a handful of gel across his hair, spiking it up. Turning his head this way and that, he grinned at the effect it had, making him look a lot younger than his forty-two years. A quick spray of lemon-scented cologne and he was ready. Max Whittaker was prepared to enjoy this outing. He had a feeling that the outcome would be far beyond the imaginings of Brogan's sister.

Marianne stepped out into the sunlight, glad of the excuse to hide behind these large sunglasses. She had twisted her hair into a russet knot, impaling it with a single clip at the back of her head. It was not perfect as a disguise, but anyone on the lookout for a woman with long red hair would be unlikely to give her a second glance. She'd chosen to wear a shorter skirt today, dark blue and tailored rather than the trademark Gypsy style that she normally favoured. A red top and a cream linen jacket completed her outfit. Swinging her handbag, Marianne felt a sense of freedom that she had long forgotten; a girlish smile made her look in a nearby window to see an attractive young woman smiling back at her, head held high. The sunlight flitted between the tall buildings as she crossed from West Regent Street to Bath Street, heading for the pedestrian precinct.

On a day like this, anything was possible, she thought, glancing at the shops as she made her way up Sauchiehall Street. She might even be able to have a normal day out like those other women who lingered by the windows, pondering the selection of clothes and shoes. Some of them, like Marianne, were dressed smartly as though they too were meeting a friend for lunch. There was a carnival feel to the city today, she thought, listening to an old woman playing the violin, her nut-brown face turned up to catch the glances of passers-by. On impulse, Marianne took out her purse and selected a handful of silver, placing it in the musician's open music case. A Romanian Gypsy, by the look of her, Marianne thought; a fugitive from some story that was now behind her. Was that why she had given her the money? Had she felt a common bond between them?

For a moment she hesitated, not sure whether she should be seeking out this stranger, Billy's old friend. What if he were to pester her? Come on to her with lascivious intent? Then, remembering his voice and his name, she quickened her pace. Max. It was a good name, a safe name and suddenly the shadow that had crossed her mind had disappeared in the brightness of this September day.

She knew it was him right away, standing, hands in his pockets, looking up and down the street. He was a man of average height and build, nothing outstanding but, as Marianne drew closer and their eyes met, she could see from his smile and outstretched hand that there was a kindness and strength about Max Whittaker, traits she needed in a friend right now.

'Marianne,' Max said, stepping forward and taking her hand lightly in his own.

'At last.' He smiled and she noticed the tiny flecks of gold in his light grey eyes. 'I've been looking forward to meeting you so much.'

CHAPTER 29

Billy Brogan sent up a prayer of thanks to whatever god might be listening. All night he had begged the powers that controlled the wind and waves for mercy, his head bent over a foul-smelling bucket. Now that line on the horizon gave him the first sign of hope. Hands clutching the post beside his wooden bench, Billy glanced up to see Carlos coming towards him, the Spaniard's grin splitting his weather-beaten face.

'You see? Land ahead. Not long now and we will have reached the shore,' Carlos told him, slapping his back in a friendly manner. 'One night we stay with family of Juan,' he jerked his thumb in the direction of the wheelhouse where the other sailor sat, navigating the boat through the choppy waters. 'Then back home again.' The old man gazed back across seas that seemed just endless lines of crested surf to Brogan. The man from Glasgow couldn't get his head around it: why would someone actually want to make a living from being constantly tossed up and down on this rotten boat? But he kept such thoughts to himself.

'How long . . .?'

Carlos shrugged. 'An hour, maybe a little more, depending on the tide. We have to anchor in a small cove that I know, then we take the little boat ashore.'

Billy twisted round, looking for another boat.

Carlos laughed. 'Maybe you help me find it, Meester?' He pulled out a box from under the rows of wooden seats and opened it, turning to Billy with a grin.

'See? My leetle boat!' he exclaimed proudly, showing off the folds of grey rubber concealed inside the box.

Billy gave a sickly grin. An inflatable. That was all he needed, he thought, imagining it bouncing high across the open sea.

'I have a pump,' Carlos was saying. 'You help me, yes?'

So it was that Brogan was too occupied with the foot pump to notice that the dark smudge against the horizon had taken shape and become a curve of ochre hills against a pale sky that looked bleached of colour in the midday sun. But it had also kept his mind off the constant nausea and by the time the inflatable was ready, he felt restored to his normal optimism.

'That Marrakesh over there?' he asked, leaning on the rail behind Juan.

The sailor gave him a grin that showed several missing teeth, shook his head and giggled.

'*Ay amigo mio, estás tan atontado. Te estamos tomando el pelo y no te enteras,*'* Juan told him, giggling again as he saw Brogan's face. *Ah my friend, you are such a moron. You have no idea we are totally taking the piss out of you.

'Oh, aye?' Brogan said, his face creasing in a smile as he turned to look at the approaching land.

'*Mirate sonriendo, pensando que somos tus amigos. No te das cuenta que te vamos a engañar,*'* Juan said, tipping a wink at the Scotsman. *Look at you grinning away, thinking we are friends. You don't realise that we are going to fool you.

'Amigo, aye sure, amigo,' Brogan replied, putting an arm on

Juan's shoulder. 'But what's the name of that place we're coming to?' he asked.

Juan merely shrugged and spread his hands as though he didn't understand.

Maybe it was just a wee village not on the big maps, Brogan told himself consolingly. He shrugged. Wouldn't be long now anyway, he thought, watching as the flecks of white on shore became visible as houses and the darker green shapes turned into palm trees lining a muddy looking shoreline. As the boat entered quieter waters, Brogan heard the change in engine note and knew that Carlos was looking for a good anchorage. Soon they were rocking gently in a dark lagoon, small darting fish appearing in the clear waters, and Juan beckoned to Brogan to help him carry the inflatable to the stern of the boat.

The small craft entered the bay with a single splash, its rope still fastened to the larger boat.

'How do I . . .?' Billy looked down into the water, trying to estimate its depth, wondering how they would make that leap from one boat to another.

Juan giggled at his expression then pointed to what looked like a bundle of rope. With a flourish, the Spaniard tossed it over the side and Brogan saw that it was in fact a length of ladder made from thick strands of rope.

'Baggage?' Juan asked, miming the backpack that Brogan had taken on board.

'Oh, aye, be with you in a mo,' he said, then headed back to the spot where he had spent all these hours of misery. He heaved the pack onto his back and returned to where Juan stood above the inflatable.

'No carry,' the man said, pulling at the pack. 'Baggage go first.' Then, before Brogan had time to protest, the Spaniard had taken the pack and flung it into the stern of the dinghy, climbing as nimbly as a monkey after it.

'Now, come,' Juan told him, beckoning with his sun-darkened hand.

Brogan hesitated for a moment then, with a deep breath, swung his leg over the side, clinging to the rope ladder with two white-knuckled fists. He breathed hard as he made the descent, feeling his feet slip against the rounded rungs, fearful of letting go. At last he reached the dinghy and the sailor's outstretched hand then with one leap he was in the boat, making it rock violently.

'Sit!' Juan commanded and Brogan sat where he was told, next to his luggage, shifting to make room for Carlos who was suddenly there as if by magic. Brogan clung on to the rubber handles on each side as the outboard motor roared into life, bucketing them across the final strip of water towards the shore. For once the motion did not make his stomach heave and he felt a mixture of relief and exhilaration as salt spray was flung across his face.

Brogan looked at the strange houses that were built just above the shoreline, their flat roofs showing cables and masonry as though each of them was in the process of being constructed. Had he known it, this was a traditional method of building: each new storey ready and prepared for an expanding family that included the older generation, something that typified the culture of North Africa.

But Billy Brogan knew nothing of this, and even less about the village beside which they were now landing. *Near Marrakesh*, he had supposed, not knowing that Carlos had actually sailed his boat many hundreds of miles away from Brogan's desired destination.

Billy had never known such hospitality, even in Glasgow, a city famed for its kindness to the strangers within its gates. They were seated on cushions around a low square table in the main room of

230

the house that belonged to some distant relation of Juan's. Brogan couldn't make out what was being said but he reckoned from all the back-slapping, smiles and hugs that Juan had received from the men and women of the house that he was a long lost cousin of some sort. And any friend of Juan's . . . he grinned, sipping the strange tasting tea that he had been offered. It was like drinking peppermints and treacle, he thought, eyeing the dark green liquid floating in the tiny gilt-edged cup. They had been sitting here for what seemed like hours now and were at that stage when after-dinner sweetmeats were being offered and the hookahs brought out to smoke. Food had been conjured up from a kitchen some-where and the younger women had carried enormous, brightly painted bowls of spicy meats and fragrant rice to each of the men sitting cross-legged around the central table.

None of the women had joined them for food, Brogan noticed. But some of them had looked at him with shy almond eyes, gig-gling as he attempted to thank them in his broad Glasgow accent. *They haven't a clue what I'm saying*, he thought. And for the first time Billy Brogan felt a pang of homesickness for the place where everything he said and did was understood. A nod, a grunt or a particular gesture could speak volumes when you were with your own kind, he realised wistfully, listening to the excited voices raised all around him.

A tap at his back made him turn and there was Carlos, standing grinning down at him.

The Spaniard made a motion with his head towards the door and Brogan rose to follow him, bobbing a little bow to the rest of the company as he made his way from the smoke-filled room.

'Now is time to settle our account, Señor Brogan,' Carlos smiled at Billy. 'And then we go on our way,' he waved a hand at the boat whose hull was glistening in the sunshine out on the bay.

'Eh, sure thing, Carlos. What do I do?' he asked, looking around him. All Brogan could see was a narrow trail disappearing around a corner of the shoreline. 'Is there, um, a bus . . . like . . . that I can get to Marrakesh from here?'

'Bus, yes. Get a bus at the next stop around the corner. Maybe a mile along the road,' Carlos assured him, wagging his head.

'Right, pal,' Billy said, delving in to his pocket and taking out the dollars that he had kept folded inside his pocketbook. 'What we agreed, eh?' he said, frowning slightly as Carlos licked his thumb and flicked through the notes to check on the amount.

The Spaniard gave him a grin as the money disappeared into a leather bag on a string that he kept around his neck, hidden under the same blue cotton shirt that he had worn for the entire journey. '*Me haces reir*,'* Carlos said suddenly, giving such a guffaw that Brogan began to laugh with him. *You make me laugh.

'What time's the bus?' Billy asked as Carlos made to walk away.

'Oh, you stay here until tomorrow,' Carlos told him. 'Juan's family be *very* upset if you leave them too soon. *Comprendes?*'

'Aye, *comprende* right enough,' Brogan agreed. The laws of hospitality were the same the world over, after all; to fail to show appreciation of one's hosts was to give offence. He grinned back at the Spaniard who slapped his back as they returned to the house.

Billy woke up, trying to figure out where he was. The swell of the boat was making him sway from side to side, but as his eyes opened, he saw that he was lying on a couch in an unfamiliar room, silken curtains blowing gently at the windows. It was not the boat that was making him feel so weird, but perhaps, Brogan reasoned, he was still feeling its motion. A scent of something sweet filled his nostrils and he saw twin wisps of smoke coming from a dish beside the couch. Joss sticks, he thought, smiling in remembrance of the many times he'd had pals round for a session. In Glasgow you burned them to mask the smell of the joints; here they were part of the ambience. Brogan let his eyes close again with a sigh of contentment.

He had little recall of the previous evening, a smoke-filled haze of laughter and girls dancing to the music of tabor and sitar. But he did have a memory of gentle hands guiding him along a darkened corridor and a black pointed lantern pierced with stars that swung to and fro as he staggered away from the throng.

Suddenly he remembered that he hadn't said goodbye to Juan or Carlos. Sitting up, he swung his legs over the edge of the couch and felt the tiled floor beneath his bare feet. Padding towards the window, he parted the curtains and looked out across the palm fringed bay.

The boat was gone.

Brogan twisted his mouth into a moue of disappointment. Och, well, they had a long way to go, he told himself. But the idea of being quite alone with people who could not understand his speech was disconcerting, no matter how kind they had been.

He dressed quickly and made his way down a narrow wooden staircase that was painted in stripes of red and green.

The room where he had spent such a joyous time last night was empty. The square table had been spread with a piece of embroidered linen and someone had stacked the cushions in a corner, neatly, out of the way.

'Hello?' he called out, but his voice fell dully against the whitewashed walls and somehow Brogan knew he was alone in this house. Whoever had lit the joss sticks couldn't be too far away, though, he reasoned. Sauntering through to the back, he found a small kitchen with a refrigerator that hummed loudly as though its thermostat were working overtime. The table in the middle of the room had been swept clean of crumbs and on one side was a mat of fringed cloth laid with a bowl, a spoon and a plate. Had they all gone to work? Brogan wondered. And was this their way of saying help yourself to breakfast?

Shrugging off a feeling of unease that was threatening to make him nervous, Brogan opened the fridge and drew out a jug of milk and a carton of orange juice. He gave a sigh of relief. His throat felt as though someone had sandpapered it during the night. Pulling open the corner of the carton, he swallowed greedily, wiping the drops that fell over and under his chin.

A cupboard high up on the wall revealed a packet of cornflakes that had been tied up with a pair of knotted shoelaces. An expression of puzzlement crossed his face until he remembered the pavement cafes back in Cala Millor and the hosts of tiny ants that had gathered under the tables. Nodding to himself in sudden understanding at the makeshift precaution, Brogan dumped the cornflakes onto the table and began his meal.

He'd emptied two bowls full of cereal before he thought to look out of the front door to see if anyone was around. Raking a hand through hair that was already damp from the heat, Brogan opened the door on to a wide veranda that looked out onto the ocean.

Looking from left to right he could see nobody at all on the deserted sand, not even one of the old folk who had grinned toothlessly at him from across the table the previous evening.

'Right, Brogan,' he said aloud. 'Time to move on.' He grinned as he squinted up at the acres of blue above him, as fathomless as the stretch of water he had so recently crossed. 'Marrakesh, here I come.'

Less than a quarter of an hour later, Brogan was whistling as he walked down the path that led away from the little village, pack on his back, feeling like a real adventurer.

It would be hours before he came to the next sign of civilisation, foot-sore and weary, but Brogan had no notion that he was on the coast of northern Algeria, nor of the immense distance that separated him from the western tip of this great continent.

CHAPTER 30

'Come in, Fathy, sit down,' Lorimer beckoned the young man who had knocked on his door and now hovered on the threshold.

'Any news of Marianne Scott?'

Fathy shook his head. 'Not yet, sir, but there are still a few departments we have to visit.' He cleared his throat nervously. 'It was on a personal matter that I wanted to see you, sir.'

Lorimer sat up a little straighter, looking quizzically at the detective constable. The thought came to him that Fathy had been a bit quieter than usual during team meetings. And now, seeing the younger man twisting his fingers together on his lap, Lorimer realised that there was something seriously amiss.

'I wanted to tell you why I left Grampian for Strathclyde,' Fathy began. He looked down at his hands and clasped them together as though to keep them still and calm himself. 'I was the target of some racist incidents,' he mumbled.

'That doesn't sound so good,' Lorimer frowned. 'I suppose the persons responsible were properly dealt with?'

Fathy looked up, his eyes full of appeal. 'That's just it, sir. I never told anybody about what was going on. I just asked for a transfer and came down here.'

'Well you should have,' Lorimer insisted. 'Grampian would want to make an example of whoever targeted you.' His eyes narrowed. 'Do you want me to do something about it now?'

Fathy looked embarrassed. 'That's not what I came to say, sir. You see,' he took a deep breath before continuing, 'it's begun to happen again.'

'What d'you mean?'

Fathy drew out the notes and laid them on Lorimer's desk. 'I found that first one in my locker here,' he said, pointing to the note. 'Then I had a series of letters through the post, all saying the same thing, see.' He lifted them one after the other, displaying the similar words.

'Good Lord,' Lorimer sat back exhaling as though he had been winded. 'I find it hard to believe that someone in this police office would do such a thing.'

'It's true, though, sir,' Fathy's mouth trembled for a moment as he met Lorimer's eyes. 'And I think it must be linked to what happened up in Aberdeen. Same sort of notes, same kind of messages.'

'Well,' Lorimer shook his head as though finding the man's words hard to fathom, 'I'll need you to complete a proper statement about this. You do realise that, don't you?'

Fathy nodded, his shoulders slumped in what Lorimer recognised as plain misery. 'If we ever find out who was responsible for this then it'll be a matter for the procurator fiscal.' He leaned forward. 'Do you have any idea who is behind this?'

Fathy shook his head, still looking down at his hands as though he were the guilty party in this affair. Lorimer knew the signs; the man was feeling tainted by it all, dirtied.

'I don't know who would do anything like this, sir,' he said at last, looking up to meet that familiar blue gaze. 'I did try to find out up there . . .' he tailed off with a tired shrug that spoke more than all the words he had yet uttered.

It was hopeless to think that anyone in Grampian might be able to help Fathy now, Lorimer thought. But it was not too late to set up some sort of surveillance to catch someone at this end.

'Look, leave this with me,' Lorimer told him. 'Write me that statement but keep this completely to yourself for now. If we are to find out who's been up to this . . . this *nonsense*,' he spat out the word as though it was a bad taste in his mouth, 'then you can be sure it'll result in a disciplinary hearing for them at the very least. Okay?'

Annie Irvine stole a glance at her sidekick as he sat back at his desk. His dark face was flushed and there was something about the tilt of his head that made her continue to stare until he turned to catch her looking at him.

'What?' Fathy asked.

Annie grinned at him. 'Nothing. Just that you seem more your old self today, that's all. And here's me thinking that you were getting all worked up about not finding Marianne Brogan.'

Fathy grinned back at her. 'Well, I don't share the boss's opinion, you know that.' His smile slipped as his expression became more thoughtful. '*I* think she's alive.' He turned towards Annie. 'Don't you?'

It was Annie Irvine's turn to become reticent and she mumbled an unconvincing *dunno* as she turned back to her computer screen. In truth, Annie knew that she was becoming more and more engrossed in the background to this case. And she desperately wanted Marianne Brogan to be somewhere in the world, still warm and upright.

'You know about stalkers, don't you?' Fathy continued softly. 'I saw your face when these photographs came back.'

239

Annie gave a non-committal shrug, not daring to turn and face him.

'What do you know about stalkers, Annie?' Omar Fathy whispered gently.

There was a silence between them for several minutes as Fathy waited for a reply.

Then the policewoman turned towards him. 'That's why I joined the force,' she said, her face darkening. 'And if you knew what I'd been through, you'd understand a lot more about that poor woman,' she nodded towards a blown-up photo of Marianne.

Omar slipped his hand across their desks, covering Annie's fingers and giving her an enigmatic smile.

'Maybe I understand more than you realise,' he said, squeezing her hand gently before releasing his grip.

Marianne felt the wind on her face as the car breezed down the dual carriageway towards Loch Lomond. She had let down the window a few centimetres and now she smelled a freshness in the air as they passed green fields on either side. Sheep and fat lambs grazed amiably and for a moment Marianne envied them their simple lives of feeding, growth and reproduction, so different from the complexities of human existence. The landscape changed to over-hanging cliffs on one side and soon they were slowing down at the signs for Loch Lomond Shores. She leaned back as they circled the roundabout that went on to Balloch and Gartocharn, smiling at Max as he continued to drive north.

She had suggested Duck Bay Marina for no other reason than it was scenic, a lovely day and they could be guaranteed something nice to eat. Earlier Max had asked her for directions and she saw that he had a good memory since he hadn't needed to enquire again. He was a bright man as well as good company, Marianne thought to herself. Older than he had sounded on the phone, but then she had expected someone of Billy's age, hadn't she? He had short hair, thinning a little, but his features were regular and strong, something Marianne found reassuring.

Suddenly the woman found herself thinking about the slight, dark Asian and a pang of guilt coursed through her. Should she have run out on Amit like that? Had these latest dreams been no more than fantastic shapes whirling around her brain? Shaking her head, Marianne tried to put all such things out of her mind. Lines from last year's English class flitted into her brain.

These deeds must not be thought after these ways; so, it will make us mad.

And surely that was true? She had to put her night-time thoughts away from her. Doctor Brightman had shown her the way out of these dark places. Now, Marianne told herself, as the sunlight streamed through the windscreen, it was time to begin somewhere new. And perhaps Max Whittaker was the man to lead her there.

Solly lifted the green file and put it into his already bulging brief-case. Dreams, he smiled to himself. That had been one of the more successful in his series of lectures to last year's undergraduates. Now he had updated it to include references from Shakespeare, and the Bard's plays were still to the forefront of his mind. Last night he and Rosie had discussed possible names for the baby. Again. It was a pity, he thought, that they had not yet come to any agreement about this. His recent foray into Shakespearean literature seemed to have influenced his own preferences: *Miranda, Imogen, Harry* and *Anthony.* They all sounded fine when conjoined with his surname. But Rosie had wrinkled her nose. Her own choices had Celtic overtones: *Siobhan, Mhairi,*

Ruaridh and *Euan*. He'd smiled as usual, shrugged them off and suggested they both look at the well-thumbed book of children's names once more.

'You will know what his name is when you see him,' Ma Brightman had said when he had revealed their dilemma to his mother. She was so sure it would be a boy, he laughed to himself: a little new Brightman to continue the family tree.

Solly had dreamed about the child last night. A boy, certainly, but not a newborn. This was a little lad who had walked by his side, blonde head uncovered, shining in the sun. And although the details of that dream were now hazy, Solly still retained the powerful feeling of paternal love towards the boy who had slipped into his unconscious mind.

He smiled as he lifted the briefcase and headed towards the door of the flat. Dreams, indeed!

'*A Midsummer Night's Dream* is all about the quarrel that Oberon and Titania have over the little changeling boy,' Maggie told her class. 'The whole of the natural world is turned topsy-turvy as the quarrel persists, making the summer weather wet, foggy and stormy.'

'Aye, jist like Glasgow durin' the Fair,' Jimmy Lang piped up and everyone laughed.

Maggie smiled too. The two-week trades holiday was notorious for having poor weather. 'Don't think that's the fault o' the fairies,' someone else called out and again a ripple of giggles ran through the class.

As the bell to end the period rang out, Maggie raised her hand to prevent a charge towards her classroom door. 'Now remember to tell your parents about the theatre trip. We need to have the forms filled in and returned no later than next week. Okay?'

She smiled as they filed out into the corridor, some of them grinning up at her, others saying 'See you, miss,' as they passed her by. This was by far the nicest group of first years she'd had in a long time, Maggie thought, closing the door behind them and settling down for a rare period of preparation.

Her smile faded as she regarded the notes on Shakespeare's well-loved play. Why had she chosen to highlight the changeling boy? Was it some subconscious desire on her part to elevate the child to a position of importance? Surely not. She smiled again, remembering the little faces that had just looked up at her. These would be her family, kids who passed through her life for five or six years. She sat, thinking about the future. Soon both she and Bill would be forty and that landmark birthday seemed to Maggie to be a kind of watershed in their lives. She could go on teaching for more than twenty years, hundreds of kids receiving the benefit of her tuition, she mused. Would she still be here, in this school? There was no ambitious streak in the policeman's wife to go chasing promotion. Their only ambition had been to have children one day and now that possibility was fast drawing to a close.

Maggie drew a sigh. She was so lucky compared to many of her friends; like her colleague, Sandy, with a messy divorce behind her and a teenage son who drove his mother demented. And if her husband worked long hours and had sometimes to cancel social engagements because of work, she could still treasure the knowledge that she was his only love and that they would always share a unique and special bond. The notion brought her back to the warring lovers in A *Midsummer Night's Dream* and Maggie settled back to prepare lessons for the following weeks.

'No he isn't here at present. No. Would you? Oh, well, thanks for that, ma'am.'

DCI Lorimer put down the telephone and looked at it thought-fully. The deputy chief constable had expressed both the horror and outrage that he himself had felt over DC Fathy's revelation. Talking to Joyce Rogers had been a good idea since she had taken such a personal interest in their Egyptian detective constable. *We need more ethnic minorities representing our forces*, she'd told him more than once since Fathy had transferred from Grampian. But if there were racist elements at work within their divisions then something was seriously wrong.

Lorimer wondered just how to begin to tackle this. There were known groups, football casuals among them, that were blatantly racist. It might pay to ask a few questions in those quarters. But since the first incident had actually happened here, in the locker area, just yards from the charge bar where officers came and went at all hours of the day and night, he really should begin with their own division. If it was an incident involving serious crime, then he could have used some technology, like hidden cameras, but that was completely out of the question given the number of officers using the locker area. And, since Fathy hadn't a clue who his attacker was, they had to keep any investigation very low-key indeed. Any officer worth their salt would have taken precautions to keep his (or her) DNA off the materials sent to Fathy through the post. But he might just call up a favour from his chum in the Scottish criminal record office to have the letters and note dusted for prints. Even the most forensically aware person could still make mistakes, he reasoned. Lorimer would make enquiries, he'd promised Joyce Rogers, keep it as discreet as possible, see if he could avoid putting it through official channels just yet.

The DCI pursed his lips as he thought about all the things going on right now; Fathy's problem, the hunt for Billy Brogan, and his wife's difficulty in coming to terms with her operation.

Then there was Solly and why he was being sidelined when such skills as his were invaluable. His frown changed to the faintest of smiles. Solly would soon be immersed in fatherhood and Lorimer was certain that the psychologist would make an excellent dad.

Should he be feeling a pang of envy? Or was he so wrapped up in this job that he simply never had the time to think of what he was missing?

CHAPTER 31

'Aaaagh!'

The man's scream bounced off the walls, tripling the sound of his agony.

'No nice tae grass up yer mates, Jaffa. No nice at all,' the man standing over Jaffrey whispered softly, chuckling as he watched the pain twist the man's face.

'C'mon Raj, let's git oot o' here,' a voice behind him insisted. 'He's grassed wance, he'll mibbe grass us anither time.'

'No, Vik,' Raj replied. 'Jaffa won't do that, will you, son?'

Jaffrey's frightened face looked up and he shook his head, opening his mouth to beseech his tormentors.

But Raj had already raised his knife, plunging down hard, cutting off any coherent words.

The high-pitched scream of pain ended in barely a whimper.

Then the two men turned and walked away from the shadows of the deserted factory into the bright afternoon sunlight.

Raj heaved the metal door shut then secured it with the large padlock that had dangled from its hasp. The derelict building had a row of windows set high up on one side, all of them broken like stars from a toddler's drawing book. Weeds grew up against the ruins of a pathway around the place, feathery willow herb and thistles, their fluffy seed heads floating skywards. He let his eyes roam over the area round about. Several dark brown bottles that had been kicked into the undergrowth glinted in the afternoon light, evidence that people had been here. Probably jakeys from up in the village over that nearby hill, he told himself, then grinned. Nobody would find Jaffa any time soon. And by the time they did, he would be past telling anything. He swaggered to where Vikram was waiting by his Beamer, nodding to himself in satisfaction.

'Hey, dinna mess the car, man,' Vikram whined, stepping in front of Raj, who still clutched the bloodstained knife in his left hand.

'Aye, nae sweat,' Raj replied, bending down to push the blade into the tussocky ground beside the black BMW before wiping it on the grass. 'Now, c'mon. let's split before onybody clocks us.'

The big car accelerated from the patch of rough ground and sped off around a bend past a copse of mottled sycamores. Somewhere, unseen, a blackbird began to call; an insistent warning cry, signalling danger. But all that could be seen on that September afternoon was a swirl of dust settling back onto the dried-up earth. The bird flew out of the thorn bush, its dark shape a swift arrow against the fading blue sky.

And no sound issued from behind the wooden doors, where a man lay bleeding quietly to death.

CHAPTER 32

'He's not come home,' the woman said, her voice breaking into the threat of a sob. 'What should I do?'

Young Jaffrey looked around him as a crowd of tourists passed by the pavement cafe. The sun that shone down on the busy Mallorcan street made the boy resentful as he listened to his mother and that plea in her tone that suggested he should pack up now and return home. His mouth drooped into a sulk as he thought how to reply.

'Well, don't do anything foolish, will you?' he said at last. 'That's not what Dad would want, now, is it?'

'Oh, I was hoping . . .' the woman's sentence tailed off but there was no need for her to finish it. Young Jaffrey knew fine what she was wanting him to say: that he'd come home, sort things out.

'Don't worry. He'll probably have a good reason for staying out.' He bit his lip, wondering as he spoke just what such a reason might be. 'Ring me when Dad comes back. All right? Have to go now. Bye.'

The boy clicked his mobile off, looking thoughtful. Was this something to do with that murder case back home? He'd let Dad know about Brogan, after all. And his own snooping had produced results. That gossipy girl behind the hotel desk had let slip that the Spanish police were trying to find Brogan. But the trail here had gone cold, neither the police nor his own furtive enquiries were producing any sign of the Glasgow dealer.

It was all wrong, the boy told himself. Their kind should stick together, not mix with guys like Brogan. The dealer had many friends within the Asian community, though, didn't he? And rumour had it that he was well in with the Hundi, a personage who commanded huge respect from everyone young Jaffrey knew. He frowned. Would Dad have done anything stupid to upset the fragile balance that existed between families like their own and the powerful men who controlled the ebb and flow of drugs in the city? The thought made him blanch under his tanned skin. Whatever was going on back home, he was better off right here away from it all.

'The PD-100 Black Hornet has the advantage of almost total silence,' the man said, turning his head to make eye contact with his audience.

Lorimer tried hard not to fidget. The man's presentation at the Pitt Street assembly hall was going quite well so far and he had that knack of every good speaker for engaging his audience with humorous anecdotes. Most of these had been relevant to his subject which was what their attention was focussed upon: a tiny helicopter smaller than a cricket ball. So far the man had shown the senior officers some video footage of the device at work. Powered by an electric motor, the helicopter had rotor blades that measured a mere ten centimetres in diameter. Lorimer had been a little sceptical at first, especially when his neighbour had nudged him, remarking that they were being shown a clip from a Harry Potter film and that the PD whatshisname was really the Snitch in disguise.

Now Lorimer was paying a bit more attention as the speaker began to demonstrate the little machine's other facilities.

'The microphone has now been fully tested and it can "eaves-drop" on conversations at a range determined by its controllers. This adds to the benefits of it being used in situations that call for extra care like the hostage situation I mentioned earlier.'

The DCI was sitting up straighter now taking notice of all the pictures being shown on the screen. A close-up of the device made it look far too simple but in the videos he had seen how it could whirr silently, unnoticed by the men inside the building who had been part of the mock-up incident. It looked good, he had to admit. *One more tool for the box*, he could almost hear his old super saying. And it was right that the force should be looking to technological developments to help in fighting crime. If a wee helicopter like that could film a crime scene that was under sur-veillance then perhaps it should be given a place in their budget.

'More toys for the boys,' Helen James remarked wearily as they filed out of the hall afterwards. Lorimer smiled at her politely, not wanting to get into an argument about it. He recognised the woman as a DCI from another division who had been up to her ears with the press lately on a series of missing girls who were known prosti-tutes. Helen's dough-coloured pallor on a skin that was stretched tight over sharp cheekbones was something that every one of her fellow officers could recognise – too much work and too little sleep. That she had taken time to attend this presentation surprised Lorimer. Perhaps she was simply escaping for an hour? He knew how that could work. A brief respite that was still within the descrip-tion of work could always help to focus back on a difficult case like the one she was on. Nodding to her as they walked out into the day-light again, Lorimer hoped that it might do the same for himself.

Solly turned the key of his office, smiling in appreciation as he entered the room. It was a different office from the one he had occupied for much of his tenure at the university and reflected his status as professor designate. He nodded approvingly at the light that flooded in from the two tall windows, art deco ovals etched onto the upper parts of their frames. It was, Solly told himself, a handsome room. Yes, handsome was certainly the correct word to choose.

Putting down his briefcase, Solly wandered around the room, touching the edge of a huge rectangular table that sat in the centre of the room. It was easily big enough for any of his seminars and as Solly stood there he imagined a group of young faces laughing and chatting as he encouraged their developing thoughts. The bookcases that lined almost every wall had begun to fill up with his books; the summer had seen him make lots of trips between his old, modern office and this large airy room.

He strolled across to the window, looking down the length of University Avenue, past the line of parked cars next to black painted railings. A small smile of satisfaction hovered on the psychologist's lips. Down there on the left was the department of forensic medicine, its sand-blasted walls a honey tone just visible behind the trees. In winter he would be able to look out and imagine Rosie when she was in her office; her time being divided between the campus and the city mortuary. His eyes drifted across to the buildings opposite, the crow-stepped gables jutting out from moss-covered roofs. Funny how this place felt so much like home to him. London was part of his past now, though he would surely continue to make family visits. Solly moved away from the window, checking the small desk where his new computer lay ready to be switched on. The departmental website would soon have his title changed from doctor to professor. How would he feel seeing that every time he logged on? Or came around the turn of the stair to see it emblazoned upon his door?

Professor Brightman sounded quite right to his ears and probably preferable to Doctor once his child had grown up and talked about him to his friends. (*His* again, Solly grinned above his dark beard. Surely a subliminal wish?) Being mistaken for a doctor of medicine was simply not on, especially when Rosie already had that distinction. Anyway, his new title would be conferred during this coming session. The Senate would be sitting soon and Solly was not sure that he would actually enjoy the little ceremony that was to confirm his new status. It would not alter very much except a title and the welcome increase in salary that went with it; his research and teaching would remain pretty much as normal since this professorship was an internal, personal chair. And it would not affect the two weeks' paternity leave that he had ahead of him. That would be something of a watershed in his life. Once the baby was here and Rosie was settled into her period of new motherhood then he could return to the department and resume his teaching life.

The new post was not something he had mentioned to Lorimer, nor to anyone outside of his family or academic circle. Perhaps it might have given him a little more cachet in his dealings with Strathclyde Police, he mused. Having a professor of psychology to assist them might have been hard to resist. He knew how human nature worked, after all. But perhaps it could also have been counter-productive in his quest to remain on their payroll: might having a Prof for profiler be seen as way outside their budget?

When the telephone rang, Solly blinked, shaken from his thoughts back to the present.

'Doctor Brightman,' he said. As the familiar voice of the departmental secretary spoke to him, the psychologist's eyebrows rose in a speculative expression.

'And they'd like to see *me*?' he asked.

Putting down the phone, Solly stroked his dark beard thoughtfully. Officers from Strathclyde Police were in the departmental office and wondered if he could spare a minute to see them. Curiosity and his own better judgement overcame a sudden childish notion to say that he was too busy. The name of the officer was unknown to him, not one of Lorimer's team, he decided, walking along towards the main office. But as he opened the door and saw DC Irvine standing beside a slim, dark young man, Solly had to revise his first thought. The other detective's elegant features marked him out as North African, the psychologist decided, and his body language told Solly that the man was both respectful and ill at ease. Had he heard about Solly's dismissal as a profiler? That could certainly cause a slight sense of embarrassment, he told himself as Annie Irvine made the introductions.

'Sorry to bother you, Doctor Brightman,' Irvine began. 'But we wanted, that is, *I* wanted, to let you know what we were doing here,' she began.

Solly smiled at the woman. He liked this officer. She had been one of Lorimer's team on several of the cases he had been a part of and it was sensitive of her to go out of her way to keep him in the loop.

'Good of you,' Solly murmured. 'Perhaps we can talk in my office?' he suggested, leading them back along to the bright and airy room that overlooked a delicate row of silver birches swaying in the afternoon breeze.

'We're investigating the murder of Kenneth Scott and the double shooting in the West End,' Irvine told him, sitting down on the chair that he had pulled out for her. 'But you know that of course, sir,' she gave a rueful grin. 'Mrs Brightman did the postmortems,' she added, turning to address Fathy.

'We're looking for the sister of the drug dealer who's disap-peared,' she went on. 'Seems she applied to the university a couple of years back and was given an unconditional acceptance. Only thing is, we haven't been able to find her name in any of the registration lists so far. So we're trawling through all the depart-mental records instead.'

'That's a lot of work for you,' Solly nodded then, looking at them both in turn, he asked, 'What does my good friend think?'

Irvine made a face. 'Lorimer thinks she's dead,' she told the psychologist.

'And you don't?' Solly said, looking from one officer to the other.

Irvine shook her head. 'But he isn't being pig-headed about that, either.'

'Which is why you have come to talk to the secretarial staff?'

'Yes, sir,' Fathy answered for them both. 'I just have this feel-ing . . .' the young Egyptian broke off.

'And feelings are important,' Solly replied immediately, encouraging the officer. 'They can tell us things that are not on the surface but are of value nonetheless,' he continued, wagging his head sagely.

Omar Fathy sat opposite the psychologist seeing eyes that twinkled behind their horn-rimmed spectacles. So this was the legendary Solomon Brightman? Solomon the wise, Fathy thought, noting the man's keen intelligence. Here was a man he felt he could trust. On impulse he blurted out, 'We're looking for a woman who called herself Marianne Scott. Was Marianne Brogan before her marriage,' he said, pulling the well-thumbed photograph from his inside pocket. He stopped suddenly, aware of the change that had come over the psychologist's face.

For a long moment none of them spoke, Solly staring at them

255

owlishly as though he had retreated inside himself. The ticking of an old-fashioned clock on the wall seemed unnaturally loud.

'Marianne?' Solly said at last, swallowing as though the word stuck in his throat. 'Marianne,' he paused for another moment, sighing as if it were an effort to continue, 'is one of my students. Or at least she was,' he tailed off, eyes gazing into space at something neither of the police officers could see.

'I've seen her,' he told them at last, still looking into the distance. 'And she was happy. Happier than she ever was last session.'

Turning to Irvine and Fathy Solomon Brightman's face grew serious once more. 'I would hate to think that anything bad has happened to that young woman.'

CHAPTER 33

'C'mon, doon here,' Geordie Mitchell beckoned his pals. 'This'll do fine,' he added, grinning as the other two boys picked their way carefully through the broken glass that littered what remained of the pathway. 'Here, Rab, gonnae you gie's a haun tae git up tae thon windae?'

'Ye cannae git up therr, Mitchell,' Rab replied. 'Thur's way too much glass still in that one.'

'Well let's finish it aff,' the third boy said gleefully, setting down his backpack with a clink that betrayed its contents. He was by far the smallest of the trio, a dark-haired boy, quick and otter sleek, but he had shouldered the pack manfully down the steep track that led from their village. 'Better inside where naebody can find us, eh?'

The three boys scrabbled in the tussocky grass, finding suitable sized rocks to aim at the already broken pane of glass above them.

'Geronimo!' Rab shouted, 'See thon wee bit up tae the left? Got it a bull's eye so ah did!'

'Ah'll finish it aff fur youse n'all,' his pal boasted.

'Bet ye cannae, Chick. Ye're too wee!' Geordie scoffed.

The challenge flung out made the smaller boy's face tighten with concentration as he pulled back his arm then let the stone fly through the air.

With a tinkling sound the remaining shard fell inwards, leaving a blank hole big enough for them to scramble through.

'See!' Chick yelled in triumph, offering his open hand for a high five.

'Right, let's get in there,' Geordie told them. Who's gonnae gie me a leg up?'

Geordie Mitchell heaved himself upwards from Rab's clasped hands, scrabbling his feet to find some purchase. Then, seizing the edge of the windowsill, he thrust his body forwards into the gloom.

For a moment he could see nothing, blinded by the contrast from the sun's glare outside. Then his eyes began to register shapes beneath him. And a smell that made him wrinkle his nose in disgust.

'Three laddies, sarge,' the officer told the mobile phone in his hand. 'Down at Brockenridge's old place. Foot of Rowan Glen. Aye, that's the place.'

The uniformed policeman turned to the boys sitting behind him in the squad car. 'You all right, lads?'

The three boys nodded in unison, silenced by the enormity of what Geordie had found in the old factory. Thoughts of being punished for dogging off school had long vanished. Fear of something more dreadful had made them scramble up the hill to the main road where, as chance would have it, they had managed to flag down a passing patrol car. Their earlier bravado had vanished; now they were three wee laddies whose natural instincts for what was right and what was wrong had reasserted themselves. Breaking already broken windows and having a few bottles of Buckfast was nothing compared to what Geordie had found. That was wrong in anybody's book.

'Can you describe the man to us, Geordie?' the officer in the front passenger seat turned to ask.

Geordie Mitchell swallowed the bile that threatened to shame him before his mates. He'd never forget that sight as long as he lived. Yet trying to describe that body covered in blood with its dead, glaring eyes was beyond him. He shook his head, refusing to meet the eyes of his pals who were looking at him with unashamed curiosity.

'*It's a deid man!*' he'd screamed, falling down on top of an astonished Rab.

There had been no time for discussion. Geordie had turned to run back the way they had come, the other boys following his lead, galvanised into action by the expression of horror on his chalk-white face.

Marianne wiped her mouth with the paper serviette and smiled at the man opposite. He'd been quieter than she had imagined an ex-soldier would have been, this Max Whittaker, but he had made up for that by being attentive and a good listener. She had told him lots about her first year at the university and as the meal had progressed, Marianne had even let slip her hopes for the future.

'Why America?' Max had asked, gesturing in the air with his fork. 'Aren't there enough opportunities here?'

Marianne had shaken her head, pretending to know more about that than she actually did. A gulp from her water glass had given her time to think up some spurious comment about psychologists being better paid and Max seemed to take her fantasies for the straight truth.

He hadn't said much about himself and Marianne's curiosity had been satisfied by the few comments about travelling around the UK as a consultant and the tedium of staying in travel lodges that looked the same no matter what city you were in.

She let her fingers stray on to the table, playing absently with the pair of white ceramic ducks twined together to provide salt and pepper. Years ago a friend who had worked for British Airways cabin crew had pinched one of them and sent photographs of the duck from places all over the world. Marianne pondered for a moment whether the staff had missed the lone duck and what they had done with its partner.

'Glad you came out with me today,' he said gruffly, breaking into her thoughts and putting a light hand over her own. It was the nearest he had come to an intimate moment and, absurdly, Marianne found herself blushing like an awkward schoolgirl.

'I've enjoyed it,' she said truthfully, looking at him with a new appreciation.

Max Whittaker wasn't drop dead gorgeous, but there was something appealing about these regular features and his light grey eyes, especially the way they held her own as though he wanted to say more but was too shy.

'Better get the bill,' he mumbled and began to reach into the inside pocket of the jacket that was slung on the seat behind him.

She felt a spasm of disappointment as keen as real pain. That was it, then. They'd drive back to the city and he would disappear from her life. Suddenly Marianne knew that she wanted more from this man, this stranger who had made her feel like a girl again, full of hopes and possibilities. Reaching behind her head, she unclipped the barrette and shook out her long, russet tresses, watching under her lashes for some reaction. Men had always remarked on her hair, finding something fascinating in the way it cascaded round her shoulders, falling onto her breasts.

'Maybe we could find a movie? Or something?' she asked,

hearing the deliberate huskiness in her voice, watching the man's face to see if such boldness was overstepping the mark.

When Max smiled and nodded, Marianne let out her breath, her cheeks glowing with a mixture of relief and pleasure.

As they rose to leave, Marianne accidentally swept the two salt-and-pepper ducks off the table.

'Oh!' she cried, her hand flying to her mouth in horror as one of the ducks shattered into bits on the stone floor.

'Come on. Someone'll clear that up. Don't worry about it,' Max told her, a slight irritation in his tone.

Marianne nodded and hurried out after him, but for some reason the incident had cast a shadow over her spurt of optimism like a cloud suddenly covering the sun.

He knew that she was looking at him even in the darkness that shrouded them from all the other cinema goers. That was good. As his lips curled upwards the hit man wondered what the woman would make of the thoughts that prompted that smile. He had hardly mentioned Brogan; just a couple of questions thrown out casually. *Hope my old pal Billy might be around next time I'm up in Glasgow.* And, later, *When did you last see your bad wee brother?* That had been said with a grin that was meant to tell her that Max knew the score with Billy Brogan. He'd seen something like relief in Marianne's face: this old friend, Max Whittaker, was straight but didn't hold Billy's wayward lifestyle against his sister. It had been a nice little conjuring trick, letting her think that he understood how she felt.

His grin widened. If only she knew what had really prompted that smile. Should she manage to make contact with Brogan, the dealer would be happily surprised that Max Whittaker had turned up out of the blue. Billy Boy hadn't seen or heard from Max for years, thankfully.

The hit man chuckled to himself. Private Whittaker might be dead and gone, one of the casualties of the Afghan conflict, but his name still had its uses.

He laid a casual arm across the back of the seat, fingering Marianne's long red hair, feeling her body edge closer to his own.

This was a different sort of war he was involved in now, and there would doubtless be more casualties before the end, but whether this woman was to be numbered amongst them depended on his new paymasters.

CHAPTER 34

'Sahid Jaffrey. Aged forty-nine. Lived at 20 Maxwell Road. No previous convictions,' Detective Sergeant Wilson looked up at the team as he recited the dead man's statistics. 'And that's just because he was good at ducking and diving,' he continued grimly.

'How's that?' DC Fathy asked, puzzled.

'Ach, Jaffrey was pretty well known to us,' Wilson explained. 'Used to be a small-time dealer. Rumour has it his missus threatened to turn him in so he went straight. Sort of. But we know he'd maintained links with some of his old mates. Worked to our advantage and he was one of the more reliable snouts on our books. In fact,' he sighed heavily, shaking his head as he turned to address the entire team, 'he was the one who was instrumental in telling us about Brogan.'

'But I thought it was from a call box,' Fathy frowned.

'Aye, that was just for the record, son. See, we don't give away our sources that easily. One trip to court and Jaffa would have been a sitting duck for the bad guys.'

'Well it looks as though it was one of the bad guys who found out that he'd been dealing with us,' Lorimer broke in. 'Those knife injuries to his knees suggest a very personal sort of punishment.'

It was two days since the discovery of Jaffrey's body. The

officers from K Division had sent in a forensic team to the Gleniffer Braes where the body had been examined then taken to Glasgow City mortuary. The SIO on the case, DI James Martin, had been astute enough to recognise DS Wilson's name from the stack of cards inside the dead man's wallet. Now the two divisions were collaborating on the man's death since it could very well have some link to Scott and the men in Brogan's flat.

'DI Martin's Family Liaison Officer has told us something else that might be of interest,' Wilson went on. 'Seems like Jaffrey junior's been doing his gap year over in Spain.' He paused to let his words sink in. 'A place in Mallorca called Cala Millor.'

'So that's the link with Brogan!' DS Cameron exclaimed. 'I wondered how on earth he had that sort of information.'

'We need to speak to the boy as soon as possible. Family Liaison have advised us of his return flight,' Lorimer nodded to Wilson. 'We have to lift him the moment he steps off that plane. Okay?'

Thomson Holidays had asked their passengers returning from Palma if any of them would give up their seat to a young man whose father had died suddenly. The airlines had a special budget for such acts of compassion and an obliging lone traveller could sometimes find himself with an extra day's holiday plus a few hundred quid to spend. Such a person had not been hard to find and Jaffrey junior was now booked to fly home, arriving at Glasgow International Airport later that evening.

'What about Mrs Jaffrey?' DC Irvine asked. 'Do we know what she's told Family Liaison so far?'

Wilson shrugged and spread his hands in a *who knows* gesture. 'She certainly didn't report him as a missing person. And the pathologist reckons he's been dead for several days.'

'I think it's a good idea to speak to her before the boy gets home. Otherwise he'll maybe do all the talking for her,' Lorimer said.

There was a murmur of agreement in the room. It was well known that many Asian families continued the tradition of the male being head of the family, the woman often choosing to be subservient to him. With the death of her husband, Mrs Jaffrey might well look to her teenage son to speak on her behalf.

Annie Irvine made a face. There weren't many women nowadays who'd let their men folk get off with that sort of behaviour. She thought back to Mrs Galbraith. There was one mother who hadn't minced her words. Would Mrs Jaffrey have the courage to tell the police anything she knew about her dead husband and his secrets?

She was suddenly aware that the DCI was looking in her direction.

'Irvine. You and DC Fathy go and see her,' Lorimer told them. 'See what you can find out.'

Mrs Jaffrey opened the door just wide enough to let the chain tighten. DC Irvine saw a tiny woman, caught sight of a dark purple sari banded with a design of red and gold, a matching scarf covering her head. But it was the expression of fear in the woman's eyes that caught the policewoman's attention.

'DC Fathy, DC Irvine, Strathclyde Police, ma'am,' Fathy said, holding his warrant card out in front of him.

The woman was silent as she fiddled with the chain, hands visibly shaking. The two officers exchanged glances. She was still in a state of shock and no wonder. A missing husband who had turned up brutally murdered was enough to numb the mind of any anxious spouse. The door was pulled back as though by a tremendous effort and as they stepped in, Mrs Jaffrey swayed where she stood.

Annie caught the woman's sleeve before she could collapse.

'Come on, dear, through here,' she whispered, guiding her back along the corridor to where she could see a glint of light under a door. Under Annie's grip, the woman felt like a thin bundle of bones hidden beneath the swathes of clothing. There was no one else in the house and Annie wondered when this woman had last eaten anything. The brightly lit room turned out to be the woman's bedroom and Annie reckoned from the state of the place that Sara Jaffrey had been lying in her bed, fully clothed, when they'd rung the doorbell.

'Here, sit down, are you okay?' Annie asked, helping the Asian woman into a chair beside her unmade bed. A tumbler of water lay on the bedside cabinet and Annie picked it up, setting its rim to the woman's lips, letting her swallow until she began to splutter. Mrs Jaffrey gave a little cough then murmured something that Annie couldn't catch. As though exhausted, she leaned back, her eyes staring wildly at the two officers.

'Have you got him?' she asked, clasping her hands to her chin in a gesture that was so pitiful that it made Annie bite her lip.

'Have you found my husband?'

Annie looked up at Fathy. *This was going to be a hard one*, his expression said.

'Make some tea,' she hissed at him, then, taking the other woman's hands in her own, Annie knelt down beside her.

'Mr Jaffrey's been found, Sara. He's not coming back, though. You know that, don't you?'

The black eyes full of tears stared at Annie uncomprehendingly. 'You'll find him, yes?'

Annie shook her head. 'He's not coming back, Sara,' she repeated gently. 'The other officers who came here, they told you that, didn't they?'

Sara Jaffrey continued to look at DC Irvine, eyes wide with disbelief then the first tears brimmed over and a quiet keening noise issued from her lips.

'We have to ask you things about your husband, Sara,' Annie continued gently. 'But if it's too much we can always come back?'

The woman looked blank for a moment then gave a ripple of sobs that ended in a long sigh.

'What can I tell you?' she replied, her voice thick with emotion.

'When did Mr Jaffrey disappear?' Annie asked.

There was a short pause and Annie realised that Sara Jaffrey was probably struggling to remember what day of the week it was.

'He didn't come home on Friday night,' she said at last. 'My son . . .' she broke off as Fathy entered bearing a tray of steaming mugs. 'No, thank you,' she said, a tremulous smile directed at the handsome young Egyptian. 'Perhaps later . . .'

Fathy set the tray down on a small table next to the chair and stood beside the door, nodding his compliance at the two women. With Fathy in the room a small change had come over Jaffrey's widow; a man commanded respect and she should comply with that, her straightening back and folded hands seemed to say.

'You were telling us when you saw your husband?' Annie prompted the woman once more.

Sara Jaffrey drew her scarf a little closer to her face in a gesture that both officers recognised: there was something she wanted to keep from them.

'My son thought his daddy would come home soon,' she said at last, casting her eyes downwards.

Perhaps that was half a truth, Annie thought. More likely she'd been told not to contact the police.

'So you didn't worry?'

Sara Jaffrey's eyes flashed and they caught a flicker of indignation. 'Of course, I worried!' she told them. 'What am I? A wife without feelings?'

'But your son told you not to worry, surely? Didn't he, Sara?' Fathy said, adopting an utterly reasonable tone.

'Yes, he did,' Sara agreed.

'What was he doing out in Mallorca, Sara?' Fathy asked.

'Oh, he was on his gap year,' the woman told them, her voice more confident now that she thought they were on safer ground. 'My Rashid will be going to Caledonian University,' she added proudly.

'And he bumped into an old family friend while he was there, didn't he?' Annie said.

Sara Jaffrey gave a little frown as though she were unable to remember.

'Billy Brogan, Mr Jaffrey's good friend,' Annie prompted, smiling.

The woman's face cleared. 'Ah, yes. Mr Brogan is big family friend,' she nodded. 'Well liked by many of our neighbours, here in Pollokshields.'

'Just a coincidence that he was taking a wee holiday while Rashid was there, then?'

Sara frowned again, looking from one to the other. But whatever she saw in the two officers' faces must have reassured her. 'Yes, of course. Rashid had no idea that he was there. We thought . . .' she put her hand to her mouth as though she had already said too much.

'Yes, Sara, where did you think Mr Brogan would have been instead?'

But the woman was looking away now, fingers fidgeting on her lap.

'How about that cup of tea?' Annie suggested. 'Then maybe you can tell us more about Billy, eh?'

Solly sat with his head in his hands, staring at the pattern on the carpet. For the life of him he could not begin to understand what the woman had meant.

'She said she was grateful to me,' he murmured.

'Well maybe she meant that you'd been a great teacher?' Rosie suggested.

Solly raised his head and looked mournfully at his wife. 'No. It was more than that.'

His sigh seemed to fill the room. 'Lorimer reckons I saw her the day after her husband was killed.' He raised his eyebrows in a mute appeal.

'So what does that tell you?'

'I don't know,' Solly shook his head. 'She was so . . .' his eyes lost their focus as he paused to remember. 'Animated. Yes, that's the right word, I think. Quite unlike the student I recalled from our seminars,' he insisted.

'And you think she was happy for a reason?' Rosie asked slowly. 'If her husband had been stalking her and she knew that he was dead, maybe that would be cause enough,' she went on.

'But why thank me? I didn't stop any of the things in her life,' Solly replied, though in truth he was speaking more to himself now than to Rosie.

'No, there's more to it than this,' Solly nodded.

'Well you've told the police all you can,' Rosie continued reasonably. 'And it confirms that Marianne was still in Glasgow after Scott was killed.'

'She must have been living in constant fear,' Solly went on. 'That's why there was no trace of her name on the university register. Somehow she managed to slip through that particular net, though God knows how she did it.'

'Well, it's in Lorimer's hands now,' Rosie said, her tone hinting that the subject ought to be closed. She looked over at her husband, noting that expression of concentration she knew only too well. 'Come on, Solly,' she wheedled. 'It's not your case. Strathclyde Police aren't hiring you for this one, remember?' But as the psychologist continued to stare into space, Rosie knew that her words were falling on deaf ears. Solomon Brightman had decided that he was involved in this woman's fate and in the death of her ex-husband. And Rosie knew in her heart that this time it wasn't a matter of being brought in to dispassionately examine a case. This time it was personal.

'Doctor Brightman saw her in the bookshop,' Lorimer said. He was sitting opposite Superintendent Mitchison, the afternoon sun shut out behind the vertical blinds so that what light there was made faded shadows over the room. Being in this room was like being inside one of these old sepia photographs, Lorimer decided, the furnishings were all browns and tans, even those colours being leached out by the lack of daylight.

'A coincidence,' Mitchison said, nodding his head as though it had been Lorimer who had suggested as much and he was simply agreeing with him.

'It places her in a specific place and time,' Lorimer went on, trying not to show the irritation that he felt. 'We believe Scott may have been stalking his wife prior to his death,' he continued.

Mitchison smiled, his eyes narrowing. 'It's usually the one who is stalked that ends up dead,' he laughed mirthlessly. 'So how does this give you any more information about who killed Scott?'

'Marianne Scott's brother disappears suddenly,' Lorimer said.

'She goes to ground.' He raised his hands. 'Isn't it possible that they were in it together?'

'You think Brogan killed his former brother-in-law to stop him following his sister around?' Mitchison's voice was full of derision. 'Come on, Lorimer. That's the most risible theory I've heard in a long time. Brogan's a known drug dealer who's been lucky enough not to have been caught. Two men dead in his flat, remember?' he sneered. 'Or have you forgotten that little matter? It's about drugs,' he added, clenching a fist and tapping it lightly on his desk as though he were reminding a foolish pupil of the correct way to do his homework. 'When the Spanish police finally bring Brogan to ground then you'll see I'm right,' he nodded again. 'Till then I don't want to hear any more nonsense about Doctor Brightman and his theories. He's not on our payroll, remember?'

Lorimer strode out of the building and headed for his car. He was still seething after his encounter with Mitchison. The man was a total prat, he told himself. Hidebound by budgetary constraints, blinkered by his desire to see every other murder case in terms of drug dealing. Okay so the city was awash with the stuff. And there were always demands to show that the police were tackling crime of that sort. What Mitchison wanted was a difference in statistics, something to boast about. But did he really think that one less dealer on the street would equate to a drop in drug usage? Aye, right, Lorimer thought cynically. Mitchison hadn't even given consideration to the facts. There were signs that a hit man had been used to effect at least three of the killings. Okay, so Sahid Jaffrey's murder showed a different MO. But he'd had dealings with Brogan, hadn't he? Mitchison hadn't even bothered to acknowledge that connection.

But even as he drove out of the car park, Lorimer realised that the two senior officers were at loggerheads for a very different reason. The superintendent wanted the figures to add up while all that Lorimer wanted right now was to find a dangerous killer and justice for his victims.

CHAPTER 35

Marianne woke from a dreamless sleep. Her eyelids flickered, their grittiness making her blink. The room was bathed in sunlight, fine cotton curtains blowing gently at an open window. She looked around, wondering for a moment where she was, feeling more relaxed than she had for years. As her eyes registered the rumpled sheets Marianne saw the hollow in the pillow where his head had rested next to hers.

'Max,' she said aloud, savouring the name. It was a word redolent with possibilities: *maximise, maximum* . . . surely it mirrored that feeling of complete satisfaction that flowed over her right now? Their coupling had surprised her, mainly because it had happened at all. Somehow he dispelled all her fearfulness, treating her like an ordinary woman whose desires matched his own. Her hunger for his body had shown how starved she had been for the merest affection.

Marianne frowned. Amit had been kind to her, shown her an innate courtesy, hinted that he, too, might release that pent-up need that had been locked inside her for so long. But they had made a pact, hadn't they? The tiny creases on her brow smoothed out as a smile appeared on her lips, in her eyes. Amit was almost history now. Max, she thought, hugging her arms around her cold shoulders, was her future.

There had been no restless night punctuated by smothering dreams, a good omen surely? Even Amit had featured in her nightmares, encouraging her to distrust the gentle Asian whose destiny had become entwined with her own.

A faint peeping sound from the handbag across the room made her stiffen. Someone was trying to call her mobile. She laughed as she remembered; Max had her number. Perhaps he'd gone out for some food and was wondering what she would like. Drawing a sheet around her naked body, Marianne tiptoed across the room, fishing the mobile from her bag.

'Hi,' she said, waiting to hear Max's English accent. But it was a voice far more familiar than her new lover's.

'*Billy?*' Marianne clutched the phone closer to her ear. 'Where the hell are you?'

Billy Brogan was sitting in a small pool of shade under a tree, watching as an army of ants circled madly beside his feet. He shifted his bottom then swept the frenzied insects away with his foot, sending them tumbling down in a small cloud of grey dust.

'I'm in trouble, Marianne,' he said solemnly.

'You can say that again,' his sister answered tartly.

'No, I mean real trouble. The police are after me. They think I had something to do with Fraz and Gubby . . . I mean, come on . . . would I do anything like that?'

There was a pause and he began to fidget, watching the ants regroup to return their assault. Did she really think he had anything to do with these killings?

'I know,' Marianne said at last and he heard her sigh. 'Things haven't been exactly fine here either,' she said dryly. 'Anyhow, where are you? Why haven't you been in touch?'

Brogan sniffed, putting out a foot to bar the ants' progress. 'I'm in Algeria,' he said at last.

'*What?*'

'Algeria. It's a long story. Remind me to tell you some time if I ever get out of this godforsaken place. Anyway, I need your help. Are you listening?'

'Aye, go on,' Marianne replied, a trace of wonder in her tone.

'See if you can find the Hundi for me. He'll fix things.'

'Like he fixed things for Amit?'

'Look, that was okay, wasn't it? You did no' too bad out of that arrangement, eh?'

'And how am I supposed to find him? Look up directory enquiries?' the sarcasm in his sister's voice made Billy sigh.

'Ach, okay, I know he plays this hard-to-get act. See if you can locate him through Amit.'

There was another pause then Marianne said quietly, 'I'm not seeing Amit any more, Billy. That's all over now.'

'Oh, well.' He stopped to think then said, 'Go and find Jaffa. You know where he lives, don't you? He'll arrange for you to see the Hundi.'

'How can I contact you again?' Marianne asked anxiously. 'You left without even telling me what was going on,' she added. 'I know you've changed your mobile. C'mon, Billy. What's your new number? I need to know,' she insisted, angry with him now that the shock was subsiding. 'What if we get cut off?'

'I'll call you, okay?'

'Right,' she said, then there was another pause that her brother took to mean that the conversation was over.

Billy grinned and clicked off his mobile, standing up and shaking a few ants from the hem of his trousers.

He never heard her last words telling him about his old friend or that Max Whittaker had been asking after him. Stepping out into the blazing African sun, he adjusted his shades and sauntered towards a group of dark-skinned boys who were lying in wait for him. One of them held the rope tether of a sleepy-looking donkey in his small fist.

'Taxi,' they yelled as he strode past their outstretched hands, 'air-conditioned taxi!'

Brogan grinned as their yells surrounded him. The donkey was the only air-conditioned taxi they possessed, but he appreciated their sense of humour all the same.

It was not long past midday and the streets were thronging with people. Entering the narrow bazaar was like running the gauntlet, hands tugging at his loose sleeves, eager faces turned his way, voices shouting as the vendors tried to entice Brogan to sample their wares. The noise was deafening, donkeys braying, *tuk-tuk*s puttering round the adjacent streets and the occasional camel train sauntering past, the animals looking disdainfully down their rounded noses. His feet were sore and dusty from the long days walking since he had been abandoned at the village, and all that Billy Brogan wanted now was a bottle of cold mineral water, preferably one with its cap still intact. Above him the daylight was obscured by goods hanging high on wooden rails that crossed from one side of the alleyway to the other, a selection of *galabayas* floating like headless dolls, their hems richly bordered in designs of golden thread. Vendors in white robes or European dress sat at the entrances to their tiny shops, every inch of space crammed full of goods, selections of garishly printed T-shirts suspended from unseen hooks. Some shops had windows made of glass behind which Brogan could see large brass lamps, hexagonal tables and cabinets inlaid with mother-of-pearl and jewellery twinkling against velvet stands, too expensive to risk being at the mercy of passers-by, too enticing for the tourists to ignore. Most, though, were open to prospective purchasers, three sides of a small, high space stacked high with linens, basket works, vegetables and spices.

Brogan paused for a moment beside a tea and spice vendor who was relaxing with a sheesha, its red and gold pipes connected to the bubbling pot beside him. Packets of warm spices were stacked into the shelves of a wooden cart behind him; saffron, fenugreek, cinnamon and chilli next to less familiar packets of bright blue and muddy green, fragrant smells tickling his nostrils, making him suddenly homesick for a curry in dear old Glasgow. A large basket sat on the ground at the vendor's side, full of some dried flowers the colour of old blood. Herbs of every hue packed in clear plastic dominated an entire wall of the shop and several feet above them was a rail of the ubiquitous cotton T-shirts and signs in Arabic that Brogan could not understand.

'Water?' he asked, shuffling to one side away from a group of men who were coming towards them down the narrow street, one of them so fat that he was like a huge ship in full sail under his galabaya.

The vendor followed Brogan's eyes as the men passed them by.

'Water?' Brogan repeated.

The man grinned at him, showing a set of stained and cracked teeth, then handed over the sheesha as he rose.

Brogan looked at the pipe suspiciously. He wouldn't half mind a wee puff of the old sheesh, but the buzz of flies rising from a stain on the ground made him wary. His stomach was still delicate from the boat trip and the unfamiliar food he had eaten over the last few days, so he wiped the end of the pipe with the hem of his shirt before he took it between his lips.

The vendor returned, a bottle of ice cold water in his hands, its plastic surface dewed with droplets as though he had just taken it from a cooler in the back of the shop.

'How much?' Brogan asked, offering a handful of cents.

The vendor's grin widened as he selected some of the coins.

'American?' he asked.

'Naw, pal, Scottish,' Brogan replied. Then, seeing the puzzled look on the other man's face he laid down the bottle and sketched an impromptu Highland Fling, miming a set of bagpipes under his armpit.

The vendor giggled and clapped. 'Scoteesh!' he said, then nodded as Brogan took the water and headed back into the crush of bodies.

Other eyes followed the Scotsman's progress as he made his way through the bazaar, wondering if a man who didn't haggle over the price was worth the bother of chasing for a few yards to offer their bargains.

Brogan tightened his grip on the pack. He had swung it to the front of his body before entering the street, fearing any light fingers that might slip under its straps. It contained everything he owned, though his money and passport were carefully secreted about his person, his mobile shoved to the bottom of his hip pocket. The man in the hotel had told him to look for a sign at the far end of the bazaar. He would see a goldsmith's shop then an opening into another street. That was where he would find the travel agent's office.

Sure enough, the familiar green sign loomed ahead, advising passers-by that here was the agency of American Express.

'My son works there,' the hotel manager had told him. 'He will be able to help you with tickets,' he had nodded, looking at Brogan suspiciously as though the request to purchase rail tickets was something illicit. But a couple of dollar bills had changed the man's expression to one of ineffable sweetness and he had been only too eager to give Brogan directions to someone who might escort him to the ticket office as his translator.

The city of Algiers was not somewhere that Brogan wanted to stay in for much longer. Too many foreign faces made the Scotsman uneasy, too many jabbering voices talking in a tongue he would never understand. Even the French words were beyond him; Billy Brogan's limited experience at school hardly progressing beyond *parlez-vous français?* So it was with some relief that the dealer passed the swinging sign into the travel bureau, the young man grinning as he came forward, hand outstretched.

'Train ticket to Marrakesh?' the guy was asking as he ushered Billy into the back shop. 'You got a passport?'

'Aye,' Brogan replied and the young man nodded his approval.

'Come,' he said, beckoning towards a door that led out into a narrow alley. 'Quicker this way.' He grinned again, his dark skin complementing a set of fine white teeth. 'No crowds here,' he explained.

Brogan followed him out along the shaded street. Piles of wooden pallets were stacked at several of the closed doors, bags of rubbish at others, colonies of flies buzzing madly at every untidy heap. A small yellow cat darted past, making Brogan jump: it was little bigger than some of the rats Billy had seen in the Glasgow slums when he'd been peddling gear to junkies. A thin trickle of something that might be water ran down the slope towards them and Brogan stepped over it, shuddering; the smells here were sour and fetid, no doubt wafting up from the rubbish discarded in these bin bags.

'Here,' the hotel manager's son motioned to Brogan as they stopped outside the back door of yet another shop. It looked like all the others save for the fact that its entry was not obscured by any garbage.

The lad knocked the door and they waited for what seemed like several minutes until a grating sound showed the door being opened. Brogan peered into the dim interior, his eyes trying to focus. Gradually he made out three steps below him and a figure who stood at their foot, waiting.

'Ticket office,' the young man encouraged him, smiling and waving his hands to usher Brogan forwards.

But in the split second that it took Brogan to sense that something was wrong here, the man below had leapt forwards, grasping Brogan's arm and dragging him into the darkness.

CHAPTER 36

DCI Lorimer stood in the arrivals hall of Glasgow International Airport watching the automatic doors as the trickle of passengers became a steady stream. Young Jaffrey's flight had landed some time ago and many of his fellow passengers had already made their way from the baggage carousels to this inauspicious part of the airport. To one side was a small coffee shop, its chairs probably occupied by folk waiting for family and friends, their gaze shifting from the arrivals board to these frosted glass doors. An avenue of sorts had been created between rows of seating on one side and the bookshop on the other for the passengers to wheel their luggage out, families hovering as close as they dared to the doors that were now constantly opening and closing with a sibilant swish.

He saw Rashid Jaffrey the moment he stepped out into the brightly lit hall. The boy was dressed in wide-fitting jeans that had abandoned their hold on his waistline, sliding down well past the edge of a pair of black boxers and causing him to shuffle along, his trainers almost hidden by the ragged hems. It was the fashion still for some youths to wear their jeans like this, Lorimer knew, and looking at Jaffrey he suddenly felt not just old-fashioned but simply old. With his fortieth birthday looming ever closer, the policeman could not help but reflect that he was nearer in age to Jaffrey's late father than to his son.

'Rashid?'

The boy stopped in his tracks, letting the handle of his pull-along suitcase rest against the edge of a seat.

'DCI Lorimer. Strathclyde Police. Thought you might be able to spare us a few minutes before you go home,' he added gravely.

Rashid looked into Lorimer's blue gaze, his own dark eyes widening in a moment of panic but then he looked down at his feet and gave a shrug. The gesture seemed to say he wasn't bothered one way or the other but Lorimer, who knew how to read body language better than most, saw the sagging shoulders and guessed that the lad was bowing to the inevitable. He stepped alongside the boy, ushering him out into the Glasgow night and across to a waiting police car.

'We've got a family liaison officer with your mum,' Lorimer told him as they settled back for the drive into the city. 'But I'm sure she'll be glad to have you back home again as soon as we're finished.'

Rashid nodded mutely and turned his face away as though to reacquaint himself with the bustling motorway and the skyline over Paisley.

'Sorry about your dad,' Lorimer added, touching the boy's shoulder. Rashid flinched as though he had been stung but Lorimer affected not to notice, continuing in the same friendly tone as before.

'How was the flight?'

Rashid half turned back towards the man at his side and looked at him for a long moment as though he were reassessing this tall policeman.

'Okay, I suppose. The flight attendants were nice . . .' he broke off but not before Lorimer could hear the sound of a smothered sob in his voice. Being nice to the newly bereaved was almost guaranteed to bring their emotions to the surface. It was something he remembered from his own experience. He'd been younger than Rashid when his own dad had died and he could still recall the solicitude of various aunts and neighbours and his own useless efforts to remain tearless.

'Mallorca must be great this time of year,' Lorimer went on, deliberately making small talk to bore the lad into a semblance of calm. 'Cala Millor, wasn't it?'

'Aye,' Rashid nodded, stifling a yawn.

'Thought Cala d'Or might've been more up your street, young lad like you,' Lorimer joked. 'More nightlife, eh?' he smiled conspiratorially. 'How come you ended up in a quiet place like that, then?'

Rashid turned away once again, the shrug meaning that he wasn't going to answer that particular question.

'Of course, you've got family over there, haven't you?' Lorimer said, slapping his knee as if the thought had just come back into his head.

'Aye. My uncle's got a business and I've been giving him a hand over the summer,' Rashid replied with a sigh.

'Nice way to spend a gap year,' Lorimer continued. 'Lucky you, having family there. You'll be able to go whenever you fancy, I suppose?'

'S'pose,' Rashid echoed.

They were entering the approach to the city now, signs from the overhead gantries advising drivers to keep a safe distance from other vehicles, rows of red tail lights twinkling ahead out of the inky blue darkness.

'Funny running into Billy Brogan like that,' Lorimer mused.

Rashid gave him a sharp look but the policeman's face seemed so completely innocent of guile that the boy nodded. 'Aye, it was. Could've knocked me down with a feather, like, when I saw him walking along the market. Know what I mean?'

Lorimer smiled but said nothing, giving the boy a chance to elaborate on his story. 'My dad had been trying to phone him for ages and getting no reply so I called him and told him I'd clocked Brogan on his holidays,' he added with just a hint of smugness.

'Funny how a chance encounter can have such far-reaching consequences,' Lorimer murmured.

'How d'you mean?' The boy's eyes were wary.

'Well, there you are minding your own . . . sorry, your uncle's . . . business and along comes the very person your father had been looking for.'

'Yeah, coincidence, yeah,' Rashid agreed.

'Then someone else decides that it wasn't such a good idea of your dad's to tell *us* where to find Brogan,' Lorimer said. His tone was light but there was a steeliness of authority in his voice that made Rashid shift uneasily in his seat.

'It wasn't my fault that happened!' the boy protested. 'I just wanted to tell Dad where he could find Brogan so's he could tell . . .' he stopped suddenly, mouth still open wide.

'So he could tell someone else?' Lorimer asked.

The boy nodded unhappily into his hands.

'I think we should carry on this conversation on a more official basis, Rashid,' Lorimer told him. 'There's quite a lot we'd like to know about what Brogan's been up to lately.'

The Hundi paced up and down, glancing from time to time at the large watch on his left wrist. The man was late in calling in and the Hundi was not used to being kept waiting, especially for those who

284

were numbered on his payroll. It wouldn't do, he told himself, turning his well-shod foot on the thick Persian carpet, it wouldn't do at all. Smith, or whatever his real name was, should have been in touch hours ago and his lack of contact was making the Hundi clench and unclench his fists as he made yet another circuit of the room.

Their friend, Amit, had become more and more nervous since the woman's disappearance, thinking no doubt that she had suffered a similar fate to that of Sahid Jaffrey. No amount of reassurances from Dhesi or indeed from the Hundi himself, had helped but perhaps the company of Dhesi's niece, newly arrived from Lahore, might help to distract the wealthy businessman. Amit was one of their own now, Dhesi had insisted, and it was important that he make a good marriage, settle down and become part of their growing community. Nalini was just the tonic for a lonely man adrift in a strange land. The Hundi grinned. He remembered the girl's luxuriant hair caught up in a net of tiny sparkling jewels, her lovely doe eyes lowered demurely as Dhesi had made the introductions. There were no parents left to arrange a marriage to a suitable man, just Uncle Dhesi with his generous dowry and his good friend, the Hundi, who would see that Nalini's future was secured. It would be a good marriage and serve to bind Amit even closer to his new friends.

But first Marianne had to be found. He looked at his watch again, shaking his wrist impatiently as though somehow it was the fault of the Rolex that Mr Smith had failed to keep his telephone appointment. The furrow on the man's brow deepened. Smith was a professional, anyone could see that. So why was he so late in calling in the latest news about his assignment: an assignment that would sever the tie between Amit and Marianne for good.

Rashid was tired beyond anything he had ever felt before. The emotions that had surfaced during the journey and the unexpected

285

trip downtown to these police headquarters had taken their toll and now all the boy wanted was to go home, see his mum and fall into bed, hopefully to a dreamless sleep. Informing that tall policeman with the kind voice all about Brogan hadn't been what Rashid intended at all. But those hypnotic blue eyes seemed to be telling him that the policeman already knew much more than he was letting on so it had all come tumbling out. He cursed himself softly as the tears began to flow. Maybe playing at informant was something that ran in this family. What was the point of hiding it any more, anyway? Dad was dead and, when he'd spoken to her on the phone, his mum had sounded so different from the bustling little woman she'd been when he'd left home just a few months ago. What could anyone do to him to make life worse?

Lorimer's blue eyes seemed kindled with a pale fire as he read over Rashid's statement. Now they were getting somewhere!

The DCI looked up, hearing a small knock on his door.

'Fathy. Still here? Come in,' Lorimer beckoned the detective constable to a seat opposite his desk.

'Anything I can do for you or would you like to see this?' Lorimer grinned making his face suddenly younger and less careworn. 'It's young Jaffrey's account of Billy Brogan's recent activities,' he continued.

'Right!' Fathy leaned towards his boss, his own face lighting up, infected by the mood of renewed optimism. 'I was going to . . . but it doesn't matter. May I . . .?'

Lorimer handed over the sheets of paper and folded his arms, watching to see the younger officer's reaction.

Fathy looked up, his eyebrows raised in astonishment. 'Brogan was dealing with big, big money,' he said at last. 'And young Jaffrey reckons he's scarpered off to the continent owing . . . how much?' he looked at the paper again as though unable to believe his eyes. 'That's not possible, surely?'

Lorimer nodded. 'We think Brogan's been acting for certain members of the Asian community as a conduit for the proceeds of some VAT fraud. And yes, these figures are probably correct. We're talking huge sums, here.' He leaned forward again, steepling his fingers against his chin. 'Brogan buys and sells drugs in quantity. We've suspected for a long time that much of the heroin coming into the city was down to a middleman like him but till now Brogan was thought of as fairly small beer, a dealer in hashish, mainly.'

'Rashid Jaffrey says he was responsible for all of the drugs coming into Pollokshields. How would he know that?' Fathy asked.

'He's probably exaggerating. I can't see one man having such a grip on the supply. But go on, read what Jaffrey tells us about why Brogan left in such a hurry.'

Fathy bent his head obediently and skimmed the rest of the young man's statement. He handed it back to Lorimer in silence.

'Galbraith and Sandiman were owed money, as well as members of the Asian community that young Jaffrey has refused to name,' Lorimer said. 'According to the boy, Brogan siphoned off all of the profits of his trade into some scheme that went wrong. You can see how he was either genuinely hazy on the details or he's keeping something back. I'm inclined to think he really doesn't know what happened to Brogan's money.'

'So Brogan skips to avoid paying his debts . . .'

'. . . and just happens to have the bad luck to run into young Rashid when he's over in Mallorca.'

'But where does that leave us with Galbraith and Sandiman?'

Lorimer nodded and gave a sigh. 'Aye, that's one thing we know now. Given the timing it's pretty certain that Brogan couldn't have killed them. And it probably means he didn't pull the trigger that killed Scott.'

'So, what . . .?' Fathy spread his hands in a questioning gesture.

'What it means,' Lorimer said slowly, 'is that we're looking for a professional hit man. Assuming Brogan was the killer, given his experience from his ex-army days, may have thrown us off on completely the wrong direction.'

'So, hunting for Marianne Brogan was all a waste of time?' Disappointment sounded in the young man's voice.

'No, I don't think that at all,' Lorimer countered. 'She may well hold the key to her ex-husband's death. *And* to her brother's present whereabouts. Electing to vanish as effectively as she has shows that she has plenty to hide,' he nodded. 'And so continuing to locate her is still one of our top priorities.'

Fathy listened, noting his boss's words. It was almost as though Lorimer were rehearsing what to say to his own superior, choosing his words for maximum effect.

'Anyway,' Lorimer said suddenly, 'what did you want to see me about?'

Fathy smiled a tired smile and shrugged. 'Nothing that can't wait, sir. Thanks.'

The Hundi tipped back his head and swallowed the last of the whisky then set down the heavy crystal glass. He was sitting on the pale beige leather settee that was squashed to one side under the man's bulk, a deep frown creasing his forehead.

There had been no phone call. And now the Asian was beginning to wonder whose side this man called Smith was really on.

CHAPTER 37

'I'm worried,' Solly said, turning away from the window, the brightness from the setting sun's last rays making him blink owlishly behind his horn-rimmed spectacles.

'It's that girl, Marianne, isn't it?' asked Rosie, shifting her position on the easy chair. Despite the cushions wedged at her back the discomfort from the Braxton Hicks had continued all afternoon. Her mouth twisted in a small grimace; nobody told you about the minutiae of pregnancy, did they? Until you read up on the baby manuals, it was all a bit of a mystery, even for a qualified medic like herself.

Solly stood with his back to the window, his face now in shadow. Sometimes, Rosie thought, he was too concerned about the frailties of human suffering for his own good. She smiled at him, a sudden tenderness welling up inside her. He was so generous and kind to her, caring for her every need. And he'd be a splendid father – anyone could see that. She reached out a hand and Solly came over to where she sat, cuddling in at her side, his fingers lacing in her own.

'I keep wondering if it was something I did. Or said,' he murmured.

'What d'you mean?' Rosie asked.

'She said she was grateful to me . . . no . . . what were her exact words?' Solly broke off, frowning. A minute passed then his brow cleared and he sat up, his eyes bright. He turned to Rosie, and as he spoke she could hear the edge of excitement in his voice.

'She said she had a lot to thank me for. That was it!' he beamed, wagging his head. 'I thought she meant that I'd been a good teacher, or something like that. But there was . . . how can I put it? So much *more*. It was as though she was saying that I had helped her *personally*.' He stopped, a faint expression of embarrassment on his face. 'That sounds rather egotistical, doesn't it?'

'Go on,' Rosie urged. 'If you don't probe more deeply into this encounter you'll never arrive at the truth.'

Solly smiled at her fondly. His wife's words were an echo of what he himself had said on many occasions and hearing them coming back was an affirmation of just how close they had become as husband and wife.

'I remember Marianne as a faded, sad sort of young woman. So much so, that I hardly recognised her in the bookshop. She was . . .' he tailed off, trying again for the right word to describe the memory in his mind's eye. 'She was so *alive*,' he said at last. 'It was as though something wonderful had happened to change her from that nervy creature who sat through my seminars last session into a lovely, confident young woman.'

'Was it just an emotional change or was there something different about her appearance?' Rosie asked.

'Her hair,' Solly said simply. 'She has long red hair and it used to be scrunched up in a tight knot as if she didn't care about how she looked,' he said slowly. 'But that day it was loose and flowing, like some Pre-Raphaelite figure. Even her clothes had more colour,' he murmured, remembering.

'Sounds like she'd found a man,' Rosie laughed. 'Love does

that to a woman, you know,' she said, snuggling closer to Solly's side.

'But *I* was not that man,' Solly said. 'And she told me she had a lot to thank me for . . .'

'Didn't you lecture on love, maybe?' Rosie asked.

'Yes, the usual one I trot out on St Valentine's day,' Solly replied. 'But she was such a mouse-like creature all the way through the session. I don't think it could have been that.'

'What, then?' Rosie asked.

'I don't know,' Solly said slowly, 'but I'm determined to find out.' He looked at his wife who was beginning to yawn.

'Come on,' he said gently. 'Bed time for you. That child of ours is taking its toll tonight, isn't he?'

Marianne rolled over onto her side, listening. Max was breathing deeply and she watched him sleeping as his chest rose and fell. The faint veining on his eyelids began to flicker and Marianne could tell he was dreaming. Rapid eye movement, she thought, remembering Doctor Brightman's lectures. What was her lover dreaming about? Was it something from his past? Or simply a collage of the day's events? She smiled, thinking about their day away from the city. Max had told her his business could take a rest for a few days and that he needed a holiday, but Marianne suspected that he simply wanted to be with her.

Yesterday they had stood on deck as the ferry crossed from Wemyss Bay to the Isle of Bute, wind blowing her hair into a tangle until Max had told her she was a wild woman. He had drawn her closer to his side, murmuring that he liked wild women. Her heart had beaten faster at that and Marianne had felt such a sense of abandonment and freedom as she had never known before. This man would take her away from all the things that held her to the city, just like this ship sailing to the misty island. Wouldn't he?

She gazed at Max's sleeping form, noting the twitching eyelids. Perhaps, she thought fondly, he was dreaming of her?

Lorimer heard the tiny sigh that escaped his wife's lips and, though he knew she was sleeping, the sound made his heart ache for her. It was hard to think she would be undergoing major surgery so soon and his mouth narrowed as he began to imagine all the things that Maggie had not told him. She'd made light of the operation, telling him it was one of the most common procedures nowadays. But though she'd pasted on a smile, he had heard the fear in her voice. And not just fear, a despair that finally their hopes of having a family of their own would be gone for good. 'I'm too old anyway,' she'd joked, not saying what both of them knew, that mothers were becoming older and older these days as more women postponed the start of bearing children.

He'd wanted her to talk to Rosie but that suggestion had been met with a definite shake of Maggie's head. Seeing a friend who was carrying a longed-for child of her own was simply too much for Maggie to bear. Besides, his wife had reminded him sadly, Rosie should not be concerning herself with thoughts of the surgery to remove a womb; not when her own was doing what it was meant to do.

Lorimer sighed. It would all be over and done with in a few weeks' time, their lives continuing as before. Meantime he had other things to think about in the darkness of this night. Who had killed Sahid Jaffrey? And was that killing linked in any way to the men who had been shot in Brogan's flat? Ballistics had come up with some suppositions. One candidate for the murder weapon was a Glock self-loading pistol, possibly the model 19. The ballistics expert had given some details of a pistol suppressor, the Jupiter Eye, that was compatible to all 9mm pistols and how it might have been used in the first but not the second shooting. That made sense of the theory that Galbraith and Sandiman had been shot in a moment of random panic whereas Kenneth Scott's death bore the hallmarks of a premeditated and carefully planned assassination. Nothing had been heard by Scott's neighbours so a silencer had obviously been used, hadn't it?

Lorimer's thoughts chased themselves around his head like screaming children on a Ferris wheel, round and round in a rhythm that was beginning to make his head ache. It was no use. Sleep would be long in coming so he might as well be up and about, looking at the documents he had left downstairs one more time just to see if anything new occurred to him.

Chancer, the ginger cat, gave a meow of recognition from his basket under the kitchen table as Lorimer switched on the light.

'Hi, you,' Lorimer said softly, stroking the cat's fur as he passed by into the kitchen area. He took a bottle of mineral water from the fridge then padded quietly back to the desk by the window, already remembering the contents of the folder. The BBC's editorial people were totally on the ball when it came to briefing any officers before the *Crimewatch* programme. He flicked over the papers that had been downloaded from his office email address; everything that he needed was here. Everything, that is, except answers to the questions that were keeping him awake. It was not Lorimer's first visit to the BBC studios but much had changed in the programme since the last time he had made a public appeal during a murder inquiry, including the presenter. She was a Scots lass, bonny and blonde, but with a no-nonsense attitude that Lorimer enjoyed any time he had the chance to watch the programme. Tomorrow he and other members of the investigation team would be winging their way down south and expecting an overnight stay after the programme went out live. He flicked through the papers, wondering if this would be worth the time spent away from the investigation. Heaving a sigh, Lorimer reminded himself that the rest of the team wouldn't fall apart without him; they were all good officers, doing their best to come up with answers to the problems surrounding this case.

Lorimer rolled his shoulders, feeling the tension around his neck. The tick of the clock made him look up. It was only three thirty-six. He yawned, his eyes watering so that he had to rub away the tears. Maybe he should go back to bed after all, see if he could drop off for a few more hours. Suddenly the need to sleep overwhelmed him and he switched off the desk lamp then made his way up the darkened staircase.

Solomon Brightman woke with a renewed sense of purpose. Today he would find it, he told himself. Marianne had attended every one of his seminars and there were notes on all of the students' participation somewhere on file. They might help to jog some memory, Solly thought.

His own recollection of these hours was somewhat hazy, given the numbers of students who passed through his office every week. And Marianne had not been one of the most forthcoming of his undergraduates, had she? It was human nature to remember the ones who tended to be outgoing, funny even. One lad from Liverpool, Barry something-or-other, had a waggish sense of humour and each seminar that he attended was guaranteed to be lively. The fact that he had been in Marianne's seminar group was a tad unfortunate since the girl was more able to let herself do that vanishing-into-the-woodwork act that so many shy people liked to do. It was Solly's job, though, as their tutor, to try to draw them all out. But coaxing Marianne to participate had been an uphill struggle and Solly had to admit that in spite of his efforts she had let herself be overshadowed by more vocal types like Barry.

He was still in his pyjamas and dressing gown when Rosie passed his desk, handing him a mug of tea. Letting him concentrate while he worked on something was something his wife had learned to do and Solly was grateful for it, even though the tea that was silently given was often left to grow cold on the coaster beside his keyboard.

'Right,' he murmured to himself, scrolling down the file that he wanted to read. 'Let's see what we can see.'

Marianne's name had figured in every one of the seminars, her attendance perfect, unlike quite a few of her fellow students who seemed unable to get out of bed for that nine a.m. class. What had he written about her? Solly stroked his beard as he read the scant notes about the missing woman. Each seminar seemed to tell the same story; the psychologist repeatedly noting his suspicions that this particular student was a bit out of her depth and was struggling to keep up with the ebb and flow of conversation and arguments that enlivened the meetings. He sighed and shook his head. Was this all a complete waste of time?

Then the final seminar subject heading appeared on his screen: DREAMS.

Solly sat up, thumping one fist into his open palm.

How could he have forgotten?

It had been towards the end of the session, hadn't it? When examinations had been looming and students and staff alike had been under considerable pressure.

He read the notes he had written after the seminar.

At last!!! Marianne has come out of her shell. A topic that seems to interest her. Was more animated than at any other time in the session. Hope she has the sense to choose this in the exams.

And she had, he remembered. On examination day she had written a good essay on dreams. Did he still have it?

Solly sat still for a long moment. Anyone seeing the psychologist gazing at the wall in front of him might have been forgiven for thinking that he was absorbed in the picture above his desk. But it was not the little watercolour of New Zealand's snowy peaks that Solomon Brightman was seeing. Instead his eye was turned inwards to a different time and a different place.

Barry had been on good form that day, full of little quips dispelling the pre-examination tension that always seemed to build up then. They had been discussing the veracity of dreams, Solly remembered now. The psychologist had quoted passages from the Book of Genesis telling of Joseph's ability to interpret dreams and how he had saved the chief butler but had been unable to save the chief baker, who had been hanged. The conversation had centred around visions and their interpretation and Solly had been keen to point out the charlatans who had written so-called 'dream' books based on nothing more than random mixtures of symbolism and myth. Things had become quite heated during the seminar, with some of his students questioning just how far dreams could influence one's behaviour.

They had talked around the subject of death and premonitions, each one of them offering more lurid and fanciful stories until Marianne had spoken up.

'*What if you dream that someone is going to kill you?*' she had asked. Her tone had been so serious, Solly recalled. And now he remembered with shame the words he had spoken to her.

All he had wanted was to restore some light-heartedness to the seminar, hadn't he? And so he had answered back, '*Oh, bump them off first and then it can't happen,*' his quick riposte meeting with a general outburst of laughter. And, of course, he should have added *in the dream*, not in cold blood.

Solly sat very still, recalling every moment of that seminar. The girl had participated well up to that point but after his comment she had said nothing. But he remembered her eyes shining as she listened to the others.

He felt a chill growing over his bones.

What had he done?

I've got a lot to thank you for, she had said.

Was that it? Had that throwaway comment sown a seed within the girl's mind? She had been a different woman that day in the bookstore, the day following Scott's death. Surely she hadn't . . .?

Solly gave a sigh that became a groan. *A lot to thank you for*, the woman's voice echoed in his brain. His fingers clasped the mug of tea and he drank it slowly, grateful for the warmth seeping into his cold hands.

If this was what had happened, and surely it was a very large if, then he had to make some form of reparation. Solly blinked as if to waken himself from a reverie. It was such an odd thing that he knew a little of Marianne's history through his wife. The missing woman's former husband was dead, killed by a professional gunman, Rosie had told him. But he hadn't known then that it might have involved one of his own students.

Might even have involved *him*.

Solly shook his head again in disbelief. His own wife had performed the post-mortem on the ex-husband . . .

These two CID officers, the nice girl Annie Irvine and that handsome young Egyptian, hadn't been terribly forthcoming about the woman they were seeking. She had been hiding away from someone or something, managing to have her details erased from the data banks in registry. He would have to find out more.

Had he been part of the team ... but he wasn't wanted by Strathclyde Police right now, Solly reminded himself. Still, he mused, stroking his beard thoughtfully, that didn't preclude him from carrying out some investigations of his own, did it?

CHAPTER 38

DCI Lorimer and his fellow officers walked into the studio accompanied by a tiny girl who had assured them that she was indeed the producer's assistant even though she looked about fourteen. *I'm getting old*, Lorimer reminded himself yet again, looking around him. All of these runners and gofers looked as though they had been let out of school on a work experience project. Take this young lady, who was struggling to keep up with the policeman's stride; she was wearing a pair of thick black tights under a pair of dark grey denim shorts and a too-tight black knitted tank top over a white blouse with little puff sleeves. Her face seemed devoid of make-up and her dyed red hair was tied into a spiky ponytail with an elastic band. A wee lassie, Lorimer told himself. But the girl's appearance had been belied by her detailed knowledge of the programme that was to take place. She had to have a mature personality for something like this.

Lorimer grinned suddenly. Wasn't that what he was always telling his own officers to avoid doing? Judging someone on their appearance? His smile faded as he spotted the blown-up photograph of Marianne Scott née Brogan that would be going out on national television that evening. Glancing around, Lorimer saw other images being thrown up on a screen one after the other, a series of mug shots of men wanted for various criminal offences. Most of them were dark skinned and this alone made the tall policeman purse his lips and wonder why.

Had Britain been seen as the land of milk and honey for many of these fellows from overseas? And had they turned to lives of crime in their disillusionment? Who knew the answer to that one? He thought of DC Fathy and the young Egyptian's privileged back- ground. Frowning to himself, Lorimer began to wonder if the man had been targeted not for the colour of his skin at all but because he came from a wealthy family, unlike most of the officers who joined the police force. It was an angle worth considering, he told himself, mentally filing that thought away for future consideration.

'Detective Chief Inspector, how nice to meet you,' a slim blonde woman approached him. Lorimer took in the sleepy eyes that regarded him from under her long lashes and that curving smile. Kirsty Young put out her hand and he took it, noting the firm handshake and the way she looked so steadily at him as though they were quite alone and not surrounded by technicians, cameramen and youngsters passing in and out of the dark walled area. His first thought was what a great police officer this woman might make. There was something about her that reminded him of a quotation from *King Lear*: 'you have that in your countenance which I would fain call master. What's that? Authority.' Yes, Kirsty Young had such a quality, Lorimer thought, following her as she led them out of the studio into a corridor leading to a large room where rows of chairs had been set out.

'We haven't had the pleasure of working together before,' Kirsty said, her husky voice still holding a trace of her Scottish roots. 'But I believe you did a programme when Nick was here? And of course you know Alex Loughran,' she added as the pro- gramme's editor passed with a wave of her hand.

300

'That's right,' Lorimer replied, taking a seat beside her as she motioned towards the end of a row.

'A couple of soft drinks, Pamela,' the presenter asked the tiny girl with the bright scarlet hair. 'That all right with you, Chief Inspector?'

'Fine,' Lorimer replied. 'We had a series of young girls found strangled and left in a Glasgow park,' he went on, picking up the thread of their conversation. 'Your programme was hugely instrumental in finding the killer,' he said approvingly.

'But this is quite a different sort of case, isn't it?' Kirsty asked, crossing one leg over the other, her navy linen trousers draping in loose folds as she clasped her hands over her knees.

'You're right. This is altogether trickier. We want to see if we can locate a woman, Marianne Scott. Her brother, Billy Brogan, is somewhere overseas and we have reason to believe he's involved somehow in the murder of Marianne's former husband.' Lorimer stopped, biting his lip. 'It's a bit complicated. Brogan was thought to be a small-time drug dealer but our current intelligence suggests that he was involved in the drug scene in a much deeper way altogether.'

'Go on,' Kirsty nodded, her eyes still holding his own, showing that she was genuinely interested.

'We think the ex-husband, Kenneth Scott, had been stalking his former wife. He was found shot in his own home, he's got no record nor has he any known association with criminals other than the fact that Brogan was his brother-in-law.' Lorimer took a deep breath. 'Then a couple of other Glasgow dealers are found shot dead in Brogan's home and we get the nod that Brogan has skipped to Spain.'

'You think Brogan killed all three men?' Kirsty asked.

Lorimer gave a mirthless laugh. 'That's just it. We did at first, but we don't think that now. Timing for the second two is all wrong and we've got ballistics evidence to suggest that all three were killed by the same weapon.'

Kirsty re-crossed her legs and frowned at him. 'So why are you putting out an appeal for the sister? I don't quite understand.'

'She's deliberately gone into hiding. Even made sure her name was taken off Glasgow University's registry database while she was a student there. Something's wrong,' he said, leaning forward. *She may even be dead*, he almost told her, but stopped himself in time. *Had Marianne Scott been targeted by the same hit man?* This was a question that Lorimer did not yet want to utter aloud, his mind full of so many doubts and possibilities. But what if she were still alive?

'If we can find her and question her, or anyone who knows her or has seen her, we may be able to locate the brother.'

'How will that help to find the killer, though?'

'Brogan owed a lot of money to some very dangerous people. And only he can give us their names. That isn't the whole story, though, I'm afraid,' he continued. 'A man called Sahid Jaffrey was brutally killed on the south side of the city recently.' Lorimer looked hard at the woman across the table. 'He was the police informant who let us know that Brogan was in Spain.'

'This gets more and more complicated,' Kirsty said. 'How do you suggest we put such a lot of information across to our viewers?'

'We don't,' said Lorimer shortly. 'What I want to do is to appeal for information for any sighting of this woman whose ex-husband was found dead. If we can slant the appeal to that sort of angle, suggest without actually saying that she may be a suspect, then perhaps we will have some response.'

'And you don't think she actually had anything to do with these killings?' Kirsty asked, slowly.

'They were done by a professional,' Lorimer replied. 'Brogan's ex-army and we thought at first it might have been him.'

'But the timings were wrong,' Kirsty said, echoing Lorimer's earlier statement. 'So what do you actually know about this woman, Marianne Scott?'

'She was a mature student at the University of Glasgow. That's why we asked the editors to have footage of the campus as part of the appeal,' he said. 'Anyone who knew her in that context might want to give us a ring.'

'How odd that she was able to have her name taken off the registry,' Kirsty remarked.

'Aye,' Lorimer replied. 'We're looking into that as well. And we'll find out just how she managed it, believe me.'

'Well, Chief Inspector, this is certainly going to be a little bit different from our usual appeals. Still,' her eyes twinkled at him, 'we *are* accustomed to senior officers giving out only part of their case histories. Wouldn't do to give too much information to the criminals, after all. That's not what we're about.'

'Indeed,' Lorimer nodded. 'So, this is what I have drawn up.' He handed over a slim sheaf of notes from the folder that was on his knee.

Maggie set down her empty coffee mug on a coaster and tapped in the numbers she knew off by heart. Almost immediately she heard her friend's voice. Rosie sounded tired, Maggie thought guiltily. 'Hi, it's me. Hope you weren't lying down or anything,' she added lamely.

'Don't worry, the phone's beside the sofa,' Rosie replied. 'Nice to hear from you. It's been a while. Busy as always?' she chuckled.

'Yes, you know what it's like,' Maggie said vaguely, twisting a dark curled strand of hair through her fingers. 'Sorry I haven't been in touch,' she said. 'Anyway, just wanted you and Solly to know that Bill's on *Crimewatch* tonight. It's not a reconstruction, just an appeal,' she said.

'Oh, right. That wouldn't be anything to do with these three chaps whose PMs I did recently, would it?'

'Yes, same case. The one that involves a man called Brogan, I think. Bill hasn't told me too much about it,' she replied.

'Great,' Rosie said. 'Well, thanks for letting us know. If I'm off to bed before it's on I'll get Solly to record it. He's up at the uni just now,' she added.

'Oh,' Maggie replied. There was a silence between the two women as Maggie struggled to put her thoughts into words. She couldn't tell Rosie why she hadn't been in touch, she simply couldn't.

'Well,' Rosie said at last in a tone that Maggie realised was forced brightness. 'Maybe we'll see you pair up here one of these days when life's calmed down, eh?'

'Mm. That would be nice. Maybe once Bill's less busy with this horrible case,' she added.

'You're welcome to come up on your own, you know,' Rosie said briskly, 'if you have the time.'

'Thanks,' Maggie replied. 'I'll do my best, honest. But, listen I've got to go, someone's at the door. Bye.'

Clicking the phone shut, Maggie Lorimer bit her lip at the sudden deception. It wasn't in her nature to tell such lies, especially to a friend like Rosie. There was no knock at the front door, no sound at all, only Chancer who had somehow found her lap when she wasn't looking and was now purring happily. Maggie stroked his soft fur absently, feeling more wretched than before. If only she could tell someone how she felt: how the prospect of this operation was making her feel that she would be diminished as a woman. It was bad enough to be barren, but to lose that part of her . . .

At any other time Maggie would have sought comfort and advice from Rosie, but not now. Not when the pathologist was about to give birth to a child of her own.

Amit turned on the television and flicked through the channels. There was nothing much on that he really wanted to see. Maybe the radio would be a better option, with some music to soothe his troubled spirits. He flicked back to BBC1, intending to switch off but then something stopped him.

It was not the woman's low, seductive voice that halted the Pakistani, but that familiar name on her lips. Amit froze. He knew this programme, *Crimewatch*, and had seen bits of reconstructions of some violent crimes that reminded him far too much of things that he preferred to forget.

Suddenly there were scenes he recognised; the dark red sandstone of the university, its spires against a cloudless blue sky, the quadrangles with their gothic arches, then the scene changed to the streets around the library and Wellington church, students thronging the pavements. He'd walked there often with Marianne in these first days, tentatively finding his bearings around the campus and the streets that comprised Glasgow's West End. And she had been kind to him, hadn't she? Always making sure he could find his way back to the flat he had rented for her.

Amit listened to the presenter's voice and watched as she turned to the dark-haired man at her side. It was a police officer from Strathclyde, Amit realised, hearing the man's accent; some senior officer called Lorimer. And now he, too, was talking about Marianne.

Amit clutched the edge of his seat, fingers trembling. What had happened to her? He listened as the officer recounted the facts. Marianne's ex-husband had been shot dead in his own home and the woman appeared to be deliberately trying to hide from the authorities.

What was the man saying? That Marianne, *his* Marianne, had killed this man? This Kenneth Scott? Amit blinked as though to clear his vision. But the policeman's face was drawing closer to the television screen as a camera zoomed in on him, filling Amit's head with all sorts of ideas.

'We would especially ask any of her friends from Glasgow University or anyone who was close to her to make contact with us,' Lorimer was saying. 'No matter when you last saw Marianne Scott, please get in touch.'

Then he paused and Amit saw his blue eyes staring intently as if he were speaking directly to him.

'If you are watching this yourself, Marianne, please call us or go to your nearest police office. We very much want to speak to you.'

Amit sat very still as the numbers appeared on the TV screen. A faint ringing sounded in his ears and he licked his lips, feeling how dry they were.

He knew what he could do. More than that, he knew what he *should* do.

But there was only one question drumming a beat in his brain: had he the courage to give up everything he had gained since his arrival in this city?

Lorimer sat staring at the screen in front of him, his fist closed over the handset. All over the country phones would be dialling the *Crimewatch* number, texting or emailing messages. A lot of them would be a complete waste of time, many simply hoaxes by stupid people who got a kick out of sending duff information. The police were used to that sort of behaviour, though. The Yorkshire Ripper case had been dogged by bogus intelligence to the extent that Peter Sutcliffe had managed to select another victim before he had eventually been apprehended and shut away for good.

'Thanks for calling,' Lorimer said, putting down the phone on a woman whose voice had betrayed her genuine eagerness to help. She'd been a fellow student at Anniesland College and now her details were to hand should she be needed again.

The day seemed to be going on for ever, he thought, glancing up at a clock on the wall. Since their arrival that afternoon, Lorimer and the members of his team had been briefed about the programme, undertaken a preliminary rehearsal, had dinner (which seemed like hours ago) followed by a dress rehearsal for the nine p.m. live programme. Now each of his hand-picked officers was responding to the calls that were coming in, urged on by Kirsty Young's usual polished performance. But, as yet, nothing had come through that would give any clue as to Marianne's whereabouts and the DCI began to gnaw his lower lip anxiously. Just what had become of Ken Scott's ex-wife?

Amit looked around the room and saw all the things he had accumulated since his arrival. Nice things, expensive things, that he had hoped would delight Marianne. And the part ownership of the restaurant, the car outside, his very future . . . all these things would be taken from him if he lifted the telephone and made that call.

Suddenly he remembered the night that they had come for his

father. Now he could vividly recall the stern, unyielding faces of the officials who had beaten the old man until he was senseless; he could remember the wailing cries of the women who begged them to stop; remembered his own tears running down his face. They had left Papa Shafiq there at last, a crumpled heap surrounded by his weeping family.

That battered and bleeding body with unseeing eyes staring heavenwards was a sight that Amit had tried so hard to banish to the darkest parts of his mind. But now it was as if it had come back to tell him something.

His father had led an exemplary life, had enjoyed wealth and the respect of many of his peers. But in the end everything had been taken from him.

What was it all about, this little life that was rounded by a sleep? Amit shook his head, wondering. Then, with a sigh that seemed to come from his very soul, he lifted the telephone and dialled.

He listened to the instructions on the line then a voice asked him to speak.

'My name is Amit Shafiq.' He paused to clear his throat, amazed to hear the sound of his own voice and how strong it sounded. 'I'm calling about the *Crimewatch* programme,' he said at last. 'It's about the woman they are calling Marianne Scott,' he continued.

'That's right,' the operator said. 'Do you have information about her?'

Amit swallowed, then licked his lips.

'Yes,' he said softly, 'she's my wife.'

Pamela tiptoed around the tall policeman from Glasgow, trying to catch his eye. He was speaking into the telephone right now and didn't look as though he would want to be interrupted. But it was part of the girl's remit to brief this man on what was happening elsewhere in the studios, and really, he would want to know about this call in particular, wouldn't he?

CHAPTER 39

The hit man picked up the passport and flicked the pages until he came to a reasonable likeness of himself. Stern and unsmiling, Michael Stevens, aged forty-two, glared back at him from the square of plastic. It was a name he rarely used when he was working but sometimes it became necessary to be himself again for overseas business where the pickings were richer. Here in the UK he could make plenty though. *If* the punters hiring him paid up, he reminded himself sourly, remembering Billy Brogan. But for now he was Max Whittaker to the woman and Smith to his Asian paymasters. Only someone like Brogan himself would be able to tell the real story about Mick Stevens, the sniper who had made such a name for himself in the Iraq conflict.

He laughed silently. The army had taught him plenty, hadn't it? How to kill being one of its main lessons.

Stevens listened to the rush of water from the bathroom next door. Marianne was taking a shower, washing away their night of pleasure. The hit man grinned to himself. She had been so easy to beguile, he could hardly believe it. Ripe for picking. In a way he could almost imagine someone pitying the woman for setting her cap at him. But pity was not an emotion that a man like Stevens ever allowed himself to feel. He slipped the passport into the duffle bag beside the items he would need for the journey back down south. Being ready to leave at a moment's notice was something else he had learned in the forces.

Sitting back on the bed he fondled the gun, its familiar shape fitting snugly in his hand. His eyes moved from the Glock to the bathroom door, anticipating the look on her face when she emerged, naked and utterly vulnerable.

Marianne hummed as she twisted the bath towel over her hair, tucking in the ends. Max hadn't mentioned what they would do today, but she was already thinking of suggesting another journey away from the city, maybe to St Andrews where they could walk along the sands at Tentsmuir, a quiet estuary out of the town. She imagined the smell of the pine trees and how they might run along the beach together, hand in hand, listening to the North Sea surf rolling in.

The picture of the water's edge and the copse of sweet scented trees was switched off abruptly as her brain commanded Marianne to take in what she was really seeing.

The man lying back on the bed had a large pistol in his hand and it was pointing straight at her.

'Max?' she hesitated, drawing the thick bath towel more closely around her. 'What are you doing?' Marianne shook her head. 'Is this some sort of joke?' She made to move towards the bed but then stopped, frozen by the expression on her lover's face.

'No joke, darling. No joke at all,' the hit man drawled. 'Now just you step over there nice and slowly,' he added, motioning with the gun. 'And do keep quiet like a good girl, won't you? This little beauty is loaded,' he told her, smiling. 'All ready to use if you don't do exactly as I tell you.'

*

312

Amit sat twisting his hands together below the surface of the table, feeling the dampness on his palms. He had been spoken to politely by the officers who had met him at the front of the police station, had even been called 'sir'. One of them had led him into a corridor with a row of chairs that were fixed to the wall and there Amit had sat, waiting, watching the clock as it ticked through almost twenty-five interminable minutes.

Had it really been necessary to make him wait all that time to see the senior officer, Lorimer? Wasn't it all part of a strategy to unnerve him? When at last he had been ushered into this small square den of a room, Amit had felt like one of the criminals he had seen on that programme.

'Mr Shafiq? DCI Lorimer.'

Amit stood up suddenly, the scrape of his chair on the floor sounding unnaturally loud.

The tall man who entered the room made the Pakistani feel very small as he shook his damp hand and motioned him to sit back down again. He was not what Amit had expected. There was nothing harsh about this man's face, though the lines showed signs of worry and fatigue that Amit supposed must be inevitable given his choice of profession. As he flicked a lock of dark hair back from his brow, Amit saw a keen intelligence in the policeman's blue eyes and something else, something that reassured him. A trace of what would he call it . . . sympathy, perhaps?

'It's good of you to come in, sir,' Lorimer began. 'We really appreciate it.'

Amit's eyes flicked to the other man who had sat beside Lorimer. He was very dark, a Nubian Egyptian by the look of his beautifully sculpted face, Amit thought. And a policeman, here in Scotland?

'Detective Constable Fathy,' Lorimer said and the younger

313

man leaned across the table to shake Amit's hand, the stiff little nod of his head serving as a bow.

Amit breathed a long sigh of relief. It was going to be all right. These people were on his side, surely? They wanted to find Marianne as much as he did. And hadn't she often told him that the British police were a different breed altogether from the kind of men who had taken his father's life away? Besides, these men wore no intimidating uniform. Lorimer's shirt was a little rumpled and the knot on his tie had been loosened a little as though he had been hard at work and needed to be comfortable at his desk, somewhere else in this building.

'I will have to ask you rather a lot of questions, sir,' Lorimer told him, 'so please bear with me.' He looked at Amit and smiled encouragingly. 'I know this must be very hard for you.'

Amit nodded, taking a deep breath. He felt calmer now that this process had begun and was mildly surprised at his feeling of relief that some larger authority was taking over the burden he had been carrying around for those long days since Marianne had disappeared.

'It might seem like a strange question, sir, but can you give us any proof that this woman is indeed your wife?'

Amit tried a tremulous smile as he passed the folded paper across the table.

The policeman took it and frowned as he read the marriage certificate.

'You were married in Las Vegas?'

Amit's smile faltered. 'Yes, sir.'

'But why? I mean, why go there?'

The Asian shrugged. 'It was her wish. And one does not deny a bride-to-be her heart's desires.'

Lorimer gave a short laugh. 'And what did you make of Vegas?'

'Not a very nice place, sir. It was . . .' he broke off as though the memories were ones he would prefer to forget. 'Not what I had expected for my own nuptials, sir,' he sighed at last. 'It was over so quickly. But then, perhaps my bride had reasons for wishing to be married somewhere like that. Somewhere anonymous . . .' Amit bit his lip as though he was finding it hard to speak.

'When did you last see your wife?'

Amit cleared his throat and told them about finding that deserted room. Then, without warning, he put his head in his hands and began to weep.

'Forgive me,' he mumbled. 'It has been a bad time . . . I did not know what to think . . .'

'Perhaps it would be better to start at the beginning,' Lorimer suggested, 'then we can build up a clearer picture, hm?'

Amit nodded, unable to speak. Then, taking a freshly laundered handkerchief from his pocket, he blew his nose.

Lorimer had listened patiently, never once interrupting as Amit Shafiq had told his story. It had begun in far-off Lahore with the murder of his father by political opponents and Amit's flight to freedom in Scotland. The tale unfolded as the man spoke about the contact he had made; Dhesi, a kindly beneficent man with whom he had forged a business partnership in Glasgow. It was a stroke of luck, Amit had explained, seeing Lorimer's eyebrows raised in a question.

'Before that I was also introduced to a Scotsman,' Amit went on. 'A Mr Brogan. A good friend of the Asian community, I believed,' he murmured.

Lorimer noted the way the man's voice tailed off. What had happened to change that belief, he wondered? And was there something else that he wasn't saying?

'Go on,' he said quietly, as Amit fell silent, his eyes cast down.

With a sigh the man continued. 'Mr Brogan said he could help me to find permanent residence in Glasgow. Said I would be able to become a British citizen. Arranged for me to meet his sister.'

Lorimer listened, understanding what it must have been like for this man, frightened and alone in a strange city, desperate for some form of security.

'I met Marianne one day in the park,' Amit said softly, his eyes shining with tenderness at the memory. 'She was a kind lady, very lovely, and I could see that she was willing to be a friend to me,' he raised his hands and looked at the officers in expectation. 'You see, I needed to stay here and Marianne offered me that opportunity,' he said simply.

'Yours was a marriage of convenience?' Lorimer asked.

The man nodded. 'Yes. It could have been described as that, I suppose. Certainly it was convenient for me and I suppose the money I gave my wife made it convenient for her,' he said, his tone suddenly cynical. 'But we were not like a business partnership,' he insisted. 'You see,' he went on, smiling a sweet sudden smile, 'after we returned from the United States she became my friend.'

Lorimer nodded in understanding. Marianne had become his wife, had been set up in a rented flat so she could pursue her studies, then all of a sudden this man had found himself in love with her. What had begun as a means to an end had become an affair of the heart, at least on the part of Amit Shafiq.

'So you see, I must find her,' he went on. 'I worry that something dreadful has happened to make her run away from me. But I did not know anything about the death of the man who had been her previous husband,' he said quietly.

Lorimer looked at him intently. He believed him though what a jury might make of his statement was another matter. He

316

wanted to ask about Brogan but knew it was more important to let this man tell his story first.

'What did you think might be the longer term prospects for you and Marianne?' he asked instead.

'I had hoped that she might be my wife in the proper sense, not just on the paper we both signed,' Amit said and it was not hard to hear the wistfulness in his voice.

'Marianne was a student at the University of Glasgow when you first met, is that right?'

'Yes. She wanted to study psychology, become a doctor of some kind. She even spoke about travelling to work in America one day. I thought . . .' he shrugged as he tailed off.

'You thought she might have gone to the US when you found her flat empty?'

Amit nodded, exhaling slowly in a sigh of resignation. 'I wondered if I would ever see her again. Then I heard you and the lady speak about her on the programme . . .'

Lorimer asked a few questions about the date of their marriage, where it had taken place, making scribbled notes on the pad in front of him, though there was a tape running to record the entire interview. Sometimes doing a trivial thing like note-taking brought a sense of formality to an interview situation. And right now he could see that the Pakistani needed something like this to rise above the emotions that threatened to overwhelm him.

'And you paid her a sum for the privilege of marrying you?' he asked, his mouth crinkling at the corners as though Amit might share in the joke.

'Yes. Ten thousand pounds.' He shrugged. 'I am a wealthy man, Mr Lorimer. It was a small price to pay for my freedom. That,' he said solemnly, 'is something on which no man can put a price.'

'And I presume you supported your wife as well?'

Amit nodded, his back stiffening as though he had been offended. 'But of course. Marianne required a place to live and I paid for the rent as well as giving her a modest allowance. It was a satisfactory arrangement.'

'For her,' Lorimer answered sharply.

'And for me,' Amit replied. 'I had a legal reason to remain here and build a new life for myself.'

'How often did you see her?' Lorimer asked.

'Once a week, perhaps less. We met in the station sometimes for coffee. It was what she liked,' he explained. 'Marianne did not like being seen with me over in the West End where we both lived. Perhaps it was . . .' he shrugged, glancing across at Fathy, the words unsaid. *Perhaps she didn't like to be seen with an Asian.*

'Tell me about Billy Brogan,' Lorimer said at last.

Lorimer watched as the man walked away from the building. He had given the Detective Chief Inspector a lot to think about. Shafiq was a well-educated man, that was clear from his speech and the innate courtesies he had shown during the interview. The story about Lahore was chilling; it was not an unfamiliar scenario by any means, yet coming from this man who was riven with anxiety for his wife, it had made Lorimer flinch inwardly as the story had unfolded. It also explained why Shafiq had not called the authorities when he had found Marianne missing. He would be kept under surveillance from this moment on, hopefully unaware of the undercover officers who would dog his footsteps day and night. Had that been his father's experience? Lorimer wondered. Had the old man been watched by these faceless people who had waited for him to make one small mistake before they had entered his home and bludgeoned him to death in front of his family?

318

His tale about Brogan had been nothing short of astonishing. Just how the drug dealer had become embroiled in the Asian community's affairs was unclear, but undoubtedly he had some influence there. Marianne had offered to marry Shafiq in order to allow him to become a British citizen and stay on legally in Glasgow. What had been her motivation for that? Her brother's influence? Lorimer shook his head, remembering the photograph of the red-haired woman. She was an educated woman and had never been in trouble with the law. Surely she was not the sort to be pushed about by Brogan. So, it all came down to money. And that, as the DCI well knew, was one of the prime motivations behind such a lot of crime.

Ten thousand pounds was a lot of money, but perhaps for Shafiq it was worth it. Besides, hadn't he admitted his own personal wealth? Ten thousand pounds. Lorimer tapped a pencil against his teeth.

Interesting that it should equate to the price of a hit in this gun-ridden city.

'Ten thousand pounds,' the hit man told her. 'That's what your brother owes me.'

Marianne sat rigid on the wooden chair, her eyes staring at the man with the gun. The last few minutes had taken on nightmare proportions, more terrifying than the worst excesses of her hateful dreams. Max had made her put on her nightdress, watching her every move, his grey eyes cold with something that she had not seen before in the man. Now, her arms fastened behind her, ankles tied tightly so that the bonds cut into her flesh if she made any movement, she was his prisoner.

At first she had thought it a game, Max working out some sexual fantasy that would end up with her screaming at the height of their passion. And she had laughed uncertainly, moving towards him. But that gun, that gun . . . Marianne knew without having to ask that it was not only loaded but that she was Max's intended victim. The room was warm, but the sweat trickling down between her shoulder blades felt chilled.

'So, just you tell him from me, babe, that his little sister gets it for free if he doesn't pay up,' the man-who-was-not-Max said, his voice full of a sneering tone that made Marianne shiver.

'I don't know where he is,' she said at last.

'Don't give me that,' the hit man replied, waving the gun closer to her face. 'Brogan wouldn't keep his whereabouts from you of all people.'

Marianne felt her eyes begin to swim with tears. That was exactly what Billy had done. He'd run out on her, left her to face the consequences of his thieving ways. But wasn't that how it had always been? Marianne bit her lip, willing herself not to break down. Even when they'd been little hadn't she been the one to cover up for Billy's misdemeanours? Her loyalty to the wee brother she'd adored had never really been rewarded, even now. *Especially now*, a little voice insisted. She had thought that all her nightmares would cease once Ken had been blown away. But now the nightmare had come to life, facing her with this gun, its dark eye staring at her.

'Billy ran out on me too,' Marianne whispered. 'Honest. I . . . I didn't know he was gone till . . . till I heard the tone on his mobile . . .' she gulped, unable to continue. 'And he's blocked the number, so I can't call him.'

The hit man nodded, never taking his eyes off her. Did he believe her, then? Marianne swallowed hard. Max, or whatever his real name was, hadn't realised why he had been commissioned to kill her ex-husband. She breathed fast, telling herself that she would be okay so long as he continued to be unaware of her part in all of this. Billy must have arranged the hit, never mentioning just why it had been necessary to kill Ken. A hit man probably didn't ask too many questions, anyway; he just carried out the deed, took his money and vanished.

'Well the first call you have from brother Billy you just let him know how much his little sister is worth, okay?' He grinned, then, and to Marianne's relief, laid the gun down beside him on the bed and pulled his own mobile from his pocket. Perhaps it would be okay. Perhaps he was only trying to frighten her. Perhaps . . . Marianne felt the tears trickling unbidden down her cheeks . . . he would touch her again, gently as he had before, telling her that it was all a big mistake.

CHAPTER 40

The Hundi put down the phone, nodding to himself. That was good. The man called Smith had agreed a fee for getting rid of the girl. Brogan had been a thorn in their flesh and his sister's existence was only bringing more trouble into their world. He screwed up his eyes. There was no room in his world for sentiment. This was purely a matter of business. He had nothing against the red-haired woman whose compliance had allowed their new friend, Amit Shafiq, to remain here, part of his thriving business network. Brogan had had his uses too, as a way of laundering money from certain sources. But Brogan himself was a marked man now. And if he ever set foot again in Glasgow . . . the Hundi's grin widened. Perhaps Mr Smith would be happy to undertake that particular commission for free? The man rubbed his hands together, feeling the heavy rings on his chubby fingers. It would all work out. Money always made everything work out.

Billy Brogan opened his eyes to see a fan spinning on the pale ceiling, its sweeping rhythm soothing his emerging senses. Everything he saw was white: walls, ceiling, the vertical blinds keeping daylight from penetrating the room where he lay. He blinked, then felt his fingers touch the cool cotton of the sheet that was covering him. Where was he? Turning his head a fraction, Brogan saw a table against a wall with a large white jug covered in a square of cloth. Above it was a picture of Christ, hand out-stretched, lines of yellow radiating from the circle above his head. Brogan blinked again. This was weirding him out, big time. There was a strange metallic taste in his mouth that made him search around it with the tip of his tongue, feeling a gap where two of his front teeth should have been. He screwed up his eyes as saliva flooded his mouth. His gums were sore and tender, throbbing as though the teeth had been wrenched from his mouth. What the hell had happened to him? He tried to sit up, but as soon as he moved a pain shot through his skull.

Then the memories began to return. That darkened alley, the man in the half-opened doorway . . .

Billy groaned as much from the ache in his head as from the realisation that he had been taken for a mug. Yet he was here, in a quiet place, alive. And, apart from his missing teeth, still in one piece. He turned his head slowly, fearful of another blast of pain, and saw a door with a sheet of paper attached. It was in some lan-guage that Billy couldn't understand. But the familiar symbols required no interpretation. There were little pictures, interna-tional hieroglyphics, that showed emergency exits and fire extinguishers. So, he was in some sort of an institution. A hospital, Brogan supposed, raising a hand to touch the place where the pain was worst. He felt the soft padding someone had placed under a swathe of bandage, confirming his suspicions. Somehow he had been rescued from the men who had assaulted him and patched up while he was still unconscious.

Brogan let his hand slide back under the bedclothes, feeling only skin against the sheets. 'Christ!' he exclaimed, then looked guiltily at the picture to his left as though the image had overheard and disapproved. 'Sorry,' he mumbled, reminding himself to say a proper thank you for actually waking to find himself safe from his attackers. But it *was* a bit of a shock to find himself stark naked, his eyes told the picture.

The room appeared to be empty of any furniture save a small bedside locker, the type that one always found in hospital rooms. Perhaps his stuff was in there? Steeling himself, Brogan pushed himself into a sitting position, then stopped, panting with the effort, waves of agony shooting through his head. He felt the sweat running in rivulets down his chest and he was glad of the fan's blades swishing round and around, cooling his fevered body.

He had to get up, see if everything was still there.

He turned around in the bed, letting his legs fall into mid-air, feet searching for the floor. With a huge effort, Brogan slid off the bed and tried to stand up. Immediately his legs buckled under him and he slid to the floor, only saving himself from crashing down by grabbing at the sheets. Head pounding, he let himself rest for a few moments, his back against the side of the bed, trembling with a weakness that threatened to overpower him. But he had to see if his things were still there, had to know . . .

The locker had two compartments; a door and a drawer. Brogan tried pulling at the door but his hands were too damp with sweat and his fingers slid uselessly off the wooden handle. Wiping them on the sheet that had come off the bed, he tried again. The door opened and Brogan's mouth opened in a gasp of dismay. The compartment was completely empty. Shaking now, he pulled at the drawer, praying to any gods that might hear him.

Inside there was only one familiar object. Not his wallet stuffed with dollars, not his passport, only the cheap mobile phone he had bought before leaving Mallorca.

Hands still trembling, Brogan lifted it out and flicked the

device open. The battery still showed full. Brogan flicked a gaze at the Christ on the wall. That was something to be thankful for, at least.

He tapped out her number then pressed the green button and waited.

For a few moments Brogan listened as the ringing tone pounded in his head, biting his lips, willing his sister to pick up her phone and answer it. She wasn't there, he thought, dismay making him shiver as he sat there on the tiled floor.

Then the ringing stopped and his face creased in a smile as he anticipated Marianne's *hello*.

'Who's this?' a voice asked suddenly, making Brogan frown.

Did he know that accent? A shudder went through his body. No. It couldn't be . . .

'It's me. It's Billy,' he said slowly, hoping that his instincts about that voice were wrong. 'Will you put Marianne on?' He heard his own words come out, thin and reedy, like an old man's.

A chuckle sounded from the line. 'Oh, she's been hoping to speak to *you*,' the man told him. 'Haven't you, Marianne?'

Brogan heard his sister's muffled reply but he was unable to make out her words.

'Is that you, Stevens?' he asked, suspiciously.

'Who did you think it was, Brogan?' the hit man replied. 'Santa Claus?'

The dealer sat, stunned into silence. How had Stevens managed to find Marianne, of all people? After the pains she had taken to ensure that nobody could find her; these repeated changes of address, her name deleted from that registry file. *Nobody but Amit*, Brogan reminded himself. Was that how Stevens had located her?

'Hello?' Stevens said, and Brogan heard the man's fingers tapping against the plastic casing of his mobile.

'I'm still here,' Brogan said, resisting the temptation to add 'only just.'

'Well, listen to me, pal, and listen good,' Stevens told him.

Brogan nodded then wished he hadn't, the throbbing in his skull making him feel as though he might pass out if he moved again.

Stevens' voice continued, telling Brogan what he expected him to do, telling him what would happen to Marianne if he failed to comply with his demands. Warning him to keep the police out of it.

Then the man stopped speaking and Brogan heard a small cry in the background.

He winced, trying to imagine what was happening to his sister at the hands of this man, a man he knew to be capable of unimaginable horrors.

'Billy? Billy?' Marianne was sobbing into the phone, her breath coming in short bursts.

'Aye, I'm here,' Brogan said, pulling the crumpled sheet around his shivering form.

'Please,' she cried. 'Please do as he says, Billy,' Marianne begged. 'He . . . he's got a gun. And he says . . .' her voice tailed off then returned in a whisper. 'He says he'll kill me if you don't get him that money.'

'Where are you?' Brogan asked, urgently. 'Just tell me where. And I'll fix everything.'

Marianne had just given him the name of a city centre hotel and their room number when Brogan flinched, hearing her let out a yelp. As he heard Stevens shouting at her Brogan stiffened, wanting to square up to the hit man, sudden rage boiling up inside him.

'You heard what she said, Brogan. You get that money to me by tomorrow or she's dead meat. Understood?'

'I'll need more time,' Brogan protested, hearing the blood pound in his head.

But the connection had been cut and he sat there looking at the phone in his hand, wondering how the hell he was supposed to get out of this mess.

CHAPTER 41

The leaves were falling in swirls, withered and brown, as Solly watched from the window of his new office. Summer was past and the new session was beginning. Already students had arrived back in the city, many of them looking for accommodation or books from their lists, trying to prepare for the autumn term that lay ahead. His postgraduate students had never really left though, working on dissertations that never seemed to be curtailed by the familiar markers of the academic year.

Marianne's name had not appeared in his class lists so far. Where was she? Solly had watched the recorded *Crimewatch* programme with Rosie, his concern for the woman growing as he had listened to Lorimer's appeal. He had sat through to the end, seeing pictures of criminals who had slipped out of the reach of police in several different parts of the country. Many of them went by aliases, Solly noticed. And that had given him something to think about. What if Marianne had changed her name, too?

So far he had not made much progress with his own investigation but today there was one thing that he thought he might do. He turned around, his eye falling upon the many boxes of textbooks laid neatly below his bookshelves. Among them were several from the library that he had borrowed and must now be returned. Solly bent down, taking the books out of their boxes, opening every one to check its return date before placing them in a tidy pile. Perhaps, like him, Marianne had had to visit the library, to take back books? It was worth a try, Solly thought as he gathered up the textbooks into a hessian shopping bag.

Several students were walking down the path towards the students' union as Solly emerged from the door of the psychology department and he smiled at their laughter, hearing the sound of enthusiasm in their voices. Freshers, he thought, nodding to himself. Their lives were on the threshold of something new and wonderful and on this windy day when the air tossed the leaves skywards, Solly found their eagerness quite infectious. Quickening his stride, Solly turned left, following the path to the library, a modern building that was tucked between the Hunterian Museum and the curve of University Gardens.

The library was already busy with students sitting at tables, poring over books or laptops. As ever, Solly found himself relaxing in this place where quiet study was carried out day after day. He handed over the books, watching as the librarian checked to see that the dates tallied as they should then he cleared his throat.

'Perhaps you might do something for me?' he asked, smiling hopefully.

'Of course, Doctor Brightman,' the librarian replied. 'Is there a book you want us to reserve for you?'

Solly shook his head. 'No, no, nothing like that. I'd like you to do a little detective work,' he said, tapping the side of his nose conspiratorially. 'It's one of my students. She seems to have changed her name.' He shrugged as if this was a matter of little import. 'It was Marianne Scott, but perhaps you don't have it on record?'

'Oh, we have everything on record, Doctor Brightman,' the woman replied briskly. 'Now, what year is she in?'

Solly told her and waited as the woman worked at the keyboard, her eyes on the computer screen.

'Ah, yes. Marianne Scott. She was in here less than a fortnight ago,' the woman told him. 'Told us she had changed her name from Scott to Shafiq. Must have married a foreigner,' the woman said, her eyebrows raised in mild surprise.

'Well, thanks for that. I'm sure she'll let us know the details in due course but our secretaries will be glad to put it right for now. For class lists, you know?' he murmured.

Gathering up the empty bag, Solly left the library and made his way back down to the main road, his heart beating a little faster. She had married! Rosie was right, then. Her woman's intuition had suggested that Marianne's personality change was down to that old black magic, after all. Plus she *had* alerted the library to that change of name. So, he reasoned, Marianne had intended to resume her studies here.

The television programme had suggested that she might be involved in her ex-husband's death, but how could that be? If Marianne had hoped to continue at university as normal surely she would be afraid of detection in such a public place as this? The psychologist stopped at the edge of the pavement across from the main university gates and stood still, staring into the sky, quite unaware of the curious glances he was receiving from passers-by.

Motivation was everything in a crime, he told himself. Why a person chose to commit an evil deed said so much more about them than the deed itself. *If* Marianne had killed her own husband then what could her motive have been? She had been legally divorced from Scott so she did not need to be rid of him to marry this Shafiq, whoever he was. Yet, she had thanked Solly for . . . for what? Suggesting that she rid herself of some bad dreams? In the clear light of this autumn day such a notion seemed absurd, but, until he knew more, Doctor Solomon Brightman could only theorise about the reason behind Marianne's change from the timid student she had been into the vibrant woman he remembered from the bookshop. And was that simply down to finding the right man to love?

Solly noticed the orange lights of an approaching taxi and he stepped forwards on to the road, one arm raised. Perhaps it was a little rash of him, a little presumptuous, but it had to be done.

'Into town, please,' he told the driver. Then, stepping into the cab, he gave him the address of Lorimer's divisional headquarters.

Sitting back, Solly stroked his beard thoughtfully, wondering what sort of reaction his unexpected appearance would provoke.

Lorimer sat on the edge of a desk, facing the members of his team. All of them had been brought up to date with the *Crimewatch* results. There had been some tuts of disapproval as the team learned that one of Scott's neighbours had phoned in, distraught yet full of apologies, telling them that she had gone into the house to tidy up, as she had put it. Hadn't meant to cause any bother. The mystery of the neatly made bed was a mystery no longer. That was one box at least that could be ticked. But the best result had been the Asian's call and now Lorimer was relating Amit Shafiq's part in the investigation.

'We've got him under surveillance partly for his own protection,' he explained. 'After what happened to Jaffrey we can't afford to take any risks,' he said gravely. 'Hopefully the people who were Brogan's associates will make contact with him, but that may take time . . .' he broke off as the door to the room opened and a harassed looking uniformed officer entered, a familiar figure in her wake.

'I'm sorry, sir, but he wouldn't listen when I said you were in a meeting . . .'

'Ah, Lorimer,' Solly neatly sidestepped the woman and came forward, beaming as though the senior officer would be equally delighted to see him.

'Doctor Brightman,' Lorimer replied formally, sliding off the desk and taking the man's outstretched hand. 'We are, as you see, in a meeting . . .'

Solly looked around him, nodding at the officers he knew well. 'Yes, yes, that's fine. I thought it best to come right away, you see. There's such a lot you all have to know,' he told them, standing just in front of Lorimer as though to take his place, a strategy that was quite deliberate on the psychologist's part.

'Forgive the sudden interruption,' he added, glancing at Lorimer with a sweet smile that he knew was not nearly apologetic enough. 'But I have information relating to the disappearance of Marianne Scott.' He turned to Lorimer again. 'Or should I say, Marianne Shafiq?'

It gave the psychologist a moment of satisfaction to see Lorimer's jaw drop at the mention of that name.

'How did you know . . .?'

'Your good people came to see me, remember?' Solly waved a hand in the direction of Irvine and Fathy. 'I was made aware of the fact that you were looking for one of my students, a young woman whom I had come across by chance during the summer vacation,' Solly continued, drawing Lorimer to his side as he addressed the assembled officers. 'I had been puzzled for some time by something that she said to me,' he went on. 'Something rather strange.' He paused and looked at them intently while they waited, most of them accustomed to the sudden little silences in the psychologist's flow.

'Perhaps,' he said, turning to catch Lorimer's eye, 'it might be easier to understand if I begin at the beginning.' He took off his spectacles and polished them with the end of his tie, looked to see that they were clean, then replaced them. 'Marianne Scott began studying with me a year ago. She was a mature student but the difference in her age was not what marked her out from the rest of her class.'

There was complete silence as Solly continued, the officers keen to hear whatever new information he might have.

'Marianne was a very quiet, withdrawn sort of creature. One who liked to keep to the back of a seminar, remain unnoticed,' Solly said, nodding his head as though he were trying to recall her exactly. 'I remember her as a plain looking woman; hair pulled back from her face, no make-up, rather drab, actually,' he said, a note of apology in his voice as though he were stating some political incorrectness. 'With hindsight, I think that this was a deliberate ploy on her part.'

The quizzical looks that were directed towards him made Solly nod once more.

'When I saw her a few weeks ago, she was a different person altogether. Vibrant,' he murmured to himself. 'That's the word I keep coming back to. It means being full of life and energy,' he explained. 'And she was. Her hair was long and loose, that lovely Titian red . . . she wore something brightly coloured . . . I can't recall just what it was . . . but it was her expression that stays in my mind most of all,' he said, folding his arms across his chest. 'She was so full of animation, excitement, joy . . .'

Solly broke off again but this time Lorimer filled the pause. 'How is this supposed to help us find the woman?' he asked, a note of irritation in his voice.

'I was coming to that,' Solly replied mildly. 'She said she had something to thank me for,' he told them. 'Her exact words were, *I've a lot to thank you for.*' He nodded again, this time unsmiling. 'Later I was to find out that I had met her just one day after the death of her ex-husband,' he said.

There was a murmur amongst the officers who did not notice the psychologist's sigh as he spoke. But Lorimer had heard it and came to stand beside his friend.

'You know something about all of this, Solly, don't you?' Lorimer asked.

'Yes,' he replied sadly. 'You see,' he continued, 'I fear it may have been something I said that prompted Marianne Scott to have her husband killed.'

'What?' one officer asked, clearly incredulous at the psychologist's statement. Others began to frown and mutter amongst themselves.

'Okay, let Doctor Brightman explain,' Lorimer waved an authoritative hand, silencing the officers' reaction.

Solly began to describe the scene he had remembered from the seminar on dreams, taking care to repeat his own words, explaining why he had said them.

'It was a careless, throwaway remark,' he shrugged. 'Something to elicit a laugh. But I fear that the woman may have taken it seriously. You see,' he broke off again, his gaze sweeping the room, 'I think she was haunted by particular dreams of her own death. I believe,' he continued, 'she may have thought her ex-husband was going to kill her.'

A derisive snort came from the back of the room and a male voice called out, 'Well, if you saw her having so many mood changes she probably was a bit unstable. Do we know if she had mental health problems?'

'Problems?' another voice burst out. 'Of *course* she had problems!'

Everyone turned to see DC Annie Irvine standing, red-faced, her eyes bright with anger.

'Do any of you know what it's *like*?' she asked, thrusting her hands forwards in appeal. 'Day after day after day not knowing if he's going to be behind you in the street or the bus or a queue at Starbucks? Jumping every time the phone rings in case it's another load of filth you have to hear? Leaving the home you love just to get rid of him . . .?'

Tears were streaming down the policewoman's cheeks now but she seemed totally unaware of them.

'You don't know, do you, any of you?' she said, whirling to look at her fellow officers in turn. 'Marianne Scott was probably out of her mind with the strain of it all. Being hounded like that must have been bad enough, but to be unable to sleep because of him infiltrating her dreams . . .' She broke off in sobs and Fathy came to stand beside her, proffering a large white handkerchief.

There was an uneasy silence as several of the officers eyed her curiously, others too embarrassed at her outburst to even look in her direction.

'Is that why you joined the police force?' Solly asked kindly and nobody was surprised when Annie Irvine nodded, hand holding Fathy's handkerchief to her face.

'I'm sorry,' she gulped, 'I shouldn't have . . .'

'No, don't apologise,' Lorimer told her. 'Perhaps we need to understand a little more about Marianne Scott and her ex-husband in order to see how Doctor Brightman's story is possible.'

'Maybe it was the only way she could imagine being rid of him,' DS Cameron suggested.

'And if she was having such awful, recurring nightmares, she probably wasn't what you would describe as being in her right mind,' Fathy put in.

'If what we have heard is true, and remember it is only a theory – we can't present something like Doctor Brightman's notions as hard evidence – then this woman may need help,' Lorimer said. 'We need to look into old hospital records, see if there is anything that might suggest injuries from abuse by the husband. She deliberately absconded from what Shafiq saw as a place of safety. Now why is that, do you think?'

There was no answer from the room.

'Well,' Cameron said at last. 'If she knows that her brother is being sought by the police, surely it follows that she's afraid we'll bring her in too.'

'She's still hiding,' Annie said firmly. 'She may have thought that everything in her world was working out when you saw her,' she nodded towards Solly. 'Thought she could sleep peacefully at last.'

'Well, let's hope that Shafiq might lead us to her. No matter what he says, I think someone in the Asian community may have a good idea of her whereabouts,' Lorimer said firmly. 'Brogan's links involve his sister, I'm sure of that.'

Billy sat on the edge of the bed and wept, his shoulders heaving as the sobs racked his body. If only . . . he sighed, remembering the words of his mum. *If only you were more like your sister*, she'd scolded him on a daily basis. *Instead of running with that bad crowd*. Poor old Mum had succumbed to the cancer that had ravaged her body, long since, dying in that hospital where he had rarely visited, knowing he was unwelcome, the black sheep of the family. He hadn't been able to face that, either, had he? It had always been the same: he'd run away from anything hard. Had she always seen him as a bad lad? Probably, he thought, tears of remorse trickling down his face. Dogging off from as young as ten, trying

337

dope before he'd even reached the end of primary, selling it by the time he was in high school. And while Marianne sat and passed all of her exams Billy Brogan had been receiving a different sort of education altogether. How to hustle, how to drive a good deal, how to ingratiate himself into an established group of businessmen.

Until that time when someone had been stabbed in a fight amongst a rowdy lot of football casuals, out of their heads on a mixture of booze and drugs. That had been the end of it for da, hadn't it? There was no welcome home for his boy after that.

Billy Brogan had been lifted with the rest of them, thrown into the cells for a night he didn't ever want to repeat. The threat of a longer spell in prison had driven him into the army and into the company of men who seemed to understand how he felt about life. Many of them were from far more impoverished backgrounds than he was, Billy remembered, shivering as he sat with the sheet wrapped around him. Guys who thrived on three decent meals a day, loved the camaraderie and even took to the harsh discipline as though they had been waiting for someone to give some form or structure to their lives. Even in the scary situations when lives were on the line (and sometimes blown away, though you never dwelt on that) Private Billy Brogan had seen lads who'd once been young hoods like himself turn into brave and honourable men. *If only he'd stayed in the army . . .*

Meeting Stevens had been the turning point for him, though. The older man's biting cynicism had made him laugh. Had made them all laugh, some uneasily, as he recounted stories about picking off his human targets out on patrol. At first Billy had thought the man's tales a load of bullshit, but gradually he'd realised that Stevens was not just a trained sniper, but that being good at killing was something of which the man was inordinately proud.

'Found my vocation, haven't I, Billy boy?' Brogan remembered him saying after one particularly bloodthirsty patrol when several young Iraqis had fallen under Stevens' fire.

'When this is all over, I'll be coining it, won't I?'

And when Billy had asked him 'How?' Stevens had told him.

'Once a killer, always a killer, Billy boy. And there's plenty will pay for me to do jobs they can't or won't do themselves, know what I mean?'

If only he hadn't kept in touch with the hit man. If only he had ignored Marianne's pleas for help. If only bloody Ken had let her go . . . There were so many if onlys in his life, Brogan thought wearily, wiping his eyes with a corner of the sheet. Now it looked as though he'd have to face all the bad choices he had made.

'Hello?'

The door opening made Billy look up, startled out of his thoughts.

A woman dressed in white, with a veil billowing over her shoulder, had entered the room and was advancing to him.

Billy pulled the sheet more closely around his body, suddenly shy.

'Who ur you, hen?' he muttered, his Glasgow accent sounding suddenly strange to his own ears.

'It's all right,' the woman said and Billy felt a sudden relief at her English accent. 'I'm your nurse. I'm here to help you.' She smiled, seeing Billy's uncertainty. 'Glad you've woken up at last. You've been sleeping for quite a long time, you know. We were worried that you might have had a more severe head injury,' she nodded, glancing at his bandaged skull. 'Now just sit back against the pillows while I change that dressing.'

Brogan pushed the breakfast tray to the foot of the bed with a sigh. Funny how a decent bit of food and the prospect of some fresh clothes could make you feel less desperate. He'd been picked up off that back alley and taken to the hospital, one British citizen robbed and beaten; no identity since all of his personal things had been stolen. All but his mobile phone and that hadn't helped them much since it appeared that he hadn't stored any numbers. Brogan had breathed a sigh of relief when the nurse had told him that, her pretty face creasing in a frown. He needed to keep certain things to himself, especially now. Things like Marianne. What was happening to his sister?

Connie, his nurse, had promised that a car would be made available to take him to the British Consul. Did he feel up to it, though? Thinking of Stevens' threatened deadline, Billy had assured her he was feeling brand new, thank you, barely concealing the panic he really felt. Now all he had to do was dress in these borrowed garments and head off to where someone could help him sort out this mess.

The sunlight filtering through the blinds reminded Brogan of the glare of the African sun beating down outside on these foreign streets. Only they were the streets of Algiers, not Morocco. *Stupid, stupid*, he berated himself. Only a moron would make a mistake like that, he'd told himself more than once. Palma, Mallorca was a very long way from Las Palmas in the Canary Islands and the nearby Moroccan coast. And he deserved to be punished for such stupidity now.

Brogan took a deep breath. He was done with running away from his responsibilities. Now he had to get back home as soon as he could. No matter what the final consequences.

CHAPTER 42

Marianne woke with a start. Somehow she had slept through the night with no dreams to disturb her for once. Was it because she was so exhausted, physically and emotionally, or had she simply found that reality was far more terrifying than all the images that had swirled uncontrollably around her brain?

Max (she couldn't stop thinking of him as Max) was not in the hotel room. The bed they had shared was neatly made, but not by one of the hotel staff. He had made sure of that, letting the *Do Not Disturb* notice dangle from the door knob outside. Hearing their sexual frolics night after night must have made the staff think they were newlyweds or something, Marianne realised. Had it all been a ploy, then? Had Max bedded her to make the hotel think they were on their honeymoon? He'd certainly beguiled *her* into imagining that all of these endearments and caresses had been real. She bit the inside of her lip, trying not to cry, but the gaffer tape caught at her skin, tightening its grip.

The hit man had secured her to the only wooden chair in the room, one she'd sat on in front of the mirror to brush her hair, put on her make-up. He had set it deliberately away from a wall so that Marianne could not thump her elbows or wrists against the adjoining rooms. Nor could she tilt it over, making it crash to the floor, he'd seen to that, too, roping the back of it firmly to the brass bed ends.

She swallowed hard, feeling the dryness in her throat. How long had it been since she had drunk anything? Hours and hours, she told herself, glancing at the television's digital clock. Despite that, she badly needed to pee.

Marianne closed her eyes and began to pray. *Please, please let Billy come home.* Would Billy come back, bringing the money that Max asked him for? Or would he leave her there, running away from something difficult as he usually did?

That's not fair, a little voice reminded her. *He helped you to get rid of Ken, didn't he?*

Marianne shivered, remembering the nightmares and the days when she had been too scared to turn around to see Ken following her, stalking her wherever she went. She'd been terrified he'd get hold of her once again; torture her in those insidious ways he had devised. No matter how often she changed her address he had always seemed to find her. *I'll sleep like the dead once he's gone for good*, she'd told Billy once, and her brother had laughed at the phrase.

Max had killed those two men in Billy's flat, Galbraith and Sandiman. The hit man had shrugged it off, telling her they had been an accident. But his words had chilled her. There had been no tone of remorse whatever, just a matter-of-factness that had made her wonder at the nature of a man like this. What would Doctor Brightman have made of him? she wondered. Did he fit the description of a psychopathic personality? Marianne didn't think so. Her Max Whittaker, Billy's Mick Stevens, was so frighteningly normal, wasn't he? As a companion he'd been able to make her laugh. As a lover he had been able to make her swoon with pleasure. And all the time he had been planning her imprisonment, calculating Billy's response to his threats.

342

She sighed, hearing her breath tremble as she exhaled. It was crazy, but she still felt something for the man she had met that day by the car park, some remnant of longing. (And of lust, though it shamed her to admit it.) What was it they called it? That odd relationship that a prisoner forged with their captor? Something to do with being in thrall to them, being a hostage, something like that? Despite the hours of sleep, Marianne felt dog tired, and her brain was unable to summon up words and phrases.

Somewhere she heard the ring of a phone, far away, as if it was coming from the next room. Perhaps it was. Perhaps she could hear the guest next door speaking on his mobile? Perhaps if she made a big enough noise he would hear her and alert the hotel staff . . .?

But as the door opened and Max walked in, his ear to her own mobile, all thoughts of rescue faded. Over one arm he carried a plastic bag, its contents bulging. The woman's eyes fell on a bottle top. Water! She watched as he threw the bag on to the bed, totally ignoring her as he spoke into the telephone.

'Aye, Brogan. Just you do that,' Stevens was saying, making Marianne's eyes light up with sudden hope.

'You want to speak to her?' He turned to Marianne with a grin across his face. 'Not sure if she can manage conversation right now, let's see.'

Marianne screamed as he tore the duct tape from her mouth, her head swung roughly to one side.

'That do for you, Brogan? Hear it loud and clear?' Stevens was saying into the phone. 'Well, maybe you'll not hear her voice for much longer if you don't get your arse back here with my money. Got it?' he tossed the phone onto the bed and pulled a bottle of water from the bag.

Slowly he unscrewed the top, tilting it up to take deep gulps.

'Ah,' he sighed. 'That was good.' He watched as she licked her lips, knowing that she was unable to take her eyes off the bottle.

'Thirsty, are you, darlin'?' he asked then laughed softly. 'Want some?'

Marianne nodded, hardly daring to breathe.

He came so close to her that she could smell the familiar mixture of sweat and aftershave lotion.

'If I give you some, you'll have to promise to be a good girl. Okay?' His voice was soft and low, a lover's murmur in her ear.

'I promise,' she said, meeting his gaze with her own, hoping as much for his lips to brush against hers as for the bottle of water that he held aloft.

CHAPTER 43

Lorimer moved the telephone from his ear for a moment, covering the mouthpiece with one hand as he turned to the man who sat patiently beside him.

'It's the British Consul in Algiers,' he whispered. 'They've got Brogan with them. He wants to talk to me.'

Solly nodded. 'Perhaps the *Crimewatch* programme has spread its . . .' he fell silent as Lorimer shushed him, waving his words aside.

'Detective Chief Inspector Lorimer,' he said. 'Mr Brogan?'

'Aye, you've been looking for me, Lorimer, haven't you? Well, I jist want to say I had nothin' tae do wi Fraz and Gubby, okay?'

'We know that, Mr Brogan. But I think you also know that we want to talk to you about the death of your former brother-in-law, Mr Kenneth Scott,' Lorimer told him, speaking as calmly as he could to temper the drug dealer's initial belligerence.

There was a pause then Lorimer could hear the man sigh down the line.

'Aye, well, that wasnae me, neither.'

'Not directly, perhaps,' Lorimer conceded.

'Look, Mr Lorimer, I huvnae time tae waste wi' all of this, right? Ye c'n charge me wance I'm hame, but meantime . . . ye huv tae do something fur me.'

'I'm listening,' Lorimer said, hearing the urgency in the man's voice.

Brogan drew a deep breath before continuing. 'There's this man called Mick Stevens. He's the one you're looking for. He's got my sister. And he's going to . . .'

Lorimer frowned at the handset, wondering if the line had suddenly been cut off, but Brogan's voice returned, high-pitched and nervy.

'Mr Lorimer you've got to do something quick. Or Stevens is going to kill her.'

'We have very few choices,' Lorimer told the superintendent. 'Either we allow this man, Stevens, to stay in the City Inn armed with God knows how many weapons, threatening the life of a young woman, or we go in after him.' He paused then gripped the sides of Mitchison's desk, willing the man to agree with him for once. 'We've got one strategic advantage, sir. And that's the hotel's proximity to Anderston police station. We can call on as many of their officers as they have available right now.'

Mitchison nodded. 'You're right. It's a class A situation; public safety must be our primary concern. What do you suggest?'

DCI Lorimer took a deep breath and began to outline his plan.

Omar Fathy fastened on the Kevlar vest, glancing at his fellow officers as they prepared themselves for danger. It was all part of the job, he reminded himself, feeling the buzz of adrenalin shooting through his veins, nothing to get too worked up about. Omar gave a wry smile. It was just this sort of scenario that had caused his parents to have so many misgivings when their son had announced his decision to join the police force. Far too dangerous, his mother had scolded him, but Omar had simply grinned and told her to stop watching so many TV cop shows; it wasn't like that in real life. But now the young man was in a situation that had begun to resemble some of these celluloid adventures. And he found that it was thrilling.

'Ready?' Annie Irvine was not smiling as she came to stand by his side.

'You bet,' Omar replied. For a moment they looked at one another, two colleagues ready to face a dangerous situation. And suddenly Omar wanted it to be more than that; his fingers itching to take Annie's hand in his, to reassure her that everything would be okay. But then a voice commanded them forwards, the moment was gone and she turned towards the police transporter van that was to take them into the city centre, leaving Omar feeling slightly dispirited.

'Got your taser?' Annie asked and Omar nodded, giving it a tap against the belt that contained his equipment. He had never been supplied with a weapon before and had been surprised when Lorimer had insisted that they be issued for their own safety. Still, there was to be a proper firearms unit there as well, men who were trained to shoot on command. These hand-picked officers were already on their way to the scene, the hotel's staff having been alerted to evacuate the premises.

Fathy had been amazed at the speed with which Lorimer had managed to make all of these things happen, though having Anderston so close by was a huge bonus. Now, entering the white van and wedging himself next to his colleagues, he squared his shoulders, returning the nervous smiles and glances that were directed his way.

For the first time since arriving in Glasgow he felt truly part of this team. No matter what happened today or the next day or the week after that, Fathy knew that nothing would stop him being a police officer, not even the malicious notes he was receiving with such painful regularity.

The hit man had selected his location well, thought Lorimer as they approached Glasgow's City Inn. If he had planned to be in a siege situation, Stevens couldn't have made a better strategic choice. The hotel was bounded on one side by the river and there was a police launch just out of firing range, in the lee of its southern bank. The Squinty Bridge and the main road to the Scottish Exhibition and Conference Centre had been closed to traffic with police cordons set up around the adjoining streets, the road block at the slip road to the M8 causing most of the disruption for motorists.

Looking up at the pale blue sky and a single gull floating over the river, Lorimer wondered at how calm it all seemed. There was little sound of traffic save from the distant rumble across the faraway bridges.

His decision to call this operation 'eyeball in the skyball' had been met with curious looks from those officers too young to remember *The Perishers* cartoons. But it had seemed an appropriate tag for this hostage situation, especially when the new technology of the PD-100 Black Hornet was to be utilised. It might have seemed like a waste of an afternoon at the time, but now Lorimer found himself pinning a lot of hope on this new, untried device. He grinned as he remembered the superintendent's raised eyebrows: for once Mark Mitchison had been in total accord with all of Lorimer's proposals.

The window of Stevens' room was at an acute angle from their present position, but they would be able to see when the Black Hornet was activated and watch its flight upwards to the hotel's top floor then listen to what was happening inside. An additional advantage was that this tiny helicopter could send images back to the monitor that was secreted inside the police vehicle where Lorimer sat with Wilson and Solly.

'Lucky that Brogan knew which hotel they were in,' DS Wilson murmured to Lorimer as they sat waiting in the patrol car opposite the hotel car park.

'More than lucky for us,' Lorimer replied quietly. 'Especially when his sister told him their room number into the bargain.'

Both officers kept other thoughts to themselves: that sometimes luck played a part in bringing an investigation to a satisfactory close. But it was far from being ended and much could still be played out against the backdrop of this riverside scene. It was hard to imagine that Strathclyde Police now had this place surrounded, the quiet was so intense.

'What's happening with Brogan?' Wilson whispered.

'Being flown back to the UK under escort,' Lorimer replied. 'Right, looks like we've got all our ducks in a row,' he added, spotting the officer who was to launch the Black Hornet. 'Radio silence, all units, please,' he said, nodding to the members of his team who watched and waited from the confines of their vehicle.

Mick Stevens was completely oblivious to the tiny helicopter whirring silently past the window of his bedroom, hovering to a place just out of his direct line of sight. But he did know that things had begun to happen.

The fire alarm had been set off half an hour ago, making him look out into the corridor. The frightened face of a porter met his as the man rushed towards the nearest exit. And in that one look, the hit man had seen something he recognised. Fear. And not just the fear of some bogus fire. It was fear of *him*. The hit man. Mick Stevens.

So now he knew it was happening. Everything had caught up with him yet all he felt was a strange sense of calm, as though this day had been inevitable.

When he heard the loudspeaker announcing the police presence, Stevens had been savvy enough to keep out of sight from the window. There would be police marksmen all over the bloody place, ready to pick him off the moment they saw his face.

'Let the woman go, Stevens!' a voice commanded, its booming tones reverberating in the cold air outside his room.

'What d'you think, darlin'? Should I let you go?' Mick smiled sadly at Marianne whose eyes bulged with terror at the pistol pointed at her. 'After all, Billy's been a bad boy, bringing the cops after us, hasn't he?' Stevens reasoned, waving the gun at her. 'Deserves to be punished,' he went on. 'And what better way,' he brandished the weapon closer to Marianne's face, 'than to leave him a little message?' he laughed softly, pulling one finger back.

Marianne shrank further into the chair, her body slick with sweat under the thin covering of her nightdress. He was going to kill her. Any minute now he was going to press that trigger . . . she closed her eyes, terror numbing her senses, her only prayer that it would be over quickly.

'Right, you're coming with me, darlin',' Mick crooned softly. 'A little walk upstairs. See if you'd like to fly instead.'

Lorimer and Wilson exchanged glances as the couple left the hotel bedroom and disappeared. The Black Hornet's microphone had picked up the hit man's words perfectly but it was unable to do any more unless he appeared by that window.

'The roof,' Lorimer said, shortly. 'He's taking her up onto the roof.'

The DCI shifted his position to get a better view of the upper level of the hotel, then spoke into the mouthpiece. 'Attention all units. No firing until you are absolutely sure that the girl is out of Stevens' way. And as soon as we have sight of them get the Hornet up to their level!'

'Oh my God,' Wilson whispered. 'D'you think . . .?'

Lorimer's face was grim as he replied. 'I think he may be going to jump,' he said. 'And take Marianne with him.'

Amit had watched the men following him, aware of their presence at every street corner. Didn't they know how adept he had become in those frightened weeks after his father's death when spies had dogged his every footstep? Here in this strange city he might have been considered an easy target, but Amit Shafiq knew all about the art of surveillance.

Hiding from these undercover officers was not an option, so the man from Lahore had decided to adopt a different strategy altogether.

He was not going to be hunted all of his life. No, he would turn this to his own advantage. Now, whenever he saw them, Amit simply turned and walked back towards them, across busy roads, in and out of the subways, smiling to himself as they moved away, shiftily, as though they hoped their cover was still intact.

So it was that the hunters became the hunted and Amit Shafiq had let several of them pick up his trail, hoping that they might eventually lead him to where Marianne was hiding. Practising that U-turn, he had followed different men and women all over the city until this morning. One of them, a woman in jeans and a sweatshirt, ostensibly out jogging on Byres Road, had put one hand to her ear as if she was adjusting her iPod. But it was the expression on her face as she stopped mid-stride, rather than the tell-tale action, that immediately alerted Amit. Something was happening.

Suddenly ignoring the Asian, she broke into a run, fled across Great Western Road, one hand waving frantically as she hailed a taxi.

Amit was not far behind her.

He grinned as he got into his own cab, feeling almost like a boy again as he told the taxi driver, 'Follow that cab!'

The road at Houldsworth Street had been closed to traffic but the woman's taxi stopped a little beyond the police tape and Amit saw her get out, brandishing what he took to be a warrant card at the officer who bent towards the taxi driver.

'Here,' Amit whispered to his own driver. 'You never saw me. All right?' Then thrusting a couple of twenties into the man's hand, he slipped out of the cab and walked cautiously past the empty car park at PC World, and the deserted forecourt of the Citroën garage.

'Sorry, you can't go past here, sir,' the uniformed officer told Amit.

'DCI Lorimer needs me,' Amit told him firmly. 'I'm with that other officer but we got split up back there,' he lied, pointing to the woman in running gear who was now quite far ahead, almost at the corner where the road forked right towards the City Inn.

'Need to see your ID, sir,' the man replied firmly.

'Of course,' Amit said, putting a hand to his inside pocket. Then, as though he had spotted someone behind the policeman, he smiled and waved. As the officer turned, Amit broke into a run, arms pumping hard by his sides, heart thudding at his own audacity.

Marianne felt her legs buckle beneath her as Max pulled her off the chair, her bonds cut free by a knife he had produced from somewhere.

'Come on,' he told her, flicking her hair back from her face with the blade of the knife. 'Get going.'

As the hit man pocketed the knife and picked up the gun again, Marianne bit her lip. She had to go, she just had to . . .

Too terrified to reach out and touch his arm, the woman watched his every move until finally she caught his eye.

'Please,' she begged. 'Can I go to the toilet?'

He seemed to hesitate for a moment then shrugged. 'Okay, but make it quick.'

With a sigh, Marianne sat on the pan and closed her eyes. It was humiliating to have him standing there, watching, but the relief as her bladder finally gave up its contents overcame any residual embarrassment.

'Right, move it,' the hit man told her.

Somehow she managed to stumble towards the doorway and out into the darkened corridor. All the lights were out, she noticed. Had the hotel staff cut off the power? A flicker of hope entered the woman's heart. Maybe the police outside would save her from the man who was pushing her steadily along, that gun pressed into her back, urging her towards the end of the corridor. Or would Max relent? Tell her it was all a mistake? That he never intended to harm her?

The fresh air made her gasp as the door was thrust open and Marianne was bundled onto the roof. Her nightdress billowed upwards, exposing her bare legs and for a moment Marianne feared that she would be blown straight off into the river below.

'I can't . . .' she said, holding back, her eyes pleading with the gunman.

'Move,' he said, twisting her arm painfully so that now she was in front of him, a human shield, protection from whoever tried to fire on them.

'Please,' Marianne whimpered, her bare feet taking steps against their will. Sharp bits of gravel cut into the soles, making her wince.

The edge of the roof began to come so close. Too close . . .

'No!' she said, struggling in his grip. 'Don't make me! Please!'

But her words blew away in the wind as he forced her nearer and nearer to that dizzying drop.

Amit walked slowly around the corner of the street, aware at any minute that he might be made to return. The undercover policewoman had disappeared and there were several police vehicles parked around the outside of the hotel.

He stopped, lingering in the shadow of a building, wondering what was going on. Ahead of him, crouched low beside a white van, was a police marksman, his rifle trained on something he could not see.

Amit looked up.

Just as two figures appeared on the roof, Lorimer's voice sounded from a nearby loudhailer.

'Stop right where you are, Stevens. Leave the woman and come back down!'

'Stay back or I'll shoot her!' the hit man yelled.

Amit took a step forward, eyes fixed on the man who was drawing closer to the edge of the roof and the woman he held in his grasp, her red hair blowing in the wind.

Then he began to run.

'Marianne!' he called, waving his arms at them. 'Marianne!'

The moment he saw the little Asian, Detective Constable Omar Fathy leapt from the transporter. Where the hell had this crazy man come from?

'Stop!' he cried out, lunging towards the running figure. 'Don't go . . .' but his words failed as Stevens' shot rang out.

'No!' Annie screamed, feeling other arms pulling her back as she tried to leave the van and reach her friend.

'No,' she whimpered, her eyes refusing to believe what she was seeing. 'No, please God, no . . .'

Omar lay there, motionless, arms flung out, one dark stain bloodying his forehead.

Annie stared at him, willing the Egyptian to move. 'Get up, Omar. Please get up . . .'

Then, as strong hands turned her away from the sight, she began to sob into the shoulder of the officer next to her.

There was a man dead at his feet. Amit could see that. A young man, dark-skinned. His life taken by a bullet that had been meant for him.

Amit stood there, shock rooting him to the ground.

Then he heard a second crack of gunfire ripping through the air.

He watched as though in a dream, that figure tumbling from the edge of the roof, a dark shape outlined against the pure, pale sky then falling with a thud onto the concrete below.

When he looked back up, Marianne was crouched on the rooftop. Her thin, eerie wail floating down to the scene below, shattering the silence.

Then, as he saw other figures come up behind her and take her in their arms, Amit sank to his knees beside the body of the young policeman and wept.

CHAPTER 44

'Let me speak to her, first,' Solly said quietly, his hand on Lorimer's sleeve.

They were back in divisional headquarters. It was hard to believe that it was barely two hours since they had left, such was the difference in the place. Before, there had been that tense anticipation when adrenalin and testosterone filled the veins of so many officers; now there was only a sullen silence.

Solly had taken his body armour off with the others, waiting to hear murmurs of regret, anything that would ease the pain of this deathly hush. That would come, he told himself. Maybe tonight when the police officers could feel safe in their own homes, maybe tomorrow when they reported for duty. Or perhaps not until they stood at the graveside watching as Omar Adel Fathy's body was laid to rest with all the panoply that surrounded a police officer's funeral.

Lorimer gave no sign of having heard him and Solly patted his arm, seeing the way his friend looked out of his office window. It wasn't difficult to imagine what he was seeing. The sight of his fallen officer would be imprinted on Lorimer's brain for a long time to come, Solly knew. But there were things that still had to be done even though the Senior Investigating Officer might wish to forget about them entirely.

'May I talk to her, take Detective Sergeant Cameron with me, perhaps?' Solly asked.

Lorimer gave a great sigh then wiped a hand across his eyes as though to clear that unwelcome vision.

'It's totally out of the question, Solly. I can't authorise a civilian to undertake something like that.' He gave a faint smile. 'Even you.'

Solly nodded. That was what he had expected and, though his request was genuine, it had been phrased to elicit a particular response. To shake the man back to his responsibilities.

'I'll go down myself,' Lorimer said at last, straightening himself wearily from the window sill where he had been leaning. 'But I can let you sit in on the interview. Even ask some questions if you like. It'll all be on record, anyway.' He shrugged. 'Come on, let's get this over with.'

Marianne held the polystyrene cup in her fists, feeling its warmth seep right through her bones.

She was alive. And for now that was all that seemed to matter.

Those moments when she had looked down at the greyness of the pavements way below, sick with fear, still remained, however. The uniformed policewoman who had wrapped a blanket around her as they sat in the back of the car had held on to her shoulders, murmuring soothing words. Marianne had let the tears fall, then, too choked to utter a single word.

Now, though, her mind was full of questions. How had Amit got there? Who had been shot? (She had seen the stretcher and the shape of a body beneath that white sheet.) And was Billy safe?

Marianne had stopped considering her own fate. What would come to pass was surely something that she deserved, after all? That she would be sentenced to a lengthy stretch in prison was inevitable. But somehow that wasn't important.

'Mrs Shafiq?' A tall man had entered the small room where Marianne was sitting on a bench seat, the same female officer sitting near her.

'Detective Chief Inspector Lorimer,' the man told her. 'Please would you come with me?'

Marianne met his eyes for a second, light blue, piercing eyes that seemed to look straight into her soul. Then she nodded, rising from the bench, feeling the woman's hand on her arm, helping her up. They had been quietly kind in that first police station, providing some clothes for her to wear; jeans that were too big at the waist, a navy fleece and a pair of socks and trainers. Where did they get all of these things? she had wondered, too afraid to ask, just grateful to have that stinking nightdress taken away with the promise of a shower *once everything had been sorted out*. A vague phrase that she had accepted, too numb to look ahead. Now, though, following this man with these broad shoulders under that dark suit, Marianne felt grubby. Raking fingers through her hair, she felt the knots and tangles and was suddenly ashamed.

'In here, please,' Lorimer ushered them through a door marked Interview Room 2.

The room they entered held a surprise.

'Doctor Brightman!'

'Marianne,' he replied, rising politely from a chair in the corner of the room. He gave her a stiff little nod, but did not come forward to take her by the hand. She glanced back at the two police officers, the tall man and the kindly woman, suddenly at a loss.

'What . . .?' she began.

'Sit here please,' Lorimer told her, indicating a place to one side of a formica-topped table. She sat on the plastic-covered chair, hearing its metal legs scrape along the floor, frowning at her surroundings. Surely this was where criminals came to be questioned?

Marianne watched as Lorimer switched on a recording machine then gave his name, rank and the date and time then she blinked as the enormity of the situation began to dawn on her. *She* was the criminal about to be questioned.

Solly's face was grave as he watched the changing emotions flit across the woman's face. *She'll still be in shock*, he had advised Lorimer. But that had not seemed to concern the policeman. Was Fathy's death making him vengeful? Could he really have no consideration for this young woman's sensibilities? All of the psychologist's questions had been swept aside as Lorimer had taken the decision to interview Marianne himself, with Solly in attendance. Yet now he could understand why. This woman was vulnerable, certainly, but she might be far more compliant as a result of that, yielding up such information as they needed to know in order to make total sense of the case.

'Marianne,' Solly said, making her look at him. 'There's something I would like to know. The seminar about dreams,' he paused as her eyes widened. 'Was it my fault, giving you that idea?'

She nodded. 'Yes,' she said. 'It seemed so simple really. If I could have him taken away, out of my life somehow. Then you said, *why not have him killed?*'

'Please explain the background to this for the record,' Solly heard Lorimer say, his voice stiff with disapproval.

'Oh, sorry,' Marianne said, turning to look at the recording machine.

'I had these terrible dreams,' she began.

Lorimer closed the door to his office with a sigh. It had been too easy, really. Once Solly's question had prompted her, the floodgates had opened and Marianne had told them everything. How

360

Scott had followed her everywhere, making her change her address in a series of bedsits, until she was almost at screaming point; how the chance to earn some serious money had come her way when Billy had suggested that she help out this wealthy man from Lahore. Then she had enough money to pay for *that matter*. She hadn't referred to it by any other term, Lorimer had noticed, never even calling Stevens a hit man, always referring to him as Billy's friend. When he had at last charged her with conspiracy to murder, Lorimer had noticed no change in the woman at all, only a vague nod as though this was something she had expected to happen, part of a process she was willing to undergo.

There was still so much to be done, he thought, suddenly longing for home with Maggie there, waiting as she always did. He still had to speak with Amit Shafiq and arrange for Brogan to be brought up to Glasgow once his plane touched down in Heathrow Airport. There were hours before he could see her, touch her hair, bury himself in her caresses. And all this while Maggie was worried sick about that operation, miserable because she thought it might make her somehow less than the beautiful woman he knew her to be.

Standing there in the room that had become almost a second home to him, Lorimer suddenly came to a decision. Sometimes changes were inevitable, like Maggie's operation, but he knew right now that it was time for him to change his career, put all of today's tragic events behind him. He would accept Joyce Rogers' proposal, take the job in the Serious Crime Squad. There would be some conditions attached, though. First he would take the leave that he was owed, making sure that it coincided with Maggie's time at home after her surgery. Then, he thought, with a sigh, he could make a fresh start again, seek out new challenges.

CHAPTER 45

Mr and Mrs Fathy were sitting side by side in the family room when Lorimer walked in. The first thing he noticed about the mother was her resemblance to Omar. Mrs Fathy had that same angular face, smooth dark skin and natural grace that he remembered so well. He swallowed hard. This was not going to be easy.

'Detective Chief Inspector Lorimer,' he said, moving forward. Mr Fathy stood up and accepted the outstretched hand but his wife remained seated, tense fists clutching a large handbag on her lap.

'Thank you for coming, Chief Inspector,' Mr Fathy said, his voice gruff with emotion. 'It means a lot to us.'

'Omar was a fine officer,' Lorimer began, then, giving a sigh, he passed a hand over his own eyes. 'I can't tell you how sorry I am . . .'

Mr Fathy touched his sleeve. 'I can see that,' he murmured. 'It is good that you show this.'

'He was tipped to go far in his police career,' Lorimer continued. 'Even those at the highest level recognised that.'

'That is some comfort,' Mr Fathy replied, though it was hard for Lorimer to tell whether Omar's father was uttering mere platitudes or whether he really meant it.

'He should never have joined up in the first place!' Mrs Fathy cried, looking at Lorimer, her face twisting in pain. 'I tried to stop him. I *really* tried!'

Lorimer nodded, his blue eyes meeting her own dark gaze. There was something in that look, some unspoken, guilty secret.

Then, as though she had said too much, she dropped her gaze and opened her bag, rustling around for a handkerchief.

And at that moment it came to him, the answer to Omar's persecution.

It was you, his own mother, Lorimer thought to himself, but he did not say the words. How she had managed it, was anyone's guess. Bribing officers within Grampian and Strathclyde to put notes in her son's locker, perhaps? Sending messages to his home address? Anything to try to stop him in the career that she hated.

Thank God he hadn't had time to put anything officially into motion.

Whatever had been going on, it simply didn't matter any more. They'd got off with it, but Lorimer hoped that somewhere in Aberdeen and Glasgow there would be officers whose consciences would weigh heavily upon them for the rest of their careers.

Perhaps, though, Omar's mother would always feel a sense of vindication. The danger she had feared for her beloved son had come to pass in the most tragic way, despite what she had seen as her best intentions.

Lorimer cleared his throat. 'Omar is to be given the police medal for bravery,' he said. 'It's something that is often awarded posthumously,' he added gently. 'And, with your permission, we would like his funeral to be conducted with full police honours.'

Mr Fathy nodded. 'He would have liked that, wouldn't he, Mother?' he said, turning to his wife.

364

But Mrs Fathy simply bent her head and wept, her racking sobs reaching into Lorimer's heart like a knife.

Billy Brogan twisted uncomfortably against the handcuffs that were pinioning him to the metal walls of the prison transporter. The journey from North Africa hadn't been so bad. He'd managed to chat to the stiff-looking English officer who had met him from the consulate and taken him back by plane. Being cuffed to the man had been okay, except when he'd had to go to the tiny onboard toilet. *How did couples manage to join the Mile High club?* he'd joked, but that had cut no ice with his poker-faced companion.

Now he was almost back in dear old Glesca Toon, but whether Billy Brogan would see much of the city was doubtful. Barlinnie prison was his destination and, as far as Brogan knew, that high-walled institution gave no views of the surrounding landscape. The transporter rumbled along, giving Brogan no clue as to whereabouts they were and he suddenly realised that this was how it was going to be. No matter what sentence was handed down to him for conspiracy to murder, he'd lost control of his own destiny for a long time to come.

And Marianne? What of her? Nobody had let him know a thing about his sister. Perhaps once he was incarcerated and part of the system he could find out what was going on from his brief. Brogan shrugged. Stupid thing to do, really, hiring Stevens to get rid of Ken Scott. Seemed to make sense at the time. Surely helping his only sister get rid of a filthy stalker would cut some ice with a jury? he told himself, trying to justify his actions.

The vehicle slowed down and Brogan felt his body sway as it turned a corner. Instinctively he knew they had arrived. He took a deep breath. 'Right, Billy boy,' Brogan murmured to himself. 'Time to turn on the charm.'

Amit was walking beside the Hundi. It was autumn now and the city had wrapped itself in a mistiness that chilled him to the bone.

'We have to be careful, my friend,' the Hundi told Amit. 'There are many who would wish us to perish like our friend, Jaffrey.'

Amit nodded sagely. This Hundi had been good to him, hadn't he? Introducing him to Brogan and Marianne so that he could stay in this country, ensuring that his financial needs were taken care of and now, giving him the sort of fatherly advice that the younger man respected. Instinct had warned him to say nothing about the Hundi to that tall policeman, only mentioning Brogan's part in the transaction. And that was good, wasn't it? Amit felt the big man's hand rest upon his shoulder as they strolled through Kelvingrove Park, past the pond where a heron stood motionless, waiting to strike.

'Everything is fine with Dhesi?' the Hundi asked and Amit nodded.

'He is a good friend to me,' he said simply. 'And an honest business partner.'

The Hundi smiled to himself. Just so long as Amit Shafiq thought along these lines then all was well. It was unlikely that Brogan or his sister would mention him to the police. After all, what could they say? That a nameless Pakistani gentleman had fixed things for them? Where was this man? the police would want to know. And that was a question that they would be unable to answer. No. Their community had closed ranks against the likes of Brogan and even young Jaffrey would be too afraid to talk.

'Dhesi is a good man,' the Hundi continued. 'And he is concerned for your welfare.'

Amit nodded again, his eyes fixed upon the path.

'Once your ... *marriage* ... is terminated perhaps you might think of taking another wife?'

Amit swallowed hard as a sudden vision of the laughing red-haired woman came into his mind.

'You've met his niece, the lovely Nalini?' he said, patting Amit's shoulder once more. 'She would make a man like you very happy, don't you think?'

Amit looked up at the man. What did he see? A large Asian dressed in an expensive suit and overcoat, cut to hide his immense girth; a man whose very presence dominated this narrow path.

No, that was not all that Amit Shafiq could see. He had learned to look past those outward trappings. Now he could see those little piggy eyes sunk in layers of flesh glittering with a hint of malice. And, as he saw the Hundi looking back at him, Amit felt an overwhelming sense of despair.

Had he come so far only to meet a different kind of evil?

Was it the same everywhere, after all? And was there never going to be any escape for someone like him?

'Perhaps,' Amit said at last with a sigh of resignation. 'Perhaps.'

CHAPTER 46

'Solly, wake up!' Rosie nudged her husband. 'Things have started to happen!'

Professor Solomon Brightman sat up in bed, hearing the note of excitement in his wife's voice. It was dark still. But what was it his mother had told him? *Babies have a way of beginning in the night.*

'Are you sure?' he asked, rubbing the sleep out of his eyes. 'The baby isn't due for another two weeks,' he protested.

Rosie chuckled. 'Tell that to this little critter,' she said. 'Oh! That was a big one!' she exclaimed as a painful contraction seized her. 'Come on, Solly,' she urged, sweeping the bedclothes aside. 'Time to get me over to the hospital.'

'Maybe you'll meet Maggie Lorimer there,' Solly mumbled.

'What? Why will she be there?' Rosie frowned.

'Oh, dear, I wasn't supposed to tell you in your delicate state, was I?' Solly bit his lip. 'Maggie's had a hysterectomy,' he replied. 'Lorimer told me.'

'Och, the poor thing,' Rosie said. 'So that's why she's been avoiding me,' she nodded then her face twisted in pain once more. 'Ooh, come on Solly, shift yourself. This wee one's not going to wait much longer.'

*

369

Maggie sat up in her bed, feeling the whirr of the fan that was wafting cool air over her sticky body. The first thing she had felt after waking up was a wonderful sense of euphoria that had taken her completely by surprise. She was still here, maybe not exactly in one piece, but alive and full of a calm acceptance that she had never expected to feel. Was it the aftermath of a general anaesthetic, perhaps? Or the human spirit's way of adjusting to change?

'Mrs Lorimer,' the nurse came into Maggie's room, her face wreathed in smiles. 'There's someone to see you.'

Who was here to see her? Not her husband, surely, for it was not visiting time yet.

Maggie looked towards the open door and the nurse's smiling face then gasped as she saw Rosie being wheeled into the room by Solly, a tiny bundle held in her arms.

'Oh,' she said at last, her eyes searching hungrily at the folds of cloth surrounding the newborn. 'Oh, I didn't know . . .'

'Meet your god-daughter,' Rosie said, grinning up at her. 'Abigail Margaret Brightman.'

'Abigail!' Maggie gasped. 'It's a wee girl!'

Solly gave a boyish smile. 'Her name means *father rejoiced*,' he said, his voice full of pride.

Then, as Solly lifted the tiny bundle from his wife and placed Abigail into her arms, Maggie's tears began to flow.

'You *will* be her godmother, won't you?' Rosie asked, her eyes bright with anticipation.

Maggie nodded, too full to speak, as she gazed down at the little face with its tiny button nose and feathery eyelids against closed eyes.

'She's perfect,' Maggie whispered, cradling the baby against her breasts. She watched as Abigail gave a sigh and nuzzled against her, the little bow mouth opening expectantly.

Then everybody laughed.

'Come on, lady, back to your mum. Looks like it might be feeding time,' Maggie said tenderly, looking back at her friends.

Then, as Solly carried his daughter back to Rosie, Maggie put out a hand to touch his arm.

'Thank you,' she said.

Once they were gone, Maggie lay back against her bank of pillows, a radiant smile on her face. She had a god-daughter. Little Abigail Brightman would be a very special person in her life from now on.

Things never stayed the same, did they? Maggie thought, gazing out at the blue sky and the clouds that drifted past her window. Solly was a professor now, Rosie a mother; Bill was leaving his old job for that new promoted post at Pitt Street. And she had become a godmother. Life had a way of surprising you in all its vagaries, twists and turnings, she told herself.

Then, closing her eyes, Maggie Lorimer settled down to enjoy the peace of a dreamless sleep.

Acknowledgements

I would like to thank the following people for their help during the research and writing of this book. Professor Willie Maley for a nice afternoon at Glasgow Uni and for allowing Solly to pinch his office and set the department of psychology where I wished it was! Detective Inspector Bob Frew and DC Mhairi Milne for their willingness to answer all my questions concerning police procedure; Alistair Paton for being such a whizz at keeping me right with all things ballistic; Doctor Marjorie Black for casting an expert eye over Rosie's post-mortems; Asif Ali of the Shish Mahal Restaurant (still Glasgow's best!) for inspiring me and letting me know more about the Asian community; my dear friend Shafiq of the Shimla Cottage, Bridge of Weir (best restaurant in Renfrewshire, ever!) for allowing me to borrow his name; June and George McKenzie for their expertise in nautical matters and for the fun we had deciding to send Billy Brogan to North Africa; Alex Loughran and Kirsty Young for allowing me to use them as themselves in the *Crimewatch* episode; Helen MacKellar for some notable Spanish phrases; my agent, the one and only Jenny Brown, for her unstinting encouragement; my lovely editor, Caroline Hogg, who is such a blessing to me and keeps me right on all the details; Kirsteen, Moira (what would I do without you?)

and all the fabulous folk at Little, Brown (never forgetting the wonderful David Shelley) who work so hard on my behalf to make it all happen; my family for putting up with me through it all, especially Donnie whose patience with me (if nothing else) should gain him sainthood.